Cynthia Harrod-Eagles won the Young Writers' Award with her first novel, THE WAITING GAME, and in 1992 won the Romantic Novel of the Year Award. She has written over fifty books, including twenty-two volumes of the Morland Dynasty – a series she will be taking up to the present day. She is also creator of the acclaimed mystery series featuring Inspector Bill Slider.

She and her husband live in London and have three children. Apart from writing her passions are music, wine, horses, architecture and the English countryside.

Visit the author's website on
http://www.twbooks.co.uk/authors/cheagles.html

D0030909

Also in the *Dynasty* series:

DYNASTY

19

The Hidden Shore

Cynthia Harrod-Eagles

WARNER BOOKS

A *Warner* Book

First published in Great Britain in 1996
by Little, Brown and Company

This edition published by Warner Books in 1997
Reprinted 1998, 2000

Copyright © Cynthia Harrod-Eagles 1996

The moral right of the author has been asserted.

A CIP catalogue record for this book
is available from the British Library.

ISBN 0 7515 1934 0

Typeset by Palimpsest Book Production Limited,
Polmont, Stirlingshire
Printed and bound in Great Britain by
Clays Ltd, St Ives plc

Warner Books
A Division of
Little, Brown and Company (UK)
Brettenham House
Lancaster Place
London WC2E 7EN

SELECT BIBLIOGRAPHY

Acton, W. *Prostitution Considered in its Moral, Social & Sanitary Aspects*

Battiscombe, G. *Shaftesbury: A Biography of the Seventh Earl*

Chesney, K. *The Victorian Underworld*

Cole, G.D.H. *The Common People*

Havitt, W. *Rural Life of England*

Hibbert, C. *The English: A Social History 1066–1945*

Pearsall, R. *Night's Black Angels*

Rawlinson, R. *The Ormskirk Board of Health Report, 1850*

Samuel, R. *Village Life and Labour*

Webb, S. and B. *English Poor Law History*

Webb, R. K. *Modern England*

Woodward, E. L. *The Age of Reform 1815–1870*

Young, G.M. *Early Victorian England*

THE MORLAND FAMILY

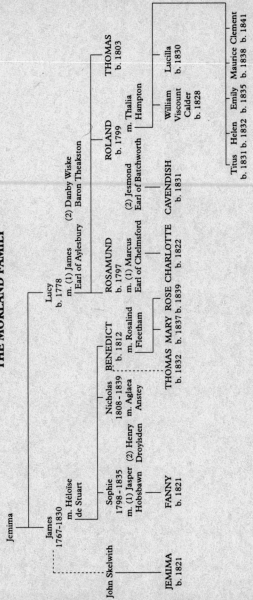

BOOK ONE

The Voyage

Ah, what pleasant visions haunt me
As I gaze upon the sea!
All the old romantic legends,
All my dreams come back to me.

Sails of silk and ropes of sandal,
Such as gleam in ancient lore;
And the singing of the sailors,
And the answer from the shore!

Henry Wadsworth Longfellow:
The Galley of Count Arnaldos

CHAPTER ONE

April, 1843

The garden of Heath Cottage was small and dull, but at the bottom only a low bank and a hedge separated it from the marsh. The hedge was threadbare and sometimes cattle broke into the garden, to the detriment of the few struggling plants it sported. Through one of the gaps they had left, Charlotte escaped now and then to walk under the wide sky and 'stretch her lungs', as Ellen said.

She felt guilty for thinking of it as escape. She knew that Aunt, if she were still alive, would say that a good daughter would delight in service to her parent, particularly a father so grievously crippled as Papa. But the cottage was low-ceilinged, cramped and dark, and she was a tall girl – 'gawky' and 'clumsy' had been Aunt's preferred epithets. Even though she wore fewer petticoats than Ellen said was fashionable, still she hardly seemed able to move without knocking something over, and any loud or sudden noise taxed Papa's nerves.

So she escaped out onto the marsh when she could, where there was a vastness of sky and the horizon was so distant it seemed you could see forever. She walked briskly, swinging her arms, rejoicing in the freedom of movement: she would have run, but it wouldn't have been seemly for a person of twenty. Today there was a mildness in the air for the first time, which said spring was coming at last. The great bowl of sky was filled with windy light, and between the loose, rushing clouds there were glimpses of a pale and rainwashed April blue. And there was birdsong: the marsh did not quite rise to a skylark, but there were peewits, and a chaffinch throbbed and whirred in the blackthorn like a wind-up bird on a musical box lid.

Despite its name the marsh was not marshy. It had been drained for grazing these hundred and fifty years by a network of narrow ditches crossed by plank bridges, which the farmers moved from time to time to change the pastures. Here and there a more solid, permanent structure with a gate at either end marked a sluice; lines of gorse, stunted thorn, willow and sedge marked the cart tracks, and the wider canals were dense with rushes.

The willows were still bare, but a flush of palest green was softening the blackness of the thorns. Grey-green and brown the marsh was, under a rushing sky; not alive yet, but coming alive, like the princess in the first instant after the kiss. She hoped there might be daffodils today – the little, short-stemmed wild ones with the back-turned petals, like dogs with their ears streaming in the wind. The local people called them 'affadillies'. She wanted to bring some to Papa to cheer him.

In search of them she walked further than she meant, and did not notice the sky darkening. Then, suddenly, the clouds were a seamless blanket, low and black. Rain was coming: the edge of a distant beam of light touching the far marsh was silvery with it. Charlotte turned and hurried back; but even though she took a short cut through the village, the rain caught up with her when she was still a good way from home.

At least in the village there was a tree, a lone horse chestnut so much prized in that naturally treeless corner of the country that when the road had been widened, it had been preserved by common consent, and the traffic parted round it like a stream round a large rock. It was rather a public place to shelter, in the middle of the street, but her mantle was thin, and Ellen got cross if presented with extra work like drying clothes.

'You'd have been more use to me a few weeks later,' Charlotte told the tree, squinting up against the silvery drops falling fast through the branches. The leaves were still furled, only just breaking out of their sticky buds. She was soon very damp and beginning to feel cold. She wondered if she ought to make a dash for it, but her mind wandered off into a calculation of whether more drops would land on her if she were moving or still, and she stayed where she was, getting wetter by the moment.

She was not unobserved. The nearest house, just across the road, belonged to Doctor Silk, the physician who attended her father. He had gone to the front window to look at the rain, and called to his wife, who was sitting by the fire knitting.

'My dear Mrs Silk, do you see who is sheltering under the tree – for what shelter it affords at this time of year.'

'No, my dear,' his lady replied comfortably, without moving.

'It's the poor little Meldon girl – Mr Meldon's daughter.'

'No, is it? But I thought she never left the house.' The interest of the idea was enough to rouse Mrs Silk from her chair. She joined her husband at the window and stared. 'So it is. Well, well! They say she is not right in the head, poor child. That must prove it, to be sheltering under a bare tree.'

'No, no,' Doctor Silk said in wounded tone, 'she's not simple. Whoever said so?'

'Everyone says so. Why else would they keep her shut up in the house like that? She never goes out, and never speaks to anyone.' She peered with interest through the rain. 'She must have escaped her keepers. They say lunatics are cunning.'

'You must not repeat such tattle, Mrs Silk,' the doctor said firmly. 'I've hardly spoken ten words to her, but I can assure you she is quite sensible. Mr Meldon is a recluse and his daughter keeps him company, that's all.'

'But Martha says the butcher told her that when he called one time and Miss Meldon opened the door to him, she looked frightened to death and ran off into the house, and the next minute the servant came and spoke very sharply. They don't want anyone to find out that the girl is – you know.' She tapped her muslin-bowered head significantly.

'Martha is a romancer,' the doctor said. 'And the child will catch her death in that rain. She must come in.'

'Ask a madwoman in, Doctor Silk?' Mrs Silk said, opening her eyes very wide.

'I assure you she is not mad,' the doctor said testily, and strode to the door. 'Martha! Martha! Miss Meldon is standing under the chestnut tree soaked to the skin. Take the big umbrella and go and ask her to come in.'

Charlotte was startled out of her reverie to find a large black umbrella hurrying towards her, calling her name breathlessly. Martha was middle-aged and comfortably stout, and in the way of house-servants she hated going out of doors except on the balmiest of days. She picked her way past the puddles with the dainty distaste of a cat, the umbrella well down over her head and shoulders. The hand that held up her skirts was red and wet, and her bare forearms were spangled with fish-scales: she had been gutting herring when interrupted by this mission of of mercy, as Charlotte's nose soon confirmed.

'Doctor says come you in, my maiden, till that stops,' Martha gasped, tilting back the umbrella to eye Charlotte with undisguised fascination. The Meldons had long been a talking point in the village, with their mysterious, secretive ways.

Charlotte was embarrassed. Forbidden to speak to anyone, she was sure that to enter a strange house would be a serious offence. Yet the servant had issued the invitation with the force of one who does not expect to be denied; and out of the corner of her eye she could see the doctor himself at his front parlour window, beckoning and nodding to reinforce the imperative. It would be rude to refuse – but how could she possibly accept?

'Oh, no, thank you – you're very kind – but I do very well here,' Charlotte said unhappily. 'Please thank the doctor for me.' She met the servant's obdurate gaze and looked away to add hopefully, 'I think it's stopping.'

Martha looked around at the increasingly lowering sky. 'That hent,' she contradicted flatly. 'That'll come down stair-rods pren'ly. Come you in the house, miss, do. You'll starve o' cold.'

Charlotte struggled with the social dilemma. 'No, really. I can't. Thank you, but I mustn't. Papa said—'

The servant laid a dank hand on Charlotte's forearm. 'Don't you fret, my maiden. Your pa woo'n't want you to catch a fever. He know Doctor well enough, don't he? So come you in and get dry.'

Charlotte felt she could resist no longer. The doctor came to the door as they made their dash, and with his own hands removed Charlotte's wet mantle, shook it, and handed it to the servant. 'Take that to the kitchen fire, Martha.' Then he ushered Charlotte into the front parlour, where the fire, which he had just poked up to brightness, made the day outside look darker by comparison. Mrs Silk had removed herself upstairs, her fear of lunatics stronger than her curiosity.

'Treacherous, these April showers – and I'll swear they're wetter than any other time of year,' he said comfortably. From treating children he knew the value of a gentle stream of conversation for soothing the fear of the unknown. 'Come, sit ye down in this chair. Put your feet up on the fender, that's right. We can't have you catching cold, that would never do. Are your stockings wet?'

'No, sir, not at all. I have very stout boots,' Charlotte said in a small, shy voice. 'I was growing cold, though,' she added, not wishing to seem ungracious. 'You are very kind.'

'No, my dear, I'm a selfish old man who craves amusement, and I know the value of an unexpected visitor on a wet day at this time of year.' His voice, deep with a faint Scottish burr, was very soothing. Charlotte watched passively as he fetched two tins from the chimney-cupboard and swung the kettle over the fire. 'Now I'm going to make you some tea,' he said, 'and we'll have some of Martha's plum-cake with it, for as we say in Scotland, "What's tea wi-oot a piece?"'

Charlotte felt one last protest working its way up like an unwelcome hiccough. 'Oh, but really, I mustn't stay—' But it was so cosy here, and the predicted stair-rods were bouncing off the road outside, and she was in a permanent condition of pining for company. Even to her own ears, the protest lacked conviction.

Doctor Silk straightened up and stood looking down at her, the stiff white commas of his eyebrows drawn down more in thought than disapproval. It was not for him to countervene the legitimate authority of a father over his daughter, but he had been a rebel all his life, and could never resist bending what he saw as foolish rules when he encountered them. Besides, he was full of curiosity about Heath Cottage.

'Why, I'm your father's physician, lassie,' he said. 'Where's the harm in setting with me a while, just until the rain passes? Don't you see me often enough at your own house?'

Charlotte nodded doubtfully. It sounded perfectly reasonable, but still Papa's rules weighted her spirits. A child accepts its circumstances without question, until it has other experience to measure against, and Charlotte, lacking experience of any sort, was a child in spite of her score of years. For as long as she could remember, she had been kept apart from all people, living in seclusion at first with her aunt and Papa, and for the last three years since Aunt died, with Papa alone. She did not know why contact with other people was forbidden, but Aunt had always hinted that it was Charlotte's fault. Thus a sense of guilt reinforced the obedience which was a child's Christian duty towards her parent.

So Charlotte obeyed the rules, keeping to the unfrequented marsh when she went for her walks, and minding her tongue when she spoke to the servants. But it was hard, for she had a sociable soul which longed for company and conversation; a mind full of curiosity about the world; and a tongue primed with a thousand questions.

She was easy prey to the doctor, who was skilled at drawing out his subjects. At first he made all the running, chatting lightly of the weather and the local farmers' complaints, requiring no answers from her, until she was lulled into a sense of security. Then when he finally did ask her a direct question, it was one she was able to answer comfortably.

'And how is your good father? I assume, since I haven't been called to see him, that he's no worse since last week?'

'No worse,' Charlotte assented, 'but no better. He always gets restless at this time of year, when the evenings begin to draw out. It must be so dreadfully boring to be an invalid.' Silk nodded sympathetically, and she was emboldened to add, 'He so much enjoys playing piquet with you. It's kind of you to spare him the time.'

'Not kind at all,' Silk said. 'I enjoy a game, and your father is the dickens of a player. I swear to myself that one day I'll beat him, but I know I never will.'

'He doesn't say anything, but I know he looks forward to Wednesday evenings,' Charlotte said, eager to secure pleasure for her father.

'Do you not play cards with him?'

'I'm not very good at piquet, though I almost always beat when we play cribbage.'

'If you think he would like it,' Silk said, 'I could come more often. Perhaps we could organise an exchange: you could come and chat to Mrs Silk while I sit with your father. She pines for female company.'

Charlotte coloured and looked down, the social dilemma rearing its head again. 'I'm afraid that wouldn't be possible,' she said awkwardly.

'Ah. I see. I'm sorry.' He wanted to provoke a reaction. 'It was presumptuous of me to suggest it. Of course a lively young lady would find it dull work to chat to an old woman.'

Charlotte looked so stricken, he was almost sorry. 'Oh, no! I didn't mean that. I should like it very much. But – oh dear! It's so difficult.'

'What's difficult, my dear?' Silk asked gently.

She hesitated, torn between loyalty to Papa and a dislike of hurting anyone's feelings. 'I'm afraid I'm not allowed to visit anyone. I shouldn't be here now. Oh please, when you see Papa next, don't tell him I was here. It would vex him so much, and you know he oughtn't to be upset. I'm very sorry,' she added dismally. Little as she knew about society, she was sure it was not the done

10

thing to oblige someone to conceal the fact that one had visited them.

The doctor looked at her with an ache of pity. 'I won't say anything. But my dear, why does he keep you from everybody, do you know? Can you tell me?' She shook her head. 'I only ask because I am concerned about you both. Would it not be possible for me to speak to him, to suggest that a change of society would do you both good?'

'Oh no,' she said in alarm. 'Please, it would upset him and put him in a rage and then we'd have to—'

'Yes? Have to what?'

Charlotte hesitated, but in the end felt it better to tell him than to risk his saying anything to Papa. 'We'd have to go away,' she said in a low voice. 'It's happened before. If anything upsets Papa like that, we have to move away to a new place where no-one knows us.' Three times in the past she had grown too friendly with outsiders, and it had caused a hasty departure. Leaving behind the servants she had grown used to grieved her, and she had endured months of silent reproach from Aunt; but worst of all, she felt guilty about the suffering caused to Papa. 'I don't want to have to move again,' she finished.

'What made your father choose Chetton Farthing?'

'The last time we moved was from Leicestershire. We lived in a valley by a stream, and Doctor Hopkins, who looked after Papa then, said it was too damp and we should come to the east, because of the lower rainfall.' She and the doctor looked as one out of the window, and then at last she laughed. It was like the breaking of a barrier: he saw her shoulders relax from their watchful tension.

'Well, I'm glad you did, for without your good papa I should have nothing but labourers to doctor. Three cottages and an ale-house, that's all there is to Chetton – hardly a carriage-family in the district. But as I suppose

11

you know, there's not much to be done for him besides using common sense.'

'I'm glad you think like that,' Charlotte said quickly. 'I'm sure some of the other doctors did more harm than good, with their "sovereign cures", and pretending to know more than they really did.'

Doctor Silk smiled as he said, 'Whereas I always admit to knowing very little. It's my greatest virtue!' She smiled uncertainly, and he added seriously, 'Alas, when your poor aunt fell ill, I was pretty sure it was her liver, but beyond that—' He shook his head.

'She didn't like it here,' Charlotte confided. 'She started to get aches and pains as soon as we settled in, and she was never really well that whole year.'

'It has left you very alone,' Silk suggested.

'Oh, I have Papa; and Ellen and Steven, and Alice during the day—' Charlotte said lightly. They were straying near forbidden subjects.

'Servants are not company,' Silk said. 'And your papa, I suspect, is not much company either, for a young lady. What do you do with your hours of leisure?'

'I don't understand you,' Charlotte said uncertainly, and the very question touched Silk painfully.

'In the evenings, say, when you are not attending to your papa – what do you do to pass the time?'

'I take up my work, generally,' Charlotte answered. 'I have all the fine sewing to do, because Ellen only does plain work. And I play the piano, when Papa wants it.'

'But for pleasure,' Silk insisted. 'What do you do for pleasure?'

'Oh, I read. I love to read.'

'So you should,' Silk said cheerfully. '"Reading maketh a full man."'

'Sir Francis Bacon,' Charlotte supplied.

'Quite right. You are well taught, my dear. Have you

12

finished with your governess now? I suppose you did not go to school?'

'No, I had a governess at first, when we lived in Middlesex. But we left Miss Hendrop behind when we went to Huntingdon, and Aunt taught me after that. But I'm too old for a governess now. I'll be twenty-one in December.'

Silk shook his head. 'You will think me an old fool, but I took you for about fifteen. You are a grown woman indeed! I beg your pardon if I have not spoken to you with sufficient deference.'

Charlotte didn't know how to respond, not having come across this kind of affectionate teasing before, so she went on, 'Since Aunt died, I've tried to improve myself with reading. Some of Papa's books are very dull, but he has lots of military books, and I enjoy them.'

'Yes, there's nothing like a great battle for proving what men are made of,' Silk said, filling her cup again. 'What are you reading at the moment?'

'General Mercer's *Journal of the Waterloo Campaign*.'

'It sounds most interesting,' Silk said, and went on to draw her effortlessly out. Having access only to her father's library, she was well-read in history, philosophy and theology, medicine and physiology, military tactics and engineering, but she had never had a novel in her hand. She talked intelligently, but she hardly seemed to know how to laugh. Silk was perplexed. It was his opinion that the balance of Meldon's mind must be disturbed to keep this gentle girl a virtual prisoner, but there was nothing he could do about it. One could not interfere between a man and his daughter. But perhaps if he spent more time with Meldon, he might be able to persuade him at least to include him and Mrs Silk in those she was allowed to speak to.

An increase in light showed the rain to be finally easing,

13

and Charlotte suddenly discovered how long she had been sitting there, and grew flustered with apprehension and guilt. She resisted the doctor's blandishments, and shortly set off down the wet street under the lessening rain, her mind a turmoil of new impressions, seasoned with fears and doubts.

Ellen was at the door. There was a smell of soup on the air. 'Oh miss, where have you been? I was at my wits' end. The master's wanting his dinner.'

'I got caught in the rain,' Charlotte said, taking off her mantle. 'No, no, I'll hang this up while you get the tray ready. Go, hurry.'

'Best do something to your hair before you go up,' Ellen said over her shoulder as she hurried away. 'That look like a rook's nest.'

Charlotte hurried into the parlour for the looking-glass over the fireplace. Usually she looked at herself without seeing much, but today after her meeting with the doctor she wondered how she seemed to an outsider. The face in the looking-glass was pale, with hazel eyes, strongly marked eyebrows, a wide, full-lipped mouth, fair hair with a good deal of red in it (strawberry-blonde, Ellen called it) drawn back into a knot with the side-curls held by combs. Was it an attractive face? Would it be called pretty? She thought not. Alice, the day-maid, was pretty – according to Alice – and she had a round, full face and a snub nose. Alice had had lots of beaux, and a very good young man from the next village was saving up to marry her, so she ought to know.

Charlotte knew from scraps of overheard conversation between Ellen and Alice that they thought her life strange and unnatural. She wondered what it would be like to go out to dinner, or to a ball, or to a theatre. What would it be like to have a beau? What did one do with them? Alice, with a great deal of giggling, called it 'walking

14

out', but Charlotte was not such a simpleton as to think there was nothing to it but walking. Still, someone to go for walks with would be pleasant – though she thought she would sooner walk with someone like the doctor, someone sensible to talk to, rather than a young man. The only young man she knew was Steven, and he—

He appeared in the doorway behind her, and met her reflected eyes in the glass with a silent stare.

'Is the master calling for me?' she asked, and he nodded, once each way, up, then down, like a bullock. Perhaps it was unfair judging all young men by Steven. He was Papa's nurse, his duties being to help Papa wash and dress, to carry him and push him in his chair, and to run errands. Aunt had chosen him, perhaps as much for his tiny brain as his huge strength, for he could be depended on not to stray or to gossip. Steven had no family and no friends, never wanted time off, never even left the house except on errands for Papa. When he was not actually working he sat and stared at nothing. His only pleasure seemed to be eating. He ate enormous amounts, but very slowly, which drove Ellen mad. She said it was purgatory to have to take her meals with him, for he never spoke and never smiled, just filled his mouth and chewed endlessly.

All young men could not be like Steven, Charlotte thought as she started up the stairs, or what would the world come to? And then, suddenly, a memory came back to her, something she had not thought of for years, and she stopped to consider it. She had met a young man once, when she was just a little girl. That was when they lived in Middlesex, just before the first of their sudden moves. She had been playing in the garden, and he had suddenly appeared up in a tree beyond the garden wall and talked to her. Was it a memory or was it a dream? Young men did not really appear up in trees. But she

15

remembered his face with extraordinary clarity, and his strange words. 'I shall never be far away, even when you can't see me.' And he had said that they would meet again one day. No, it must have been something she'd made up. It was so long ago—

'Move along, miss, do,' said Ellen peevishly from behind her with the laden tray.

'Sorry, Ellen.' She hurried on up, opened the door to Papa's room for Ellen, and followed her in.

'Ah, there you are! And where have you been?' he greeted her crossly. He sat in his chair by the fire, covered from the waist down by a rug of tartan wool: even in warm weather he always had his legs covered, unable to bear the sight of their mutilation. His face was drawn, and Charlotte realised with sinking spirits that he was having a bad day, which always made him snappish. She abandoned immediately any hope of introducing her meeting with the doctor into the conversation.

'Just walking on the marsh, Papa,' she said – which was true, if not all of the truth. 'I wanted to get you some daffodils, but I couldn't find any.'

'You would do better to observe punctuality. I've been kept waiting for my dinner.'

Charlotte said nothing, helping Ellen to arrange his meal as he liked it on the small table, which Steven then placed before his chair. Charlotte's was laid on the table in the window. She was ravenously hungry after her long walk and exciting adventure, and the dinner before her, plain and meagre as it was, would have been wolfed down in minutes if she had been alone. But she could not display such healthy appetite in front of her father, for whom eating was a pleasureless drudgery.

He was watching her over his spoon. The window framed her, and the setting sun, breaking through the

16

clouds at last, illuminated her hair with a coppery light. 'You're a good girl,' he said more kindly. 'You look—'

She turned her head, knowing that he had been going to say, 'You look like your mother,' and knowing equally why he did not finish the sentence. Her mother had died when she was a baby, and Papa never spoke of her. It was one of the many restrictions which made conversation hazardous. Aunt's taboos had been legion: there were things improper and things unladylike, things a Christian would never even think, things a daughter would not say to her father, and things a child would not say to an adult. When you added to that a whole series of specific prohibitions about their circumstances and Papa's past, and anything to do with her mother, it left very little. Commonplace chatter about the household or the weather was all that was definitely safe to venture on.

'I'm sorry, Papa,' she said on an impulse.

'For what?' he asked.

There seemed a perilous moment of contact between them, and she wanted to say, for everything, for being the cause of all your pain, for being the reason we have to live in this cramped cottage, miles from anywhere. But it was beyond her. In the end she said, 'For being late.'

But he looked as though he understood. He didn't smile, but his expression softened a little. He said, 'Eat your dinner,' and that was acknowledgement enough.

She ate, unaware of the taste as she thought how little she knew about her own father. She knew his first name was Marcus, for she had sometimes heard Aunt calling him by it. Marcus Meldon – a name. Of his family she knew nothing. He was an educated man, that was obvious; she thought he had once been a soldier; and Aunt had hinted they had been wealthy, but now they lived in a very small way, so she supposed all the money had gone. And he had been badly injured in what Aunt

17

had always referred to as 'the accident'. What sort of accident she did not know, and must not ask.

Successive doctors had marvelled that he had lived so long, and every winter gloomily predicted that he would not see another spring. After the doctor in Huntingdon had cut off his leg, even Aunt had believed he would die. Charlotte hated to remember that dreadful time – the hideous, dehumanising butchery of the operation, the appalling effects of the shock, which had left him for weeks afterwards in a black despair that nothing could touch. But he had recovered, and in the end it was Aunt who had gone. Poor Aunt had suffered 'a disappointment' many years ago, unspecified but never forgotten, for which she blamed Charlotte. Of course, as a Christian, it was Aunt's duty to forgive her niece, and forgive her she did, whether she liked it or not. Charlotte thought guiltily that it was really much more comfortable now poor Aunt had gone.

Glancing covertly, Charlotte saw her father had put down his spoon, having eaten almost nothing. Emboldened by compassion she said, 'Is it bad today?'

He evaded the question. 'It's hard to have any appetite when one sits in a chair all day long. *You* might amuse me more,' he said, moving his head with the impatient, helpless movement of an invalid. 'God knows, you have the lightest of duties and nothing to vex you. Is it too much to ask that you distract me a little now and then?'

'Shall I play to you?' she asked cautiously. In this mood, he was hard to anticipate.

'Have you finished your dinner? Yes, play, then. Something lively – a waltz by that damned Frenchman.'

All Frenchmen were damned to him, but he liked Chopin's waltzes. They were the only modern music in the house, sent up from London by the mail. She wondered vaguely as she sat and played who sent them –

books, too. She came to the end of the piece and looked across to see if he wanted more. The music had soothed him. He was almost smiling.

'A pity you can't play and dance at the same time,' he said. 'You used to dance for me when you were a little girl – do you remember? – round and round with your skirts flying and your cheeks flushed.' He lapsed into thought for a while, and then said abruptly, 'Twenty years old, and never been to a ball. Is it a dull life for you? Are you restless, little bird? Do you long to stretch your wings and fly away?'

She scented a trap. 'Where should I fly to?'

'Where indeed?' he replied, equally lightly; but there was a tension in his expression.

'Shall I play again?' Charlotte asked, hoping to escape the subject.

'No, no more music. Come and talk to me instead.' His watchful gaze followed her as she came to take the seat opposite him. 'I wish to know what is going on in your head,' he said. 'I know the furniture of my own too well, and I ache with boredom. Distract me, child. You have been thoughtful since you came in. Tell me what you are thinking.'

She hesitated, sensing danger; but it was too good an opening to pass up. 'I was thinking that perhaps Doctor Silk might come and visit you more often than once a week. A man's company would entertain you more than mine.'

'He would not like to spend more time with me,' Marcus said flatly. 'A poor cripple, good for nothing—'

She fell into the trap. 'Oh no, Papa, he doesn't think like that! He would be *glad* to come!' She stopped abruptly, too late.

'And how do you know so much about the doctor's state of mind, miss? What have you been doing?'

'I – I spoke to him today.'

'Where?'

'In the village. It was raining so hard, and he sent out a servant to bid me shelter in his house, and—'

'You went into his house? You disobeyed my instructions – my specific instructions? You went visiting a stranger behind my back?'

'Not a stranger, Papa—'

'You took advantage in the meanest way of my immobility.'

'Oh no, Papa!' she cried, shocked.

'Oh yes, Papa! If I had been able to follow you, if I had not been confined to a chair, would you have dared to flout my rules in that way?' She hung her head, miserable with guilt. 'After all I've sacrificed for you – your aunt's sacrifices too – all our care! Christian duty means nothing to you. Your own desires are everything. You care nothing for anyone but yourself. Oh, this is ingratitude!'

The awful word struck her to the heart. She sat silent, close to tears, rigid with pain.

'Who else have you been talking to and visiting?' he demanded.

'Only the doctor, Papa, I swear it. And I wouldn't have, except I didn't know how to refuse when he insisted so. I didn't want to seem rude, and I was very wet, so I couldn't say I wasn't. He asked after you so kindly, and said he would be glad to come and play at cards with you more often, because he enjoys it so. And I thought it would be pleasant for you—'

'It is not pleasant for me to have you discuss me behind my back,' he said sharply. A tear escaped, and she knuckled it away quickly, not wanting to provoke him further. There was silence for some time, and then he said in a more even voice, 'Come, come. Stop crying.'

She tried, but the suggestion of softening made her cry more. 'I'm sorry,' she managed to say.

'I didn't mean to make you cry, child,' he said at length. 'I was afraid, and fear makes my tongue rough. It is a bitter thing to be betrayed, and the bitterness never grows less.'

'Oh Papa, can't you tell me what it is you're afraid of?'

'I can't tell *you*: you are at the heart of it.'

'If I'm all you have to fear, then you're as safe as houses. How could I harm you?'

'You could destroy me with one word.'

'Then tell me what the word is, and I'll never say it.'

'I will make very sure you never know it – that is my security. *Our* security. I have kept us safe for too many years to let go now. You shall not destroy us, by accident or intent. I will not show you where to plunge the knife.' He was growing agitated again.

'I would never hurt you, Papa. I would never do anything you did not like,' she said, trying to soothe him.

'But you knew I did not want you to speak to anyone, and you did. It seems I can't trust you out of my sight.'

'I didn't do it deliberately, Papa, and it was only the good doctor, who is our friend. Wouldn't you like him to come and play piquet with you, and chat to you?' she coaxed. 'I'm sure it would amuse you.'

He looked at her narrowly for some time, calculating her state of mind and the risk involved. He sensed a difference in her. He had hoped to keep her hidden for ever, but he had always known the difficulties. Had the moment come? Was she trying to break free? Could he still keep her, if he played the line? Perhaps a little touch of the doctor would ease the itch for freedom. The old Scotch physician was harmless enough, and the concession might keep her from wanting stronger potions.

'Perhaps,' he said. 'I will think about it. Yes, perhaps we might have the doctor over now and then. The three of us might play cribbage together. Or I might teach you whist. Would you like that?'

'Don't you need four for whist?' Charlotte asked.

'We would play with a dummy. It's more interesting that way. Yes, a good thought of yours, child. I shall send the good doctor a note. And now you may play to me again.'

CHAPTER TWO

Summer came, a grey, disappointing one. Papa's spirits remained as low as the barometer. Pain made him restless, and he often snapped at Charlotte, driving her from the room because she irritated his nerves, and then calling for her peevishly when she was out of sight. If she tried to amuse him, he would tell her to leave him alone and stop fussing him; if she then went out for a walk, he accused her of indifference and neglect.

But there was help at hand: Doctor Silk kept his promise, and called at Heath Cottage three or four evenings a week. He played cards or chess with the invalid, or simply sat with him and chatted, and sometimes Charlotte brought her work in and sat with them, and a conversation would be skilfully engineered between the three of them by the good doctor. His delicacy in choosing subjects was much appreciated by Charlotte. He spoke of local affairs, of the political situation, of the new railway which was building between Norwich and Yarmouth – anything that was not personal or particular to the Meldons; and like a skilled horseman with a nervous colt, he gradually and gently accustomed Papa to his presence and his voice.

For Charlotte, despite her anxiety for her father, it was the happiest summer she remembered, for she was enjoying the first friendship she had ever known. Whenever she could get away, she would slip out of the cottage and run down to the doctor's house.

Silk had been born and studied medicine in Edinburgh, and had moved south by degrees all his life. He had been in Manchester in 1806 at the time of the cholera outbreak, and had caught a lifetime's interest in the connection between the conditions of poverty and disease. The country-wide cholera epidemic of 1832 had found him in Leicester; his subsequent moves to Peterborough and Norwich had interested him in rural poverty; his final semi-retirement in this secluded corner of the world had roused an interest in the problems attending the agricultural workers, particularly the gangs, which in this area of sparse population were brought in to do the open-field work.

These things he discussed with Charlotte, flattered by the interest of someone young enough to be his granddaughter. She had lived all her life with sickness and doctoring, and the subject was not a blank to her. And she was reading her way through his library, which naturally contained many medical books. Her understanding and knowledge grew rapidly, so that sometimes Silk forgot he was talking to a female – and a young female at that.

Of Mrs Silk, Charlotte saw little. The doctor's lady was a wife in the old-fashioned mould, whose concerns went no further than her house, her garden and her servants. As she could neither read nor write, she had no opinions on any subject outside her direct experience, and though she accepted the doctor's word that Charlotte was not a lunatic, she found it tiring to have such a moving, talking creature in the same room, demanding a response from her she could not give. Besides, Miss Meldon was Doctor's friend first and foremost, and Mrs Silk was happy to leave her to him, and take herself off to her kitchen or her greenhouse when the young lady appeared.

She appeared very often as the summer progressed. It was the greatest delight to her to bring her eager thoughts and opinions to the doctor, and to know he did not find them contemptible, to discuss not just medical matters, but anything that caught her hungry attention. It was real intercourse, a thorough interaction with another human being, and it made her feel glowingly alive. And though the doctor seemed to understand instinctively what must be kept from Papa, there were no forbidden subjects with him, no sudden frowns, no chill rebuffs. She was a different person in the doctor's company; she felt it, and though it gave her guilty pangs that she was being disloyal and ungrateful to her father, still it was too important to her to give it up.

There was one subject she did not discuss with the doctor, and that was the future. The way she lived, being all she knew, was not something she had ever wondered about before. Living from day to day, taking care of her father, taken care of by him, was after all what most women did. A woman was the absolute property of her father until she married, and then she was the absolute property of her husband. But Charlotte was sure that Papa never meant her to marry – and living as they did, how could it even be possible?

It was as if she had been in an enchanted sleep, like the snow princess wrapped in a thousand years of winter. But now the ice was melting, she was coming alive, and it was agony to feel her mind fill with energy and purpose and endure the frustration and tedium of her life as it was. She needed to work, she needed to strive, she needed to achieve something. She ached with the boredom of doing nothing and going nowhere, as sometimes her legs ached with sitting in a chair all evening when Papa wanted company but no conversation. The world was full of things to see and do, and if she was not destined for pleasure, still there was so much of good that needed to be done. But she knew he would never let her go.

This lay as a shadow over her thoughts through that cool, damp summer. She told herself that she should be grateful for what she had, and think of how much she had gained, not what was beyond her grasp. She had had long training in being grateful for small mercies, and patient in adversity. Doctor Silk, cannily aware of much of what went on unspoken in her mind, often praised her quiet cheerfulness to Mrs Silk.

'She's an example to us all,' he would say, and Mrs Silk would answer placidly, 'Yes, my dear,' without having much idea what he was talking about.

There was a warm, sunny spell towards the end of July, but then the rain returned. Charlotte could not give up her walks just for the weather, but there was little pleasure in struggling through the rain along increasingly dirty paths; and the damp air affected her father, brought on his pains worse than ever, shortened his temper, and made the household miserable.

One rare dry day in August she came back from her walk and saw the doctor's pony-trap standing at the door. She walked down the side path to speak to the pony – an elderly, bony, flea-bitten grey, with jutting hip bones like a cow, a jaundiced eye, and a pendulous lip. 'Luckily for you,' she addressed him, 'I took some crusts out with me today to feed the ducks. I think I may have a crumb or two left in my pocket. Yes, there we are. How do you like that, poor old pony?' The pony flapped his lips over her palm, and took up the fragments of bread with a hint of teeth against her flesh, as though to say, I am not biting you, but I very well might, so be grateful.

Charlotte smiled, and stroked his neck. Doctor Silk must have come to play cards with Papa, though it was not his day. The pony shook her hand away. 'No, I haven't any more bread,' she said. 'I wonder the doctor should have kept you standing here, though. Steven could have walked you back to your stable.'

And then the house door opened, and Ellen appeared. 'Oh miss,' she said in a cracking voice, 'thank God you've come back!'

Charlotte looked at her, and then ran.

'He may regain consciousness,' Doctor Silk said to her gravely. 'If he doesn't come to himself in the next twenty-four hours, I'm afraid there's little hope.'

Charlotte stared at him, searching for different answers in his face. 'Do you mean – he might die?'

Silk nodded. 'My dear, he is worn out. A man with a weaker constitution would not have reached his age. And given the conditions of his life, can we begrudge him to God?' Charlotte struggled with tears. The doctor longed to touch her, to comfort her, but it was not possible. He went on, 'Frankly, child, it may be a blessed release if he does go. I've been worried for some time about that other leg.'

Charlotte put her fingers against her mouth to stop it trembling. It was some time before she could speak. 'What must I do?'

'Sit with him. Talk to him – one cannot tell what a patient hears in this state. But think of him, my dear, not of yourself. If it's his time to go, let him go. You're a grown woman now.'

She didn't feel it. If Papa died she would be all alone in the world. What would she do? How would she live? She sat by his bed and tried not to be selfish, tried to think of him. She looked at his face, which in the way of faces very close to one, she had ceased really to see. Now she saw in detail how old he was, how grey, how furrowed with long pain and suffering. He must have been handsome once. She tried to imagine him a dashing cavalry officer at Waterloo – dancing at balls, playing cricket, picnicking in the forest – but there was no reality to it. The only Papa she knew was the invalid, sometimes cheerful and kind, sometimes gloomy, cross, or withdrawn. She had no memories of him from early childhood.

His breathing was very shallow; his skin was shiny and bluish grey, like some strangely coloured wax. The hair around his temples, which she had thought grey, was in fact white. She knew suddenly with certainty that he was going to die; that very soon – today, tomorrow – he would be gone, completely and for ever. This time, whatever now remained, was all that she would ever have of him, and he was all she had to love. She willed him to wake. She didn't want him to go without saying goodbye; she needed very badly to have him say that he loved her, that she had been a good daughter to him, that he would be sorry to leave her.

But he did not stir, only slept away their last precious moments together. And then she remembered what the doctor had said: 'We do not know what he may hear.' So she took up his limp hand and folded his fingers through hers, and said, 'Can you hear me, Papa?' The sound of her own voice made her feel foolish; she stopped, bit her lip, but then went on. 'I'm sorry if I have been a trouble to you, or a disappointment. I wish you will forgive me. I love you, Papa. If you could give me a sign that you forgive me – if you could squeeze my hand—'

She waited, but nothing happened. He lay insensible. The door opened and Steven came in, bearing towels and a ewer of hot water, fixing her with a resentful eye, silently demanding her removal so that he could wash the patient. It wouldn't matter any more to Papa if he was washed or not, Charlotte thought; but of course it mattered to Steven. Papa had rescued him from certain poverty and probable degradation, and he was not so imbecile he did not realise it. He had been faithful, and deserved his moment with his master.

She prepared to rise, placing Papa's hand gently back on the sheet; and at that moment, just as she was detaching her fingers from his she felt them squeeze hers slightly. She stopped dead, staring eagerly at his face; but there was no change or movement, and the hand was now quite limp. Had she imagined it? she wondered as she left the room and went downstairs. She hoped she had not. She thought she had not. He had heard, he forgave her. All was well.

The sad little funeral was over. There was no church in Chetton Farthing, which was hardly more than a hamlet; they had to go to Chetton St Peter, less than a mile away across the marsh – you could see the spire from the Meldons' house – but nearly four by road, which meant hiring both a hearse and a carriage. Arranging matters had at least kept Charlotte busy for a time – and taught her how much difference Doctor Silk had made to her life, for without him how would she have managed? It was he who directed her towards a livery stable, and told her how much she ought to pay; who stopped the coffin-maker bullying her into a more luxurious coffin than she could afford – and afterwards neglecting her as not worth his business. Doctor Silk could not do anything about the rector, however, who declined conducting the service in person for people who had not been regular communicants at his church. It was left to the curate, a poor, ragged creature who seemed to Charlotte both half starved and half witted.

Steven, Ellen and Alice walked to the church across the marsh, and Doctor and Mrs Silk accompanied Charlotte in the carriage. The six of them constituted the only mourners, and with the verger, the only congregation. The curate mumbled his way through the service, coughing and sniffing in the dank atmosphere of the church. Outside in the dripping churchyard the sexton and his lad leaned on their shovels with an air of barely restrained impatience, as though it was beneath them to dig for a gentleman of so little consequence. Ellen kept stealing glances at her young lady, not so much solicitous for her state of mind as for her dress. Ellen had dyed it for her, but she was afraid the black had not taken properly: it was both greenish and streaky, and the rain falling on it was not improving its appearance.

The service was concluded, the sexton and his lad leaped into action, shovelling for all they were worth, and Charlotte turned away from the bare gash in the earth feeling utterly at a loss.

'You will come back to our house, of course,' Doctor Silk said, and Mrs Silk, warmed by pity for the poor young lady, added her endorsement.

'Of course you will, my dear. There's a little nuncheon waiting. Your servants too. Martha will make them comfortable in the kitchen.'

Charlotte accepted gratefully. She did not much want to go back to Heath Cottage without Papa. In the days since he had died, she had found herself expecting to see him in the usual places, and was continually catching herself up and re-remembering the awful truth.

'It's like going up a step that isn't there – do you know that feeling?' she said to the doctor when they were once again in his front parlour, with a cheery fire to take the dankness out of the wet August day.

Doctor Silk nodded. 'It's natural, my dear. You know how your father used to feel the foot he had lost quite clearly? Your intellect—' he tapped his forehead – 'knows he is gone, but your heart hasn't realised it yet. It will take time.'

Charlotte obeyed his invitation to sit down. 'I'm so very grateful to you both for coming with me,' she said. 'I don't know how I could have borne it otherwise.'

'It was a great pleasure to be able to do anything for you, my dear,' Mrs Silk said. 'I'll just go and see how things are in the kitchen.'

She bustled out, and Doctor Silk took the seat opposite Charlotte and leaned forward confidentially. 'I hope you will forgive an old friend for asking a delicate question, but will you be able to pay funeral bills when they come in? If there is a difficulty—' He coughed significantly and patted his pocket.

'Oh, thank you,' Charlotte said, warmed by his kindness, 'but I can pay them. I've found Papa's money.'

'Found it?'

'Yes. You see, I knew Papa had money in the house, but I didn't know where it was, and Steven wouldn't even let me into Papa's room at first. I don't think he quite understood for some time that Papa was – gone. But when he finally understood, he took me straight to it. It was in a locked chest under the window-seat.'

'He knew where it was, then?'

'Oh yes. He was Papa's legs: when there were things to buy or bills to pay, it was Steven who did it for him. What a good creature he is! Papa being helpless, he might have run off with the money at any time. But he took his duty so seriously that it was the hardest thing to persuade him Papa would want me to have the money.'

Silk cocked his head. 'There is something about that that troubles you.'

Charlotte looked down. 'When Aunt was alive, it was she who knew about the chest, and took the money from Papa, and paid the bills.'

'And when she died, your father took Steven into his confidence instead of you?' She nodded, her head still

31

bent. Silk ached with pity for her. 'Dear child, don't take it to heart. I'm sure it wasn't that he didn't trust you. Parents find it hard to remember that their children grow up. Probably he still thought of you as a little girl.' He sought to distract her from that train of thought. 'So you opened this treasure chest – and found, I hope, a vast deal of treasure?'

'Not a vast deal, but enough to pay the immediate bills and to keep us for a few months, if we are careful. I shall have to let Alice go, but she'll be getting married soon, so I hope she won't mind. What little there is to do about the house, Ellen and I can do.'

'And Steven?'

'Steven is a difficulty,' Charlotte sighed. 'What am I to do with him? Without Papa, I haven't work for him, and if I keep him the money will run out much sooner. But he has been so faithful, I can't turn him out. Where would he go? He has no family, and how would he find another place? He'd starve.'

'No, you can't allow that, I do see,' Silk said thoughtfully. 'If you can't find another place for him, you must keep him on. But when the money runs out, what then?'

Charlotte looked at him starkly. 'I don't know. I don't know what to do, or how to live. I greatly fear that I am – that I am destitute.' The dreadful word shook them both.

'But surely what is in the chest cannot be all there is? Your father must have had his income from somewhere?'

'I don't know where. Steven says the money came by the mail – twice a year, but he doesn't have much sense of time, so it may be less or more often. And he doesn't know where it came from. I've searched Papa's room without finding the slightest clue. He was very secretive.

He received letters sometimes, but Steven says he burned everything once it had been dealt with.'

'If money was sent, probably it came from your father's man of business,' Silk suggested.

'Do you think so? I didn't know he had one.'

'He never mentioned a name to you?'

'Never.'

'Did you never happen to catch sight of a direction on the letters when they came?'

She shook her head. 'Steven collected the letters and took them straight to Papa. I never had them in my hand. And Steven can't read or write.'

'You have no relatives that you know of?'

'None,' she said. 'I am quite – quite alone.' Her voice shook.

'Not that, never that,' Silk said, feeling such a protective fury for her rising inside him that he positively hated his former patient for a moment. He took control of himself, cleared his throat, and said, 'Things may not be as desperate as you think. If money came by the mail before, presumably it will come again. Then you will know who to write to.'

'Unless there was something that Papa did to make the money come. And what if the income died with Papa? What if they want the last lot back?'

'Well, well,' said Doctor Silk, 'there's no need to get into a fret now. Let things take their course for a week or two. I am very much mistaken if someone does not write to you before long.'

'But I must plan! I can't use up all the money before I think what to do next.'

'No, I do see that – but today is not the moment for worrying about it. You will not be thinking clearly for a day or two. Let the wound heal a little, and then we shall see. You are not quite alone, after all.

Mrs Silk and I will always do everything we can to help you.'

She smiled a pale smile. 'Thank you. I am very grateful to you – for everything.' She hesitated. 'There is one other thing. May I trouble you with it?'

'Of course.'

'Papa was afraid of something. You know how we lived, hidden away from the world. It has always been like that, ever since I can remember. He was afraid that some harm would come to us if it were ever known where we were. But he never would tell me what the danger was or where it would come from. And now he's gone, and I don't know what to do about it.'

Doctor Silk looked at her levelly. 'Do you want me to answer frankly?' he asked. 'Then, my dear, I must tell you that I think the balance of your father's mind was disturbed. It was not to be wondered at, given the grievous hurt he had suffered.'

'You think poor Papa was mad?'

'Not mad, no. I've talked with him a great deal these last few months, and he was quite rational about most things. But the contrast was very marked between his thoughts on general subjects and on those personal subjects he didn't like to have touched on. He wanted to keep you hidden away, that's very clear, and I believe he thought it was for your own good; but I think – I am quite sure myself – that the danger existed only in his mind.'

'Thank you. I hope you're right.' She looked thoughtfully into the fire, and sighed. 'I used to long so to go out into the world and meet new people, but now I shall have to do it, it scares me.'

'It's natural. But you must make a life for yourself, and whatever has to be done to that end, you will do.'

She spread her hands in an eloquent gesture. 'But what can I do? I must find a way to support myself, but I'm not trained for any kind of work. I suppose – I suppose I must become a governess.'

He did not make light of it. The fact of the matter was that a gently born young woman with no father to provide for her was in a horrible position. Governess or lady-companion, the genteel version of going into service, was all that was open to her. But a housemaid was better off than a governess, better valued and better treated. And no-one expected a housemaid to be grateful for being given a home.

'Did your father have no friends?' Silk asked as a last, desperate resort. 'Did he never mention the name of any friend?'

Charlotte smiled suddenly. 'He talked a lot about the Duke of Wellington. Perhaps I ought to write to him?'

Silk laughed, glad to encourage a more cheerful frame of mind. 'I think we might find help closer at hand than that! I have an idea – I shan't tell you yet, until I see if it's practicable – but one way or another we shall see you comfortably settled. Ah, here is the nuncheon we were promised! Miss Meldon, will you place the table, while I stir up the fire. I think the rain is coming on again. What a drear August this is!'

It was a week later that Doctor Silk called at Heath Cottage, and was received by Charlotte in the dining parlour.

'It's a pleasanter room than the parlour,' she said. 'What sunshine there is falls on this side of the house.' It was an excuse not to light a fire. Silk looked at her keenly as he took a seat at the table, cater-cornered to where she had been sitting with her work before he came in. Her face had always been a little thin, but he thought it looked thinner. He hoped she was not economising on food already. Despite the sunshine, the air smelled damp;

these cottages needed a fire all year round. Rheumatism and bronchitis were the most common ailments in the village. He didn't like to see that empty grate.

But he had news which he hoped would ease her fears of destitution. 'Firstly, about a place for Steven: since all he knows is nursing, plainly he must go on being a nurse.'

'In a hospital?' Charlotte said. 'I've heard they're terrible places!'

'No, not that. A private nurse is what he must be. Wealthy people who have an insane relative generally don't care to send them to an asylum, but prefer to keep them at home, or in a private house, and it's hard to find a suitable nurse who will do the work without abusing the poor patient. Now Steven's great strength and calm temperament would make him an excellent lunatic nurse, and you would be able to give him a good character. There's always a great demand. He ought to find himself in a comfortable house with light duties and very good wages.'

'Do you think he could manage it? Would he be happy?'

'I am sure he could; and he would be happy, once he had adjusted to the change. He won't want to leave here to begin with, but it must be, sooner or later.'

'Yes, and sooner would be better. He does eat such a lot!'

He laughed at this descent from tender concern to practicality. 'It's already in hand. I've a large acquaintance amongst medical men, and trusting in your approval, I've put out an enquiry for a suitable place. I have every hope we shall hear of something soon.'

'Oh thank you, thank you! I've been so worried about Steven.'

'More so than about yourself?'

'He is our servant,' she said simply.

'Just so.' He smiled to himself. 'I've been busy on your behalf as well.'

She looked rather frightened. 'You've found me a position?'

'Not as a lunatic nurse.' It did not raise a smile. 'I took the liberty of discussing your situation with Mr Lovelace – do you know who I mean?'

'I've heard Ellen talk about him to Alice. Isn't he the squire of Chetton St Peter?'

'Squire? Not quite! No, Sir Ernest Bachelor owns Chetton St Peter and most of the surroundings. But Lovelace lives in St Peter. He's a patient of mine, and a wealthy man with a bent for good works, and he wants to help the poor. He can't do anything in St Peter, because Sir Ernest is a jealous landlord, so he looks to us as his nearest neighbours. He and I have been talking for some time about starting up a school.'

'A school?'

'For the poorest children, to teach them to read, write and reckon, and lighten the profound gloom of their ignorance just a wee bit. Poverty breeds crime and sickness, and ignorance breeds poverty. If we can teach them anything at all, they might be able to better themselves. And any addition to the sum total of enlightenment must make the world a better place, don't you think?'

'Oh, yes! When I think how much books have meant to me—!'

'You're not to be imagining any great thing,' Doctor Silk said. 'Little will be achieved, and that with a great deal of effort. But Lovelace's money and my local knowledge can set it up. What's needed is a suitable teacher – someone patient and determined, someone who can find satisfaction in very small triumphs.'

'You mean me?'

'If you would like to try it, I can't think of anyone better.

The salary will be nothing great, but it would be the means of supporting yourself respectably – and far better than becoming a governess. As a teacher you will have your own home, however humble.'

Charlotte was so relieved to think the problem of her future was settled that she almost embraced him. 'Oh thank you, sir, thank you! It's wonderful!'

'It certainly is not that,' Silk said firmly. 'Think about it for a day or two. There's no hurry. You must be clear about the task before you accept. These children will be very rough and low. It will not be easy work, and it offers only the most meagre of livings. It is not heaven I am offering you, my dear – more a sort of purgatory.'

Still she smiled. 'I understand. But I'm not afraid of living in a small way, or of hard work. If I can keep myself, and do some good at the same time, I shall be happy.'

Putting himself in her position, Silk could see that having a means, any means, of supporting oneself would be the greatest boon. He wondered whether Meldon had ever taken thought to what would happen to his daughter when he died. Had he made plans which the suddenness of his death had prevented his putting into action, or had he simply ignored the problem? Silk rather suspected the latter: a careful father would have anticipated that death does not always give fair warning. He hoped against hope that something would turn up to rescue this poor, eager child – for whatever she said, he did not believe she could have an idea how dreary the life would be. If there were any justice in the world, Meldon's man of business would write within the next half year. Doctor Silk did not hope for a vast fortune, just a competance to keep Miss Charlotte and the wolf on opposite sides of the door.

Mr Lovelace met and approved of Miss Meldon. He had a horror of over-bold modern females with opinions (though he had never met any, he had read about them with disgust) and he particularly liked Miss Meldon's blushing maiden modesty, which proved she had been brought up as a genteel girl should be. In truth, Charlotte had been near paralysed with shyness at first, Lovelace being the first stranger she had shaken hands with in memory.

There was to be a trial period, to see whether the thing was feasible before any large sum of money was put into it. Doctor Silk was to use his local knowledge to select just six children to begin with. There was a dairy-room at the back of the doctor's house which was not in use, and, if scrubbed out, whitewashed, and provided with a table and chairs, would do very well for a few months. A trifling expenditure on chalks and slates was all that was needed; and when the weather turned colder, coals for the copper in the corner, which would serve to keep the place warm. If by Christmas everyone was satisfied with the experiment, a suitable building could be acquired which would be both schoolroom and school mistress's house. In the mean time Charlotte would continue to live at Heath Cottage, and Ellen with her. Privately, Doctor Silk was not without hope that something would be heard from Meldon's agent or man of business, or whoever had been sending him money, which would render the continuation after Christmas of no concern to Charlotte. If nothing were heard by then, the experiment could be put on a permanent footing, and Ellen would have to find another position.

Silk had his own problems. Choosing the six was not easy. Children as young as three and four could earn money at simple tasks like stone-picking and gate-minding, and many parents would not forgo the income. Others were suspicious of 'book-learning', and feared their children would be made proud and set themselves above them if they could read. And some children were too debilitated by poverty and disease to be capable of learning.

When the chosen six presented themselves on the first day, they were greeted by shrieks of horror by Martha, who disapproved of the whole affair, and had positioned herself close at hand to watch over Miss Meldon. She drove them back with a broom, declaring that they were too dirty and verminous to enter Christian folks' houses; and summoned by the noise, Charlotte found them held at bay in a corner of the yard, wailing dismally with fright. Argument and negotiation with Martha followed, after which the two of them set about the unfortunate urchins with comb and scissors, scrubbing brush and quantities of water from the kitchen pump. The children howled and struggled, and only their natural fear of gentry-folk – and the tactfully introduced bribe of an apple each if they stood still to be cleaned – prevented them from running away and never coming back. It was not an auspicious beginning.

After considerable discussion amongst the principals, a new regime was worked out. Martha, Ellen and Charlotte cut out and sewed six smocks of stout Holland, and when the children arrived in the morning they left off their outer garments, washed themselves (not under the pump, though, at Charlotte's intervention, but at a wash-stand brought down from one of the spare bedrooms and with soap), and put on the smocks for the duration of their lessons. When they went home, they resumed their own clothing; the smocks stayed, and Martha satisfied her frustrations by washing them far more often than was necessary.

Even so it was not two days before Charlotte found a flea in her own clothing. Ellen shrieked and begged her to give up her association with the filthy pauper children; she refused, but after that prudently kept a dress for teaching in and changed it in the scullery on her return home, where Ellen took it up with the washing tongs and inspected it at arm's length for livestock.

After a further week Charlotte was obliged to point out to the 'committee' that they could not expect much in the way of learning if the children were faint with hunger, as she had discovered was the case. Thereafter a breakfast of porrage followed the washing, which largely reconciled the brats to the unnatural proceedings.

Charlotte was learning as she went along how to deal with the children and the situation. At first simple awe kept them quiet and subdued, so much so that it was hard to get them to respond at all; and when they did respond she had the greatest difficulty in understanding their speech, which was broad and very colloquial. Then when the awe wore off a little, some of them became bumptious, which meant that she had to reverse her former encouraging kindness and become stern and remote again. Two of the children proved to be unmanageable, and after persevering for a while she found it impossible to stop them either running away after they had had their breakfast, or disrupting the lessons if they stayed. Reluctantly she asked Doctor Silk to remove them, for the sake of the others; he did so, and two new recruits were found.

After that, things settled down. The rest of the class, sobered by the dismissal of their colleagues, minded their manners and began to learn lessons of punctuality and obedience they had not been troubled with before. Charlotte sometimes feared that those might be the only lessons they learned; anything more intellectual taxed them mightily. One child simply could not grasp the concept that the marks on the slate had a connection with the spoken word. Poor Billy tried, especially as Miss

Meldon was the most beautiful and kind creature he had ever met, and he would have died to save her the least annoyance. But the letters were never more to him than random scratches, and the notion that they represented sounds seemed wild nonsense. The only letter he ever learned to recognise was 'o'. When asked to name any other letter, he would generally, in the hope of pleasing Miss Meldon, suggest 'o'. It was not a letter to him but a piece of magic which sometimes worked and sometimes did not, sometimes producing a smile and sometimes a sigh of disappointment from his goddess.

But all in all Charlotte felt the experiment was a success; Doctor Silk and Mr Lovelace called in from time to time, and seemed impressed with the improvement in the children's behaviour and alertness. It was undoubtedly doing them good; and Mr Lovelace now talked of the school proper as a settled thing, to be set up as soon as the building was ready.

A suitable house had been found in the village, and repairs and alterations were being discussed. Charlotte had been to see it, and though it was very small even compared with Heath Cottage, it would be snug enough, and would at least be her home, not dependent on anyone's whim, but her own exertions.

Ellen refused to look at it. She did not want to leave Heath Cottage or her mistress's employ, and for some time had argued that Miss Charlotte would need a maid just as much when she was a school mistress. Charlotte pointed out that she could not afford a maid on a teacher's salary, but Ellen could not believe it was necessary for her to teach at all. Miss Charlotte was gentry, and somehow the gentry always had money enough, that was her reasoning.

'Only wait, Miss Charlotte, something will come up, you'll see,' she said again and again. Though Charlotte had warned her that her employ would end at the end of December, she would not look for a new position, convinced that God would provide, as before.

Steven had gone to his new place at the end of September. Doctor Silk had found it through a colleague: Steven was to look after a poor mad gentleman, son of a respectable family, in a large house near Cambridge. He said at the beginning that he did not want to go, Heath Cottage being the only place he had ever been kindly treated; but Doctor Silk had described it all so fully that Charlotte was sure he would be happy once he had got there. However, his gloom grew more profound day by day. In her eagerness to reassure him, Charlotte had been at pains to tell him that he was going to a better place, unaware that those were the words Ellen had used to explain to him what had happened to his master. Steven was therefore convinced his days were numbered, and the misunderstanding was only resolved when Charlotte found him in tears in the woodshed, and he confessed brokenly to her that even though he had loved his master, he did not want to die.

At the beginning of December Charlotte's birthday came: her twenty-first. She insisted that it was kept secret, and Ellen reluctantly agreed, but on the morning gave her a birthday present of a handkerchief which she had embroidered herself – a labour of love indeed, since Ellen hated fine sewing. It was only consideration for Ellen that prevented Charlotte from bursting into tears, for it made her realise how alone she was in the world. Papa was gone, Alice and Steven, and soon Ellen would be gone. She was officially of adult years now, responsible for herself. It seemed a melancholy occasion. Ellen still insisted that 'something would come up', but she no longer said it as if she believed it, and Charlotte learned from Martha that Ellen had been looking about for a new position.

43

On the day after her birthday, Charlotte came home from school feeling low. She was resigned to her new life as a teacher, and was grateful that she would have a salary and a home to go to, but it looked like being such a solitary life, that everything that had gone before seemed richness in comparison. The children were fond of her, and she of them, but they were not intellectual companions; and any evening that Doctor Silk did not rescue her from her own fireside, she would spend utterly alone and silent, from next month onwards for the rest of her life.

She saw that Ellen was waiting in the doorway, looking out for her, and as she drew nearer she saw her maid was flushed of face and in a state of considerable excitement. 'Oh miss!' she cried as soon as Charlotte was near enough to hear, 'It's come! It's come!'

'What has?'

'Oh miss, the letter! I went to the post office today to look at the advertisements, and Mr Petty said there was a letter addressed to the master. It must be what you've been waiting, for, mustn't it? Oh Miss Charlotte, do come in and open it and see what it says! I always said something would turn up, and this is it, I feel it in my bones. You weren't never meant for a schoolteacher, not a proper lady like you.'

CHAPTER THREE

The response was remarkably rapid. Within a week of her sending the carefully worded letter to the post, a reply was in Charlotte's hands.

> *Madam,*
>
> *I beg to ackowledge rcpt of yr letter of the 6th inst and to tender my most profound condolences on the loss of yr Noble Parent.*
>
> *I have had the honour to be for many years past yr esteemed Father's man of business, and as such have charge of, and am Sole Executor of, his Testamentary Disposition.*
>
> *Gvn tht there are considerations involved of heavy import and considerable delicacy, I wd esteem it a favour if you will find it convenient to call in person at my offe as above to discuss sd Testamentary Disposition.*
>
> *One of my clks will wait upon you on Tuesday in the forenoon to attend yr journey to London. He will furnish all the expenses of yr journey, & I will take the libty of securing elgbl accommodations for you in London until our business is concluded.*
>
> *I am, Madam, yr most obdt servt,*
>
> *Emml Joh Tarbush*
> *Tarbush & Blaxall*

The letter, with its curious mixture of business abbreviation and high-flown sentiment, left Charlotte torn between tears and laughter. Matters of import and delicacy? What could that mean – that Papa had been all to pieces, and had left her a mountain of debts? But they would hardly pay to bring her to London only to tell her that, would they? Yet what else could *delicacy* mean? And the adjective *heavy*? It sounded ominous.

Ellen was hovering nearby with an anxious face, and Charlotte handed the letter over to her without comment. Ellen was not a great reader, and it took her time to work her way through it.

'Why, miss, what a strange one this Mr Tarbrush must be! What can his kirsted name be? Is that Emily, do you think?'

Charlotte laughed aloud, and felt some of the strain fall from her. 'Tar*bush*, Ellen. And it's Emmanuel, I should suppose, and Joh is short for Johannes, which is Latin for John.'

'A Latin gentleman, is he, then?' Ellen said doubtfully.

'No, foolish! Lawyers speak Latin, that's all – it's the language the law is written in.' She could see puzzled questions fluttering about Ellen's lips, and foresaw a quagmire of explanations – four months a teacher had taught her that much. She went on hastily. 'But what do you think it can all mean?'

'This Testy Disparition, Miss Charlotte – what would that be? Oh, Master's Will, is it? Then it *is* the news you've been waiting for. But Tuesday – that only gives us two days to prepare. And you haven't a thing that's fit to wear in London. Oh miss, however shall we manage?'

'What's to become of the school, more to the point,' Charlotte countered.

'Bless you, miss, you don't need to worry about them

46

little heathens. It won't make any difference whether they go to school or not – they were all born to be hanged, and that's a fact. But London is full of desperate fine people, and what will they think of you if you go in that mouldy green dress of yours?' She looked wistful. 'I suppose you couldn't come out of mourning, just for the time? Your blue worsted is rightly smart, and I could trim the hem up with some new ribbon—'

'What an idea! To be discussing my father's Will out of mourning, and not even six months past? People would think me heartless.'

Ellen sulked. 'Well they'll think you a beggar or a gypsy, then, that's all! Your father wouldn't have let you go to London looking such a figure.' She brightened as an idea struck her. 'Us've got two days, miss. If you was to go in to Norwich today and buy a nice bit of cloth, we could make you something up between us, with your blue as pattern.'

Charlotte shook her head. 'I dare not spend the money. Suppose there's nothing coming to me? We'll just have to do the best we can. If I keep my cloak on all the time, no-one will see my shabby dress. It is December, after all.'

Half an hour later, in the doctor's front parlour, the doctor read the letter and pronounced it a curiosity. 'But then your father's life was full of mystery.'

'Do you think it's bad news?' Charlotte asked anxiously.

'Well, on the whole, I think probably not,' Silk said thoughtfully, weighing the letter in his hand as if the heaviness of the paper might reveal the heaviness of the situation. 'You aren't bidden to travel by the public coach, so there's money somewhere – lawyers don't pay *that* sort of expense out of their own pockets! No, I think it's more likely there's some odd secret to be revealed – but you might have guessed that.'

47

'I think I must go, sir,' Charlotte said apologetically.

'Good Lord, of course you must! What's your difficulty? The school? Nothing at all! We'll close it until after Christmas – give the brats a holiday! That should give you time to conduct your business.'

Charlotte wanted to talk about the letter and hear more of Silk's ideas about what it might mean, but he wouldn't be drawn. He said only, 'At the very worst, they must pay your carriage back home, and you will have had a holiday in the Great City, which you might otherwise never see.'

'But if I come back penniless?'

'You've already faced that possibility, child. If there's no money, you will be Mr Lovelace's teacher, and live in the schoolhouse.'

Charlotte had no idea how long she might be obliged to stay in London, so she had to take enough clothes to last. Over the next two days, everything had to be laundered, mended, darned, pressed, and carefully packed in her trunk, which had not been out of the box-room since they moved from Leicestershire. Ellen insisted that she must sew black ribbons on the sleeves of her two good nightgowns, in case she stayed at an inn and a chambermaid saw her. The ribbon came from two black silk cravats of Papa's which Ellen cut up, and she used it to good effect, to improve the sleeves of one of Charlotte's dyed dresses, and to retrim her winter bonnet. Martha came bustling over to offer the loan of a black lace mantilla, a present from her late husband who had served in the Peninsula.

'To put over your bonnet, for a veil,' she explained. 'That's all very well to run about the village as you do, miss, but you can't travel all the way to Lunnon without a veil, and you in mourning.' She stitched it on herself, and with a lighter hand than Ellen's turned the last of the ribbon into a neat rosette for the side. Charlotte tried it on, and found it did give a certain dignity to her figure.

'That suit you a treat, miss,' Martha said.

'It's not everyone as can wear black,' Ellen agreed.

Charlotte was shocked at herself. 'Oh, how can I be interested in clothes, and Papa hardly cold in his grave?'

'Don't you fret, miss, that's nacherel,' Martha said soothingly. 'Life do go on, wolda-nolda. Your pa's had his time, now that's yourn.'

The day arrived, and Charlotte was up well before dawn, having no idea at what time the clerk would arrive for her. Ellen made her breakfast. Charlotte was too excited to want to eat, but forced herself, reasoning that she had no idea when she might eat again; London was a long way off, and she had no idea what arrangements were commonly made for food while travelling. For all she knew she might be fasting for the next two days. Ellen prudently put a packet of bread and cheese into the side-pocket of the valise, just in case.

It was dry, but cold. As the light came, Charlotte went out into the garden to smell for snow. The marsh had a strange and silvery look at this hour, and everything was very still; the cattle were lying down, flank-deep in mist, and there was no sound but the gentle stirring of the rushes, and an occasional bird cry, oddly echoing in the fluky light of dawn. A wistfulness crept over her. She had grown fond of this place, and now in the face of an uncertain and frightening future it seemed something familiar and sure. She did not want to leave it; she did not want to go to London, where perhaps embarrassment and shame and the confirmation of penury awaited her.

Two hours later she would have been glad only to get it over with, for the waiting was worse than anything. By the time the coach finally pulled into view, Charlotte was sick

49

with anticipation, and had paced back and forth so much her legs ached. It was a large, old and shabby coach, sold into slavery at the break-up of its noble owner's estate, as the coat-of-arms, ghostly through the paint on the panel, proclaimed. When it stopped, the door opened and the occupant jumped down without bothering with the step.

In spite of her upbringing, Charlotte stared. She had never seen so odd a creature. He was so small and thin he seemed younger than her, almost a child, and yet there was such an air of ancient wisdom and self-possession about him that he might have been eighty. He had a sly, pinched, screwed-up face like an ape, and he wore a tall hat cocked at an indescribable angle. From under it his hair hung long and straggling over his high collar; his greatcoat almost brushed the mud. It and his coat hung open, revealing a waistcoat whose many colours were augmented with food stains, and a cravat of bright yellow with crimson spots, tied in an enormous bow. His thin legs were clad in trousers of yellow, brown and red check, and his square-toed boots had thick soles and stacked heels, presumably to correct the vertical deficiency of nature.

And he was to be her travelling companion! She felt as she might have if told she was to travel with a performing bear. His roving eye took in the cottage, garden, and surroundings with a profound lack of approbation, and darted back to Charlotte as his only hope in an alien world. He swept off his hat with an air.

'From Tarbush and Blaxall. Miss Meldon, is it? Hany time yore ready, miss, we can git horf.' He replaced the hat, and as if feeling the demands of polite society had been met, he straddled his legs, thrust his hands deep into his greatcoat pockets, and said, 'Gor, whatever possessed you to live in a place like this? Nothing but mud, I swear my oath; and hanimiles, a-mooing and a-booing at you. Never a house nor nothing comfortable for mile after mile.'

Charlotte felt a smile tugging at her lips. 'You are from London, I suppose, Mr—'

'Orrock, miss.' He bowed for his name. 'Yes, miss, London born and bred, and if I never see the wrong side o' Primrose 'ill again, it'll be too soon for me! I thought I'd never get here – and if it's all the same to you, miss, we can't start back too soon, for Mr Tarbush ain't allowed enough time for the journey, and that's a fact. But if *he* ever pounded his situpon to a patty in a bone-rattler over roads like these, then I'm a Chinaman!'

Ellen was staring with her mouth open in complete incomprehension at this rapid stream of words, and even Charlotte had to concentrate, for the youth spoke so quickly and his accent was so strange it was like a foreign language. However, she managed to pick out the essential part, and said, 'I've been ready to leave since six o'clock. I'll go as soon as you like – but don't you want to rest? And what about the horses?'

'Oh, they ain't gone ten miles, miss, since the change. And it'll rest me better to be heading back home than hanging about here any longer, thanking you all the same. So as soon as you're ready – into the kerridge, hif you please.'

Charlotte nodded, told the postboy where he could turn further up the lane, and went inside to put on her mantle and bonnet. Ellen came to tie her ribbons for her, and had to blink rapidly at the tears that filled her eyes.

'Oh miss, do you think you'll be safe with that young limb? I can't understand a word he says, and he don't look the thing to me at all.'

'He's from the lawyer, so he must be all right,' Charlotte said. 'I shall do very well.' The bow was tied; and as Ellen made to step back, Charlotte impulsively threw her arms

51

around her. Ellen was startled – it was the first time Charlotte had ever touched her – but after the briefest pause she put her arms round her young lady and hugged her too.

'God bless you, dear miss,' she whispered, the tears now a serious threat. 'Come back soon.'

'God bless you too, dear Ellen. Take care of everything for me.'

The carriage came back; the bags were put up; Orrock let down the step smartly, saw Charlotte in, and hopped up nimbly onto the box. Then there was a jolt, and the carriage was rolling. Charlotte hastily let down the window and leaned out, and waved as the cottage, with Ellen standing at the gate, retreated into the distance, and finally disappeared round the bend. She put up the window and settled back against the squabs, feeling very unsteady inside.

When they took a change at about midday, Orrock came up to the carriage door and suggested she might like to stretch her legs for five minutes. He helped her down, and then stood at a polite distance, his hands in his pockets and his lips pursed in a soundless whistle. When she had walked about a bit and came back to his vicinity, he turned to her and said cheerfully, 'Well, miss, going in the right direction at last! But a teejus long journey it's a-going to be, so I won't deceive you. Gor, what a place! You haven't even got the railway!'

'They say the line to Norwich will be finished next year,' Charlotte said humbly, feeling her home country had badly let down this sophisticate.

'Issat so, miss? And where might Norwich be, hif I might make bold to ask?'

'It's the county town of Norfolk, Mr Orrock. About twenty-five miles away from Chetton – where we started.'

'Five an' twenty miles, miss?'

'Perhaps thirty.'

Orrock made an indescribable sound of horror and disbelief. After a while he said, 'Well, miss, you might as well be dead as live that far from the railway, that's my opinion. Post all the way was Mr Tarbush's orders, and everything of the best for the young lady—' He bowed. 'But post beyond Hipswich there ain't – not what *I'd* call post – nor post-road neether.'

Six hours later, when they finally crawled into Ipswich, Charlotte saw his point. The roads had been uniformly bad, the post-houses sleepy, the horses slow. The last change had been made in the dark, and Orrock had beguiled the bait with bloodcurdling stories of highwaymen who preyed on travellers; but nothing more than the roughness of the road disturbed them, and they reached the White Horse unharmed by anything but exhaustion and hunger.

Charlotte was dizzy with fatigue, and had never ached so much in her life: her situpon, as Mr Orrock had called it, was as tender as a bruise, despite her petticoats. The landlord's wife, seeing her condition and her quality in one glance, hurried forward to help her in to the parlour, chased a gaitered worthy away from the fire, and set her there before a good blaze.

'You just warm yourself a bit, miss, and I'll bring you something before you go up. A drop of hot brandy and water, miss? Or would you prefer a dish of tea?'

'Oh, tea, if you please,' Charlotte said eagerly. She was very thirsty. It came quickly, and she sipped, observing through the wavering steam that the other occupants of the parlour – three of them – had gathered at the farther end to stare at her silently. It made her feel very awkward. She had lived so secluded a life that she could almost count on her fingers the people she had ever met face to face. Now suddenly there were strangers everywhere.

What were they thinking? Might they speak? How would she answer? She felt threatened, weary and tearful, quite unable to enjoy the novelty of the situation.

At last Orrock came in, accompanied by the landlady. 'Everything's settled, miss,' Orrock said cheerfully. He had not found it necessary to remove his hat, but had pushed it well to the back of his head as a concession to being indoors. 'Your room's ready, this-here dame's sent up hot water, and dinner is hordered for a-past seven, if that's conwenient to you, miss. A slap-up dinner, too,' he added confidentially, 'and tomorrow the kerridge is hordered for six o'clock sharp, and the roads being better from here on, and hif the weather don't turn bad on us, we should make London in time for dinner.' He spoke the last half sentence with such reverence and relief that Charlotte smiled despite her tiredness.

The landlady took her up to her room, which was small but clean, and whose beamed ceiling was so low she had to crouch a little. A hot wash and half an hour lying on the bed restored her a little, before the maid knocked to say dinner was ready. She felt a little dizzy when she stood up, and the floor felt as though it was moving under her feet, but as she descended the narrow, low, crooked stairs, the smell of food rose up from the kitchen regions, and she was suddenly ravenous. A table was laid for her in the parlour, and the other occupants had gone, for which she was grateful. The landlady bustled in saying, 'Don't worry, miss, you shall have the parlour to yourself from now on. I've told my man to keep the men in the coffee-room until you're done.'

Charlotte had supposed that Orrock would sit down and eat with her, but the table was only laid for one, and from the kindly chatter of the landlady as she placed the dishes, it emerged that the clerk was eating in a style of his own in the coffee-room. 'Put away the best part of a beefsteak pudding already,' the landlady marvelled, 'to say nothing o' potatoes. You'd never think it to look at him, such a rasher o' wind as he is, miss. Now, miss, if there's anything else you need, just ring the bell and I'll come in direc'ly.' She moved a little handbell closer amongst the dishes, and went out.

Charlotte was so hungry she hardly waited for the door to close before starting on the fried chicken. There were pork cutlets besides, and fried cabbage, pickled beets and chapped potatoes. There was also a thick slice of currant duff with sugar-sauce, and a dish of macaroons. It was certainly a slap-up meal to one who had always eaten so little and so plainly, and she ate every scrap.

When her hunger was assuaged, she began to feel homesick, but the feeling did not last long. As the warmth of the food spread through her, she found herself very sleepy; and soon she was climbing up the stairs to her room in a delicious stupor of fatigue, to fall into bed, and a sleep that twitched and jerked as trees and fields streamed past her in a seamless reel.

When the maid called her the next morning, she woke fresh as spring. She dressed quickly, packed her overnight things in the valise, took her mantle and bonnet in her hand, and groped her way downstairs. There was a tiny window halfway down and through its thick greenish panes she could see moving lights in the stable-yard – the ostlers were up at least. The parlour where she had eaten last night was empty and dark, the fire not kindled, and a smell of chilly staleness hanging about it. Warily she pushed open the farther door and found herself in what she supposed must be the coffee-room. There was still an odour of stale cigars, but a newly lit fire roared under the inglenook, jumping and spitting, and making the shadows leap about in the corners. One of the shadows turned out to be the landlord, busy clearing and wiping tables, and they both jumped.

'Oh, miss, you down already?'

She was afraid she had done wrong by coming in here. Never having stayed in an inn before, she did not know what rules there might be. 'The fire isn't lit in the parlour – may I sit in here a little, until we leave?' she asked timidly.

'O' course you can, miss,' he said with hearty kindness which took away all her doubts. 'Come and sit over here by the fire. There isn't hardly anyone astir so early, 'cepting the gentleman waiting for the down coach, but he hasn't 'peared yet. Will you have a bite o' breakfast, miss? I can fry you up a beefsteak in no time, if you could fancy it. A nice beefsteak and onions? Or a bite o' cold pie, mebbe?'

Charlotte contemplated with wonder the state of her appetite. 'Do you know, I really think I *could* fancy a beefsteak.'

'Course you could, miss,' the landlord said with huge approval, his hand twitching in its desire to pat her like a good horse. 'And a couple o' nice fresh eggs by the side? Though I says it as shouldn't, I can fry an egg fit for the Queen to eat.'

'I've never eaten beefsteak and eggs for breakfast in the whole of my life,' Charlotte laughed.

'It's the travelling, miss,' the landlord said wisely. 'Sets you up sharp for your vittles. That's why 'orses eats so well. Will you take tea or coffee, miss, or a pot o' small beer?'

She was just finishing when Orrock appeared – or rather staggered in, looking as though he had slept in his clothes. His crapulous face was unshaven, and took on a green tinge when he smelled fried onions. Charlotte glanced at him under her eyelashes, and concluded that the temptation of charging to Mr Tarbush's account had been too much for him, and that the vast meal he had dispatched last night had been accompanied by vaster quantities of drink. A lurking devil, which she had never suspected she had, woke in her.

'Good morning, Mr Orrock. I trust you slept well? I've just had the most delicious breakfast. I think there's still time for the landlord to fry some eggs for you – shall I ring the bell?'

'For God's sake,' Orrock said in a low moan. 'I'd take it as a pertickler favour if you wasn't to mention fried heggs.'

'Cold game pie and pickles perhaps?'

'If you please, miss, no mention of wittles in any shape or form.'

Charlotte smiled to herself and let him be. He sat down on a stool near her, so far gone he did not even ask her permission. The landlord brought him coffee with a knowing air, and as he bent to clear away Charlotte's dishes, he tipped her a ghostly wink, making her smile. It was delightful to be in on the joke – any joke, after the solemnity of her upbringing. Aunt had regarded laughter as a threat to the immortal soul.

'It's five minutes to six, miss,' the landlord said. 'Your traps is down, and the boy's putting them in the chaise this minute.'

'Thank you, I'm quite ready.' Charlotte put on her bonnet and mantle and went out into the yard, Orrock trailing after her. It was pitch dark, with that clear, liquid darkness that comes before dawn; cold, but not freezing. Lights spilled out from various windows in orange-yellow patches, and the air quivered with sounds which seemed the more sharp-edged and important because they came from unseen sources – voices, a sudden laugh, the plosive sneeze of a horse; the scrape of horseshoes on cobble, the clank of a bucket. Charlotte felt herself vibrate like a plucked string with the promise of the day, the keen anticipation embodied in those sounds. A journey! What a thrilling concept! To travel out of the darkness into the dawn, to see the grey shapes of day emerge from the nothing, as they must have done at the Creation; to be going on, and on, always something new, something different; and at the end of it, London, the greatest city in the world!

The coach was coming, clattering on the cobbles, its lamps swaying in the blackness. 'Oh, I do think travelling is the most exciting thing!' she exclaimed, unable to hold it in any longer.

Orrock's only reply was a feeling moan.

Charlotte had no idea what London would look like, and several times a group of houses close to the road persuaded her it was approaching. But when they did reach it, there was no doubt about it, for it was immeasurably vaster than anything she had ever seen before, spreading about in all directions, the houses joined up in one ribbon, with hardly a break or a glimpse of green. The traffic grew heavier, the coach slowed to a walk, and they pulled in off the busy street into an inn yard. Orrock jumped down and came to open the door.

'Whitechapel. We change here into a hackney, miss,' he announced, folding out the step. He thrust his fingers into his fob and brought out a battered watch. 'Two o'clock, just on,' he said with satisfaction. 'Now, the question is, miss, would you wish to take a bite to eat here, or go on immediate to Lincoln's Inn? This here 'stablishment does a werry tasty ordinary, so the boy tells me,' he added hopefully.

Charlotte was hungry, but the closeness to her destination made her anxious to find out what she had been summoned for. 'We'll go on, if you please.' Orrock's face fell, and he turned sharply away as if abandoning all hope of improving her character.

Ten minutes later they were in a cabriolet and rattling onwards. Orrock, now seated beside her, punished her with a lofty silence. Charlotte didn't mind. There was so much to see out of the window – such turmoil, she wondered how Londoners managed to hold on to their sanity. Carts, carriages and herded animals filled the road from side to side like a solid stream, yet more were still trying to get out of the narrow side-streets and insert themselves into the mass. Drays seemed to stop where they liked, without regard to anyone else's convenience, to load up or disgorge their freight of barrels, boxes, baskets, bales, and livestock. Cabriolets forced their way through the traffic in contrary directions as if their sole purpose in life was to make bad worse, and the drivers indulged in such crackings of their whips and such streams of profanity that it was no wonder the poor horses wore such a wild and strained look. She had wondered at first that the horses were all so thin and scrawny, but now she thought they must be bred that way on purpose, for a fat horse would never have got through the traffic.

Orrock stretched and yawned and smacked his lips with a great show of ease, and said, 'This is something like, eh, miss? A bit o' life at last!'

What could be seen of the sky was dark, and every chimney added to it, pumping out a stream of yellow-brown smoke. A thin drizzle began to fall – dirty and full of slimy smuts, some of them as big as snowflakes. Soon the surface of the road was wet, and the fresh heaps of horse-dung being added every moment were dissolving to spread in a slippery mire over the cobbles. The long-suffering horses were soon splashed to the blinkers.

Things were not much better for the pedestrians. The pavements were almost as full as the roads, and the people moved at such a pace they might have been fleeing from a fire, but in mutually hostile directions. There were such clashings of umbrellas, such frequent collisions, such shoving and dodging, that Charlotte thought walking about in London needed to be taught in a special school. She noted the dreadful state of the crossings and the fate of unfortunates who lost their footing in the morass; calculated the courage, nerve and nimbleness it took to get across a thoroughfare between the hooves and wheels. And the streets were so crooked, and crossed by so many others – to say nothing of the narrow alleys and courts down which, as they passed, she caught a glimpse of a life even less favoured.

'Quite a place, ain't it, miss?' Orrock said, with enormous pride. 'Takes your breath away, I dessay, you being from the country?'

Charlotte composed her features. She had been feeling almost sick with bewilderment of the senses – the days on which she saw more than four or five people, and them not all at once, had been very few in her life – but she was not going to let this inky ape, now wearing his tall hat so far back that it looked like a chimneypot about to topple, come the superior over her.

They seemed to have broken free of the traffic at last, and were now moving more briskly along a wider thoroughfare. The height of the unbroken houses on either side made it unnaturally dark, but in the normal course of things, the short December day was closing. Suddenly they slowed and turned sharply left through an archway, and abruptly they were in a quiet square of tall, old buildings, a lawn in the middle and beautiful great trees all around. The contrast was extraordinary.

The cabriolet was pulled up in front of a narrow house

with a flight of stone steps whose centres had been worn into dishes. Orrock helped Charlotte down, and escorted her to the door, which opened onto a narrow, panelled staircase. With a polite, '*Hif* you please, miss,' he led the way up to the first floor where he rapped at another door and opened it, saying, 'Miss Meldon, Mr Tarbush.'

Charlotte felt her stomach drop away from her with fear. Now it had come, the moment she had dreaded: she must meet her father's man of business face to face, and learn whatever dread secret he had been keeping from her all her life. She screwed up her courage, put back her veil, stuck out her chin, and stepped in.

It was a handsome, panelled room, lit by a good fire and pairs of candles in brackets around the walls, which had the odd effect of increasing rather than dispersing the perception of darkness. The yellow flames were reflected in the uncurtained windows, and glinted from the gilding on the books which lined the whole of one wall. A massive wooden desk, piled high with papers and books, was to one side of the room. The ancient Oriental carpet was worn almost through in places, the leather of the high-backed chairs was scarred with use. There was an air of shabby comfort about everything which made Charlotte feel more at ease than finished luxury would have done.

Charlotte had imagined Mr Tarbush – purely from his name – as being a very round, portly, jolly sort of man, with large whiskers. But the man who came towards her was tall, thin and crow-dark, clean-shaven, and with his hair so closely cropped she took him at first glance to be bald. He was younger than she had expected, too – or perhaps it was the keenness of his face and the quickness of his eyes. He shook her hand and invited her to the fire.

'Come and sit down – you must be very weary from

your journey. May I help you remove your mantle?' The door behind them clicked closed on the departing Orrock, and Tarbush glanced over her shoulder and then suddenly smiled at her, as though the new access of privacy had freed him. 'I hope my clerk took proper care of you, your ladyship?'

'Yes – thank you,' Charlotte said, loosening the fastenings of her mantle; then caught up with what he had said. 'Your ladyship?'

Tarbush bowed. 'Yes, your ladyship. I have so very much to tell you.'

Wine and biscuits had been placed on a little table at Charlotte's elbow, but despite her hunger, she did not touch them. Her attention was all on tiptoe; her mind was stretched wide open, like a fledgeling gaping for food.

'Your father,' said Tarbush, 'was not plain Mr Meldon. Indeed, Meldon is not strictly a name at all, but one of his titles: eighth Earl of Chelmsford and Baron Meldon. His family name – and yours too, of course – was Morland.' He looked for a reaction. 'You have never heard the name? The Morlands are one of our oldest families, armigerous since the fifteenth century, and connected to many of our great houses. You need not be ashamed to bear it, I assure you.'

Charlotte was dazed. Her name was Charlotte Morland. She was not who she had thought she was. 'My father was an earl?'

'He inherited the title in 1815 from his cousin, the seventh earl, who died in Brussels after Waterloo.'

'Did Papa fight at Waterloo?'

'Indeed he did. He was one of the Duke of Wellington's staff officers.'

'I thought he was a military man,' she said, glad that something she had always believed had turned out to be true. It was something to hold on to in this new mutability of her life.

Tarbush looked at her quizzically for a moment. 'Your father and grandfather were both military men,' he said, since that point seemed to be important to her. 'Indeed, your grandfather fell at Waterloo – otherwise the title would have gone to him first, of course.'

'All that time,' Charlotte said wonderingly, 'we were living in a tiny cottage with only three servants, and Papa was actually an earl!'

'The Chelmsford estate is a large one,' Tarbush went on. 'There is no ancestral seat, but there is an establishment in London – Chelmsford House in Pall Mall. It stands empty, however, and I'm afraid it may be out of repair. You might perhaps remember it?'

Charlotte shook her head. 'I knew that we lived in London once, but my memories are very vague – just that there was a big, dark house, and a cherry tree in the garden.'

'I don't know about the tree,' Tarbush said. 'But I do remember seeing you there, at the house, when you were very tiny – three or four years old, perhaps.'

She smiled at him shyly. 'You knew me as a child?' He bowed, looking a little embarrassed, and she was embarrassed in her turn. Perhaps one was not meant to speak of personal things to a lawyer. 'I'm sorry,' she said.

Tarbush looked at her uncertainly. He had never faced such a situation before, and was as much at a loss as she, particularly as he had no wife and no sister, so he was unaccustomed to dealing with females. His client had kept his daughter in absolute ignorance of everything to do with her past, even her identity, and now it was left to him, Tarbush, to unpick that ignorance and knit it up into a garment that this confused young creature could put on to cover the nakedness of her mind. He coughed, and took refuge in plain and lawyerly talk.

'Apart from Chelmsford House, there is other property in York and in London, which provides an income. There are commercial properties – manufactories – overseas, principally in the Low Countries and Russia, and stock in foreign companies in various parts of the world. I can provide your ladyship with a complete list at any time, should you wish it. And there is in addition a substantial sum invested in the Funds, from the interest of which your father drew his income. He drew so little, however, that the total amount has increased considerably over the last twenty years. All in all, I would say there is a very handsome fortune indeed – which all comes to you, now that you have reached your majority.'

Now she really did turn pale. 'You mean – you mean I am rich?'

He took refuge in a small cough. 'Very rich. You could live in the first style for the whole of your life on the interest alone. You are, ma'am, a very substantial heiress.'

She shook her head, bewildered. 'I thought we were poor. I thought—' Something occurred to her, and she frowned. 'But wait, I don't understand. Surely the fortune must go to whoever inherits the title – the earldom? Don't they go together?'

'Not always, but usually. In this case they do. The fortune and the title both come to you. You are now Countess of Chelmsford in your own right.'

Charlotte stared, and then shook her head. 'I beg your pardon, but – sir, surely that can't be? Females don't inherit titles.'

'It is an unusual situation. But the title was created by Charles II for an ancestress of yours, with the provision that it might pass to the female of the family as well as the male. As your father had no son, you are now Countess in your own right, and the title will pass to your son or, failing of a son, your daughter. The male line has never failed before, so you will be the first female to hold the title since the Lady Annunciata, for whom it was created.'

Charlotte stared at him helplessly, unable to think of anything to say, unable even to think of anything to feel. It was becoming moment on moment more nonsensical to her; she felt as though she were being dragged willy-nilly into the comic part of a morris dance, where anything absurd might happen next.

'I have a genealogical chart which I can show you to make it all clearer to you,' Tarbush was saying, beginning to rise to fetch it, but Charlotte held out a helpless hand to stop him.

'Please – I'm sorry – I can't take in any more.'

'Yes,' Tarbush said, looking down at her with some compassion, 'it is perhaps enough for one day. We can continue tomorrow.'

'But there is one thing I must know now.' She looked up, half frightened, half determined. 'Why did we live as we did, shut away from the world?'

Tarbush looked uncomfortable. 'I was hoping you would not ask that. But of course, it must be in your mind. All I can say is that your father chose to live away from the world, and I was charged to keep your whereabouts an absolute secret. I took care of your father's business affairs, and forwarded a sum of money to him at regular intervals. I had always expected him, of course, to reveal the true nature of things to you at some point. I suspect that if his death had not come upon him so suddenly, he would have done so when you reached your majority. That, however, we shall never know for sure.'

'But *why*?' Charlotte begged passionately. 'Please, what was Papa afraid of?'

'If you will forgive me, ma'am, I believe that part of the story would come better from someone else. I am a dry and prosaical man of the law, and I don't feel myself equal to interpreting such – such a *highly charged* matter.'

'But the danger—'

'Be assured, ma'am, that you are quite safe. All your questions will be answered to your full satisfaction, if you will be patient a little longer. Tomorrow I will take you to one who knows far more about it than I, and who will know just how to explain it all to you.'

Charlotte was feeling too exhausted and bewildered to press the lawyer any further. Tomorrow she might feel stronger, and better able to face what she feared must be a distressing revelation. Food and sleep were what she wanted now. 'Very well, whatever you think best,' she said. 'But please, can you tell me one thing: the money you spoke of, can it be touched? Is there enough to pay for my food and lodgings?'

The question seemed to tickle Tarbush; a smile over-spread his face which was almost affectionate. 'My dear young lady – any food and any lodgings in the land! I can give you this minute, into your hand, a roll of banknotes to pay your immediate necessities, until we have had time to discuss how you wish to draw on your fortune; or, if you prefer, you can charge your bills to this office, and I will settle them on your behalf. It shall be just as you please.'

'Then – I can go anywhere? I can do what I like? I am free?' It was an odd thought to one who only four months ago could not go a mile from the house, could not speak to anyone, without permission.

'In as much as any female is free, you are. But for the moment, if you will forgive me, I think it would not be wise for you to stay at an hotel, since I see you are travelling without your personal maid.'

'I haven't a personal maid,' Charlotte said wearily. 'I've never had one.'

Tactfully, Tarbush suppressed his surprise. 'For tonight at least, then, I would recommend you lodge at Mrs Welland's in Lamb's Conduit Street.'

'Who is Mrs Welland?'

'She is a respectable woman who sometimes provides bed and board for clients for me, where there is a particular need for security or discretion. The house is not luxurious, but it is clean and quiet, and you will be safe there from any impertinent curiosity. Mrs Welland is a safe hand, and a good, motherly creature besides. If you will pardon the humble nature of the accommodations—'

Humble accommodations, and a motherly creature, sounded heavenly to Charlotte. 'Oh, please, let it be Mrs Welland's,' she said.

CHAPTER FOUR

'I will send a carriage for you in the morning,' Tarbush said in parting. 'I have to be in court at eleven. Will nine o'clock be convenient?'

Outside Charlotte found Orrock waiting for her at the door of a cabriolet. It had got dark, and the carriage lamps each bore a fuzzy golden halo, repeated more dimly by the lamps which had been lit around the square. Against the light she could see the thin rain falling; it was cold, and seemed very cheerless.

Orrock eyed her sidelong. 'Mrs Welland's, eh? I had a notion the Old Man had other plans, but it's all according.'

'What old man?'

'Mr Tarbush, miss. We calls him the Old Man – and a very grand Old Man he is, I can tell you. Like a tiger. It don't do to rile him.'

'Indeed?'

'And smart as a whip, he is, too. Nobody don't never get nothing over on Mr Tarbush. They call him The Styx, miss, around the Inns – because no man alive has ever got across *him*.'

'I'm sure not,' Charlotte said, mystified.

'Oh, not you, miss! *You* got nothing to fear from him!' And he laughed at the idea. 'He'll take good care of *you*, I warrant.'

She wondered what he meant, but he was chuckling so knowingly she concluded that it would be unwise to encourage him to more familiarity. He went on chuckling, nodding and winking at intervals during the drive, evidently hoping to intrigue her, and plainly unaware that she was too bouleversée to respond.

At last the hackney stopped. Orrock peered through the window, pronounced that they were arrived. Charlotte stepped out into the clammy dark and followed him up some shallow steps to a dark door, which opened almost at once, and a cheerful voice said, 'Come in, come in – Miss Meldon, isn't it? I had a note to expect you. What a miserable night! Bags in, Peter, my dear. Look sharp now, don't let the cold in. Thank you, Mr Orrock, and forgive me if I close the door.' In an instant Charlotte found herself inside a narrow hallway, her bags whisked past her by a boy, the door shut behind her, cutting off Orrock in mid-ingratiation, and a thick curtain pulled across like a portcullis going down to keep the enemy out.

'You poor dear, how tired you look! I am Mrs Welland. How do you do?'

Charlotte found herself shaking the hand of a small, plump, smiling woman of between forty and fifty, neat as a pin, and exuding warmth and comfort as surely as a good fire.

'How do you do,' Charlotte responded. 'It's kind of you to have me here.'

'Not kind at all, it's a pleasure, I'm sure. More for me than for you, I guess, for you look fagged to death, and that's a fact. When did you last have anything to eat? I don't suppose Mr Tarbush thought to give you anything. These lawyers! Heads in the air! We have our dinner at six, Miss Meldon, so you haven't long to wait. Let me take you to your room. I've lit the fire and it won't take long to burn up, for it's a good drawing chimney. I'll send you up some hot water right away – London is such a dirty place! – and by the time

69

you've taken off your bonnet and washed your face, it'll be dinner time.'

She chatted as she led the way up to the top of the house, and opened the door on a small room with a sloping ceiling, made cosy by red woollen curtains, a red rug on the floor before the fire, and one or two well-rubbed pieces of furniture. The fire looked hopeful, and the room smelled beeswax-clean.

'Thank you. It looks very—' She didn't manage any more. It was all so homelike, and Mrs Welland looked just the sort of person any orphaned girl would choose for a mother. After the long journey and the confusion of the day she was beginning to feel very like a six-year-old who had just fallen over and barked her knee.

'I hope you'll be comfortable, my dear,' Mrs Welland said, as if she understood all that; and when she reached up and patted Charlotte on the cheek, it didn't seem at all an odd thing for a stranger to do. 'Come down when you hear the bell,' she said, and went away.

The dining-room was at the front of the house, a tall, narrow room, rather shabby, and dark with only two sconces, one to either side of the chimney. The long table was laid with such a variety of crockery that at first Charlotte could not see two pieces alike. Mrs Welland came to greet her, saw the direction of her glance and laughed. 'I call them the Lamb's Conduit Irregulars! China is not a week to last in a lodging house – especially lids, for some reason. I don't know how it is, but I haven't a serving dish in the house that still has its original lid. But as Mr Welland always says, if a man does his job like a Christian, it don't matter if he ain't handsome. Now, my dear, come and sit here, and let me make everyone known to you.'

Charlotte was ushered to a chair in the middle of the

long side, feeling very shy under so many strange eyes. Mrs Welland went round the table in order.

'This is Mr Snoddy, who has the first floor back. He is a clerk at Duxbury and Duke's.'

'Of Cheapside,' Snoddy elaborated, half rising and bowing to her. He looked to be in his twenties, a thin, pale, delicate-looking young man, with fair hair parted in the middle and well slicked down, and large blue eyes. His head and hands seemed too large for his body; his clothes were neat, but very worn. There was altogether an unsubstantial look to him, as though he and his suit were in the process of becoming transparent. 'Honoured to make your acquaintance, miss. Anything you should need in the linen-drapery way, I'm your man.'

'Mr Snoddy has been with me for two years,' Mrs Welland said, 'but Miss Cullett, here, has been my first floor front for longer than either of us cares to remember.'

The elderly lady, dressed with some formality in black with much bugle trimming, merely lifted her eyes momentarily and lowered them again, evidently even more shy than Charlotte.

'My son Peter—' This was the boy who had taken in her bags, but she saw now that he was eighteen or nineteen years old. She wondered why she had mistaken, and then he surprised her by sitting down, when she had thought he was sitting already. He could hardly be more than five foot in height.

'And my daughter Harriet—' A rather plain woman of thirty came in from the kitchen regions with a child of about two on her hip and nodded unsmilingly. She placed a sauce-boat on the table and went out again.

'Then there is Mr Gaits, who is out of Town at the moment, and our dear Doctor Anthony, who I'm afraid is late as usual,' Mrs Welland went on. 'Ah, and here is

71

Mr Welland come in at last, so I think we may as well begin. Patty, suppose you bring the gravy? We won't wait for Doctor Anthony.'

The master of the house appeared at the door, still shrugging off his greatcoat to the maidservant behind him, and getting momentarily tangled up in the newspaper he was holding. He was older than his lady, a stooping, balding man who looked kindly and worn. He greeted the company generally, Charlotte in particular, then sat down and said Grace.

There was a flurry of movement as dish-covers were removed and implements seized with the eagerness of righteous hunger. The maid brought in a jug of gravy, and planked it down amongst the dishes: a large piece of boiled beef with carrots and potatoes, a dish of faggots, a codfish with a white sauce, and a pudding with jam. Mrs Welland said, 'I'm sorry we have no sallets or fruit or anything dainty, Miss Meldon. December is a sad month.'

The food looked very appetising to Charlotte's simple habits. Her worry was quite otherwise: she had never eaten in company before, and had no idea how to go on. In desperate embarrassment she made a very slow business of unfolding her napkin and spreading it on her lap, keeping her head down and watching covertly to see what everyone else did. Mr Welland was carving the beef at one end of the table, Mrs Welland the codfish at the other. It seemed you passed your plate up for whichever of these you preferred, and helped yourself from the other dishes, which were handed up and down the table to terse requests and grunted thanks. From diffidence Charlotte accepted the offer of fish from her hostess rather than express a preference for the beef, which she didn't feel equal to in such large and mixed company. Peter Welland passed her the sauce with a friendly smile, and the vegetables came her way after no more than a look and a hesitant cough.

Silence reigned until the sharp edge of hunger was blunted. Then, as the fork-work slowed a little, conversation began to rise up, fitfully at first, but gathering strength. Charlotte noted with delight the interest these people took in each other, and the variety of ideas that was touched on – so lightly and confidently, as though every subject was equally important and accessible. She had lived all her life between hostile silences which, like bristling thorn hedges, were raised up around taboo'd subjects, so that it was hard to move without snagging oneself.

They were only halfway through the meal when the door behind Charlotte opened again. Mrs Welland looked up, and her face lit in welcome. 'Ah, come at last, Doctor Anthony! How tired you look! What was it this time?'

'The baby at Drover's Rents,' said a voice, in itself pleasant and musical, and yet full of such despondency that it made Charlotte shiver. She was enough intrigued to turn her head. A slight young man was standing in the doorway in the act of laying his hat on the side table. His hair, a dark golden brown, was tousled and sprinkled with rain-jewels; his grey-blue eyes were smudged with tiredness, his cheeks hollow under high cheekbones.

'Ah!' said Mrs Welland, as if that answered everything. 'Well?'

'It died,' he said.

'Come and sit down and eat, at all events,' Mrs Welland said in a voice brimming with sympathy. 'This is Miss Meldon, staying with us just for tonight. Miss Meldon, may I present our Doctor Anthony?'

He nodded to her civilly but without smiling. Charlotte said shyly, 'I'm so sorry about the baby.'

'So am I,' he said shortly.

Charlotte did not feel snubbed, guessing how upset he must be, but Mr Snoddy looked at her as though she ought to have, and said, 'Now, now Anthony, think about it. In the circumstances it was a mercy, from what I know of Drover's Rents.'

'You know nothing of Drover's Rents,' the doctor said impatiently.

Mrs Welland intervened. 'Come and sit down and have your dinner. Mr Snoddy, would you be so very kind as to pass Miss Meldon the pudding?'

The moment passed off. Conversation resumed, and the doctor, now seated in the empty place opposite Charlotte, addressed his dinner in silence, eating with a sort of slow desperation, as one whose mind was much distracted, but still acknowledged the needs of the body – just. As the other silent member of the company, she watched him with interest. She guessed him to be about thirty, though it was possible he was younger under the weariness. His clothes were of good quality, but old, and worn rather carelessly, as though he had dressed by feel. He seemed too thin, but there was a tautness about the line of his shoulders which suggested it was a nervous thinness – the quivering delicacy of a thoroughbred horse. Throughbred, yes – his features were very fine, his mouth firm, his whole air one of breeding. What was he doing here? she wondered. Had he no family?

He looked up and met her eye, and she blushed to be caught staring at him, though he did not seem offended. He made an obvious effort to be civil, dragging his mind back from his private thoughts. 'Do you make much stay in Town, Miss Meldon?'

'I – do not know,' she said. It was the truth, but it sounded stupid. She didn't want him to think her stupid. She didn't quite know why, but she wanted him to go on talking to her, so that she could go on looking at him.

'And what brings you to London?' he tried again.

'I – I do not quite know,' she found herself saying again.

'Miss Meldon is from Mr Tarbush's,' Mrs Welland intervened.

'Ah,' Doctor Anthony said. 'I beg your pardon.' He gave her a stiff little bow and bent his attention to his meal again. Charlotte could only do the same, feeling embarrassed, and snubbed. Why was her tongue so unready? She carried on fascinating conversations enough in her imagination; but faced with real people, she could only manage to sound like a half-wit.

When the meal was finished, the table was quickly cleared by the maid, helped by Mrs Welland and her two children, and then a brown plush cloth was laid over it, and the company sat down again to play a round game. Speculation was proposed, and Charlotte was cordially invited to join. She hesitated, not wanting to leave the company. Doctor Anthony caught the hesitation and said, 'Perhaps Miss Meldon had sooner go to bed.'

'Oh! No – really,' Charlotte exclaimed a little too hastily, and made herself blush again. 'But I've never played before. I'm afraid I don't know how.'

'Never played before?' Peter exclaimed in astonishment.

'Why, it couldn't be simpler, a child could learn it,' Mr Snoddy said gallantly. 'Pray take the seat by me, Miss Meldon, and I'll show you how in a snap.'

'Don't you do it, Miss Meldon,' said Peter, laughing as he elbowed Snoddy away. 'He always loses – hasn't an idea of the thing! You need an expert to teach you. Let me show you.'

Doctor Anthony's quiet voice cut through the teasing argument. 'The pair of you are as bad as each other. I shall undertake Miss Meldon's education myself – she deserves nothing but the best. If you please, ma'am.' And he drew out the seat next to his own. Charlotte sat down, her cheeks glowing. She had never been argued over in her life before. She had come and gone at her aunt's or her father's command, in accordance with their requirements, but it had never been so much as hinted that her presence gave them pleasure. 'It's a nothing of a game, but it serves to take one's mind away from the world's troubles,' he said. 'You will grasp it in a moment.'

It was a lively game, and even shy Miss Cullett grew pink-faced and almost voluble as it went on. Doctor Anthony was clearly the master at it, playing boldly and bidding with an amused determination. During a break in the play, when Mrs Welland had left the table to see to some crisis in the kitchen, Charlotte glanced at Anthony, and saw that he had relapsed into brooding absence. She guessed that the world's troubles had claimed him again, and sought for something to say to express her sympathy.

'What did the baby die of?' she asked at last, timidly.

He looked at her rather dazedly, coming back from a distance. 'It's hard to say,' he said at last. 'So many things were competing for him – cold, damp, dirt, malnutrition, a thousand or so diseases. You might say he died of living in Drover's Rents.'

'Is it a very dreadful place?'

'More dreadful than anywhere *you* will ever step into,' he said harshly.

She coloured at the snub. 'At home – at home I have a little school for the village children.'

He accepted the apparent non sequitur, and looked at her with more interest. 'You *have* a school? You mean you have endowed it?' She saw his eye flicker over her old and badly dyed dress, trying to place her in the correct rank of wealth.

76

'Oh, no,' she said. 'Mr Lovelace endowed it. I only teach the children. They are very poor, and do not learn well. Their homes are very low. I wondered if they were anything like Drover's Rents.'

'Perhaps,' he said, a little less impatiently. 'Poverty has the same smell wherever you go. But I doubt whether even the poorest village child suffers conditions as vile as those in our rookeries.'

'Rookeries?' Charlotte did not know the word in that sense.

'Poor tenements and lodgings of the lowest sort. Dirt, disease, hunger, crime and moral degradation all jostling each other for supremacy.' He pulled himself up. 'I beg your pardon, it is no topic for a young lady.' It was another snub, but it was more gently spoken than the last – not, she thought, because he liked her any more, but because he could not quite place her, and therefore stayed his hand out of caution. She wanted to make him talk more, but Mrs Welland had come back in, and he took the excuse to say quickly, 'Ah, now we may begin again. My deal, I think? I mean to clean you all out in the next half hour, so beware.'

Despite his words, the tokens kept accumulating in front of Charlotte, and she suspected that he was somehow cheating to allow her to win; but she was very tired, and a dreamlike air of unreality was beginning to spread over everything. The ginger-coloured pile of the table-cloth, the worn and greasy playing-cards, the glint of the tokens in the candlelight; Doctor Anthony's lean, strong hands, delicately fretted with blue veins, moving mesmerically before her as they cut and turned the pasteboard squares – a king, a seven, a knave of diamonds: these were strange, bright-edged images seen through a marsh-mist of confusion, and the voices and laughter were like the cries of unknown birds, close and faraway in the fog.

Finally Mrs Welland said, 'That's enough for tonight. I think poor Miss Meldon is almost asleep.' Obediently the party broke up. Peter cleared away the game, Mr Welland went out to smoke a pipe, Harriet disappeared again kitchenwards to attend to supper, and Mrs Welland came quietly to Charlotte's side and said, 'You go on up to your room, and I'll send the girl up with your supper on a tray.'

Charlotte accepted the suggestion with gratitude, said a general good night to the company, and received a civil one in return. Mrs Welland escorted her to the foot of the stairs, and there stayed her for a moment to say, 'I don't know your business, my dear – Mr Tarbush is tight as an oyster and in any case I wouldn't ask – but I think you are an orphan, aren't you?'

Charlotte nodded. 'How did you know?'

'Bless you, I've had enough orphans of all ages through my hands to know the look! Mr Tarbush sends me his Wards of Court and his heiresses and his scared young boys trying to be men. He knows I will take care of them.' Mrs Welland looked at her a moment longer, and then patted her arm briskly. 'God will show you what to do, my dear. All that's happened to you is for a purpose, you'll see.'

The words wandered through Charlotte's sleepy head like a little fitful breeze as she laid herself down on her bed for a moment to rest. When she woke in the morning she was still dressed, but her shoes and hairpins had been removed, and a blanket drawn over her. Whoever had brought up her supper must have done it, and taken the tray away again. She didn't remember any of it.

When Charlotte went downstairs in the morning, descending step by step into a miasma of haddock, she found that she was to breakfast alone. The others, Mrs Welland told her, had already eaten and departed to their places of work. She had slept deeply, and was physically refreshed, but the sleep lay like a barrier between her and the events of yesterday, so that they seemed distant and impossible. She tried to assimilate what she already knew, but it was like trying to believe palpable nonsense. Mr Tarbush had said she was a countess, and rich. She was not Charlotte Meldon, but Charlotte Morland. The ideas didn't fit anywhere inside her – inside she was just the same as she had always been.

Perhaps when she knew everything, it would feel more like reality and less like a burlesque. But as nine o'clock approached, she grew more and more nervous. Who was it she was to meet, who would tell her the secrets of her life? How much would it hurt?

At a few minutes after nine a rap at the front door made her jump. She had been listening for wheels, but had heard none. A moment later Mrs Welland came in with a letter. 'It was a runner from Mr Tarbush,' she said, and busied herself discreetly clearing the dishes from the sideboard as Charlotte broke the wafer and perused another of the lawyer's abbreviated epistles.

My dear Madam,

I beg to tndr my most prfnd apologies, tht ctn circmstnces hve obld me to go early to Court, & I regret I will not be able to accmpny you this forenoon as planned.

I have taken the libty of communicating with Her Lyship, who believes it wd be undesirable to postpone the meeting.

She has therefore indicated tht she will send her own carriage for you to Lamb's Cdt St at ten o'clock this am.

I trust you will find this arrngment agreeable.

I remain, dear Madam, yr most obdt servnt,

Emml Joh Tarbush.

No, Charlotte thought, staring at the paper in dismay, I do not find it agreeable. To go alone to meet the stranger who will tell me dreadful things? And *Her Ladyship?* Which ladyship? What was she to Charlotte?

'Not trouble, I hope, my dear?' Mrs Welland asked.

Charlotte had forgotten she was there. She turned. 'Only that the carriage will not come for me until ten o'clock, and I had hoped to have it over with by then.'

Mrs Welland looked at her keenly, but did not ask any embarrassing questions. 'If you have an hour to spare, perhaps we might do something about your gown. Run up to your room and slip it off and I will have Patty sponge and press it for you. And would you like Harriet to dress your hair? She has a very light hand.'

An hour later Charlotte was downstairs again, looking neater and feeling more confident, with her hair in a plaited knot which did not feel as though it would descend about her ears at any moment, and the side pieces more gracefully draped than she had ever managed to arrange them. The silent Harriet had worked with an obviously practised hand, while her equally silent baby sat on the floor and played with one of Charlotte's brush-bags. Charlotte had been grateful for her lack of curiosity, but had fallen victim to curiosity of her own. Harriet, she noted, wore no wedding-ring. Where had she come by the baby, and why, in this voluble house, was she so silent and unsmiling?

The carriage arrived only five minutes late – a chaise so glossy, drawn by such a magnificent pair, with so splendid a liveried coachman and footman, that it drew spectators to every front door and gathered around it a crowd of children silent with awe. Charlotte felt awed herself as she was helped into it, smelling the richness of new upholstery and feeling the graceful genuflection of expensive springs. Her mysterious Ladyship was evidently very rich – but then, Charlotte told herself defiantly, so am I, if Tarbush is to be believed, and if I am not really in my bed at home in Heath Cottage dreaming this.

It was a short drive, and when the carriage door opened again it was before a tall house of cream-coloured stucco. At the door a manservant in butler-black and white gloves was evidently waiting for her. Her mouth dry, Charlotte trod up the steps. She had never had to do with a real live butler before. It was the stuff of stories – but in stories heroines always knew instinctively how to address anyone, whatever their rank. She smiled nervously, but the man did not smile back, so she at once felt a fool. He bowed her in to a narrow, marble-floored hall with beautiful furniture and expensively dull paintings, with a flight of stairs leading upwards directly in front of her. Above her head a chandelier of scintillating magnificence had half its candles lit, in deference to the darkness of the day. The candles were smoother and straighter and whiter than any she had ever seen before. She turned her head to find the butler standing behind her with an air of expectation. She had no idea what he was expecting – some comment, perhaps? She said, 'It's very nice. Um – very handsome.'

The butler's eyebrows moved expressively. 'Would you care to take off your mantle, miss?'

A flood of embarrassment burned her cheeks. She turned again and let him divest her of her mantle, which he handed to a footman who had appeared as though by magic at the precise moment he was wanted. 'Her ladyship is expecting you,' the butler intoned. 'If you would be so good as to follow me.'

Charlotte's voice came out as a nervous squeak. 'If you please – *which* ladyship?'

'Lady Theakston, miss,' he said, as if she ought to have known. He trod up the stairs, and she followed him like someone climbing the steps to the scaffold. Lady Theakston? The very name sounded repressive.

She was shown at last into a lofty room so richly carpeted, so expensively, grandly furnished, that she felt her mouth open all on its own, and quickly snapped it shut again.

'Miss Meldon, my lady,' the butler said, bowing her in – a very slight bow, though, expressing his view of having to squander his highly paid deference on the shabby-genteel.

A figure rose from the sofa drawn up beside the bright fire and said sharply, 'Thank you, Denton.' The butler bowed much lower and retreated, closing the door with a heavy, soft click.

Charlotte stood rooted to the spot, wondering who this Lady Theakston could be. She was elderly but very upright – in her sixties, perhaps, but with a fine carriage and a bright, alert look in her eyes which said she would suffer fools far from gladly. She was smaller than Charlotte, but her sheer presence made her seem tall. She was dressed in a long-sleeved gown, so full-skirted it must have taken a multitude of petticoats to hold it out. The gown was of lavender watered silk, the skirt trimmed with horizontal bands of wide black lace, giving it a tiered effect. Even in her ignorance, Charlotte could see that immense time and labour must have gone into the making. Her ladyship wore a black lace shawl, which she carried over her elbows with graceful carelessness. At home, women wore shawls for warmth, and pinned them firmly in front with the ends tied together behind. This was shawl-wearing of a different order, shawl-wearing purely for decoration. Charlotte had an instinctive feeling she could not have worn a shawl so gracefully.

The oddest thing about the lady was that her hair was cropped short, covering her head evenly in a mass of grey curls, with a black velvet bandeau instead of a cap. Such near-nakedness of such an elderly head seemed almost shocking; Charlotte had to force herself not to stare.

The woman took an eager step towards her, and then stopped as though she had been jerked by an invisible leash. She stared at Charlotte with eyes that seemed to take in everything at once, from her fuzzy hair to her shabby gown, and then rested on her face with an expression Charlotte could not interpret – though she felt it could hardly be complimentary. For this woman was not only wealthy but grand, an aristocrat to her toes; the real, genuine article, before whom Charlotte felt a charlatan – clumsy, ill-dressed and ignorant. In the circumstances, the best thing seemed to her to curtsey, and to curtsey low. In any situation, you could hardly go wrong, she reasoned, by curtseying.

It provoked a reaction, at least. The woman hurried forward and drew her to her feet. Now, close-to, she was looking up into Charlotte's face, and the expression was not one of disapproval, but of emotional turmoil.

'Charlotte,' she said. 'You *are* Charlotte?' Her hand was as strong and hard as a boy's, and her grip was painful.

'Yes, ma'am,' Charlotte said.

'Yes,' she said, searching her face intently. 'I think I would have known you, in spite of everything. You are twenty-one, that's right, isn't it? Dear God! A whole lifetime past.' She broke off abruptly and said, 'You do not know me?'

'No, ma'am,' Charlotte said humbly. She felt that she was somehow failing expectations. She'd have curtseyed again, except that her hand was imprisoned.

'I was there at your birth. I was the first person ever to hold you.' The piercing eyes scanned Charlotte's face. 'I am your mother's mother, child. I am your grandmama.'

Lucy had been anticipating this moment with as much agitation as Charlotte, and for a whole week longer, ever since Tarbush had come to tell her of Marcus's death and of how he had been living all these years, he and his child, in obscurity. Lucy had been furious. 'How came you to let it happen, Tarbush?'

'My lady, his lordship was my client. I was obliged to follow his instructions,' Tarbush had protested nervously.

'Obliged, poppycock! Your client was quite clearly mad. I suppose if he had instructed you to cut your own throat, you'd have felt *obliged* to do it?'

'My dear,' Lord Theakston protested gently, feeling sorry for the man. 'There is a code of practice which legal men must follow.' Tarbush looked at him gratefully.

'Not when it's my granddaughter who's made to suffer,' Lucy retorted. 'If you had come to me, Tarbush, I could have done something.'

'She was living with her father, my lady, her legal guardian. You could not have removed her from his charge.'

'Marcus Morland was no match for me,' Lucy said grimly. 'Why do you think he ran away in the first place?' Tarbush had nothing to say. 'So he is dead – poor man,' she added with perfunctory pity. 'What took him off?'

'A stroke, I believe, my lady.'

'In August, you said? That's four months ago. The little girl, Charlotte, who has been looking after her?'

'No-one, my lady. She is not a little girl – she is one-and-twenty years old.'

This had taken some absorbing on Lucy's part, but of course she could count the years as well as anyone. All Charlotte's childhood missed; the baby she had held, for whom she had planned so much, gone for ever, and a strange young woman in her place. She felt desolate. 'But what kind of upbringing has she had? What education? You saw her letter, Tarbush. Is she sensible, or have they brought her up a clown?'

'Would you care to see the letter yourself?' he offered.

Lucy almost snatched it from him, read and re-read, trying to extract more information from it than it would bear. 'Well, she writes a neat hand, at least, and expresses herself properly. Have you answered it?'

'Not yet, my lady.'

'Why not? Get her down here at once, man. Don't leave her mouldering away in this dismal hamlet an instant longer.'

Tarbush coughed. 'I beg your pardon, ma'am, it is a little delicate. The young lady knows nothing of the truth. Lord Chelmsford's death released me from the requirement for secrecy – indeed, as she now inherits both the title and the fortune, it is my clear duty to inform her as much. But it will be a very great shock to her, and I must consider how it may best be done. That is why I have come to you.'

It was blatant flattery, but it gave Lucy pause. Certainly it was not a straightforward business. A discussion followed, and it was agreed that the family history would come better from Lucy than from the lawyer. She had, though, expected him to tell Charlotte a modicum. His letter this morning had shrugged the whole business off onto her.

And now, here was Rosamund's lost child standing before her, a tall young woman in a dreadful gown: daughter of one of the wealthiest earls in the country, with all the marks of genteel poverty about her; Lucy's grand-daughter, a stranger wearing a mocking mask in which Rosamund's face and Marcus's were subtly blended with shifting shadows of other people, some present, some past. Lucy felt almost afraid of her, as though she were a shape-shifter, who might assume the look of someone so dear to Lucy it would steal her soul from her. She could see her own mother in that face, and her father, teasing glimpses of the dear dead; every child, she thought suddenly, is the meeting place of the generations past, the confluence of so many thousand rivers.

But mostly it was Rosamund she saw, her most difficult, beloved daughter. There was Rosamund's mouth and chin, Rosamund's defiance in the face of fear. The hair was less red, more gold; the eyes were Rosamund's in outline, but a strange, changeable, uncertain colour, as though the shape-shifter had not yet learned how to hold on to the image.

But this was no ghost or deceiver. Lucy pulled herself together. The stranger standing before her, mocking her past sorrow and fragile present hopes, was a very fright-ened young girl, younger than her chronological years; in mourning for her father, bewildered by everything that was happening to her, and out of her place – that most of all. She had made an effort with her hair, Lucy saw, but nothing could redeem that gown, which had been old even before it was inexpertly dyed with cheap dye. What must she feel, to be standing here amongst more wealth and luxury than she had ever seen before, faced with a strange old woman claiming her kinship? Lucy saw the gawky girl swallow and try to keep her chin from quivering, and understood the courage that was keeping her from running away. Lucy had seen enough girls swooning and weeping and hysterical with not half the provocation. But this one, she thought, had *her* blood.

So she smiled, and held out her hand. 'Come, my dear, don't be frightened of me. Everything must be very strange to you, but that will pass. There's a great deal I must tell you, so come and sit and be comfortable.' She took her seat by the fire and Charlotte sat obediently beside her, still looking like a Parisian on the way to the guillotine. 'It is strange for me, too,' Lucy said.

'You, ma'am?' Rosamund's child had a face like clear water in which one could see everything that moved.

'You have been lost to us for so many years. I was afraid of what you might have become. But I see much to like in you, and nothing to dislike. Yes, it's true: I'm not so blind I can't see past a shabby dress. Now, if you are comfortable, I had better begin.'

Through the long morning she talked, with hardly an interruption. There was much more to tell than she had anticipated, for she could not talk of Charlotte's birth without telling her about her parents, Rosamund and Marcus, about whom she knew nothing. So she began with Rosamund's birth and childhood – 'she was a dreadful hoyden, always in trouble, and the despair of her governess, though she was remarkably clever, I don't deny' – and of her girlish infatuation with her cousin Marcus. 'Marcus never had a thought for her in those days – she was just a funny little girl in a pinafore. All he cared for was soldiering.'

As soon as Marcus was of a good age, he followed his father into the army. 'It was wartime still, of course, and every young man of spirit wanted to be doing. Marcus joined a very good regiment and went straight out to the Peninsula.'

Rosamund, then fifteen, had been heartbroken that he was going, had begged him to take her with him, disguised as a boy, to be his servant. When he refused, laughing, she had made him promise he would come back for her, and had sworn she would marry him one day.

'No-one took it seriously, of course. It's just a thing girls say at that age.'

Charlotte had agreed a little blankly. She knew nothing of love, not even of schoolroom passions, but she was glad to think there had never been anyone else in her mother's life: she wanted the love that had made her to be perfect. She wondered what it was like to love a man, thought briefly of Doctor Anthony, confused herself and thought away again.

Lucy went on, mentioning Marcus's distinguished career in the Peninsula. 'When the Waterloo campaign started, the Duke picked him for one of his staff officers – which was a pity in a way, because he was a good field officer, and there weren't enough of those.' She would not dwell on the battle, or its aftermath – even at this distance of years it was too painful to remember the generation of young men cut down like corn before the scythe – except to say that Marcus had been wounded in the battle. Lucy had taken Rosamund to Brussels for her come-out, and Rosamund had nursed Marcus, and he had fallen in love with her at last. 'His cousin the earl had died of typhoid – there was a lot of it in Brussels that summer – so Marcus came in to the title and the estate, and he and Rosamund married in 1817.'

And should have lived happily ever after, Lucy thought to herself. What had happened between Rosamund and Marcus had always puzzled her. He loved her, then and after, as much as any girl could possibly want; she had achieved her lifelong ambition and married her childhood's idol; they should have been blissfully happy. But those were troubled years, the first years of peace, and the mood seemed to affect everyone. Thousands of women were mourning their lost sons, husbands and fiancés; the country was near bankrupt, and breakdowns were common; the lower orders were restless, and there were riots, rick-burnings, and fears of revolution. In this atmosphere of national unease, something had gone wrong with Rosamund's and Marcus's idyll.

Lucy had known nothing about it. She and Danby had gone abroad just after Rosamund's wedding on a Grand Tour with her son Lord Aylesbury and Tom Weston, and had not returned for four years. When they came back, Rosamund and Marcus were living with a semblance of concord, and soon after that, Rosamund had become pregnant at last. So everything looked fair.

At this point in the narrative, Lucy stopped from a natural reluctance to tell the rest, the painful part; and the striking of the clock told her that the morning was long gone.

'You must be tired,' she said abruptly. 'Perhaps we should leave the rest for another day.'

Charlotte looked almost alarmed. 'Oh no, ma'am! I mean – if you please. I'm not tired at all.' Her urgent eyes said that she *must* hear the rest now; and Lucy, however reluctant, could see that in the same position she could not have borne to be put off.

'Very well,' she said at last. 'But we must have some refreshment. You perhaps don't realise how long I've been talking. My throat is dry. Have the goodness, will you, to pull that bell twice.'

Charlotte got up to obey, suddenly as aware as Lucy that since what had come before had been nothing anyone would want to keep secret, the worst must still be to come. Why had her father concealed himself and her with such determination? What was the dreadful crime Aunt had hinted so grimly at? And there was her mother's death to be recounted – the death that left her father so heartbroken he would never even mention his wife's name again. She turned back and met her grandmother's eyes, and suddenly there was a smile for her, a very kind smile.

'Don't look so blue, my dear child,' Lucy said. 'You're right, the worst of the story is to come; but it's old history, and once it's told, we will have done with it. The past is past now, and we have so much to be thankful for in the present. Here *you* are, after all, and I never thought I would see you again. You can't imagine how that heartens me – even if you are dressed like a washerwoman.' She shook her head with a pained expression. 'We *must* get you out of that gown as soon as possible.'

CHAPTER FIVE

A luncheon was brought with great ceremony by a whole platoon of servants: two footmen to carry the trays, another to move the furniture, a housemaid to make up the fire, and the butler to supervise the campaign. The food was laid out on delicate, beautiful china with lovely silver and crystal and lace-edged napery: a jellied soup, cold roast partridge, and a delicious pudding – a lemony custard with redcurrant jelly at its heart, which Lady Theakston told her was called Lowndes Pudding. There was also a surprising variety of fruit, given that it was December. Charlotte thought of Mrs Welland's apology, and had her first lesson in that age-old truth, that anything can be got for money.

Eating even a light meal in these surroundings, though, was much more of a trial than last night's full dinner. Charlotte dreaded making some awful blunder. She tried to eat everything a pace behind Lady Theakston, so that she could watch and copy her, but Lady Theakston ate very slowly, either from age or because she wasn't hungry. When they got to the fruit stage Charlotte felt herself on firmer ground, and when Lady Theakston pressed her to help herself from the glorious cornucopoeia, she selected a russet-streaked apple and set her teeth into it with delight. Even as she did so, she saw across the other side of the small table her ladyship's whole concentration directed towards the pear on her own plate, which she was delicately dissecting with a small silver knife.

Charlotte was deeply grateful that they were disturbed at that moment so that she could put the apple down and pretend it had never existed. The door opened, and an elderly gentleman stepped in. He was dressed in a well-cut frock with a velvet collar, skin-tight trousers held under the foot with a strap, a lilac brocaded-silk waistcoat, and a purple scarf-cravat held with a very discreet pin. Charlotte knew little about fashion, especially male fashion, but she would have been willing to bet that this was the pinnacle of it. Though he was not above middle height, his figure was trim and upright. His white hair was beautifully arranged, swept back from his brow and lightly curled above his ears; and his clean-shaven face had a look of such kindliness and geniality that when he smiled at Charlotte, she felt an extraordinary desire to run to him and hold her face up to be kissed – which was odd because she had never done that in her life, with anyone. Moreover, she had a feeling he would probably not have objected to the procedure.

Lady Theakston evidently felt a similar warmth, for her face lit when she saw him, and she at once put down her knife and held out both hands to him in a beautifully spontaneous gesture.

'Lucy, dear! Am I disturbin' you?' he said. 'Wasn't sure if you'd finished or not begun, but I thought I'd just look in.' He smiled almost impishly. 'Tell the truth, curious. Couldn't bring m'self to pass the door without takin' a glimpse at the new countess.' He crossed the room as he spoke, bent to kiss his wife's upturned face, and then turned to Charlotte with a warm smile and an outstretched hand. 'Theakston, m'dear, at your entire service. Can't tell you how delighted I am to see you here.'

Charlotte took the offered hand, and said, 'I am very glad to be here, sir.'

He closed his other hand over hers, and bent to kiss her cheek. 'Allow the privilege, I hope?' He smelled deliciously of clean linen and lavender, and impulsively she laid her own lips against the smoothly shaven cheek. He straightened up, looking pleased. 'Not a blood relation,' he said, 'but almost feel as if I was. By rights I suppose I am your step-grandpapa. By Jove, but you've a look of your grandmother about you!' He turned to Lucy. 'Don't you think she looks like you, my love?'

'You are hardly complimenting the child, Danby.'

Danby smiled at Charlotte. 'She was a tearin' beauty, you know, when she first came to London. Thought m'self privileged to be in the same company with her. Never thought I'd ever be so lucky as to marry her – but there, you never know what fate has up its sleeve! Still think she's the most beautiful woman in the world.'

'You will convince Charlotte you are nothing but a humbug,' Lucy said sternly, but Charlotte could see she was not displeased.

Theakston gave his wife a tender smile. 'Now don't let me disturb your lunch,' he said. 'I'm only lookin' in. Hope very much to make your acquaintance more fully this evenin', Charlotte m'dear. Dinin' with us, I hope? If you ain't too tired, after all the awful revelations.'

Charlotte cast a hesitant look at Lady Theakston.

'Of course she dines here,' her ladyship said severely. 'Now go away, Danby. We haven't finished yet.'

'Ah! Better remove myself, then.' He looked again at Charlotte, still smiling, but thoughtfully. 'All this must be very hard for you. But don't let it cast you down too much. Can't do anything about other people's lives, you know. My friend Brummell, for instance – got himself into fearful debt, had to flee abroad, died a pauper. Broke my heart. Couldn't help him, though. Everyone makes their own mistakes. Can't stop loving 'em on that account.'

'Go away, Danby, you're maundering,' Lucy said with authority. Theakston, still looking down into Charlotte's face, dropped a solemn wink.

'Known her since she was seventeen. Bullied me then – still does.' He took Charlotte's hand again and kissed it lightly. 'Even now I'm an honorary grandpa, and ought to be given my dignity. *A bientôt*, m'dear. Don't forget, you are with your own family now.'

When he had gone, Charlotte looked at Lady Theakston, feeling that the mood had been lightened by the interruption. Her grandmother's expression was certainly softer. She was looking into the fire with a remembering smile.

'It all seems so long ago,' she said, feeling Charlotte's eyes on her. 'George Brummell and Danby and I setting London by the ears. We were all seventeen when we first met. And yet, there's a part of you that never changes. You look in the glass, and it's a shock to see grey hair and wrinkles, because inside you're still seventeen.' She looked at Charlotte. 'You think that's impossible?'

'No, ma'am. I believe you,' Charlotte said.

It was a moment of intimacy. Charlotte felt something quivering on the air, a warmth which seemed on the brink of giving birth to something. But then a thought seemed to strike her grandmother, and a cool shadow passed over the moment.

'Pull the bell, child, if you have finished. There is much still to say, and the sooner it's out of the way, the better.'

The fire was well stoked, and the short December day was fading beyond the tall windows. The house was very quiet, no sounds nearby but the popping and spitting of the fire and the slow measured beat of the longcase clock in the corner. It gave a sense of seclusion and privacy; Charlotte took what confidence she could from it, for she was hollow with apprehension inside.

Lucy wanted to have it over. She wished Danby had not left them, but he had said from the beginning that it must be she who told the story, and alone, and she knew he was right. But it was all so painful – and she feared the reaction of this interesting young woman. She had begun to feel the tendrils of attachment stretching between them, and she wanted nothing to blight them.

'I come,' she said, 'to your father's accident. What do you know about it?'

'Nothing at all,' Charlotte said. 'He and Aunt never spoke about it. When I was little I thought perhaps he'd been wounded in battle, but when I grew older, I realised that the dates didn't fit.'

Lucy shook her head. 'No, it was nothing to do with the war – though it was not an accident. That was how it was put about, and the secret was pretty well kept. Even I did not hear the full story until some time afterwards. I tell you now what your mother told me when it was all over – not what I knew at the time.'

She stopped, and was silent so long that Charlotte at last felt she must prompt her. 'You said it was not an accident?'

The blue eyes came back from far away and fixed Charlotte with a grave, steady look. 'Your father fought a duel. He was wounded by a pistol shot. It was such a grievous wound, he was not expected to live. But his constitution was strong, and your mother nursed him with great skill, even though she was heavy with child. By the time you were born, he was out of immediate danger, though there was no certainty about his future. I was out of Town all the while, and was only called back when your mother went into confinement. I was with her all through her labour, and helped to deliver you. And shortly afterwards—' She stopped again.

Charlotte asked. 'But why did Papa fight a duel?' It sounded so strange, something out of history, a cavaliers-and-roundheads sort of idea, not anything that could happen in modern times.

Lucy looked troubled. 'My dear, there is no delicate way of putting it. Your father fought a duel because your mother had fallen in love with someone else. She had a lover.'

Charlotte was very still. She felt the words like a touch of salt, and shrank from them. All her life she had believed in the perfect love between her mother and her father – depended on it. When Mama died Papa was heartbroken, and that's why he never spoke of her: that had been her comfort, her faith. She couldn't give it up. 'It can't be true,' she whispered.

Lucy said, 'I'm afraid you are disposed to think badly of her. Well, you must make up your own mind of course, but hear the rest of the story. It is rather complicated. The affair had been going on for some time before your father found out about it. How he found out I don't know. But there was some kind of confrontation, and she agreed to give her lover up until she had given your father an heir. That is how you came to be conceived. You are your father's true offspring, you need have no doubt about that.'

It was small comfort, now she had been told that she was the product not of love but of a cold little bargain struck between her parents – for what? For form's sake? He wanted an heir, and so an agreement had been come to, between an adulteress with her heart elsewhere, and a man who had had to put his pride aside in the interests of genealogy. *That* was what Charlotte was, after all. It was bitter.

'As to the duel – it happened that your mother's lover was in Town, visiting an old friend. She didn't know that – she had promised to have nothing to do with him, and she kept her promise. But she met his friend in the street by accident, and, for what reason I don't know and can't imagine, the friend tricked her into a meeting with her lover. Your father found out and was bitterly angry. And so he challenged the friend to a duel.'

'The friend? Not the – not the lover?'

'No – and you will see how that proves her innocence,' Lucy said, almost eagerly. 'She had not tried to see her lover. Marcus believed that. It was the friend he called out, for the insult to himself – and to her. They met, shots were exchanged; your father was wounded, but the other man was killed. Even though it was a duel, the law would still have regarded it as murder. In other circumstances your father would have had to flee abroad. As it was, the story was put about that he had been hurt in an accident, and since the dead man had no family to make enquiries, the whole thing was hushed up. But you have the right to know the truth – and now you know it.'

Charlotte shook her head slowly. It was all so horrible, so sordid – no wonder her father had kept it secret from her. She wished she had never had to hear it. Her mother was an adulteress, and her father was a murderer – even if he did it for chivalric reasons. He hadn't even killed the man who had cuckolded him, which might have been some small comfort, but some other low, mean person, hardly more than a pander. Oh, how could such things be? Where was goodness? Only, she thought, in her father's intentions. She must shelter as best she could under that.

'I have almost done,' Lucy said; she was almost as exhausted as Charlotte looked. 'I will be brief. As I said, your mother nursed your father devotedly. It was largely due to her that he survived. Some months later you were born. I was there at your birth, it was I who laid you for the first time in your mother's arms, and I saw how she looked at you. Your mother loved you. I want you to know that.'

Charlotte stared at the carpet. It didn't seem to matter now.

'As soon as your mother was out of childbed,' Lucy went on starkly, 'your father threw her out of the house, and refused to allow her to see him or you ever again.' Charlotte looked up in dull surprise. 'She came to me, of course – to this house. She told me everything then. It was the first I knew of any of it, and you can imagine how shocked I was – much as you are now. I went straight away to see Marcus, to try to put things right, but he wouldn't listen to me. He shut up the house and lived there in seclusion, seeing no-one, hardly venturing out, living in the back part overlooking the gardens, so that no-one should even catch a glimpse of him or you as they passed in the street.'

Memories were coming back to Charlotte: big, empty rooms, with shutters on the windows, herself a very small child, dwarfed by the emptiness. It was always half dark inside, and you could see the bright light outside like liquid fire along the cracks, as though it was pressing against the windows, trying to get in. Holland sheets over furniture, looming in the shadows, like sleepers not to be woken. Smell of dust. A long corridor, carpeted down the centre, with locked doors either side, down which she ran, ran like a blown leaf, feeling the emptiness behind the doors, feeling the corridor lengthen as she ran, so that she would never get to the end of it, she would run for ever, alone, trapped for ever between high walls of closed doors. She had dreamed of that so often, the running, running in the dusty half-darkness; had thought it only a dream, with no roots in reality. But it had been a true thing. It was her home, that sad house full of shadows and brooding grief.

'Your aunt Barbarina was engaged to be married; when your mother was sent away, she renounced her fiancé and dedicated herself to nursing Marcus and taking care of you – with what results you will know. I imagine it did not endear you to her.'

'No,' Charlotte said. So much was making sense now: Aunt's bitterness – blaming Charlotte for all she had lost; and the terrible weight of sin Charlotte had laboured under was the tainted blood of her mother which Aunt had believed would out, if she were not constantly watched. The rigours of her upbringing had been designed to make sure she did not become a harlot like her mother.

'As you began to grow up, it became clear to Marcus that it would be impossible to keep you completely hidden in London, so he moved away, taking you and Barbarina. His one determination was that your mother should never see you again, by design or accident. To keep you from her, he changed his name, lived in the remotest places he could find, saw no-one. I believe it became an obsession with him. The rest, you must know better than I.'

And that, Charlotte thought, was what he was afraid of? That was the terrible danger that haunted him? But how could he go on year after year in the same fear – a fear so acute he would not let her speak to anyone, and forced them to flee like bedouins in the night when she grew too friendly with a servant or a tradesman? It was pitiful. More, it made no sense. It was – madness.

She looked up at last, and her expression was so lost that Lucy misgave, wondering whether she had done the right thing. Perhaps it had been too cruel; perhaps she should have invented a story, rather than plunge Charlotte into the horrible complexity that was her inheritance. But the poor child had been nourished on lies all her life, and no good ever came of that. Lucy had been brought up to believe in the importance of truth.

Charlotte said, 'Do you think that Papa was mad?'

Lucy faced the question like a soldier. 'I think – yes, probably. Considering the lengths he went to to conceal you – how you have been confined – it was not rational. But then, considering the duel – his shocking wound – I'm sure you will find it in your heart to pity him.'

'He was often ill,' she reflected, 'and in great pain. And I suppose he brooded on the past too much. He had so little to distract him. He saw nobody, went nowhere.' But it must have been madness, to go on being afraid of someone who was dead. It could be nothing else. 'When did she die? Was it very soon afterwards?'

'When did who die? Soon after what?' Lucy was confused.

'My mother. Papa said she died when I was born, and I always assumed she died in childbed. Was it soon after he sent her away?'

Lucy stared, painfully coming to an understanding of the whole situation. 'What is this? Was that what he said? He told you she was dead? Well, I suppose it made a kind of sense to him. But my dear child, she is not dead. No, no, she is alive and well.'

It was the last thing Charlotte had expected. The words, the sense, had nowhere to fit inside her thoughts. Her mother had always been dead. She could not come alive again now.

Lucy said, 'Your father divorced her some years afterwards, and she married her lover. They are very happy together. It was difficult for her at first, but she and Batchworth – the Earl of Batchworth – are accepted in all but a few places now. The steadiness of their affection for each other has never wavered.' She wasn't sure this was making things any better. Charlotte was looking unremittingly shocked. 'They have a place in Lancashire, but they spend a great deal of time in London, because Batchworth is active in the Government, and sits on a great many committees. They are in London now, indeed.' She searched the white face for reaction. 'They don't know about you. I haven't told them yet. But she has never stopped loving you, and mourning you. When I tell her the news—'

Charlotte jumped to her feet in a panic, her emotions in turmoil. 'No, no, you mustn't tell her!' She fought to accommodate the conflicting information, shaking her head like a cat trying to get free of a cobweb.

'Not tell her? What is this? She will want to see you as soon as possible.'

But Charlotte was in an absolute panic. Her mother was an adulteress, a ruined woman, a divorcée. Aunt had impressed upon Charlotte from the earliest age the evil of such people, and the shocking impropriety of those who condoned the evil by receiving them. And yet her grandmother was speaking of the couple with calm affection, expecting Charlotte to meet them. 'How could you?' she cried wildly. 'How could you be so—'

Lucy was on her feet too. 'Calm yourself, child. What ever is the matter?' She had expected shock, but had thought it would be followed by a realisation of delight, not this near-fury.

'You cannot make me meet them,' Charlotte cried. 'They are wicked, wicked people.'

'No, nonsense,' Lucy said, too surprised by the reaction to find more eloquent words.

Charlotte felt her heart thumping like a wild thing, making it hard to breathe; shadows seemed to be rushing towards her from the corners of the room. She wanted to escape, to go back to the place of certainties from which she had been so violently torn. She wanted to be Charlotte Meldon again. 'Let me go!' she implored. 'Don't make me see them! Let me go home, please let me go home!'

Lucy caught hold of her hands in consternation. 'Be still, no-one is hurting you. You are hysterical. Be still, and we will talk about it. Child, your hands are like ice. Good God – Charlotte!'

Charlotte heard no more: the shadows caught her up and whirled her away.

Lucy saw the already-pale face drain completely, even the lips whitening, and the icy hands slipped from hers as her granddaughter fainted on her drawing-room carpet.

At Lady Batchworth's house in St James's Square, Tom Weston lounged on a settle like an undergraduate, his legs stretched out before him and crossed at the ankle, his hands stuffed in his pockets. His sister faced him, her hands clenched in her lap.

'Mama's very upset,' Tom concluded. 'She feels she was to blame for not being more tactful.'

'Tact was never Mother's strong suit,' Rosamund said rather absently. 'But it's hard to know how you could put something like that tactfully. How is she now?'

'Mama? Oh, you mean Charlotte. Well, Mama had Doctor Melville in to see her the next day, and he said there was nothing seriously wrong with her, that the swoon was brought on by hysteria. He left a tonic for her nerves, and ordered her to stay in bed for a week – which needless to say Mama countermanded immediately. So she's up and about now. She isn't talking any more about going home, which is good. But she's very quiet and listless. She seems almost depressed.'

'Depressed?'

'Papa Danby says not to worry about it,' Tom said,

trying to sound cheerful. 'He says she'll come round, and when did you ever know Papa Danby wrong about people?'

'She ought to have been happy, to discover she wasn't alone in the world after all,' Rosamund said.

'You mustn't underestimate the violence of the shock of being plunged into all this. Her life before was so different. There were no visitors to the house, and she wasn't allowed to go anywhere or speak to anyone. The poor thing didn't even know how to eat her dinner – she'd never dined in company before! The only society she's ever had is in the last few months, when she's been sitting and talking with the local doctor. *That* was wild excitement to her, until now! She speaks of him as her "friend", with such a world of pride in having one, that I hardly know whether to laugh or cry.'

Rosamund said nothing. How could Marcus have been brought to such madness? What had her child suffered at his hands? And how much of it was her fault?

'Tell me what she's like,' she asked at last.

'Tallish, a little on the thin side. Something of you in her features – not much of Marcus. Papa Danby says she looks very like Mama at that age – you know that portrait of her in the dining saloon at Wolvercote? In the riding-habit?'

'Is she pretty?'

'That's a woman's question.'

'Well, give me a man's answer,' Rosamund said impatiently.

He thought. 'I wouldn't say pretty, no. But she has something. Striking, perhaps, is the word. A face you wouldn't forget. A face you could fall in love with.'

The tense lines of Rosamund's body relaxed a little. 'You like her,' she discovered.

'Yes, I like her. For all the shock she's suffered, she's struggling not to be overcome. I think she has a great deal of character.'

Rosamund got up and walked restlessly across the room, and back. 'So what happens now?' she asked at last.

'She stays with Mama, and learns how to go on in the world. Well, now she has the title and the fortune, she can't go back to her village obscurity – she sees that, or I think she does. Naturally with that upbringing she's rather awkward and solemn, and some of her notions are a little odd. Mama's concentrating on getting her new clothes made, and telling her the family history.'

'Oh Tom, I want to see her,' Rosamund said starkly.

'I know.'

'There's not a day of her life that I haven't thought about her.'

'I know,' he said again. He could have said much the same of himself. 'But you must give it time. Marcus was all she had to love in the world, and she blames you for what happened to him.'

'It wasn't my fault!' Rosamund cried. 'I begged him not to fight that stupid duel. And it was he that cast me out—!'

'I know. Dearest, don't. It's natural for her to see things from his side at present.'

'But how can she ever hear my side, if she refuses to see me?'

'Well, she doesn't exactly refuse. She'll do as she's told, like a good girl, but Papa Danby doesn't think it would be wise to force her into anything while she's in such a state of shock. When she's recovered a little—'

'But when will that be?'

'Don't be in such a despair,' Tom said with a smile. 'Where's your fighting spirit? This is not like my sister.'

'I don't feel much spirit at the moment – I seem to have been fighting for so long.'

Tom knew how difficult her life had been, both with Marcus, and afterwards. She and Batchworth adored each other, and Jes was the most tender of husbands; but for years they had longed in vain for a child, and when their only son did finally arrive, he was premature, frail and sickly. Cavendish had reached twelve years, but there had hardly been a day in his life when his mother had been able to feel secure of keeping him even to the year's end.

'Listen, dearest,' Tom said cheerfully, 'Mama has it all planned: as soon as her clothes are ready, she's taking her down to Wolvercote. Roland and Thalia aren't going down until Christmas Eve, so it'll be quiet there, which will give her time to think – and learn to ride. D'you know she's never been on a horse? I think that shocked Mama more than anything else!'

Rosamund smiled unwillingly. 'Don't tease. Then what?'

'A family Christmas. Introduce her to everyone – show her her place in the vast Morland clan. And naturally you and Jes will be there. Less daunting than meeting you separately. It will be all right.'

'Do you think so?'

'She'll have come to terms with things by then,' Tom said. 'Mama is confident that being exposed to the civilising influence of horses will bring her to a proper state of mind. And if that fails, there's a stronger influence yet which she'll never withstand.'

'What influence?' Rosamund asked, frowning. 'You don't mean religion?'

'Religion, pho! I mean Parslow,' Tom said solemnly.

'Oh Tom!' Rosamund said, laughing at last.

Meeting Tom had added to the confusion which left

Charlotte feeling so languid and tired and depressed. In the course of conversation the name of Tom Weston had come up often, but it had taken Charlotte a while to place him in the family. Grandmother had had three children by her first marriage to Lord Aylesbury – Rosamund, Flaminia (now dead) and Roland, the present Earl of Aylesbury – and none by her marriage to Lord Theakston. It transpired that Lord Theakston had adopted Tom as his son, his father, a sea-captain, having perished at Trafalgar. But Lucy referred to 'my son Tom' with evident tenderness, which was confusing. Charlotte concluded that it was just proof of a warm and generous heart.

It was before dinner on the second day that she met him. The housemaid who was dressing her had done her job quickly, and Charlotte had gone downstairs before the bell, to give herself a chance to get used to her new gown before meeting anyone. Its full skirts were held out into the fashionable bell-shape by a stiff and heavy underskirt of woven horsehair, which swayed awkwardly as she walked, and Charlotte was not sure of her balance. She wanted to get the stairs out of the way before anyone else was around, and perhaps practise walking up and down the drawing-room.

The gown was the most beautiful thing she had ever worn – of grey brocaded silk, perfectly simple, cut to perfection, its only trimming an edging of narrow black lace to the bodice and cuffs. It was, as the mantuamaker had explained to her, exactly suitable for a young woman not yet out but of age, and nearing the end of first mourning for her father. The idea that clothing could involve such subtleties of distinction was extraordinary to Charlotte. She felt she ought not to enjoy wearing clothes meant to mark sorrow, but she couldn't help liking the lovely feeling of the material and approving the elegant neatness of her outline. She felt, a little guiltily, that it made her look *almost* handsome.

She opened the drawing-room door, and there by the hearth with a sherry glass in his hand was a strange man. Charlotte's self-possession was balancing on a pin-head as it was – the presence of a stranger discomposed her entirely. She turned scarlet, felt her hands and feet grow enormous, stammered, 'Oh, I thought – that is – I beg your pardon,' and tried to back out again.

'For what?' the man asked, smiling pleasantly. 'You can't think I object to being disturbed in such a pleasant manner?' He put down his glass. 'Yes, I think I would have known you. Come, Charlotte, don't be afraid of me. I promise I don't bite.'

She advanced nervously to where he stood before the fire, a man of middling height, in his thirties perhaps, with pleasant, boyish features, smooth brown hair, delicately arched eyebrows over warm brown eyes. His face was nice and unremarkable, and she felt there was something faintly familiar about him.

'Well, who am I?' he asked teasingly. 'It is a long time since we met, but I thought I had made more impression on you. Thus is my vanity served!'

She guessed his identity – he was, after all, making free with Lord Theakston's sherry in Grandmama's drawing-room. 'Are you perhaps Mr Weston?'

'No perhaps about it. Tom Weston at your service.' He gave her a quizzical smile. 'You really don't remember me, then? I had hoped to distinguish myself from the herd, but evidently you met so many people up in trees, my face has sunk in the multitude.'

The faint, mocking familiarity of his smile slid into place. '*You* are the man in the tree?' She stared, trying to fit his reality into that dreamlike memory.

'I told you we'd meet again, though I didn't expect it to be so long.'

'You said you would never be far away, even if I couldn't see you,' she said.

'Did I? You are tenacious of memory! Yes, well, it was rather a fancifully worded promise, I suppose, but I fully intended to keep it. Unfortunately, soon after that, you and your father disappeared again.'

It was all so confusing – to discover her dream was reality. 'But why did you do it? Why did you climb the tree?'

'For the chance of seeing you, of course,' he said. 'While you still lived in London, it was possible to keep an eye on you. But then you were taken away by your father, and we didn't know where. Only his lawyer knew, and he wouldn't tell. We did everything we could to find you—'

'We?'

'Mama, Papa Danby and I. And Jes – Lord Batchworth. He—'

'I know who he is,' she forestalled him quickly.

'Ah. Well, in the end the others gave up hope. But I couldn't. Eventually – by methods I won't bore you with – I found out where you were living. I couldn't go boldly up to the front door and knock, so I climbed the tree in the hope of somehow catching a glimpse of you.'

'But why did you go to all that trouble?' she asked.

'Why? What a question!' he said, seeming put out by it. 'Because you are my sister's child.' Charlotte turned her face away. 'She grieved for you,' he went on. 'I wanted, for both your sakes, to keep contact. Was that wrong?' Charlotte said nothing. 'I only hope it was nothing I did that made your father move you on again.'

'He was always afraid,' she said. 'I thought someone had threatened him, or was trying to kill him. I didn't

108

know he was trying to hide *me*. It seems I brought him nothing but misery.'

'Charlotte, my dear,' Tom said. Her grave face, so like Rosamund's, made his heart ache. 'None of it was your fault. People do what they must, and you can't stop them. And I imagine that you brought Marcus great happiness – the greatest happiness of his life, poor man.'

She looked at him now, doubtfully. 'You pity him?'

'Who wouldn't?' He studied her for a moment, trying to understand her thoughts. 'I've known him all my life, you know. He was my cousin too.'

'I thought you'd be on – on my mother's side.'

'It isn't a courtroom; there are no sides, no criminal and victim. What happened hurt everyone, and nobody meant any harm. Sometimes things happen that seem to be unstoppable, like a boulder running down a hill.'

'But there are things that are always right or wrong, aren't there? It can never be right to – to do what she did.'

'Perhaps that's true,' he said. He knew a brick wall when he saw one, and tried to give the conversation a lighter turn. 'I'm so glad you remember me after all,' he said cheerfully. 'I ruined a perfectly good pair of trousers that day, and I should hate to think it was for nothing. You can't get moss stains out, you know. My man was furious.'

She looked, but didn't manage to smile. 'You really do exist. I thought I'd dreamed you.'

'I've sometimes thought I must have dreamed you,' he said. 'I can't begin to tell you how glad I am we have you back. The whole family will rejoice.'

'Is it a very large family?' she asked.

'Very,' he assured her. 'Cousins beyond cousins, rings of ever more remote relatives, like concentric ramparts, keeping the barbarians at bay.'

She laughed. 'How you talk! Oh, I beg your pardon—'

'No matter. Everyone says just what they like to me. I'm famous for having no feelings.'

'I know that can't be true,' she said shyly. 'Did you really search for me?'

'Really, my Charlotte,' he said solemnly.

'What – what do I call you? I suppose you are a sort of uncle.'

'You shan't call me Uncle Tom, if you please, or I shall have to take to chewing a straw and dispensing country wisdom. Just call me Tom. Everyone does.'

CHAPTER SIX

Charlotte was thrown off balance by Wolvercote. She had thought the Theakstons' house in Upper Grosvenor Street was large and luxurious, but it was at least comprehensibly a house; Wolvercote was more like a whole village which had somehow been pushed together, an accretion of buildings which, against reason, housed only one family instead of dozens.

'It's a monstrosity,' Lucy said, though with evident affection. 'Aylesbury ought to knock it down and start again.' Wolvercote had, of course, once been hers, and she seemed to Charlotte to treat it as if it still were. The only good building in the whole place, Lucy told Charlotte robustly, was the Queen Anne dower house across the park, which she asserted was a little gem and much admired; but Charlotte noticed that she had no desire to live in it rather than in the main house.

The size and complexity of the house induced a profound bewilderment in Charlotte. She had no idea whereabouts she was at any time, which way she was facing, north, south, east or west. She could not find her way from one room to another, and had to be conducted everywhere by a housemaid or footman – never the same one twice, to add to her confusion. And there was a hidden but parallel warren of servants' corridors and backstairs, which Charlotte could never catch sight of but was continually reminded of. It made her feel dizzy when a maid appeared or disappeared as if by magic out of a solid wall, or when she heard them, close but unseen, pattering up and down staircases hidden behind the wainscot. She never felt secure of being alone and private; and never opened a cupboard door without half expecting to find a stairway to the kitchen regions hidden behind it.

So she was very glad when her first riding lesson obliged her to go out of doors, where things were always what they seemed. Since leaving Chetton she had not trodden on grass, nor tasted clean air, nor listened to silence, and she discovered an appalled place in her soul that was dying for want of that great friendly solitude with which nature engulfs the lone walker. A maid conducted her from her room by convoluted wanderings until at last they reached a small, dark-panelled hall with a door opening onto sunshine. Charlotte hurried towards it, almost forgetting the maid in her eagerness to be out. Outside the chilly sun was spilling onto the gravel, a light frost sparkled over the bushes and glistened on the stone urns, and the bare trees thrust their arms up into a misty sky as pink and gold as a little girl's dream of a party-frock.

There were two horses standing there, each held by a boy. The horses looked very big to her, glossy and bright-eyed, their breath smoking on the cold air, whisking their tails impatiently as if the slightest thing would set them galloping. Was she really going to get up on one of them? She felt a mixture of elation and fear. There was also an old man in breeches and boots and a green coat, holding his tall hat in his hand, his white hair glistening in the sunlight. This, she knew, must be the legendary Parslow. She wasn't entirely sure why he was legendary, except that he had been with Grandmama since she was a young girl, but she had heard his name so often she was prepared to accept that he was. He seemed very nice and ordinary to her, with a kind face and very dark eyes.

'Well, my lady, shall we get you mounted?' He had a quiet, calm voice that she thought animals would find very soothing. 'You shan't be afraid?'

'Not of falling off – I don't think,' she added honestly. 'Only of looking foolish.'

'You won't do either,' Parslow said, as though he knew it for a fact. 'This is Ingot. You'll find him a nice, intelligent horse, who wants nothing but to please you.'

She put up a hand to stroke the glossy brown neck, and the horse turned his head towards her. His eyes were very large and benevolent, and she couldn't see any reason to be afraid of him. Parslow gave her instructions and then cupped his hands for her knee, and in a moment she was flying up, impelled by his knotty arms. When she was settled she did feel very far from the ground, with nothing but the horse's ears between her and the park; but surprisingly secure with her knee locked round the pommel.

Parslow resumed his hat, mounted, and took the leading-rein from the boy. 'Are you ready, my lady? Shorten your reins, then, and give him the office.'

She was pretty sure it was nothing she had done, but they were moving forward, two big brown horses side by side, hers attached by that comforting umbilical cord to Parslow's strong brown hand.

She took to riding, as Parslow informed her, like a duck to water. 'But I knew you would. It's in your blood.'

'I love it. I wish I had learned years ago,' she said. 'And this is such a nice horse.' She leaned forward to pat Ingot's neck. It was her third lesson, and there was no leading-rein now. She felt so at home in the saddle, she wondered anyone could find it difficult. 'He has such lovely eyes.'

'That's right, my lady. You can always tell. He's an honest one.'

113

Charlotte smiled. 'I think you like horses better than people.'

'Oh no, my lady. Well, some people, mebbe. Horses are straightforward. It isn't in them to be otherwise. Mebbe I like people who are like that too.'

'You like Grandmama.' It wasn't really a question. She just wanted him to talk.

'I've been with her since she was a girl. It was only my second position. She took a chance on me. She could have had someone much more experienced.'

'I think Grandmama likes people at once, or doesn't like them, and that's that,' Charlotte said. Parlsow nodded, impressed by her insight. 'She's a good rider, isn't she?'

'The best, man or woman, I've ever known. I do believe there isn't a horse she couldn't master – and I didn't have the teaching of her.'

Charlotte gathered this was a joke. 'I hope I shall do you credit. If you're ashamed of me, you must tell me, and I'll pretend it was someone else taught me to ride.'

'You'll do very well, my lady. You have light hands, just like your mother.'

'You taught her to ride, didn't you?' Charlotte said, feeling nervous now that the subject had arisen.

'Yes, my lady. I taught them all – Lady Rosamund and Lady Flaminia, his lordship – Lord Calder he was then – and Mr Weston. Right here in this park. But Lady Rosamund was the best by a long chalk. Very wild, she was, as a girl, but she never risked her horse's legs.'

'Were you fond of her?'

'Indeed yes, my lady.' He was silent a moment, then went on, 'The only time I was ever away from my mistress was just after Lady Rosamund married your father, and for four years I was her personal groom, while Lord and Lady Theakston was on their Grand

114

Tour. That was before you were born, of course, my lady.'

'I didn't know that,' Charlotte said. 'I wish you would tell me about her and my father.' He didn't say anything at once, and she said, 'Not if it is wrong of me to ask you, of course. But you must have known them very well, and I want to understand why – why things happened as they did.'

'It isn't wrong to ask, my lady,' he said. And so he told her; and she listened avidly, forgetting he was a servant, hearing only a wise and kind man who might have the key which would allow her to come to terms with her own life.

He told her of Rosamund's childish hero-worship of Marcus; of that summer in Brussels and how she fell in love with Philip Tantony; and how Tantony had died at Waterloo. Then, too late, Marcus fell in love with her. Everyone knew that Rosamund had always idolised him, and assumed it was a love-match; no-one but Parslow had ever guessed that in Tantony she had found an adult passion to replace her childish fancy.

'But then – why did she marry him? Why did she marry Papa if she didn't love him?' Charlotte cried.

Parslow looked at her with enormous sympathy. 'It was a good match, and it was what everyone expected. It can be hard to go against what everyone expects.' Charlotte was silent, doubting. 'I believe she would have got out of it if she could; but she could never oppose your grandmother's will. Would you have gone against your father's wishes? And she was very fond of him. She did her best, I promise you that. I was there, I saw. Once she was married, she did her very best.'

'Then, why – why did everything go wrong?'

'They weren't suited, my lady, that's all. They never

would have been, in my opinion. Her ladyship's school-room fancy was all that queered the issue.'

'You mean if it hadn't been for that, they would never have married?'

'Oh no, my lady. They'd probably have married anyway. Marriage for people of rank isn't a simple matter of fancy, and that's understood all round. But because she had fancied him from a child, everyone thought it was a love-match, and expected accordingly. And his lordship thought it was a love-match too, and judged of her more harshly. If it hadn't been for that, they would have come to an arrangement, as people in their position do.'

'You mean – they would both—?'

'Just so, my lady.' His eyes held her still so that she could not wriggle away from the knowledge. 'That's the way it happens in the great houses. Marriage is marriage, and fancy is fancy, and it's the lucky exception when they fall in the same place. In this case – things were confused, and the upshot was that your mother got the blame. That's the way it goes.'

'You don't think – what she did was wrong?'

He thought a while about that. 'When I first went into service, my lady, it was at Lord St George's stables. The head groom there was a Mr Bacon, a big, strong man, but he had two fingers missing off his right hand. Bitten off, they were, by his lordship's favourite hunter – the boldest horse you ever saw and generous to ride, but wicked unreliable in the stable. This horse was old now, but still kept on, had the best box in the whole stable, fed the best of everything and taken for gentle exercise. Mr Bacon tended him, wouldn't let anyone else touch him. I thought it was because the old horse was dangerous, but it was because Mr Bacon loved him. And I said to him one day when we were cleaning tack together, "How come you treat the horse so tender, when he cost you two fingers?" Mr Bacon said, "You love a horse for what he is, not what he does. What happened to my fingers was just bad luck."'

They rode on in silence, Charlotte frowning over her own thoughts. Parslow said at last, 'We just have to do our best with what we find to hand. We have to do our best, and love each other, that's all. There isn't enough love in all the world to be turning any of it away. Are you ready for a canter, my lady? The track's nice and smooth here.'

The week passed quickly and pleasantly, and though Charlotte still felt sometimes confused, and slept at night like the dead, she was gradually sorting through the new information and folding it into the right drawers in place of the old. There was so much to learn, that for the moment she did not look any further ahead than coping with the Christmas season. What the future would hold for her she had not yet found the opportunity to wonder.

Tom was not coming down until Christmas Eve, but Lord Theakston arrived in the evening of the third day. Charlotte was glad to see him again. She loved his gentleness, his patience, his unforced kindness. It seemed to her a testimony that Tom always called him 'Papa Danby', the sort of informality of affection she had never witnessed before; and she would have liked to call him that herself, but did not dare. But then on that first evening with him at Wolvercote, she was feeling so glad to see him that it just slipped out.

'Oh, but Pa—' she began, and stopped herself, crimsoning.

Lord Theakston only smiled serenely. 'You'd better call me Papa Danby, m'dear,' he said. 'Everyone else seems to. Bumped into Wellin'ton at my club the other day.

"Well, Papa Danby," he said, "how d'ye think the vote will go in the House today?" Did I mind? Never turned a hair, just shaped up like an old dog waggin' its tail. Find it hard to answer to anythin' else now.'

He was a great help to her in sorting out the family history, for he saw it with the clarity of an outsider. Many an hour she spent listening to his stories, or poring with him over genealogies, which he wrote out for her in his small, careful hand. He had a wonderful memory for family connections, and seemed to know who everybody's great grandfathers were.

By the end of the week she had got to know the Aylesbury children, and liked them very much. The eldest, Viscount Calder, was fifteen and a little shy of her at first, though he soon warmed to her. His eldest sister Lucilla was thirteen, a lively girl who was evidently a great favourite with her grandmother; the others ranged in age from twelve-year-old Titus down to the 'baby', Clement, who was three. Charlotte felt at ease with the young Aylesburys: their frank curiosity about her was easier to deal with than hints and innuendos would have been. She told them her story in plain terms, but they thought it wonderfully romantic. The little ones were Charlotte-mad within an hour of first meeting her, and could hardly be detached from her side. Lucilla sighed over her great good fortune, and lightly wished her own parents to oblivion so that she could be a 'lost heiress' too.

The young Aylesburys soon discovered that Charlotte knew hardly any games, and thereafter a part of every afternoon was dedicated to repairing the alarming gaps in her education. 'What will you do at Christmas if you don't know how to play?' In the evenings the little ones were banished to the nursery, but Calder and Lucilla were allowed to dine down (much to Titus's chagrin –

'he was only a year younger than Lulu, and a boy after all.' Charlotte often felt sorry for Titus – too young to be a companion for Calder, too old to want to play with his little brothers). After dinner Lucy liked to have a little music, and brother and sister played duets and sang together in an easy, companionable way. Sometimes they asked Charlotte to join them, but she didn't know any of their songs.

Only once during that week did the outside world intrude, when Mr Tarbush requested an interview with his newest client, to discuss certain essential financial arrangements with her. Lucy would have refused him, but Charlotte said gently but firmly that she wanted to see him. It was the first time she had exerted her will, and she felt the better for it. Since she came to London, she had been carried along unresisting on a stream of events; but in the few months between her father's death and her coming of age, she had enjoyed a brief taste of self-determination, and it had agreed with her. She was grateful for all that was being done for her, but it certainly felt good to be seeing Tarbush alone, and to feel that her wishes were all that counted with him.

It had also occurred to her that she had left her friends at home without a word, except for a scribbled note to Ellen to say she had arrived safely, which she had sent from Mrs Welland's. She suspected that Grandmama would not see the necessity of communication; Tarbush, however, assured her that he would see to it that any letters she wrote were sent with all possible speed.

He explained the arrangements he had made for her to draw from a banking account at Hoare's, and the amounts he had put at her disposal for the time being, until she could decide on a permanent establishment. He briefly sketched in the other dispositions he had made on her behalf, and then asked her if there was anything she wanted him to do.

'Yes, there is something,' she said.

Tarbush listened in amazement. 'But, your ladyship, there is simply no need,' he protested. 'Your desire to take care of your servant is very laudable, but to maintain a whole establishment for her is quite unnecessary.'

'It is not only for Ellen, it is for me,' Charlotte said. 'I want to be able to go back there whenever I want.'

'To Heath Cottage?' He struggled to find the words to express the incongruity. 'Even if you should ever go into that country again, which I sincerely doubt you will find time or inclination for, you will not wish to stay in such a village as Chetton, or in such a – a *dwelling* as Heath Cottage. Let me advise you to let it go. Settle a pension on your maid if you wish – though a gift of money would be in all ways better. A pension would encourage her not to seek another position, and she is a youngish woman, as I understand it, which would mean that the pension is a very long time paying.'

'It is what I wish, Mr Tarbush,' Charlotte said firmly. 'It is Ellen's home, and I want her to be able to live there comfortably. Do you tell me I can't afford it?'

'Indeed, no,' Tarbush said.

'Then will you do as I wish?'

Tarbush looked at the set of the mouth and the angle of the chin, and wondered he hadn't noticed before the similarity of looks with Lady Theakston. 'I am your ladyship's to command,' he affirmed stiffly, comforting himself that the Chelmsford estate was so vast, the cost of these follies would be felt no more than the removal of a spoonful of water from a bathtub. Unless the new countess took to gaming, or married a gamester, she would never manage to outrun her income.

'There is one more thing, Mr Tarbush. I would like to

send them each a present – Ellen and Martha, and Dr and Mrs Silk – and perhaps something for each of my pupils. I don't want them to think I've forgotten them in my good fortune.'

'Yes, my lady?' Tarbush said, with the air of one whom nothing could not surprise.

'If I told you what I wanted, could you get the things and have them sent?'

Tarbush baulked at this. He would arrange to have the things sent, but he was not going to go shopping for her. But she argued, and her estate, though she didn't know it, argued louder. In the end he agreed that if she made a specific list, one of his clerks could be spared to go out and purchase the things. The shops would pack them and send them to a carrier of his nomination and the carrier would take them to Chetton.

So she spent a happy hour writing her letters to Ellen and Dr Silk, and making a list of the presents she wanted for them: a fine shawl for Ellen, a set of ivory combs for Martha, books for the doctor – whatever was the newest novel out – a silver filagree bouquet-holder for Mrs Silk. Six boxes of candied plums for the six children, she added after some thought, and a box of cigars for Mr Lovelace. A little more thought, and finally she put down a pair of good hairbrushes, preferably in tortoise-shell, to be sent off separately to Steven.

Tarbush received the letters and the list, and took his departure, marvelling over the variety of experiences that were to be had in the service of the law. Charlotte felt immeasurably better for her little victory, and more comfortable about her situation. Whatever happened now, there would be home to go back to.

The Aylesburys arrived on the morning of Christmas Eve, accompanied by their guests. Lord Aylesbury was a rather thin, slightly stooping man in his forties with plain features. He greeted Charlotte warmly, with a smile and a kiss, and said that he was very pleased to see her, and to have the honour of introducing her to her family. He had been Earl since he was six years old, with the consequence that everyone, even his wife, called him 'Aylesbury'. Only Tom called him by his given name of Roland.

Lady Aylesbury – Thalia – was a small, sharp-featured, quick-moving woman who smiled and talked a great deal. Her enthusiasm for Charlotte was more marked than her husband's, but left Charlotte unwarmed; after gushing over Charlotte for some minutes, she abruptly asked when Tom would be arriving, and hardly waited for the answer before veering off on to the subject of the baby's cold.

The guests who had arrived with them were Lord and Lady Ashley and their children. Lord Ashley was rather a frightening-looking man – tall and grave with black hair and whiskers, a mighty nose and a mighty chin, and piercing eyes that might have flashed fire from the pages of some Bible-story. He was an Evangelical and a noted Philanthropist, and could be very stern on the subject of Duty. But he had a sweet smile, and was evidently less terrifying than he looked, for his children plainly doted on him, and he on them. His wife was a plump and pretty woman with merry eyes, and her devotion to her husband was a pleasant thing to see.

The Aylesbury children received the Ashley children with the warmth of old friendship, and dragged them off to the nursery as soon as their devoirs were paid. There was a special closeness between Titus and Lord Ashley's eldest boy, Anthony, always known as Accy. Charlotte noticed how eagerly Titus claimed 'his friend', with relief and jubilation at having someone of his own at last.

The newcomers soon wanted to go to their rooms, and Charlotte took the opportunity to put on her old, warm cloak and escape out of doors for a walk, to try to sort out the names and faces in her head. When she couldn't go to sleep, walking was the best way of coping with the confusion of new impressions. She had worked out by now how to get from her room to the oak hall, which was the nearest way out of the house for the stables. Turning the other way the path curved to the right, following the line of a large shrubbery, and gave onto the park. She walked for some time, until hunger warned her she ought to go back. It must be time for luncheon by now, and absenting herself from a meal would look impolite; and besides, Tom might have arrived, and she longed to see Tom again.

As she reached the shrubbery again on the far side from the house, she heard someone whistling close by; and turning, she saw a boy come jogging towards her from across the park. He looked about ten, she thought, small and lightly built, with very delicate features, and a skin so fine that with the sun behind him he looked almost transparent. His hair was so fair it sparkled silvery-white; his eyes were the darkest blue Charlotte had ever seen. He was dressed in country woollens, breeches and stout boots, much splashed; but he did not look like a servant's or a countryman's child. She wondered if he could be one of the neighbours' children, coming to play – or even trespassing.

The boy stopped short, looked at her appraisingly, and said, 'Hullo!' with the confidence of one who had every right to be where he was.

'Good morning,' Charlotte said. 'It's a fine one, isn't it?'

'Yes, very fine.' The boy looked her over with a faintly puzzled air that was endearing in its innocence. 'You must be the new governess,' he concluded, after what was plainly a complicated calculation.

Charlotte was amused, and evaded the point. 'I'm afraid I don't know you. Do you live nearby?'

'Oh, no,' he agreed. 'We've just arrived – just this minute, I mean, in the carriage. I asked Papa to let me out in the park so that I could walk the last bit and see if Kelder still has the tame deer.'

'Kelder?' she asked.

'He's one of the groundsmen. He has a house on the other side of the park, by the woods.'

'And did he still have the deer?'

'Rather! It's even tamer than last year – it let me stroke it and didn't seem to mind me a bit,' he said enthusiastically. 'It's a roe deer, so it's only about as big as a dog, and it follows him about and lies down in front of the fire just like a dog, too. He has a tame crow as well, that does tricks. It fetches things when he tells it, and it does sums and taps the answer out with its beak.'

'I'd love to see that,' Charlotte said.

'Would you? I'll take you some time, if you like,' the boy said, seeming pleasantly surprised at her interest. 'He had a tame fox once, he says, but it died. He says it got him into terrible trouble with the estate agent because the gamekeeper said that it would kill his birds and the poultry maid said it would get in her yard and the kennelman said it would confuse his hounds, so he had to keep it on a lead all the time to prove it didn't kill birds, and when the hunt was out he had to tie it up under his bed and keep all the doors and windows shut.'

'Poor thing,' said Charlotte, but she was trying not to laugh. The boy laughed too.

'Well, he stole it from the hunt in the first place, when it was a tiny cub and they killed its mother. He says if they ever kill a vixen again, he'll try and get all the cubs, and he said he'd give me one. But,' a sigh as realism took over, 'they'd never let me have a fox at home.'

'I shouldn't think they would,' Charlotte agreed solemnly, enjoying this luminous youngster.

'You'd like Kelder,' he went on. 'He's a great gun! He showed me how to get right up to a wild animal, so it doesn't run away. He said he would take me badger-watching next summer – only,' his face fell suddenly, 'only Mama will probably say I mayn't, because I might catch cold. Just because a person was ill a lot when they were a child,' he added fiercely, 'they never let you do anything ever again in case you get ill!'

'It must be very hard,' Charlotte sympathised. 'But parents do worry about their children. It's only natural.'

'Of course, you would be on their side,' the boy said resignedly.

'I'm not on any side. But I do sympathise with you: my father would never let me do anything or go anywhere. Sometimes I thought I would burst with frustration.'

'What did you do?' he asked hopefully, wondering if there might be a magic formula.

'There wasn't anything I could do. Children have to obey their parents – girls especially.'

'But now you're grown up, you can do anything you like, can't you? Your father can't stop you now?'

'No, not now. He's dead, you see.'

'Oh.' The boy flushed with embarrassment and looked at the ground. 'I say, I'm awfully sorry.' He glanced up into her face, and seeing no anger at his faux pas asked, 'Do you mind awfully?'

'Fairly awfully,' she said, but with a smile to relieve his anxiety.

'I should hate my father to die. He's the most splendid person in the world – as brave as a lion, and the best shot and the best rider in the whole country. And not a bit stiff, like some people's paters.'

'Well, he did let you get out in the park to go

125

and visit – what was his name? – which sounds pretty understanding,' Charlotte said.

The boy nodded. 'Yes, that's true. And he generally talks to Mama if she gets into a panic about me. You see, I almost died when I was born, and then I was ill an awful lot, and she sort of got into the habit of worrying about me, and she goes on doing it, even though I haven't been ill for ages now – not for over a year.'

'She must love you very much,' Charlotte said.

He scratched the calf of one leg with the toe of the other boot, twisting his face as easily as his young body. 'Yes, I suppose so, and there is only me, so she hasn't got any others to worry about. But a chap doesn't like to be fussed over all the time.'

'No, I can see that.'

'Oh well, I'd better go – they'll be waiting for me to go and do the pretty to everyone. Goodbye – it's been nice talking to you,' he said with a sudden burst of politeness, and dashed off into the shrubbery, taking the short-cut to the house.

Charlotte walked on the long way, round the path, feeling enormously cheered by this contact. She supposed there must be some other guests Lady Aylesbury had not told her about. She did not look forward to meeting the grown-ups, but thought the boy would make a very good addition to the nursery group. Wouldn't he be surprised when he found out who she was? She was amused that he had taken her for the governess: she supposed her old cloak had disguised her – or perhaps she had not yet achieved a haughty enough expression to be taken for one of the nobility.

As she rounded the bend of the shrubbery and came in sight of the house, she saw a man, a stranger, sitting on the low wall at the end of the terrace. He must have been waiting for her, for at her appearance he jumped down, threw away his cigar, and stood watching her approach. She had no difficulty in recognising her young friend's father: he was a tall and handsome man with the same pale hair, brushed with grey, and the same blue eyes. Down one cheek there ran the fading scar of what must have been quite a spectacular cut. A war wound, perhaps? He had the upright posture of a soldier.

When she was near enough to him he said, 'The house is in the throes of a melodrama. Well, two melodramas, to be exact. One is called The Missing Heiress, and the other is The Phantom Governess. I fancy I might be addressing the heroine of both.'

Charlotte liked the form of address – without preamble, as if it were part of a conversation they had been having for some time – and took courage from its informality, and the amusement in his eyes. 'In that case,' she said, 'I fancy I might be addressing the best father in the world. Let me see if I have it right: brave as a lion, and the best shot and the best rider in the whole country.'

The man grinned. 'Did my brat really say that? He must have been hoping you'd repeat it! I wonder what he's after?'

'A pet fox-cub, I think.'

'I knew it! That child is a Machiavelli! But you have scored quite a hit with him: he told me he thought you were hardly like a grown-up at all, which is a great compliment with him.'

'I am honoured,' Charlotte said, smiling. She felt at ease with this man, as she had with his son, and the latter was of course connected to the former. 'He obviously admires you very much.'

'He has a forgiving heart, then. When I think of the name I burdened the poor little soul with – or didn't he happen to mention it to you?'

'No, we didn't get round to introducing ourselves.'

127

'His given name is Cavendish – which is a family name of mine. It seemed somehow to suit him when he was a baby, and he couldn't very well object then. And now, of course, he has made it his own. He has even given rise to a new expression. When something that ought to go disastrously wrong gives itself a shake and a twist and turns out all right after all, we call it "Cavendish luck".' He surveyed her face, as though expecting the information to mean something to her. 'Well, I have the advantage of you, I see, because I know who you are, and plainly you don't know me.'

'I suppose you are a guest too,' she began, and then it came to her suddenly. She fell very still. She wondered how she could have been so stupid as not to have guessed before; but she hadn't known that there were any children. No-one had thought to mention that to her. 'You are Lord Batchworth,' she said at last.

'Yes,' he said, serious now. 'We arrived about an hour ago, as I suppose Cav told you.'

'Is—?' Charlotte couldn't go on. And it was a stupid question anyway. Of course she was there.

He didn't pretend not to understand. He nodded. 'I collect you are not happy with the idea of meeting her?' Charlotte didn't answer. 'Is it because you feel she did wrong?'

'She betrayed my father,' Charlotte said, looking at the ground. But it was more in sorrow than anger now – Parslow had achieved that much. *You love someone for what they are, not what they do.* She had begun liking this man before she knew who he was. Could she take the liking back now?

He said quietly, 'What your mother and I did was wrong, and I don't try to disguise it. But we didn't set out to do wrong, we didn't plan it out of wickedness. We didn't mean to fall in love – but we did. And in the end, you know, it was your father who sent her away. She wouldn't have left him. She would have stayed with him and taken care of him—'

'But she didn't love him!' Charlotte cried, from the depth of her own hunger. It surprised her, made her examine what she had said, what she had felt. Not to be loved was the worst thing of all; yes, she believed that. And underneath that, there was a worse hurt still: in the end, had her father loved her? She didn't think so. He was all she had had, and she was afraid – she knew really – that he had not loved her. She had been many things to him, and most of them were painful. She had been his burden; without her, he might have lived a more comfortable life. Whether or not her mother had started it, she had been the cause of the continuance of his madness.

Her companion looked at her with a world of understanding and pity. He seemed to hesitate over which path to choose; and then he said, very gently, 'He didn't love her, either, you know. Don't look at me like that. It's true. What he loved was an image he had of her in his mind, which bore no resemblance to reality. He tried to make her fit that image, and the attempt hurt them both.'

She thought then of the image she had carried around all her life, of the perfect, angelic, dead mother; and how trying to hold on to that image in the face of reality hurt her.

'What I am trying to tell you,' he went on, 'is that there is no blame in the case. Things happen that can't be helped.' His expression grew almost bleak. 'My dear, I have witnessed her tears these twenty-one years. No-one can know what it is to lose a child.'

'She has—'

'Cavendish? Ah, yes. Cav is himself, and dearly loved. But he doesn't replace you.' She said nothing. 'Nothing can hurt your father any longer – God rest his soul. But you and she go on hurting. Let me bring you to her. You can give each other so much.'

She looked up at him searchingly. He was her stepfather, she realised suddenly. How odd! And the boy, Cavendish, was her brother – odd again! And that made her think longingly of her mother – not the dead angel, who was an exploded myth; nor the scarlet woman, who, it seemed, was a myth also; but a flesh-and-blood mother, such as other people had. A mother was the one person who was meant always to love you, no matter what. Was it possible? Might hers love her?

'I'm afraid,' she said at last.

He smiled, as though some important question had been answered, and in the way he had hoped for. 'You will like each other, I promise you,' he said, as if that had been her question. 'You are very much alike. Will you come now?'

Charlotte looked anxious. 'Will the others be there?'

'No,' he said. 'She's waiting for you in the painted parlour. No-one ever uses it. You will be quite private.'

Lord Batchworth led the way, into the panelled hall, up the stairs and along a narrow, Tudor corridor, and left her at the door with a kindly nod. Charlotte drew a deep breath, and opened it.

A woman stood in the middle of the room; a tall woman, rather too thin, with a careworn face, and reddish hair, done up in a knot on top of her head, instead of at the back as the fashion was. It made her look as though she were wearing a crown. She was standing very straight, facing the door, her hands down at her side. Charlotte closed the door behind her and stood still, not knowing what to do or say. She did not know this woman: how could she feel anything for her?

The woman lifted her chin a little – a movement not of pride or defiance, but of endurance. Then Charlotte saw

130

that in the way these things were viewed, they did look alike, that there was a resemblance of the flesh which had nothing to do with their lives or feelings, and could never be wiped out by ignorance or absence. They were of one substance. Their eyes met at last, and suddenly Charlotte felt a jolt of knowledge, of *identity*, as though they were not two separate people, but a single thing that had been divided, now reuniting. For an instant she *was* her mother; and though she pulled back from it, almost resentfully, she knew that something had changed, and the change could not be undone.

Her mother was smiling at her, a faint, troubled smile. 'They said you looked like me. But there's a lot of your father in you.' She made a shaky sound like a laugh. 'I didn't know what you would look like. Isn't that an extraordinary thing?'

Charlotte said awkwardly, 'I don't know what to call you.'

Rosamund nodded understandingly. 'It's all very new. We don't know each other yet.'

'No,' Charlotte said. But it was not true: she had felt that moment of fusion, and she knew how her mother felt. The acre of sorrow she had found in her mother's heart was now in her too, part of her, and she didn't know whether she would ever own enough love to be able to plant it. She wanted suddenly to give her something, but didn't know what there was for such a situation. At last she said foolishly, 'I do love Grandmama. And Papa Danby.'

Her mother smiled. Perhaps it hadn't been such a foolish thing to say, then. 'They are good people,' Rosamund said. Distantly a bell rang, and an identical expression of startled dismay on both their faces made them both laugh. 'Luncheon,' Rosamund said. 'Everyone will be assembled in the blue drawing-room, waiting to see us meet each other. But we've forestalled them.'

Charlotte thought about the assembled family, and ought to have been daunted, but discovered that it would be all right after all. She would feel very shy; she wouldn't know what to say; but she could go in to the drawing-room without great turmoil. She would not be, after all, alone.

'Luncheon on Christmas Eve is always the start of Christmas proper at Wolvercote,' Rosamund said. 'Everyone assembles, children and all, and after eating we all play games together until the dressing-bell. It's the great indulgence for the children.'

'It will be for me too,' Charlotte said. 'I've never had a Christmas with people, and games, before.'

It was the hardest thing Rosamund had ever done, not to cry then. She swallowed very hard, and managed a smile, albeit rather a watery one. 'Shall we go down?'

'Yes,' said Charlotte. 'I'm ready.'

That was the beginning of the happiest Christmas – the happiest *time* Charlotte had ever had. Though she and her mother continued to feel shy and a little awkward about each other, there was sufficient company for it not to be uncomfortable. And through every meeting Charlotte kept that feeling of not being alone. There was someone especially for her – someone to whom her presence alone gave pleasure. She smiled and was gay like someone in love.

Cavendish came up to her at that first luncheon and said, 'Why didn't you say you were my sister? I thought you were the governess. I made an awful ass of myself.'

'I didn't know who you were,' she replied. 'And you didn't make an ass of yourself.'

He looked her over frankly. 'Grandmama says you look like Mama. I don't see it myself. I mean, you're young – or quite, anyway. I'm very glad you are my sister. I never had a sister before, but I always wanted one.'

'I always wanted a brother,' Charlotte said, and held out her hand. He shook it firmly, and then grinned.

'I say, what a lark! And Papa says you are a countess too, in your own right, and horrid rich.'

'I'll bet he didn't say that.'

'Well, not exactly, but you know. Will you come and stay with us next summer? Grasscroft is up on the moors, and there are jolly places to ride. If you come and stay, I'll show you where the buzzards nest.'

As the days passed, Charlotte discovered to her amusement that as she was a figure of dazzling romance to the children, Cavendish paraded his relationship with her as a source of credit. She was surrounded whenever she appeared, entreated to play, and when they were exhausted by their games and sat down for a moment, she would inevitably find some small person creeping into her lap, and her indefatigable courtiers gathering round begging for a story. But her most constant companions were Cavendish, Titus, and Accy. These three were of an age, and had been playing together at family gatherings for years. Now the other two felt entitled to share in Cav's status as particular owner of Charlotte, and every now and then they would send the little ones away so that they could have Charlotte to themselves. Then they would march her off to see some treasure, share some secret, or play some particular game of which only they knew the rules.

When she was not playing with the children, there were all sorts of other entertainments, charades and romps and games in which the whole company joined in, and lots of music. Everyone played something, or sang; Charlotte's piano playing was admired, but she knew she was no more than tolerable. Her mother played wonderfully, and was

much in demand; often Tom sang to her accompaniment
– he had a fine voice – and Charlotte would see her grandmother watching them with tender pride. Charlotte was
glad to find, too, that the real reason for Christmas was
not forgotten: there were prayers morning and evening,
and usually a reading from the Bible in the half hour
before dinner. Generally Lord Ashley was asked to do
the reading – he had a fine speaking voice, and read with
a great deal of feeling.

The weather turned on Christmas Day, and snow came
up from the northeast. Grandmama mourned loudly that
there would be no hunting – and indeed for several days
the party could not step out of doors. But there was
good humour and good company within doors, and vast
meals that outshone anything Charlotte had experienced
at her grandmother's house: she had thought Upper
Grosvenor Street dined with ceremony, but that was
nothing to Lady Aylesbury's table, where the servants
were so numerous some of them seemed to have nothing
to do but pass dishes from one to another. But Charlotte
was growing more at ease in company, and was not quite
so afraid of committing an embarrassing faux pas. Her
mother, she discovered, could be quite informal, and
even on one occasion when Lady Aylesbury tutted her
said quite sharply, 'Oh Thalia, don't fuss!' which gave
Charlotte heart.

After New Year the party broke up, the Ashleys leaving
to go down to the family home in Dorset. Tom was
going back to Town, where he had engagements. Lord
Batchworth was also going up, for goverment business,
and his family with him, though Cavendish was urgent
to be left behind.

'You have made a conquest,' Rosamund said to
Charlotte. 'He's never asked to stay behind before.'

Charlotte began to make some laughing reply, and

then suddenly realised that she felt quite natural with her mother, not shy or awkward at all, and the realisation that things had changed without her noticing made her stop short. She met Rosamund's eyes, and thought that perhaps she had just realised the same thing.

'We might manage to get down again,' Rosamund said, 'but Mother will be bringing you up in any case before the end of February.'

'Shall I see you in Town?' Charlotte asked; she wished she could call *her* 'mother', but was not yet quite so bold.

'Of course,' Rosamund said, and her face lit in a smile that was for once free of shadows. Charlotte would have liked her to embrace or kiss her just then, and had a strong sense that her mother wished the same thing, but it was not yet possible to do it. Charlotte's upbringing had not taught her a vocabulary of touching, and that restraint had created an invisible shell around her. It would take a more confident lover than a newly acknowledged mother to break through it.

CHAPTER SEVEN

Tom had never married; he had never even been in love. His situation was unusual. Because he had been brought into Society at a very precocious age, kept by his mother's side and going everywhere with her, like a cross between a pet dog and a page boy, he had seen so much of the follies of the beau monde by the age of ten that he had no more illusions.

Added to that, he adored his mother as she adored him, and the very special, intense and tender love between them had rather got in the way of his forming any other attachment. But he was not unhappy. He lived in pleasant bachelor apartments in Ryder Street, where he was looked after by his man, Billington. He had a private income enough for his needs, and as Member of Parliament for Winchendon he had business enough for his mental stimulation. His other needs had always been taken care of exceedingly willingly by a series of discreet (and discrete, he sometimes joked to himself, for each of them thought she was the only one) married ladies. He had always preferred older women, and as older single women were naturally impossible, he had to turn to those who had accommodations with their husbands. It was ironic that his young niece Charlotte plainly liked and admired him so much, while making such a piece of work about Rosamund's affair with Jes.

But that problem seemed to be sorting itself out, he noted with satisfaction. Mama's family Christmas had turned the trick – and Cavendish had unwittingly done a great deal to bring the two sides together. There was now a fairly easy discourse between Upper Grosvenor Street and St James's Square – though he thought all parties were aware that painful subjects had been set aside rather than gone through. He was not, himself, a great advocate of 'going through', and thought it would be best if Charlotte and Rosamund shut the lid on certain subjects and turned the key. Theirs must always be an unusual relationship in some respects: meeting for the first time as adults, they could not be woman and child together.

It was odd, he thought, walking home from Soho Square through a fog that was laying its taste like a coating of silver on his tongue, how things that happened to the child had such an effect on the adult – as if one was not master of one's own fate at all, but fixed like a little locomotive on rails laid down in one's childhood. Take himself, for instance. He had always taken his situation and personal arrangements for granted; but since the reappearance of Charlotte, he had begun to feel that there was something sad and unsatisfactory about it all. He had no wife, no child. He felt really quite fatherly towards Charlotte, and it reminded him that no little nipper would ever trot along by his side, clutching his finger in its whole hand, as he had seen Clement do with Roland. He would never teach a young son how to shoot, and wonder at how tall he had grown, as Roland had with Calder. He was forty years old, and what had he to show for it?

And this mood of melancholy was affecting his relationship with his current three ladies (Rosamund, half laughing and half disapproving, called them the Three Disgraces, though of course she had no idea who they were, and only knew that there were three because she had tricked him into admitting it by accusing him of having ten in keeping. 'They are only three, and I don't keep them,' he had retorted, and she had roared with laughter). Since Charlotte's return to the family, he had not seen two of them at all, and found no inclination in himself ever to go near them again. And Mrs Routledge he was just returning from, having seen her for the first time since the beginning of December, and he was rather afraid it was the end of her, too. For the first time she had struck him – it had been rather frightening – as matronly. She had greeted him with her usual warmth, but he had simply wanted to turn tail and run. The last thing he had wanted in that first moment was to bed with her: her splendid bosom seemed built for laying one's head on, not for more intimate caresses; and though she was only a few years older than him – forty-five at the most – it had seemed too shockingly like having designs on one's mother.

The strange mood had lasted only a few minutes. Once they had sat and chatted for a while, he had recovered his equilibrium and remembered why he admired her. Old habits had taken over, and the assignation had concluded happily for both parties. But trotting home now he felt nothing but dissatisfaction. It was a transaction of convenience, made tolerable by affection and respect on both sides. He had always been glad that Mrs Routledge had no desire to leave Mr Routledge for him, and that everything was conducted in such a civilised way. But now he thought, where was passion? Where was the heady, transforming madness of love? He wanted to feel, just once, that desperate longing, that frantic desire, that he had read about, before he got too old and had to settle for companionship. It struck him suddenly (and made him laugh, because he could never really take himself seriously) that he had got his life the wrong way round: he had had his sober middle age first, and was now at the age of forty proposing to embark on his headstrong youth!

Billington, opening the door of his set to him, said that Lady Batchworth had sent a messenger, asking if he could call round at his convenience. Tom brightened. Company, and someone else's fire instead of his own, were what he needed. 'I'll go straight there,' he said, reversed direction, and clattered down the stairs much more cheerfully than he had trod up them.

He found his cousin Benedict ensconced by Rosamund's fire. 'Heyday! I didn't know there'd be company,' he exclaimed, advancing with his hand out.

Bendy stood with an eager grin and seized his hand. 'Tom! I'm glad to see you. You're looking well.'

Tom extracted his fingers gingerly from Bendy's hard grip. 'Careful, old fellow, or my piano-playing days are done! Your hand is hard as a plank. All those hours in the saddle, I suppose. You're turning into a typical hunting squire.'

'What else would you expect from the Master of Morland Place?' Bendy said cheerfully. 'If you meant to insult me, you missed your mark! I might just as well say that your hand is as soft as a woman's, and expect you to mind it.'

'A little more riding and a little less soft living wouldn't do you any harm, Tom,' Rosamund joined in. 'Where were you when I sent round for you? My footman said your man was a monument of discretion, so I suppose you were out having a spree.'

'What a vulgar expression, dear sister,' Tom said. 'I shall talk to Jes – or do you mean to join in this conspiracy to abuse me?'

'Not I,' Jes laughed. 'Have some sherry.'

'Have you just arrived?' Tom asked Benedict when he was settled with glass in hand.

'An hour or two ago.'

'And are you alone? Or have you deposited the lovely Mrs Benedict somewhere?'

'No, she's still at home in Yorkshire. I came to see about hiring something for us for the Season. Rosalind doesn't care for hotels, so she means to stay comfortably at Morland Place until I have something ready for her here.'

Tom noticed the slight shadow that crossed Bendy's face, and concluded that he didn't like to be parted from his wife even for such a short time. What must it be like, he wondered, to be so much in love? He envied Bendy the experience, though not the wife: he didn't like Mrs Benedict, and didn't understand what Bendy saw in her. She was very pretty, certainly, but struck Tom as shallow, ignorant and underbred. She paraded her wealth, boasted about the rich and titled people with whom she was on terms of intimacy, cut people she thought beneath her, and flirted indiscreetly with any good-looking man she found herself in company with. He wondered Bendy didn't see it, and stop her; then he thought that perhaps he couldn't stop her, and so preferred not to see it. Perhaps he, Tom, was too sensitive. Others in the family didn't seem to regard Mrs Benedict as an embarrassment – though he felt there was no particular affection for her.

'And how are the children?' Tom asked, hoping for a more comfortable subject.

'They're very well,' Bendy said. 'Mary is studying mathematics now – you wouldn't guess how quick she is at taking it in!'

'How old is she now – five? No, six?'

'Six and a half,' Bendy said with huge pride. 'She is

simply a phenomenon. And she sings and dances too – we have a music master who comes in twice a week.' Another shadow flickered over Bendy's face. The music master was a very handsome young man, and Mary adored him, and he seemed to be teaching her well. But now Rosalind had taken it into her head that she needed singing lessons to improve her voice, and thought that Maitland might as well teach her too, since he was so good with Mary. Lots of ladies took singing lessons, it was perfectly natural, and Bendy hated himself for even thinking there was anything in it; but he did wish Maitland were not to handsome, and that Rosalind had not insisted on staying behind when he came to London.

'And how is Rose?' Tom asked.

'She's well, full of energy – full of passion, too. She screams like a locomotive when she's thwarted – the most piercing sound you ever heard; Rosalind can't stand it. And if that doesn't work, she holds her breath. You should see her, red and furious! Well, she's very rosy-faced even at the best of times. You know naughty Mary calls her Radish?'

'I must meet Miss Mary again soon,' Tom laughed. 'It is ages since I saw her.'

'Well, come up to Morland Place,' Bendy said cordially. 'You know we would love to have you at any time. Perhaps we might get up a party for race-week this summer.' He smiled at Rosamund. 'You will want to show your daughter Morland Place.'

'If I don't, Mother will,' Rosamund laughed. She flickered a look at Jes, and he smiled, knowing what she was thinking – *how strange, but how delightful, to have people talk of 'your daughter'*. 'She's determined that Charlotte shall learn the whole family history, from the Flood onwards.'

'Poor girl! There's an awful lot of it – and some not

too good for the hearing,' Bendy said. He put the thought away quickly. Not a tactful thing to have said, considering. 'I am so looking forward to meeting her. I mean to call on Aunt Lucy tomorrow – I sent her a note when I arrived. I thought it might be impolite to drop in unannounced.'

'You don't mind dropping in unannounced on me, I notice,' Rosamund remarked.

'I hoped you might prime me with anything I need to know before I go,' Bendy said. 'I shouldn't like to drop any bricks. I wonder you don't have Charlotte staying here with you, though. I'd have thought it would be more fun for her than being with the old people.'

Jes coughed, and Bendy looked at him enquiringly. 'You were speaking of bricks.'

'Oh, Lord, what have I said?'

He looked so dismayed Rosamund laughed. 'It's all right, I am beginning to grow a shell.'

'Charlotte is staying with her grandmother,' Jes explained, 'because she is the one who will be bringing her out. Ros can't do it because she is a divorcée.'

Bendy coloured with a mixture of chagrin for his mistake, and indignation for his cousin. 'Oh, but *surely*—!'

'The thing is,' Rosamund took over the story for herself, 'that I can't present her. The Queen is much less stiff about things than Queen Adelaide was, and I believe if it were left to her . . . She was under Lord Melbourne's wing when she first came to the throne you know. But the Prince is rather a stick, and the long and short of it is that on the formal occasions—'

'The formalities are observed,' Jes finished for her.

'No scarlet women,' Rosamund said, and Benedict could see that the irony was meant to cover the pain, and didn't succeed. He wanted to rush out and give the world a black eye for daring to reject his cousin.

142

'But Court isn't the whole world,' he said. 'Even if what you say about the presentation is right, surely no-one else minds any more? It was all so long ago, and you are a respectable married woman now, and – well, now Marcus is dead—'

She shook her head. 'Most people accept us, though there are still some sticklers who won't. It doesn't upset me much any more, but I don't want Charlotte to suffer for my sins. If I bring her out, but Mother presents her, the whole story will be chewed over again. If Mother does the whole thing, those who don't already know the story won't think twice about it. I'm hoping it will all pass off quietly.'

'Well, you know best, of course,' Bendy said doubtfully.

There was a moment's uncomfortable silence, which Tom broke by asking, 'Well, am I to be told why I was summoned here tonight? Or was it to meet Bendy?'

'There seems to be something of a crisis,' Rosamund said.

'Moral, financial or diplomatic?'

'Neither – none. Don't tease, Tom.'

'Diplomatic, I'd say,' Jes put in with a smile.

Rosamund frowned at him. 'It's not jesting matter.'

'I know, darling – but I can't help seeing the funny side. There we all are, planning away like ministers, and there's your mama spending I don't know how many fortunes on new clothes and refurbishing the Ogilvies' house—'

'How's that?' Bendy asked.

'Mama's house has no ballroom,' Tom answered. 'Lady Ogilvie's house round the corner in Grosvenor Square has, and she lives in the country and lets it for coming-out balls, but it's getting rather shabby. She won't spend any money on it, so Mama feels obliged – but not half so obliged as Lady O will feel, to get her house made over for nothing! So what is the crisis?' he asked his sister.

'Charlotte doesn't see the necessity of being brought out at all,' Rosamund said in a tragic voice. Tom unfortunately caught Jes's eye, and struggled in vain with a smile. 'I don't see why you all think it's so amusing,' she said crossly.

'No, not amusing at all,' Tom said, pushing the smile under for the third time. 'Tell me everything. Why doesn't she want to be brought out?'

'She thinks it's a lot of fuss and expense for nothing. Mama told her she had to be presented to Society so that she could take her place in it, and Charlotte said she was happy just to have her own family and didn't see the need for strangers.'

'Unnatural child!' Tom said.

Rosamund shot him a suspicious look. 'So then Mama explained that she would have to take her place in Society if she wanted a husband, because eligible men wouldn't be able to approach her otherwise, and in any case she wouldn't know they *were* eligible if she didn't see where they fitted in to the scheme of things; and she said—'

'That she didn't want to get married either?' Tom hazarded.

'She said she didn't see the necessity.'

'She has a point,' Bendy said slowly. 'Most girls have to marry to get an establishment, but she has all the wealth she could ever want, a title in her own right, and a large enough family for her not to be lonely.'

'Family of that sort isn't the same as a husband and children,' Rosamund said.

'You're right, it isn't,' Tom said with some emphasis, and Rosamund gave him a grateful look, not having expected support from that quarter. 'But surely she must have thought about marriage, even if only as a

144

distant prospect? Surely all girls do? And it's only very recently that she has known about her fortune.'

'That's true,' Rosamund said, 'but when Mama said much the same thing to her, she said that she never had considered marriage; she had never supposed it possible. She had thought that she would live with her father for ever; or at least, that after he was dead, he would leave her some small competence to go on living in the same place and the same style.'

'Marcus never mentioned marriage to her,' Jes added. 'And since she didn't know any men, other than servants and doctors, it simply didn't come into her thoughts at all, even as a daydream.'

'Poor child. And I suppose she still doesn't know any men, apart from uncles and cousins,' Tom said thoughtfully.

'Mother isn't the best person in the world to explain marriage to her,' Rosamund said. 'You know how taciturn she is about anything to do with feelings. And given how things were between Marcus and me, I hardly like to raise the subject: I'm not the best example in the world. I think she may be a little afraid of the idea. She told Mother that she didn't know how to go on with men, how to behave or what to say, and would be sure to get it wrong and put them off, so it would be best all round if she just went on as she was.'

'And what did Mama say to that?'

'She told Charlotte that some girls did giggle and flirt with men, but it was very unseemly, and that a sensible man wouldn't want a female who behaved any differently from the way she was with her own brothers and cousins.'

'Well,' Tom said doubtfully, and read the same reservation in Bendy's eyes.

'At all events she told Charlotte that she must just be

herself, and that would do very well, and there it was left,' Rosamund concluded. 'But Mama says she has been very quiet since then – quieter even than usual, and she's rather too solemn as it is. I'm afraid if she is really reluctant to go through with it, she just won't take. A reluctant débutante would be the worst thing in the world.' She sighed.

'She must be brought out. We see the necessity even if she doesn't,' Jes said. 'But the situation is peculiar.'

'And besides, I want her to enjoy the normal pleasures of girlhood. She ought to have the chance to dance and be merry, and flirt just a little, and dream of handsome young men, and enjoy falling in love. She's had little enough pleasure in her life so far.'

'She'll probably enjoy it all once it starts,' Benedict said.

'I just don't know what to do. That's why I sent for you, Tom. You're the sophist of the family. What do we do?'

'I deny the impeachment,' Tom said, 'but I have been thinking. The problem as I see it is not that she has never had any male companions, but that she has never had any female ones. Gently bred girls never do know how to go on with men until they meet them – but *she* doesn't know how girls go on.'

There was a brief and breathless silence, and then Jes laughed and said, 'Tom, you're a genius! Of course, that's it!'

'It may be,' Rosamund said thoughtfully. 'But even so, what do we do?'

'Get her a companion, of course,' Tom said. 'Don't you see, so far coming out has been something she is preparing to have done to her, like having a tooth pulled. She doesn't know it's meant to be pleasurable, and it's no use one of us telling her so – we're too old, we rank as the doers of things unto her. She needs someone her own age to tell her what fun it all is. Remember your own come-out, Ros? Would you have enjoyed it half as much if you hadn't shared it with Sophie?'

'No, I don't suppose I would.' She reflected. 'Dressing together, talking about the men we might meet – and talking afterwards about the ones we did meet – that was half the pleasure.'

Jes said, 'You can't force some stranger onto Mama to be brought out with Charlotte.'

'No, of course not.'

'—and there isn't anyone in the family the right age.'

Benedict and Tom met each other's eyes, both having the same idea at the same time. 'What about Fanny?' Bendy said, and 'Fanny Hobsbawn,' Tom said.

Rosamund liked the idea. It would be appropriate, as Rosamund and Sophie had been such dear friends, that Rosamund's daughter and Sophie's daughter should be too. 'But,' she pointed out the objection, 'Fanny's been out four years.'

'She's never been presented, though,' Tom said. 'I'm sure Mama wouldn't refuse to present her along with Charlotte, and she can go to all the balls and suchlike as Charlotte's companion. Fanny won't object to that.'

'You can depend on that,' Jes laughed. 'She likes nothing better than balls and parties, and she's the most shocking flirt in the country. The offer of a London Season will put her in raptures.'

'That's the point,' Tom said. 'She enjoys all that sort of thing, she has the right attitude to it, and her enthusiasm is bound to rub off onto Charlotte.'

'I agree,' Bendy said. 'It's impossible to be long in her company and not grow more cheerful. I like Fanny enormously – she's such a jolly little thing.'

'What if too much of her rubs off?' Rosamund said cautiously. There was no denying Fanny *was* a flirt.

'It won't. Charlotte's solemn character will act as a

drogue,' Tom said. 'Blend them together, in fact, and you'd have the perfect female.'

'Do you think Henry would agree to lending her?' Rosamund asked her husband.

'Of course he would. Fanny wouldn't let him refuse. He spoils her dreadfully.'

Rosamund smiled. 'You and he both. You never saw such a sight, Tom, as those two grown men fawning over that chit of a girl, making complete fools of themselves.'

But she said it with affection. Poor Fanny's father had been horribly murdered when she was only ten years old, and Sophie had been so devastated with shock Fanny had been as good as motherless, too, for many months. It was a family friend, Henry Droylsden, who had stepped into the breach, taking over the running of the mills which were the source of Sophie's fortune, being the rock that Sophie leaned on and a substitute father to Fanny. And as Sophie began to recover, Henry, who had loved her long and silently, began to pay court to her.

Rosamund and Jes had watched from the wings and wished him well, seeing how happily it would suit everyone – for Sophie was not a woman ever to manage alone. At last Henry had found the courage to propose, and after agonising hesitation Sophie had accepted him. But the death of Sophie's mother had postponed the wedding, and the inexplicable and dreadful behaviour of her elder brother Nicholas had laid another shock on an already overburdened nature. Fanny gained a stepfather, but only a year after the wedding she lost her mother.

Since then Rosamund and Jes had done their best to be a substitute family for her, helping Henry however they could, and having Fanny to stay in their town-house in Manchester and their country estate on the edge of the moors at Grasscroft. Sophie had once asked Rosamund to promise to be a mother to Fanny if anything should happen to her, and Rosamund had agreed lightly, never expecting the occasion to arise. But the fact was that Sophie had done better for her child in marrying Henry Droylsden than in any number of promises extracted from Rosamund. Henry adored Fanny, and Fanny Henry, and nothing could be more scrupulous than his care or more tender than his love. There had been little for Rosamund to do for her best friend's child, except to try to counterbalance the absurd degree of worship both Henry and Jes offered her. Fanny turned them both round her thumb; but Rosamund had to admit to herself that though they spoiled her, she wasn't spoilt. As she grew up, she corrected her own behaviour, and plainly had a much harder head than might have been expected, which resolutely refused to be turned.

Altogether, she thought Tom had hit on the right scheme. Fanny was such a merry thing, she was bound to enliven Charlotte, and would teach her to look forward to her Season and not dread it. And it would be nice for Charlotte to have a friend – assuming they took to each other. A friend such as Fanny would be a friend for life, as Sophie had been to Rosamund.

When Benedict got up to take his leave, Tom thought he had better make his excuses too; but accompanying them into the hall, Rosamund called him back for a private word.

'There's something on your mind,' she said, taking hold of his arm.

'Now why should you think that?' Tom said lightly.

'I know you of old. And there was something in the way you agreed with me about Charlotte needing a husband and children, instead of saying something teasing as I expected. What is it, Tommy? Can't you tell me? You know how I love you. I can't bear you to be sad.'

'I know, dearest, and you always worried for nothing – I was perfectly happy.'

'Was. So you aren't now? I knew I was right!'

'Oh, it's nothing. I've just been feeling a little blue. Today—'

'Yes,' she encouraged as he hesitated, wondering whether to go on. 'Where were you when I sent round?'

'Oh, you were right, I was seeing one of the Disgraces,' he said lightly. 'But I think it may be for the last time.'

'Is that it? Did she throw you off? Stupid woman! She doesn't know what she's losing,' Rosamund said with sisterly indignation.

Tom laughed, and patted her hand. 'No, no, she was as fond as ever. But somehow I – I couldn't find it satisfying any more. It seemed – oh, false and hollow and – shabby.'

Rosamund searched his face. 'I think you're growing up, dear one. You need a wife, a proper wife. All this hand-to-mouth business – well, you know what I mean,' she said, colouring, as he laughed at her choice of words.

'Yes, I do,' he said. 'And you may be right. I don't know about a wife exactly, but I feel a need to fall in love.'

'Exactly! And when you fall in love, you'll want to marry her. The one follows the other like night and day.'

'On my income? I can't afford a wife.'

'Oh pooh! If she's a nice girl, she won't mind about it. You can live perfectly happily in a small way, if you have the right person.'

'There speaks my pauper sister,' Tom said, catching her face between his hands to kiss her. 'If I never have to live in a smaller way than you, I shall be a happy man! But I fancy finding someone to fall in love with will be problem enough to occupy me.'

150

'You will. You will, darling Tommy,' Rosamund said as he parted from her. 'And when you find her, if she doesn't love you back, I'll hang her for a worthless hussy!'

'I'll be sure to tell her that,' he said at the door. 'It will prove a powerful inducement.'

The fog had thickened, and Benedict walked back down to Piccadilly cautiously, feeling his way along the railings. It was no distance from there to Dover Street, where he had bespoken a room in Shott's hotel. He was thinking of Charlotte's coming-out ball, and imagining that day in the future when he would bring out his own darling Mary. Not in London, though. He was a wealthy man, but a London Season for his daughter was not a thing he had ever contemplated. She would be Mistress of Morland Place one day – if Rosalind didn't give him a son, which didn't now seem likely – and whoever she married would have to be satisfied to live at Morland Place with her. Some spring of nobility or gentry met in London might not take to that idea, and want her to live on his terms. Better that Mary should marry a local man, who would understand the importance of Morland Place, and think himself lucky to get its heiress.

Mary's intellect was quite astonishing: at six she was as quick and clever as most ten-year-olds. There seemed to be nothing she couldn't learn, and her eagerness for instruction put her in a league apart from other children. Certainly there couldn't be a greater difference than between her and Rose. There was in the back of his mind the faintest seed of doubt about Rose. At four, almost five in fact, she still did not talk intelligibly. She didn't make much of any sound – except that dreadful screaming when she was thwarted in any way – but when she did speak it was just the same sort of baby-jabber she had always made. She was certainly healthy enough – had never ailed a thing, in fact, in her small life – ate well, and slept well and was, if anything, large for her age. But she didn't talk, and it was impossible to tell if she understood when she was talked to, either. She was like a large, strong, five-year-old baby. Rosalind shrugged and said that some children were slower than others, that comparison with Mary made her seem more babyish than she was, that as Mary got so much attention it took it from Rose and held her back – all or any of which might have been true. Probably Rose would catch up suddenly, as Rosalind said. It was just that Bendy worried from time to time; when he hadn't anything else to worry about.

His other, great worry was about to surface again in his mind when he reached Shott's, and was obliged to halt because a carriage was pulled up at the kerb and a footman holding the door open was blocking the way. Benedict waited philosophically, seeing a slim, well-shod foot and a female hand in a long kid glove emerge from the carriage door; there was a diamond bracelet about the gloved wrist, too, and a great deal of satin and velvet was following it out. Some rich provincial returning from the theatre, he thought. It was an unexpectedly young figure that was emerging: Shott's was not fashionable, and its wealthy guests were usually staid, elderly folk who were loyal to it because they had stayed there in their youth when it had been a far giddier (and more expensive) place.

The young woman had reached the footway and, holding her skirts clear of the pavement, was stepping towards the hotel door. There was something about the crook of her arm and the angle of her head that struck Bendy as faintly familiar, an instant before she turned her face towards him with a sharp intake of breath. Within the wide frame of the cloak's hood he saw the

152

bunches of ringlets and the tell-tale fuzz along the top of the forehead where what should have been fashionable smooth bands of hair had reacted to the damp air. And within the frame of hair the face seemed painted in stark astonishment, wide-eyed like an animal at bay, colourless in the unnatural mixtures of gaslight and fog.

Everything seemed to stop, so that the instant was long enough for him to see every detail as if he had a year to stare instead of a second; but a second was long enough when you knew a face well. Wide at the cheekbone, that face, and narrow at the chin, yet accommodating a wide mouth – touched these days, he saw, with lip-rouge; a little, pointed chin made for defiance; eyes like clear water, fringed with dark lashes as a river is fringed with reeds. She looked utterly astonished – and the astonishment was not all pleasurable either. She had whitened with the shock – he could tell that, even by gaslight, because the freckles across her cheekbones suddenly stood out as though she had been splashed with fine mud spray.

'Benedict!' He saw her lips move in the shape, but she made no sound.

'Sib—' he began, and then corrected himself. It was four years since he had seen her, at her come-out; she was a grown woman now, not a girl any longer. 'Miss Leytham,' he concluded, and removed his hat, and bowed. She was still staring at him when he straightened, frozen in place halfway across the footway; she curtseyed automatically, her eyes never leaving his face. He saw, now, that her face was thinner and older by those four years; more beautiful, too.

'What are you doing here?' she said at last. It came out in a kind of gasp, and he saw the footman glance at her for a instant, his attention attracted by the tone of her voice.

Benedict tried to sound hearty and natural. 'Well, it is a hotel, you know! There wouldn't be much use to a hotel if no-one stayed there.' It had come out heartier than he meant; he sounded like an idiot.

'*You're* staying here?' Well, she did too. 'But what are you doing in London?'

'I came up today on – on family business. Rather a long story. You see, a cousin of mine, or I should say a second cousin perhaps—'

He was babbling in his surprise at her reaction. She seemed to shake herself back into her senses: a little quiver, and those universe-wide eyes were reduced to human size by the lowering of lovely lids, the pained mouth formed itself into a social smile. 'Goodness! Please don't tell me the whole story out here in the street, Mr Morland. I'm sure we are blocking the footway.' And she gathered her skirts again and passed into the hotel, and he followed dumbly, like a page following a queen. She had always walked like a queen, with a horsewoman's straight back, and a proud head carriage that ought to have borne a crown.

In the foyer her maid, who had got down from the other side of the carriage, was waiting, and the manager hovered, longing to be of service. Sibella put back her hood, and he saw that she was wearing a crown, a plaited knot of her copper-gold hair. There were diamonds at her ears and round her throat, whose refulgence was brilliant enough even to shine in gaslight; her cloak was purple velvet lined with ermine; her gown stiff satin in a dark brown-purple shade that he knew was fashionable but couldn't remember the name of. She looked like a duchess, his little Sib; and now she had put on the manner of a dowager to go with it – an arch formality that seemed to hold the hint of a warning.

'Well, Mr Morland, it is very pleasant to meet with old

154

family friends, quite by *accident*. I had no idea you were staying here at Shott's, or I would have mentioned it to my *father*. He will be sorry to have missed you.'

'Is Sir John staying here?' Bendy said. 'I thought he preferred Shepard's.'

'Well, and so he does. I have just been at the theatre with him, and since we came past Shepard's first I left him down.'

This seemed curiously ungallant behaviour to Bendy – and besides, why were they staying at separate hotels? He was about to comment on it, but she forestalled him with an electric look, and turning to the manager said, 'Has Sir Samuel retired, or is he still in the smoking-room?'

The manager looked just slightly surprised, but he answered evenly. 'I believe he has retired, my lady.'

She turned quickly back to Benedict. 'In that case, Mr Morland, I fear I will not be able to give myself the pleasure of introducing my husband to you tonight. But if you are staying in this hotel, I am sure that there will be another opportunity, some other day.'

The clear, rain-coloured eyes looked into his, full of messages he could not read. Benedict felt stupid, like someone trying to follow a conversation in a foreign language of which he had only a few words.

'You're married?' he heard himself say. He knew he ought to be pleased, offer felicitations, blessings, but he could only sound astonished.

'Why, Mr Morland, is it so very surprising? I have been married almost two years, to Sir Samuel Mayhew. I wonder you should not have seen the announcement in the papers.'

He shook his head. 'May – may I offer my most sincere felicitations, Lady Mayhew,' he managed to get out. Married? Little Sib?

She laughed, a slightly unhappy laugh. 'Why, you could

not expect me to have stayed seventeen for ever. And when a woman grows up, she marries – that is the usual order of things.'

'I don't think I am acquainted with Sir Samuel,' he said.

'No, I should be surprised if you were. You do not move at all in the same circles. Well, I must bid you goodnight, sir. I wish I might stay and hear your family news, but Sir Samuel will be waiting for me. Another time, perhaps.'

'Yes, another time.' She gathered up her skirts, but did not seem to be able to go. Her eyes were all over his face, as he supposed someone might stare if they were looking at something for the last time, before they mounted the scaffold. He tried to smile, but it didn't come out properly, so he bowed instead. 'Your servant, ma'am.'

'Yes,' she said – just that; and then she was gone, lightly across the hall, swiftly up the stairs, head up, golden crown gleaming, white neck stretched for the blade. No, nonsense, what overwrought language was that? She was married, that was all – and married well, to judge from the diamonds and etcetera. As she had said, he could not have supposed that she would remain little Sib for ever. Girls grew up, and then they got married; it was the most natural thing in the world.

So why, then, did he feel such a shocking pang of loss?

CHAPTER EIGHT

Charlotte liked Fanny Hobsbawn the moment she first saw her, standing in the hall amid a mound of luggage, handing her gloves to her maid. Fanny was extremely pretty, with brown curly hair and blue eyes, and Charlotte liked to look at pretty things; but what struck Charlotte more was the sparkle in the eyes and the dimples in the cheeks, and the fact that Denton, the butler, was actually smiling! But Charlotte discovered as soon as she went down to greet her that you couldn't be long in Fanny's company without smiling, even if you were the Despot of the Lower Regions (Fanny's description of Denton). Fanny was lively, with engaging manners, and an open countenance which spoke a friendly disposition. When Charlotte offered her hand to shake, Fanny took it, looked up into her face (for as Charlotte was rather tall, Fanny was very small) and then reached up on tiptoe to kiss her.

'There!' she said. 'Impudent I know, but if I don't start off being bold, I shall lose all courage, you are such a tall, imposing creature. I am always afraid of tall people. They are by so much nearer to God, and who knows what they might whisper in His ear?'

Charlotte said, 'I can't believe you have ever been afraid of anything.'

They walked up to the first floor together, where Fanny paid her respects to Lucy and Danby, and then Charlotte was deputed to show her up to her room. They had put her next-door to Charlotte; in fact there was a communicating door between the two rooms, but Charlotte did not point it out, and Fanny made no comment on it.

Fanny looked round her room with great satisfaction, though. 'Well, this is splendid indeed! What a pretty room. I have never stayed here before, though I've visited, of course, when I've come up to Town with Aunt Rosamund.' She looked at Charlotte. 'I must say it is very kind of you to share your come-out with me, and it couldn't have come at a better time. There I was, facing a Season in Manchester without anyone new to dance with, when like a thunderbolt out of a clear sky comes a wonderful invitation to London! Balls at all the best houses, theatres and so on, riding in Hyde Park – and presentation into the bargain! I can't tell you how grateful I am!' She pulled off her bonnet and flung it on a chair, and waved her maid away with a flutter of her fingers.

'I can't claim any of the credit,' Charlotte said, wishing that she could deal so lightly with servants – she was still rather afraid of most of Grandmama's. 'I'm sorry to say until I was told you were coming I had no idea of your existence.'

'Still, you're the root cause, so you may as well take the thanks,' Fanny said. 'Oh, the excitement of being you!' she added, her eyes shining. 'It's just exactly like a fairy story – and to think I'm actually here, meeting you in the flesh! You can't imagine how I've romanced about you since I was a little girl.'

'About me? But – what did you know about me?'

'I wasn't supposed to know anything,' Fanny said, sitting on the bed. 'It was all supposed to be a deep, dark secret – but these things get out, of course. The Missing Heiress, you see—' Her face changed abruptly. 'And poor Aunt Rosamund suffered so much, I can't tell you how

158

affecting it was. She and Mama used to talk about you, and they both cried so—' She shook her head. 'But now here you are, and all is well again.' She eyed Charlotte consideringly. 'We *must* be friends, you know.'

'Must we?' Charlotte said, amused by this lively creature.

'Of course! It was planned before we were ever born. My mama and yours were the closest, closest friends. They had their come-out together and got engaged at the same time, and loved each other dearly, and always planned that they would each have a daughter and that their daughters would grow up together and be great friends like them. Well, it didn't work out quite like that – but now we have a chance to make amends, so I am quite determined to love you, do what you will!'

Charlotte laughed. 'You are absurd!'

'Am I? Will you find it impossible to love me, then?'

'No, I don't think so,' Charlotte said. 'I can't imagine anyone being able to resist you.'

'Oh, good! I'm glad you think so, for the moment I set eyes on you I thought you were just the sort of woman I should like for my intimate friend. You are everything I've always wanted to be, tall and dignified – and your lovely hair! I used to be fair when I was a little girl, but it turned dark, and just look—' she tugged impatiently at a curl – 'how impossible it is! Everyone else has smooth bands like yours, and I have this sheep's fleece!'

'I think your curls are lovely,' Charlotte said. 'I'd give anything to have proper curls, instead of fuzz. My hair is neither one thing nor the other.'

'Well I think you're beautiful,' Fanny said firmly. 'And we have a lot in common, you know.'

'We are cousins, I believe?'

'Not first cousins, of course. My grandfather and your grandmother were brother and sister. But I didn't mean that. I meant we're both orphans. I'm more of an orphan than you, in fact, because both my mama and papa are dead, whereas you hadn't a mama, and now you have one. Isn't that odd?' she diverted herself, wonderingly. 'And isn't it odd that I probably know your mama better than you do? She has been almost a mother to me, since Mama died.'

'Did she bring you up, then?'

'Not exactly, but she was always *there*, you know, which was nice. No, it was my step-papa brought me up, after Mama died. Henry's an angel! I wish you might meet him – perhaps you shall, if he comes to London before I go back. But he has a great deal of business, otherwise he'd have brought me himself. But I know you will love him if you meet him. He is the nicest person in the world, and nothing ever annoys him. He and Mama were only married a year, though she'd known him long before that – he was a friend of my father's, so I've known him since I was a little girl. He was heartbroken when Mama died. But at least he had me. Aunt Rosamund wanted to take me, but we didn't want to be separated. So she kept an eye on me from a distance. Of course, I spent a lot of time staying with her and Uncle Jes – we both did. So she's a sort of second mother to me. And darling Cav is like my little brother. Don't you adore Cav?'

'Yes, I do.'

'I thought you must. So you see, practically sharing a brother and a mother, we are almost sisters.'

'I would have liked to have a sister,' Charlotte said.

'Me too, but Mama couldn't have any more, after me. Well, there's no reason we shouldn't start now. It would make everyone very happy, I dare say. You know we have been brought together to be friends? Generally that would be enough to make me determined to hate you, but as it is, I shall think of you as my big sister – if you don't object?'

'Not at all,' Charlotte said shyly. Fanny caught both her hands and looked up at her, and everything about her was so easy that Charlotte, who was not used to being touched and had never done such a thing before in her life, bent forward and kissed the round rosy cheek before her.

Fanny laughed happily. 'Oh, I am going to love helping to bring you out! Of course, I called you my big sister, but I rather think I am older than you. How old are you?'

'I'm just twenty-one.'

'And I'm twenty-two. I'll be twenty-three in March. Almost twenty-three, and not married! Tibbet – my maid – shakes her head over me, and tells me I shall be a long time marrying. Flirts never get husbands, she says.'

'*Do* you flirt?'

'Only a little.' Then she grinned impishly. 'Well, a lot, to be honest. It's the best fun. That's why I don't want to get married yet. You can't imagine how nice it is to have all the men run after you all the time! And there's plenty of time. Tibbet thinks I shall end up on the shelf, but she forgets I'm an heiress – not as great a one as you, but I am a great catch by Manchester standards, so I shall never want for suitors – though I don't mean to marry just anyone. But one day I shall fall in love, and that will be the end of *me*,' she concluded sanguinely. 'Have you ever been in love?'

'No,' Charlotte said. 'Have you?'

'Not properly, not to want to marry. Of course, one falls in love once a week when one first comes out, but that's just practising. And I haven't been in love with anyone, not even a bit, for two years. It's very dull. I think perhaps it's time I fell in love properly – that's why this invitation comes at the best possible moment. I mean to have one last, wonderful spree.'

'From what I gather,' Charlotte said with a gleam in

her eyes, 'young women always fall in love with the wrong person.'

'Well, not always, but quite as often as not, I dare say. But these days I believe we are hardly ever forced to marry someone we don't like, as it used to happen. Not that it will apply to you, in any case – you are over twenty-one, and have an independent fortune. You may marry anyone you like – though you had better fall in love with the right sort of person, if you don't want to have your people in a ferment.'

'Do you think I might fall in love?' Charlotte asked doubtfully. 'I can't imagine it.'

Fanny looked her over frankly. 'I don't see how you can avoid it, given it's your first Season, and you'll be the most important débutante in London. Every man will be mad for you, and you're bound to have your head turned. But don't worry, I'll keep an eye on you, and make sure you don't go head-and-ears for a complete scoundrel.'

'And you'll teach me how to go on?' Charlotte asked anxiously. 'I've never had anything to do with men.'

'I shall be at your side the whole time, as close as your shadow,' Fanny promised solemnly.

'Thank you,' Charlotte said, feeling much easier about the whole thing. 'You are very kind.'

'Not at all,' Fanny said mischievously. 'I told you every man in Town will be mad for you; if I keep close I can pick up the crumbs you drop!'

Charlotte had never had a friend, not even a companion; she had never tasted before the blissful delights of chatting. Her life had been lived mostly in silence; now her days were filled with the company of someone who had a minute and personal interest in everything about her, from the curl of her hair to the state of her heart. Charlotte was a little stiff to begin with, as though using

162

an unaccustomed muscle; but practice soon loosened her up. Nothing could be easier than talking to Fanny, and the two of them hardly ever found a day long enough to say everything there was to be said. On the second night at Upper Grosvenor Street, Fanny discovered the communicating door, and thereafter most nights would find one of them sitting on the other's bed, talking, until Tibbet came indignantly to chase them away to get their sleep.

Fanny had the knack of talking to everybody, young and old, on just the subject and in just the way they liked, so the morning calls and visits of form Charlotte had been dreading passed quickly and easily. Charlotte could not help knowing that she was causing a stir of interest in the *ton*, and she disliked so much being the object of curiosity that she was deeply grateful to Fanny for distracting attention away from her.

But even so she came in for quite some staring and probing, which she was not ready-tongued enough to divert. 'But they have so little to think of, that just being a new face would be enough,' she complained.

'Now, Charley,' Fanny replied in her rapid, slightly husky voice, 'don't be petulant! You can't think how romantic you are! Here's a beautiful young woman – yes, don't interrupt me! – suddenly appeared from the deepest obscurity into one of the first families in the land – and she's rich and titled into the bargain! It's as though you had been imprisoned in a tower under an evil spell, or asleep for a hundred years, or some such thing. You are a fairy story! All that's needed is the Prince to kiss you awake – and that won't be lacking, I can assure you. Oh, we are going to have such fun!'

Charlotte was not sure about that part of it, but it was true that everything was more amusing with Fanny. Even being fitted for clothes, which Charlotte had found a bore, became tolerable, for Fanny had such a good eye for colour and style, and such an enthusiasm for seeing Charlotte look well, and was so good at drawing out Madame Bourdin, the mantuamaker, to say droll things, that the time seemed to fly by. Shopping, Charlotte's second least favourite occupation, shot up the list of pleasures like a rocket. Fanny took such vigorous pleasure in everything and everyone she saw around her, that Charlotte began to see with new eyes; and, moreover, Fanny very soon made it possible for the two girls to go out alone together, which was delightful.

Lucy at first was shocked at the idea. 'Two young girls – one of them not even out – to go out without a chaperone? It would be most improper. I wonder you can even suggest it, Fanny.'

But Fanny could charm even a Lady Theakston, and her ready tongue had arguments enough to beat down any opposition. 'Not such very young girls, ma'am. It isn't as though we are seventeen; and though Charlotte *isn't* out, and though she *is* very innocent, she's more than one-and-twenty, and I am a grown woman. No-one would be shocked to see two respectable young women walking together around some very respectable shops in broad daylight, which is all I propose – *and*,' she added, as though offering the final, unassailable argument, 'accompanied by a maid *and* a footman. And if we are put down and fetched by your carriage, Great Aunt, everyone will know whose protection we are under, and it will all be as proper as you could wish. We will, of course, only go to the very *best* shops, where you are known.'

Charlotte was amazed when Lucy agreed with very little more argument; but as Fanny explained afterwards, 'The thing was, you see, that she didn't really want to go with us. I could see from the beginning that taking us round the shops was a shocking fag to her, so she was positively

164

glad to be let off. As Henry always says, 'Work with the grain, Fan, and it's smooth going.' He is the very best at managing people of anyone in the whole world.'

Being out alone with Fanny – with only Tibbet and a footman walking behind, just out of earshot – was a delight to Charlotte, a feeling of real freedom and holiday. It was also, she assuaged her conscience, a useful exercise, for Fanny seemed to know everyone, at least by sight, and was much easier to follow than Grandmama when she explained the intricacies of the social hierarchy, which Grandmama seemed anxious she should learn. Fanny's favourite haunt was Bond Street, which not only had the best shops, but was also the place that young men of wealth and fashion liked to saunter.

'That's the Earl of Preston, walking with Mr Paulett: Mr Paulett limps – a hunting accident; the earl is the fair one. He has a dreadful stammer, poor man, which makes him awfully shy. I think that's why they are such great friends. Don't you think the earl looks rather like a horse? Uncle Jes calls them Halt and Halter – but not when he thinks I'm listening. And that's Mr Hesketh just crossing the street – he's *very* clever, they say. He married Mary Knatchbull, who's as clever as he is, so *their* children will have a merry life of it!'

'Do you see the red-haired man in the blue coat? That's Viscount Freshwater – now he might do for you, Charlotte, if you liked him, for he's just about your age. His grandpapa was a friend of Great Aunt Lucy's, so he's bound to be asked to your ball. But I'm not sure about that hair. You are a little red yourself, and think of your poor children!'

'Oh do look! That's Tom Cavendish talking to Lord Palmerston. I met him in Manchester last year when he came down to look at the factories for Lord Ashley. He's a great rattle! Shall I speak to him? But Tibbet would think

I was being bold, and probably tell Great Aunt Lucy. If we hurry across the road, we will come upon them, then he'll have to tip his hat to me. Do hurry! We'll pretend we want to look in the bookshop window – that's respectable enough.'

'There's Oliver Fleetwood – look, Charlotte! Isn't he perfectly beautiful? Aunt Rosamund came out in the same Season as *his* aunt, and I've seen him nod to her when I've been staying in London and he's passed us in the carriage. He's the old Duke of Southport's grandson and heir – his papa died three years ago, so he will be Duke himself any time his grandpa pops off, which must be soon, because he's eighty if he's a day. He is absolutely the catch of the Season – and any Season these ten years, come to that! When I was coming out, all the girls used to talk about him as if he were the prince in a fairy tale. You can't think how they envy me in Manchester because I've actually seen him in the flesh, even though I've never spoken to him.'

The young man in question was getting out of a carriage, and helping down an elderly woman, who Charlotte assumed must be his mother. They were close enough for Charlotte to get a good look at him, and she could see why, leaving aside the question of the dukedom, he might be seen as a catch. He was tall and beautifully made, with fine shoulders, and legs for which the skin-tight pantaloons of high fashion seemed to have been designed. He had thick dark hair, brushed attractively awry, and very delicate side-whiskers, and his eyes were the deepest blue she had ever seen, behind long, dark lashes which seemed to emphasise their brilliance. His nose was straight, his mouth finely cut, his chin firm – altogether there was a harmony about his features that seemed to be designed to show what faces could be like if they were got right. Charlotte liked the attentive way he helped the old lady, and the seriousness of his expression. He looked clever. A great many of the young men Fanny pointed out to her seemed like nothing more than animated clothes.

They had approached so close now that the stately progress of the dowager across the footway was impeding their own, and they stopped perforce, as did the people coming the other way. The dowager was thus walking from her carriage to the milliner's through a little corridor of spectators, which did not seem to displease her: she moved slowly and with great display which Charlotte guessed needed an audience. Her son, cradling her elbow and watching the pavement for her, seemed not to see the gathering crowds until the last moment, when the manager of the milliner's shop stepped forward from his door to take over charge of the elbow. Then, released from his task, he straightened and looked around, a brief and cool glance which seemed intended to do service as an apology for the inconvenience – all the apology that was necessary from one so exalted, it seemed to say.

But then his glance lit upon Charlotte; flickered a moment over Fanny, and came back to Charlotte's face. She coloured instantly at being looked at, but could not bring herself to lower her eyes, for he was so very handsome she wanted to go on looking at him. A faint smile seemed to turn up the corners of his beautifully formed lips – not so much of a smile as to be impertinent, but merely a slight softening of the sculpture – and he gave her a very slight bow, before following his mother into the shop.

It took only the fraction of a second, but it seemed scalded onto Charlotte's memory. She could feel her quickened pulse, and wondered what on earth could have got into her. The way was clear again and the crowds were moving forward, Charlotte and Fanny with them. Fanny was pinching her arm with excitement.

'He noticed you! Did you see? He looked and bowed especially to you! Oh, Charlotte!'

'He was apologising for holding us up, that was all,' Charlotte said – and indeed it could have been so. The cool glance had been supplemented, because they were plainly ladies of breeding, with a bow.

'No, no, that wasn't it! He was going on, and then he saw your face and was struck by it. How could you not notice? You *are* looking very well today – that bonnet particularly suits you – and a blush is becoming to you, because you are just a little pale sometimes.'

Charlotte laughted. 'Fanny, don't be absured! What are you about, trying to cook up a romance?'

'There is no cooking to it,' Fanny assured her solemnly. 'I tell you, Charley, he noticed you – and as you are not acquainted, what else could it be but admiration?'

'But Fanny, dear, you said he had seen you in the carriage with my mother. Much more likely that he recognised you.'

'Well, I dare say he did remember my face,' Fanny said modestly, 'but that wasn't it. However, if you are determined not to take the compliment, I'll have it myself. It's all the same to me!'

The number of people from whom Charlotte might now receive a bow or curtsey was increasing day by day. She was taken to the drawing-rooms of the great hostesses to be made acquaint with their sons and daughters; and on at-home days, the less great would call at Upper Grosvenor Street to watch Charlotte handing round cups. There were small private dinners and suppers, and card-parties – not parties at which card games were played, as Charlotte had supposed when she first heard the expression, but parties for which cards were sent to people who were on card-leaving terms.

There were the attendances at the Chapel Royal on Sunday, which Charlotte felt were less to do with spiritual devotions than nodding to and being seen by the right people as one came out. There were the drives out in the carriage with Grandmama for the purpose of collecting and distributing nods. And there were rides in the Park, again always accompanied by Lucy and sometimes Danby too. Charlotte enjoyed the rides most of all their activities, for since Lucy could not regard riding as a means to an end, they went out at an unfashionable hour when the paths were unfrequented. This meant that Charlotte could relax and enjoy the activity, rather than strain her attention to remember which people she knew and which she didn't, what their names were, and whether she should nod coolly or bow deeply. Fanny seemed to cope with it all effortlessly, remembering everyone's name and the exact degree of acquaintance they shared with everyone else; and Lucy was on firm ground, being under no obligation to anyone, and old enough to be excused unintentional incivility; but Charlotte had lived most of her life knowing the names of no more than a dozen people in total. Shy, feeling awkward, nervous and unsure, she needed all the encouragement of a Fanny to get through some of the outings.

But the riding was a delight. Fanny, Charlotte was impressed to discover, was allowed to ride Grandmama's second horse Copper – a compliment to her horsemanship which she appreciated just as she ought. Charlotte thought she looked very good in the saddle, taller, and very dashing in a tricorne hat with a feather. Ingot had been borrowed from Lord Aylesbury and brought to London for Charlotte's use. Seeing how dashing Fanny looked on the gassy little Copper, who never stood still for a moment and drew all eyes to himself and his rider, Charlotte felt a moment's pang of disappointment that Ingot was so well-mannered and quiet. But it was only a foolish moment, and as soon as Parslow tossed her up into the saddle, she remembered what a delight he was, smooth-stepping, intelligent, and as light to her hands as a feather. And though he did not caper and breenge like Copper, he was full of impulsion, and she longed for the chance to gallop him, and see how fast he really could go.

'Yes, I thought you'd like him,' Lucy said. 'Aylesbury bought him for Thalia to hunt, but though she took him out a couple of times she didn't take to him. He's not as easy a ride as he looks. He's a horse who needs confidence in his rider, and Thalia isn't a natural horsewoman like you.'

It was a compliment to treasure, Charlotte thought.

One day Fanny wheedled Lucy into allowing her and Charlotte to go alone in the carriage to a silk warehouse in Islington; it was a warehouse Lucy herself patronised, and if they went in Lucy's carriage and did not stop anywhere else, she persuaded herself it would not raise any eyebrows. It was the furthest Charlotte had been since she came to London, and the first view she had had of the streets beyond their own small territory, other than on that first day when she had arrived too bemused to take anything in. It was salutary, she thought, to be reminded again of how vast London was, for she was in danger of thinking it encompassed nothing more than St James's, the Park and Bond Street.

It also obliged her to acknowledge that the London of ease and wealth with which she was acquainted was not the only London: like a shadow of itself, there lay another city just behind it, parallelling its streets and squares with lanes and courts, cramped, dark and squalid, and teeming with life. Sometimes its proximity was frightening: driving along a broad thoroughfare, one would pass the opening to a side-street, and catch a glimpse of filthy children, rooting pigs, middens, bent and deformed men, tawdry half-clad women, and tenements in a state of shocking disrepair, half derelict, dripping black filth, yet evidently home to dozens of the poorest people.

But these were only glimpses. On that carriage journey with Fanny, she came upon something even more desolate. Suddenly they seemed to be travelling past a wasteland, as though in the wake of a violent, destructive army. Houses had been knocked down, vast trenches and pits gouged out of the earth, mountains of slick yellow clay thrown up. No, it was worse than the wake of an army – no mere marching men could have left such devastation. It was as if a gigantic beast with teeth of iron had clawed and champed its way through a whole neighbourhood. Streets had been burst through, roads truncated as though bitten off; tenements were split like kindling, half-eaten bridges led from nowhere to nowhere. Here the façade of a tall building reared up, its edges ragged, its glassless eyes open on nothing but the empty air behind; there a house with its top half missing hung at a drunken angle over a pit of water, from whose yellow depths poked the ends of beams, roof struts and missing chimneypots. Yet just beyond this mauled and pulverised strip was a crowded neighbourhood, where smoking chimneys and glimpses of hung-out washing, teeming alleys and steaming beast-pens, suggested life was going on as if nothing had happened.

'What has happened here?' she asked Fanny.

'Happened? What do you mean? Oh, that's the railroad workings, that's all.'

'It looks terrible – such devastation!'

'Yes, it does, doesn't it? But it didn't look much better before. It's a place called Agar Town, and it was never more than half respectable – mostly back-slums, you know, and the worst sort of lodging houses. Once they have finished, I dare say it will all be tidied up. We have railways in Manchester, and they look as if they have always been there.'

Charlotte looked out of the window again. 'What happened to the people?'

'The people?'

'Who lived there – where the houses have been destroyed?'

'Goodness, *I* don't know,' Fanny said, startled. 'Poor people, that's all.'

'But where did they go? There must have been hundreds of them. Were there houses built for them somewhere else?'

'I doubt it,' Fanny said. 'I expect they just moved on.'

'Where to?'

'Charley, I don't know,' Fanny said with a humorous look. 'Where do such people go? Where do they come from, for the matter of that? They have their own ways. It's nothing to do with us.'

She was plainly not interested in the subject, and Charlotte let it go; but the question niggled her from time to time. If such crowded housing were emptied out and destroyed, where would the displaced ones go?

At the warehouse she had her first taste of celebrity. As she went in through the door, a man in managerial black and with hair curled and oiled *just so* rushed forward, bowed himself double, and then backed before her, inviting her in with, 'Lady Chelmsford! Such an honour! Such a great honour! I am Amis, if I might be permitted, proprietor of this establishment – at your entire service, my dear ma'am! I am certain we can find just *exactly* what you are looking for!'

As he turned his head for a moment to look where he was going, Charlotte muttered in perplexity to Fanny, 'How does he *know* me?'

'The arms panel on the coach, silly,' Fanny muttered back.

Charlotte wasn't sure she liked being instantly known; she was sure she didn't like the man's silly spaniel-bowing and hand rubbing. It was not a sensible way to behave. And why did he need her permission to be who he was? She didn't know how to deal with him. A woman of fashion, just then leaving, accompanied by an elderly gentleman, looked sharply at Charlotte as Amis spoke her name, and contributed to her feeling of being unpleasantly exposed. She blushed in a mixture of vexation and embarrassment.

Fanny, however, was more interested in the young woman than Charlotte. She seized Charlotte's arm, and held her back from Amis's oily progression to hiss, 'D'you see the smart female in the hat? That's Lady Mayhew!'

'I've never heard of her,' Charlotte whispered back, distracted.

'Oh Lord, it was all the talk in 'forty-two, her marriage to Sir Samuel! She was only a Miss Leytham, but her mother was daughter to Lord Pulborough. She arranged the match, the mother, though it's said the father was against it – Miss Leytham's father, I mean. She's pretty, isn't she?'

'Was that her father with her?'

'Gracious, no! *That* was Sir Samuel Mayhew! That was the scandal, you see, he was sixty and she wasn't even one-and-twenty. He's horrid rich, of course. That's why it was rushed through before she came of age. He was mad in love with her, and they say he bribed the mother to bring it about. And now he won't let her so much as speak to a footman, for fear she might like him more than her horrid old husband – and who wouldn't?'

'Oh, Fanny!' Charlotte was dismayed rather than shocked – the lady who had passed them looked so nice – and if *she* were being gossiped about in that way, what would the world be saying of Charlotte? 'Don't talk so.'

'I didn't make it up. I only tell you what everyone says,' Fanny said. 'I feel very sorry for her. Oh, but Charlotte, do look at Amis – he's going to knock over that table if he keeps walking backwards. He must have taken you for the Queen!'

That at least made Charlotte smile, given that she was half a foot taller than Her Majesty. Amis did bump into the table, which at least made him straighten up. She thought he would oil a little less when she told him it was for Fanny they were shopping, not her, but it seemed Lady Chelmsford's Particular Friend was just about as good as Lady Chelmsford herself. Fanny found a very pretty apple-blossom silk, which Charlotte begged to be allowed to buy for her, and Fanny accepted delightedly – it was one of her nice traits, that she could accept gifts with such ready pleasure. If Amis felt any disappointment that her ladyship bought nothing for herself, he didn't show it. Afterwards in the coach Charlotte expressed how much she had disliked being fawned on, and wondered how any sensible man could do it, or suppose any sensible woman could like it.

Fanny listened, and then said abruptly, 'Better get used to it, Charley. Watch how Great Aunt Lucy deals with it: she doesn't notice 'em, any more than the horses that draw her carriage.' And then she grinned. 'Bad example! She *certainly* notices the horses!'

There was the usual traffic snarl at Holborn. The coachman, seeing a gap, forced his way into it, and then they were obliged to remain stationary for some time, as nothing was moving in either direction. Charlotte was seated on the side of the carriage nearer the footpath, and as their conversation had stopped for the time being, she interested herself in watching the people hurrying along with such intense expressions of purpose. A beggar was sitting almost opposite the carriage, with his back to the wall, and she wondered how it was he was not trodden on. But people seemed to divert round him without even seeing him – which was unlucky for the beggar. In the time they were still, she didn't see anyone drop a coin into his lap, though he was a pitiful enough object – a dirty boy in rags, with one leg ending in a stump. He had a crudely fashioned crutch beside him, and he looked about ten years old. She thought painfully of Cavendish – what a difference the fortune of birth made! She wished she could give the boy some money, but she couldn't get out of the carriage, and she couldn't throw coins through all those hurrying pedestrians. She wondered if she could call him across to the carriage to receive them, and began to lower the window.

'What are you doing?' Fanny asked; and at the same moment a man passing halted and turned towards the carriage enquiringly. Charlotte blushed to think that the man night have supposed she was trying to attract his attention; and then she saw with no less embarrassment that it was Mr Orrock. He wore the same greatcoat as when she had last seen him, and the same tall hat, tipped precariously backwards – though it differed by the addition of a long, folded document tucked into the hatband, presumably to allow Orrock to keep his hands stuffed into his pockets. His hair straggled over his collar as if trying to escape from under the hat; and as he came up to the carriage window, she thought he was wearing the same necktie and waistcoat as before, but with the addition of a few more food stains.

She emphatically didn't want to speak to him, but it was less easy to put a carriage window up than down, particularly when one was hurrying. Orrock had reached her, and was grinning and touching his hat while she was still struggling with the strap.

'Well, well, what a surprise, and a great pleasure I may add – *Lady Chelmsford*!' He spoke her name with great emphasis, accompanied by a widening of the grin, and a knowing wink. 'What could be nicer than a hunexpected hencounter with an old friend like this – and very civil I take it, to call me across and give me the meeting. Very civil, considering.'

Charlotte wished fervently that she had her grand-mother's freezing way, but she had only been a lady for three months, and it didn't come naturally to her. She could, however, say with perfect truth, 'I did not call you, Mr Orrock. I didn't know you were there.' She tried to say it coldly, but her naturally retiring manner made it sound only hesitant.

'Ho, never mind! A nod's as good as a wink, as they say,' Orrock replied obscurely, giving her several of each category. 'A lady's modesty and such-like – I compry end, ma'am, don't you worry. Cedric Orrock ain't the man to embarrass a female, especially one what he 'olds in such 'igh esteem. I am a-dying to be your servant, ma'am, your most 'umble servant!'

Fanny said from behind Charlotte's shoulder, 'Put the window up, do! It's shockingly draughty.'

Charlotte had got the tongue free now, and was grateful to Fanny for the interruption. 'Excuse me,' she said firmly to Orrock, and put the window up. Unfortunately it was another few seconds before the carriage began to move, during which time Orrock, not the least discomposed by the glass between them, continued to grin and nod at her from the footpath; and when they began to move he moved too, so that she feared he was going to walk beside them all the way home. But he came only a step or two, then stopped, and they left him behind.

Charlotte thought Fanny would ask who the horrid little man was, or take her to task for not dismissing him more forcefully; but, like Grandmama, she seemed to regard certain people as simply below notice. When she did speak, it was only of the evening's engagement.

Charlotte had plenty to occupy her thoughts, and Orrock was forgotten by the time they reached Upper Grosvenor Street. But the following morning as she was going down to breakfast, Denton came to her with a faintly frostly look, and said that there was a person to see her.

'So early?' she said in surprise.

'I did indicate that the hour was not acceptable, my lady, but the person said it was an urgent matter of business, and since he comes from Tarbush and Blaxall—'

'Mr Tarbush?'

'Not the gentleman himself, my lady, but a person from his office.'

'I had better see him, then,' she said. She supposed people of business must keep different hours: they could hardly breakfast at nine if they had a day's work to get through. She had not thought of its being Orrock, but when Denton escorted her to the library and she saw him there, this time with his hat off (Denton's doing, probably) she still thought only that he had come with a message from Tarbush.

'Yes, Mr Orrock?' she said as coolly as she could.

'Very good of you to see me, miss – my lady,' he said, bowing. Behind her Denton closed the door, and

Charlotte felt the first pang of misgiving. Good of her to see him?

'You have come from Mr Tarbush?' she said.

He grinned. 'Old Tarbush? Not much! I think he'd be surprised at my business this morning. Quite the downy one, Mr Tarbush, but he don't know everything. There are those of us which knows as much.'

'Mr Orrock, if you have business with me, say so. Otherwise I must ask you to leave.'

Orrock seemed to sense the alarm in her, though perhaps he misunderstood the cause. 'Oh, you don't need to be scared o' me, miss. I am here to do you a favour. Ain't we old friends? Just! Two days spent in each other's company in a coach – I'd say so!'

Charlotte moved towards the bell. 'I think you had better leave.'

Orrock looked wounded. 'Now then, now then, that's no way to go about keeping your friends! Pull that bell if you like, miss, but you'll regret it. I 'ave something to say to you which you ought to hear – which you need to hear. I've come to do you a favour, as I said – friendly like, and wishing to be of service, and it's a 'ard thing when a man's good hintentions is thrown in 'is face.'

Charlotte paused, entirely doubtful, and not liking this creature at all; but he couldn't mean to harm her, surely, in this house, with servants all around? Perhaps he did have something important to tell her, though she couldn't imagine what it could be. She faced him, pulling herself up to her full height. 'Say what you wish to say, but be quick.'

He grinned. 'That's better. You looks more the part now! And you are doing well, I won't say contrary. Come a long way, you have – a werry long way, considering what *we* both know. I hear great things about you all over Town, quite a splash you've made, and every grand

178

dame is after you for her son. Marriage is the game, ain't it? Marriage with the great and noble. But what would you think to looking a little lower – or a lot lower? I am here to serve you, ma'am. I admire you tremendous, and I am longing to be your servant.'

He bowed, smiling and winking, and she was utterly at a loss as to his meaning. It seemed to be leading in one direction only – a preposterous one.

'Mr Orrock, I don't understand you. You surely can't be proposing marriage?'

He laughed hugely, giving her instantly both relief and extreme annoyance. 'Marriage? Ha! Not quite!' She felt herself blushing, and was furious with herself. 'You ain't exac'ly in my style, miss. I like a bit o' meat to my bones – not but what you ain't 'andsome, don't get me wrong. But 'andsome is as 'andsome does. I deal as I find.'

'Mr Orrock, I must ask you to leave,' Charlotte said, finding levels of frost she didn't know she had.

It seemed to please Orrock. 'Is she 'aughty?' he addressed an invisible audience. 'Is she grand? Just! Go it, my lady! But what I say is, who's a-going to marry you when they finds out you're a ringer, eh? Answer me that one!'

Charlotte paused again on her way to the bell-pull. 'A what? What are you talking about?'

Orrock put his hands in his pockets and shrugged up his shoulders in a display of ease, as though it had been established that he had the upper hand. 'Yes, I thought that'd stop you! You was forgetting, wasn't you? You was forgetting I seed where you come from, and it wasn't no country seat. No, miss, and you wasn't no ladyship neether – *Miss Meldon*! Yes, that's shook you, ain't it? Thought no-one knew – forgot about me, didn't you? A dashy little cottage in a scrub of a place out in Nowhere. A place what didn't even have a public 'ouse.

Now what would Lady Chelmsford be doing in a place like that? You ask me and I'll tell you – nothing! You're a ringer, that's what you are. You ain't a ladyship at all. You're a lady, maybe, but you ain't a ladyship.'

Charlotte was stunned into silence, beginning to understand at last what he had come for. Orrock took her silence as a tribute.

'Yes, I thought you'd come round a bit when you twigged. So no more threats, eh? I come to do you a favour, like I said, so let's be pals about it. Now, this lay o' yours, you might be able to carry it off, or you mightn't – I can't say. You got some of the 'aughtiness, but not enough, and if you don't learn it quick, you'll come a cropper. But I know how the nobs go on. I've 'ad to do with 'em all me life. I could 'elp you, if you wanted, show you where you goes wrong.'

'No, thank you,' Charlotte said, struggling not to laugh. 'I can manage on my own.'

Orrock shrugged. 'Well, don't say I didn't offer. Cedric Orrock never was one to want something for nothing.'

'And what *do* you want, Mr Orrock?' Charlotte asked, though she was beginning to suspect. At least now she understood him, she was not afraid of him. She thought him merely ridiculous.

He smacked his lips and rubbed his forefinger and thumb together suggestively. 'I want a bit of it, that's what. I don't blame you for going on a flash lay, considering what's at stake. Good luck to you! But what's in it for me, that's what I want to know? Now Tarbush is a downy one, and I reckon you've paid him off all right. Just! He won't have come cheap. But I reckon I'm due something, considering what I know. I been in it from the beginning – so where's my cut?'

He thrust his hands in his pockets again and stood confidently, feet straddled, waiting for her to start bargaining.

For the fraction of an instant she wondered what figure he had in mind, wondered where she would start if she really did want to pay him for his silence – a hundred pounds? A thousand? But it was only a momentary curiosity. Mostly she wanted her breakfast. She walked across to the chimney and pulled the bell.

Orrock's face registered a mixture of astonishment and unwilling admiration that did her a great deal of good. 'Are you mad? Do you know what you're doing? I know all about you. Now, I don't want to do you any 'arm, but business is business, and if you turn me out without a penny, I shall 'ave to start talking – and believe me, I'll talk where it counts most.'

She turned to him. 'You can't do me any harm, Mr Orrock. You see, you don't know all about me. I'm not a "ringer" as you put it – I *am* Lady Chelmsford. The title and the money are mine by right, as Mr Tarbush knows very well. It's not a "lay" and I didn't pay him for his part in it. Everything is above-board, and there's nothing you can do to hurt me.'

He looked dumbfounded for a moment, but then his eyes narrowed cunningly. 'Fine words, my lady, but even if what you say is true, I can still tell things about you which will 'urt you plenty, so don't mistake me! I seen where you come from, and how you lived, and if I put that around, there'll be plenty as starts giving you the cold shoulder. Suspicion is as good as fact, when it comes to reputation, and if you don't know that, you don't know this game like what I do.'

Something in Charlotte hardened. 'Don't threaten me, Mr Orrock. I may be young and innocent, but I'm not a complete fool, and I do know that blackmail is a criminal offence.'

He grinned derisively. 'You can't tell me about the law. No witnesses, miss. It'd be your word against mine.'

'And who do you think they'd believe? Who do you think Mr Tarbush would believe?'

His grin dropped. But he said, 'Rumour'd hurt you more'n losing my job would me. Don't cross me, or you'll regret it.'

The door opened, to Charlotte's great relief, and Denton appeared, massive and impervious as always, but with, she thought, an alertness in his eyes, as if he had expected trouble.

'Mr Orrock is leaving,' she said.

Orrock went without another word, but with a final minatory glance from under his brows as he passed her. And then Charlotte was left alone, to tremble with reaction, and to try to calm herself enough to go in to breakfast. After a few minutes of pacing about the library, her agitation grew less, though she still felt sick at heart from the evil she had inadvertently swallowed. But she decided not to tell anyone what Orrock had come for. It was something she didn't want to think about, far less discuss; and she didn't think he would spread gossip about her now, not once he saw she didn't mean to accuse him, and lose him his job. She thought the one threat would counterbalance the other, and determined to put the matter out of her mind.

What did trouble her, though, was the idea that he might be right – that rumour and innuendo alone would be enough to see her shunned by Society. She didn't care about Society, really, she told herself – but it was one thing to choose not to go into it, and quite another to be rejected by it. She wondered, and continued to wonder on and off for a very long time, whether Orrock could possibly be right.

CHAPTER NINE

On the day of Charlotte's coming-out ball, Lucy decided that she wasn't happy with the sleeves of Charlotte's gown. They were complicatedly puffed and tucked, with a gauze over-sleeve cut into stitched points like the petals of a flower, and finished with a silk bow on the point of the shoulder.

'It doesn't sit right,' Lucy said, frowning at a sleeve discontentedly. The gown was hanging up in Charlotte's room. The two girls were about to start dressing; it was far too late, Charlotte thought, to change anything now. 'And I don't like the bow, either,' Lucy continued.

'It is the fashion,' Fanny mentioned helpfully.

'The fashion is what one makes it,' Lucy said firmly. 'Charlotte's shoulders are square enough without emphasising them with bows. I don't like bows anyway – I never did. No, they must come off.'

Fanny looked critically; Charlotte merely waited, not feeling her taste was sure enough to make a contribution (though secretly in her heart she was glad to find that she had never liked the bows either).

'It needs something,' Fanny said. 'It would look unfinished without the bow. How about a knot – with ribbon streamers, Great Aunt?'

Lucy also stared. 'Streamers – very thin ones. They would mingle with the points nicely. But a knot?'

'In pink silk, perhaps?' Fanny offered.

'Pink, yes – you have a good eye, child. But a rose, not a knot. A silk rose.'

'Oh yes, that would be perfect,' Fanny exclaimed. 'What a pity it is too late to alter it.'

She underestimated Lucy. 'Too late, nonsense! The set of the sleeve must be altered in any case, and changing the bows won't take any longer.'

'But will Madame Bourdin—?'

'Oh, I shan't bother with Bourdin. I hope I keep enough sewing women in the house to reset a sleeve! Norton is good with silk. Indeed, I dare say she could have made up the dress a good deal better than Bourdin's girls. I'll send her up right away.'

Tibbet dragged Fanny away to dress, and Charlotte was left alone, feeling very nervous, and wishing there hadn't been this last-minute hitch to add to her anxieties. After a few minutes the door opened and a maid came in – a pleasant-faced woman in her thirties, with quick, dark eyes. She was carrying a large sewing-basket, on top of which Charlotte could see a folded length of pale pink silk.

'I've come to do your sleeves, my lady,' she said.

'Oh, yes. Come in. Are you Mrs Norton?'

'I am Norton, my lady, yes.' She seemed a little surprised at the question, as if – Charlotte decided – she thought her name was not of any consequence. But I'm not so grand as that comes to, Charlotte thought – and suddenly decided she never wanted to be, either, not so grand that people around her could remain nameless.

She smiled and said, 'I'm sorry it has been left so late. Will you be able to do everything in time?'

Norton's expression warmed. 'Oh yes, my lady, don't worry. It isn't a big alteration, and there's plenty of time. And,' she almost smiled, 'they can't begin without you, can they?'

184

Charlotte relaxed. 'No, I suppose they can't. I am nervous, though. I wish it were all over.'

'Oh no, my lady,' Norton protested, crossing the room to look at the gown. 'Your come-out ball? You'll enjoy it above anything, once it starts. This is the gown, is it?' She fingered the material appreciatively. 'It's beautiful.'

It was, Charlotte agreed – the most beautiful gown she had ever seen. It was of white damask silk which had been specially woven for Charlotte, the figuring being a pattern of acorns and oak-leaves, the Chelmsford device (a reference to King Charles II who had created the title). The bodice was boned and cut to a long point in front, and fitted Charlotte like a skin; deeply décolleté, with a bertha of the finest, softest lace Charlotte had ever seen. The pleats of the skirt were graded and stitched under at the waistband to make it hang luxuriously full, and it had an overskirt, parted at the front, of gauze so fine it was like cobweb – the same gauze as the oversleeves.

'Yes,' said Norton judiciously, 'those sleeves'll never do. Her ladyship's never wrong. Would you be so good as just to slip the gown on, my lady, so I can see how the set needs to be.' Charlotte obeyed, and Norton began tweaking the sleeve as mantuamakers have tweaked sleeves since time began. 'I don't know how Madame Bourdin came to make such a piece of work of it,' she said, picking up her fine scissors and addressing the stitches. Then she smiled quickly up at Charlotte. 'Don't worry, my lady, it will be done right this time. All's well. And you will look lovely, if you'll pardon me. Not everyone can wear white, but with your colouring—'

'Oh, please,' Charlotte said, surprising herself, 'don't flummery. I had so much of that from Madame Bourdin, it was like being drowned in honey. Couldn't you – as a very great favour – just talk to me like a sensible person?'

Norton looked at her in surprise. Charlotte blushed. 'I'm sorry—'

'No, my lady,' Norton said quickly, 'I am yours to command. Whatever you want me to do—'

'That wasn't what I meant,' Charlotte said, with a small sigh. 'Forget about it, please.'

Norton cut a few more stitches, and then said, 'I understand you, my lady, but if Lady Theakston found out that I had presumed—'

'Presumed! There it is, you see,' Charlotte said impatiently.

Norton suddenly smiled at her, her dark eyes shining with amusement. 'Promise you won't tell, that's all.'

'Of course I won't. I promise.'

Norton nodded. 'And I wasn't flummerying. Not everyone *can* wear white, and you *have* very nice colouring. Not unlike her ladyship's – Lady Batchworth's, I mean – but more golden and less red. Easier to dress to.'

'You know my mother?'

Norton nodded. 'I've been with Lady Theakston ten years now, and Lady Batchworth has often been staying here, when they haven't wanted to open up the house. His lordship too and the little boy. What a love that child is! Though it would break your heart to see how poorly he's been over the years, and the way her poor ladyship looks at him sometimes, as though she expects him to disappear any moment. But now you are back, everything will be all right again. Now I have to fill my mouth with pins while I pin the sleeve, so I'll have to stop talking for a bit.'

'Oh no, don't stop. I like it. Please, I'll hold the pins for you,' Charlotte said. Norton looked doubtful a moment, but then handed her the box, and Charlotte held it at what she hoped was the best angle. 'Do you like it here?' she asked, to get the maid talking again.

'Oh yes. It's a very good place. You couldn't want a better mistress than your grandmama – she's fussy in her ways, likes everything just so, but she doesn't change her mind, which is a great thing for servants. You always know where you are with her; and she's always fair, doesn't take after you for nothing or because she's quarrelled with her liver, like many a grand lady will. And there isn't a nicer gentleman in the world than Lord Theakston.'

'Oh, I agree with you,' Charlotte said promptly. 'I love him so much!' Norton smiled at her enthusiasm, and concentrated on pinning in the sleeve. 'What is it like below stairs?'

'We're very well treated,' Norton said. 'The best of food, and everything is modern, which is not always the case. There's many fine people's houses hereabouts where the family side is luxurious as can be, but the kitchen regions are just like a dungeon, dark and damp and full of black beetles, as if it amused people to make their servants' work as hard as possible, and treat them worse than they treat their animals. But here there is gaslight in the kitchens, and a modern stove, and two coppers for the hot water – Lady Portman's servants have to boil kettles for every drop, would you believe it? Though I hear there's not so much bathing goes on in *that* house as you'd expect – and if it weren't for the wicked number of stairs in this house, which are misery to a servant's legs, there wouldn't be a better place in the world.'

'And what are the other servants like?'

'Well, Mr Denton is pretty fierce, but I don't have much to do with him, doing all my work upstairs as I do; though he's a stickler at meals. No-one to speak before Grace is said, then senior servants only until the meat is carved and handed, then general conversation on subjects introduced by senior servants until he gives the nod – after which you may talk to your neighbours if you wish, but never across the table. It's a trial to some of the maids, I can tell you, not to be able to chatter!'

Charlotte nodded, fascinated. 'Where do you work upstairs?'

'In the sewing-room, which is nice and out of the way. Mrs Weaver, the housekeeper, is over me.' She paused as if trying to find something good to say about Mrs Weaver, and failing. 'But she only comes to roust me when she can't find another maid to harry.'

Charlotte moved on to a point that more nearly concerned her. 'Tell me, why does my maid hate me?'

'Hate you, miss?' Norton said, surprised into a slip of the tongue. 'No, never.'

'You promised not to flummery. Pauline, the maid who has been assigned to take care of me, doesn't like doing it. She always wants to be elsewhere.'

Norton regarded her with a glimmer of humour. 'You are too quick of notice to be flummeried, and that's a fact. Well, I'll tell you, my lady, though I'm speaking out of turn, and I beg you not to repeat it. But that Pauline is a bit above herself. She was so cock-a-hoop when Mr Denton told her that she was to be your lady's maid, thinking her superiority was being noticed at last; but then when you told her you had never had a maid before, she was fool enough to repeat it below stairs, and now the other housemaids laugh at her.'

'Laugh at her? But I only told her to be friendly.'

'Ah, but she didn't want you to be friendly,' Norton said kindly. 'Servants are a terrible snobbish lot, worse than their masters and mistresses for it, as everyone knows; and a servant's standing in the servants' hall depends on how grand their master or mistress is. Pauline doesn't hate you, my lady, of course she doesn't; but if you was twice as haughty, she'd be four times as happy. There's no swank to being lady's maid to someone—'

'Who isn't a lady?' Charlotte said, suddenly remembering Orrock's words.

Norton looked angry. 'You are a lady, a real lady, and don't let anyone say different in *my* hearing! No, or anyone else in this house. Pauline's a silly little chit, with no more sense in her head than a mayfly, and it don't signify a plucked hen what *she* thinks.'

'I wish you were my maid,' Charlotte said wistfully.

Norton took another pin, and gave her a comforting look. 'Bless you, I'm no lady's maid. I'm just a sewing-maid who can't hold my tongue as I should. There, that should do for that. Could I trouble you to turn round to the light for the other one, my lady?'

Charlotte turned obediently. 'How did you learn your sewing skills?' she asked, as Norton snipped at the seams of the right sleeve.

'It was my trade, miss, before I went into service,' Norton answered. 'Why, I could tell you all about a piece of silk if I was to feel it in the dark with gloves on. There's many a thing you learn in the Nichol, but at least that's one to be thankful for.'

'The Nichol? What's that?'

'That's where I come from. It's a part of Bethnal Green, or some call it Spitalfields – it's all the same. I was born and brought up there.'

'Bethnal Green? It sounds like a country place. Was it nice?'

Norton laughed. 'Bless you, miss! It was a country place once, I suppose, but not when I knew it. The Nichol was just a poor wretched rookery – though I dare say there's worse, for at least there were decent people there, even if they were poor.'

'And were you poor?'

'Me? I was nothing but a miserable little spike.'

'Spike?'

'Work'us kid. The spike is what we called the work-house, and if you came from there, it followed you, like a surname.'

'Were you born in the workhouse?'

'Our Lord knows where I was born. I was taken to the Spitalfields work'us as a 'bandoned baby. Found on a doorstep. God knows who my mother was, but I doubt she was a lady – poor wretched sinner.'

'Oh, I'm so sorry!' Charlotte said. She knew what it was to be unloved, but at least she had never been so unwanted as to be left on a doorstep like a parcel. 'Was – was the workhouse a good home?' she asked hopefully.

'It was a hard place, I won't disguise to you, and horrid unhealthy, what with the cold and the damp. Oh, and the smells! That was the worst thing, almost – it was right next door to a night-man's yard, and the nightsoil was piled up in there as high as our roof, and the run-off soaked into our walls. And when it rained – well, I won't go into that; but you can 'magine how unhealthy. So many of us spikins died, I dare say I shouldn't have lived to see fourteen if I'd stayed so long. But when I was eight I was sent 'prentice to a silk family, and that was the making of me.'

'I've heard Spitalfields was an area famous for silk-weavers,' Charlotte said. 'They were Huguenots, come over from France, I believe?'

'That's right, miss. Mr Pertwee was my master, and that's a French name, so he told me; though they were as English as you like for all that, and they'd lived in the Nichol time out of mind. Well, they were poor folk, and lived very hard, but it was a good place. Mrs Pertwee was a true lady. That's where I learned my manners, and to 'preciate ladylike ways. The place was always spotless clean, though all around us were terrible netherkens, and the smells that come in through the windows were as bad as at the spike – worse, in a way, for in a clean place you notice 'em more.'

'Yes, I imagine so. So that's where you learned to sew?'

'That's right. They taught me everything – cutting and sewing and making-up, tassels, knots and fringes, besides knowing the silk and what it was good for. Master thought me likely, and taught me more than he needed to. And I learned to read and write, which Mrs Pertwee taught me out of hours, out of her goodness. Oh, the trouble I had keeping awake for the lessons, and how she used to pinch and slap me to keep me to it! For the hours were terrible hard, I won't disguise it, five in the morning until nine or ten at night, and master and mistress worked just the same alongside us – and for pennies, miss, hardly enough to keep body and soul together. There was never enough to eat, which is hard on a growing child. I was always, always hungry.' Norton's eyes grew distant as she remembered that time. 'It's a funny thing, hunger: you never forget it. Sometimes I still dream I'm famished, and I wake up crying out for sausages and faggots and rice pudding.'

'And you still say it was a good place?' Charlotte said in astonishment.

'Why, so it was, for a spike. Most of the others were sent to the brickfields, which there was a lot of round those parts, and that was like being sent down into Hell, except for the cold. Oh, life was terrible hard for a child in the brickfields! I've seen enough of them, stumbling back and forth in the mud like the damned, carrying bricks all day, coated with mud right up into their hair, and pinched, cold faces, and little bodies all twisted from the labour, to say nothing of the accidents. And the masters were shocking cruel there – worse than brutes, for animals would not do what was done to those children. But my master and mistress never beat us for sport, or because

191

they were drunk. They were good, Christian people, taught us the Bible on Sunday, and never let us girls be taken advantage of. For there was a rough lot of lads in the Nichol: you'd see 'em parading up and down Club Row – that's the market street – on a Sunday afternoon in their tight trousers and oiled hair, looking for girls to do harm to. But my master kept us girls pure. On the brickfields the girl and boy 'prentices all slept together in a shed, and you may 'magine what went on: if the masters didn't get you, the bigger boys would. But my master kept us separate. The boys slept in the loom-shop, and us girls slept under the kitchen table – which you may believe we got the best of the bargain, for it was the warmest place in the house!'

Charlotte was seeing it all in her mind's eyes, and marvelling at what a little benefit a person could be grateful for. Her own life, she thought, had been so luxurious and safe in comparison. 'So how did you come to go into domestic service?' she asked at last.

'Oh, that's a long story. After I left Pertwee's I fell on hard times, and the upshot is I count myself very lucky to be here. I like it in service. Some of the girls say their time isn't their own, but I say to them, if they was on the outside, they'd have to find themselves work, and somewhere to live besides, buy and cook their own food and wash their own clothes and all the rest of it. No, if you aren't rich enough to *have* a servant, you had better *be* a servant, that's my view. I've tried it outside, and I've tried it inside, and inside is better. I know.' She set a final pin. 'There, that will pass on a dark night in a rainstorm, as they say. If you would like to slip it off, my lady, I'll take it away and get sewing.'

'Oh, can't you stay here and sew, and go on talking to me?' Charlotte protested. 'I want to hear the rest of your story.' She wanted to know what could constitute hard

192

times for someone who had worked seventeen hours a day, slept on the floor under a table, and was always hungry.

'I don't know why you want to hear such dull stuff,' Norton said. 'Anyway, I shall have Mrs Weaver on my tail if she finds out I sewed in here instead of in the sewing-room.'

'It isn't dull to me,' Charlotte said. 'But I don't want to get you into trouble. Promise me you'll tell me the rest of the story another time, though.'

'I'd tell you willing enough,' Norton said, 'but I don't know when there'd be the chance. I am just a sewing-maid. It's not likely I shall ever have occasion to speak to you again after today.'

'Don't worry about that,' Charlotte said. 'I'll arrange it.' A novel thought had just come into her mind. After all, why not? She was rich and a countess, as she kept forgetting. She ought to be able to do a little thing like that if she wanted.

Norton looked at her curiously, as though she had read her thought. 'You are very like her ladyship – Lady Theakston, I mean. I see it now, though I didn't before when Mrs Weedon said so.' Mrs Weedon was Lucy's personal maid. 'But Mrs Weedon is a sharp one – and it's the greatest compliment she knows to say you are like her lady. She was niece to her ladyship's previous dresser, Mrs Docwra, who died some years back, and her ladyship sent for her all the way to Ireland, and trained her herself, though there were dozens of topping lady's maids in London who'd have died for the position. So you can 'magine how Mrs Weedon loves her. But Mrs Docwra had been with her ladyship forty years.'

There was a message in this for Charlotte, which she would need a little leisure to decipher. For the moment, she had nothing to say as Norton gathered the gown into her arms, picked up her basket, and went towards the door.

'Pauline will be back soon with the gown to dress you, my lady.' The dark eyes twinkled. 'Just be haughty with her, and you'll twist her round your thumb.'

'I'll try.'

'And – forgive the liberty – have a wonderful time tonight. It is your moment, and you deserve to enjoy it. The gown will be perfect, and you will look beautiful, I promise you.'

'Thank you,' Charlotte said. And then Norton drew on the mantle of formality, curtseyed, and left her.

Charlotte had been glad to hear that there was to be no great banquet before the ball, but that 'a few close friends would be invited to dine with the family'. The family comprised the Batchworths, Tom, the Aylesburys, Thalia's brother Lord Greyshott, Benedict and Rosalind, Fanny and her step-papa Henry Droylsden, whom Charlotte was looking forward to meeting. When she heard, however, that the guests were to be, besides the Ashleys, Lord and Lady Palmerston (Lady Palmerston was Lady Ashley's mother), Lord Melbourne and Lord Wellington, she was thoroughly unnerved. It was like sitting down to dinner with History.

'Rather a whiskery party,' Papa Danby said apologetically to Charlotte. 'Afraid you will be bored to death.'

But when it came to it, Charlotte enjoyed it very much, and was glad that there were no young people to stare at her critically and make her feel awkward. She was more at ease with older people, happy to be quiet and listen when the talk was as good as this. The Palmerstons were witty, charming, and full of interesting ideas. They had only quite recently married, and Charlotte found it very satisfying to see how much in love they were, and was touched by Lord Palmerston's evident affection for his step-daughter Lady Ashley, who seemed to sparkle even more brightly in the glow of his regard.

Charlotte had met Benedict, her Morland Place cousin, several times, and liked him very much – he was pleasant and easy to talk to, especially about horses. He also knew a great deal about railways, having been a railway engineer before he came into the family property, and his stories were always interesting. To him she put her question about where the people went when the railway destroyed their houses, with good hope of an answer, but he only said, 'I really don't know. It must mean hardship for them, I suppose – but a greater good is served by the railway. And we must have progress.' Which meant he didn't know or care either, Charlotte thought.

She didn't like Mrs Benedict Morland. She was pretty and well-dressed, but had a discontented mouth, and hard eyes which raked Charlotte from head to foot, envied her gown but pitied her looks. She seemed at their first meeting inclined to make a pet of Charlotte, gushed over her in a way that Charlotte found embarrassing, and promised to 'take her in hand' and 'make something of her'. Charlotte felt it was probably well meant, and tried to respond, but she was too little used to express herself, and had no practice at all in being insincere. Mrs Benedict soon found her reserve repulsive and left off trying to make a particular friend of her, for which Charlotte felt a guilty gratitude. She liked Fanny's open-hearted chatter, but Mrs Benedict seemed hanging out all the time for compliments, which Charlotte was too awkward to give.

She met Fanny's step-papa for the first time that night, for Henry Droylsden ran the mills from which Fanny's fortune derived, and had had too much business to be able to get away sooner. He was a thin, worn-looking man with a heavy limp and a mouth tight with long-endured pain; but he had kind eyes, and when Charlotte offered her hand, he took it in both his and gave her a wonderfully warm smile. 'Fanny has written me several *very long* letters about you, so I feel I know you already – probably a great deal better than you would like me to! But I promise never to repeat anything she has told me – especially not to you!'

Charlotte laughed. 'Thank you. I haven't yet got used to being talked about. But I love Fanny very much.'

'A person must be made of stone not to love Fanny,' he said. 'I'm only grateful to have kept her so long. I expected her to marry at eighteen; but she enjoys flirting and breaking young men's hearts too much to give it up.'

At dinner, Charlotte was seated between the two 'old gentlemen', as Fanny put it, Lord Melbourne and the Duke of Wellington. Melbourne, though actually a year younger than Grandmama, seemed much older, frail and faded; but he was charming, and chatted kindly to Charlotte on an astonishing variety of subjects. He had a droll and epigrammatic way of talking which kept her laughing; and he told her a great deal about the young Queen, of whom he seemed very, though wistfully, fond.

'You are to be presented next month, I understand?' he asked.

'Yes, sir. I'm very nervous about it,' she confided.

'No need, no need. Presentation's a lot of fal-lallery, but the Queen is a clever woman, she can see through feathers to the worth beneath. Never knew a quicker sense than hers for picking out a right'un from a wrong'un. Just like your grandmother does with horses.'

Charlotte smiled, but thought all the same, it was the Queen of England they were talking about. 'Is she very grand, sir?'

'Grandest of the grand,' he said, 'and as kind as a mother cat with a kitten. You're a tall young woman – her majesty's half your size – but if I meet you a week afterwards you'll be ready to swear she overtopped you by a foot! But you'll do, m'dear, don't worry. She likes an open face and frank manners, and you're as clear as a crystal stream, that's plain to see.' He seemed to think of something; hesitated, and bent his head closer to speak in a low voice. 'You may hear whispers. There are those about the Court with notions – find one or two under every stone – don't pay 'em any heed. Your mama's situation – you'll forgive an old man's presumption? But I didn't want you surprised by it. Your grandmama and Theakston were personal friends of King Billy's, and that's what matters to Her Majesty, so don't you mind what anyone else says. *She* knows what's what.'

Charlotte thanked him, knowing it was kindly meant, but would have been glad not to have something else to worry about. She looked down the table to where her mother was sitting, talking to Lord Ashley. In the candlelight she looked younger, almost beautiful, with her crown of hair shining like Welsh gold, her white throat encircled with pearls. Charlotte felt wistful, as though looking at something lovely and unattainable. Since Fanny came, they had met often, and Charlotte liked to witness Fanny's confident affection for Rosamund, the warm, teasing relationship between Fanny and Jes, the easy sibling banter between Fanny and Cavendish. Fanny spoke of them all as one family together, encompassing Charlotte so naturally in the idea that it brought the reality closer. But still Charlotte and her mother were adults together; she could not go back and be a child again. And, with her mother as with everyone else, Charlotte felt as though there were an invisible barrier between them, as though she were enclosed in a cage of glass, seeing, hearing, but unable to touch.

Lord Melbourne turned to talk to Lady Palmerston, leaving Charlotte to turn to her other side and the alarming fact of the Duke of Wellington. He was so eminent and famous, so much a part of history lessons, that she felt numbed with awe, as though she were meeting Charlemagne or Alexander the Great. He was ten years older than Lord Melbourne and looked ten years younger, trim, upright, firm-featured and bright-eyed. She had been surprised when she met him in the ante-room before dinner to find he was not tall, as she had always imagined him; but the hawk-nosed face, familiar to her from engravings, was just what she had expected. But though he did not have Melbourne's expansive charm, he was very kind and not a bit stiff with her, and talked to her about balls and gowns and dances as if he were not the great statesman and soldier but a favourite uncle. Charlotte found herself confessing that she was nervous about having to lead off that evening.

'I've been having lessons since I came to London, but I've never danced with a man, only the dancing master and my cousin Fanny. I'm sure it's very different when you come to do the real thing in a ballroom, with a stranger.'

He took her problem quite seriously. 'You needn't worry. A lack of polish on your part will go down very well with the hostesses – they'll think you modest and unspoilt, and treat you more kindly than if you were immediately up to everything. And as for the young men, remember they'll be as nervous as you – or more so.'

'I thought men knew how to do everything, and were always confident.'

Wellington laughed hugely, making the others at the

table look round for a moment. 'No, no, you are roasting me! Where did you come by such a notion?'

'But what can a *man* have to be nervous about?' Charlotte persisted.

'A very proper, feminine idea, which I should be sorry to divest you of! But a young man is just as afraid of being laughed at, or rejected, or not thought up to the rig. His situation is worse, for *he* is the one who has to do the asking. Can you imagine the terror of approaching a beautiful girl, who is looking at you over the top of her fan as though you were less than dust? And then when she says she has no dances to spare, you are quite sure she will say yes to the next man who comes along, and that she turned you down because she thinks you too ugly or too dull. And then you must approach someone else, knowing the second beauty has seen your humiliation at the hands of the first. Now tell me, ma'am, who is the worst off – a poor young man, crossing the ballroom floor like soldier in hostile territory with not a bush for cover, or the females standing safe in their corners, hidden by their fans and their modesty, with all the power of destroying that young man's comfort and self-esteem?'

Charlotte laughed. 'Well, you have put it in quite a different light, sir. I shan't be able to say no to anyone now! But I think the young man has the best of it all the same. The females can only wait to be asked, and hope it will be someone they like. At least the young man can approach the ladies he *wants* to dance with. It must be better to be active and determine your own fate.'

Wellington smiled. 'Now I know you a little better than I did,' he said. 'You are very like your mother. I was at her coming-out ball, did you know that?'

'Yes, sir. Grandmama told me.'

'And here I am at yours. Lord, how old that makes me feel! Well, I hope you will have better luck than she did –

she was to marry one of my young men, you know, young Tantony of the Rifles. He fell at Waterloo. It was a hero's death, but that was no consolation. You have the luck of living in time of peace. I trust and pray you will never know war.' A gleam came into his eyes. 'Your mother was a shocking dancer, a perfect trial to my young men – but she never lacked for a partner. Everyone wanted to dance with her, even if she did tread on their feet and sigh with boredom and turn the wrong way in the set. So don't worry about your dancing lessons. If you are kind to your partners, they will forgive you anything.'

'Well, how did you like your old gentlemen?' Fanny whispered to Charlotte as they stood at the top of the stairs waiting for the first carriage to disgorge its freight.

'Very much. They were kind to me.'

'You are such a nice person, Charlotte, you like everyone and always find something to be pleased with. Now I was stuck with Lord Greyshott, who is *such* a bore, and cousin Tom on my other side couldn't rescue me because cousin Thalia was whispering to him the whole time. Oh, what a dull dinner that was! Never mind, I shall have fun at the ball. I wish you may have as much, but one's come-out ball is never as good as the ones that follow, so don't expect to enjoy it too much and then be disappointed, will you?'

'Why will I be disappointed?'

'Well, you'll be standing with your grandmama, and everyone will be looking at you, and you'll have to dance with the men she chooses for you, who will be worthy but dull. You'll go up and down the set without a sound spoke between you, while I am dancing with all the wicked rakes who make one laugh.'

'Oh Fanny!'

'But just remember that this is not the pattern for the

Season, and try to endure it. You will have much more fun next time, I promise you.'

The first party was coming up the stairs; Denton was standing at the top to announce the names, Grandmama and Papa Danby were receiving; now the first introductions were being made to Charlotte. Curtsey, shake hands, smile, accept a compliment, answer a question. Charlotte tried conscientiously to keep the names in her head, but each new one thrust out the one before, and after a while she abandoned the effort. Earls, viscounts, honorables, Sir John and Lady Somebody, Lord, Lady and Mr Something Else, Mr, Mrs and Mr James Yet Another: up the stairs they came as though rising from a glittering underworld, the men in sober black and white or brilliantly coloured, gold-laced uniform, the women décolletées in silk, satin and gauze, bare shoulders, lace berthas, flowers, feathers and jewels. Eyes devoured her face and her dress – kindly or critical, they all wanted to look at her, the lost child who had been found again, the heroine of the queerest story of the Season. She felt as though she were being pecked to death, little shreds of her being torn off by every successive sharp beak of a stare. Some introductions were made by Grandmama more pointedly than others, as though she should find some significance in them, but they were all one to her. Beside her, Fanny saved the day, chatting where she was silent, deflecting impertinence, accentuating kindness.

Charlotte was jolted out of her glassy dream by Fanny's sharp whisper, 'Here's Oliver Fleetwood, Charley! He dances divinely. I wish he may ask you!'

A moment later he was standing before Charlotte, not smiling, but looking down directly into her eyes, as if he wanted to see what she was like. It was so unlike the way any of the other young men had looked at her, that it made her shiver, almost afraid. With them, the glass

201

barrier she felt between her and the rest of the world had been a protection; but he seemed suddenly very close, and very real.

He said, 'Your grandmother has given me leave to ask you for the two first, ma'am, if you would do me the honour of opening the ball with me? Though it does seem, now, more honour than I have any right to expect.'

That last bit, added in a low voice, completed her confusion. It was just ballroom talk, she told herself, who had never yet been in a ballroom. But her hand was in his, and even through her glove she felt as though she had taken hold of something that thrilled with power, and she looked into his face as if she would never be able to leave off.

'Yes – thank you, I – yes,' was all she managed to say. I sound like a silly, stammering girl, she told herself furiously. But it did not seem to have put him off. He smiled, and she thought – she definitely thought – that he squeezed her hand a little before he let it go.

'It is I who must thank you. I shall come for you when the music begins.'

He passed on. The receiving went on, and now Charlotte did her part at arm's distance from herself. 'I shall come for you when the music begins.' The words sang in her mind, with a significance beyond themselves; she didn't know what, but they were like poetry. Now the stream was slackening, the music was playing in the ballroom, and Grandmama was preparing to lead the way in, smiling and nodding to Charlotte to take her place in the procession. Fanny squeezed her arm and grinned with happy expectation, and suddenly Charlotte burst out of the bubble of unreality and found herself right there, feeling the music running down into her toes, longing to be dancing, ready to enjoy herself and quite sure she was going to.

She fell in beside cousin Tom, behind Grandmama and Papa Danby, and they walked through a corridor of applauding people into the brilliance of the ballroom – chandeliers, flowers, glasses, and the packed, dazzling colours of the guests – all the way to the far end, where they gathered in a group around the fire. The orchestra fell silent, and then struck up again, and Charlotte found everyone was looking at her. She paled. It was too much – all this for her, all these eyes on her – she could not bear it.

Lucy looked at her, and did not see the terror, only that the tall, rather too solemn young woman did her credit, and today looked beautiful, and achingly like her mother. She wanted to touch Charlotte, to kiss her, to tell her that she hoped she would always be happy; she wanted to make up to her for all the unhappiness of the past. But she could only say, 'Well, my dear, this is your moment,' and Charlotte turned those wide, changeable eyes on her with an expression Lucy could not interpret.

'Thank you, Grandmama,' she said, almost in a whisper.

And then (thank God, Lucy thought) Fleetwood appeared, walking up to Charlotte like St George come to the rescue – twice as handsome as any other man in the room, and with ten times the presence. He bowed, and offered his arm, saying, 'My dance, I believe, ma'am?'

And still Charlotte didn't smile, but she looked at him with her heart in her face, and Lucy blinked with astonishment, and thought, Good God, how did it happen so quickly? She watched with perplexity but not inconsiderable satisfaction as her granddaughter put her hand on Fleetwood's arm as though bestowing her whole self upon him; and Fleetwood received the gift gladly.

He led Charlotte, to renewed applause, out onto the floor, to be followed by Fanny on the arm of Lord Preston, and then there was a scurry of others to make up the set. The music began, the dance led off, and Charlotte was launched.

Lucy turned her head to meet Danby's gaze, and he raised an eyebrow at her.

'Well, that's that,' she said with satisfaction.

'It certainly seems so,' he said thoughtfully.

The ball went on until three o'clock, and was so far from ending because of the disinclination of the dancers that it took a further hour to get them all out of the house.

'It was the *best* ball I was ever at, Aunt Lucy,' Fanny said fervently as they all walked up the stairs together. 'Thank you *so* much!'

'You seemed to have partners enough,' Lucy said. 'And young Henry Penshurst was very attentive – Viscount Freshwater, I suppose I should call him, now that his father's come into the earldom. You had better try for him, Fanny. It would be a great match for you.'

Danby, treading up the stairs in silence behind them, intervened. 'Fanny had better not waste her fortune. I'm afraid young Freshwater may have his father's vice. George Tonbridge is a gamester, you know.'

'Used to be,' Lucy corrected.

'My dear, there's no such thing as a reformed gamester,' Danby said gently. 'Take it from me. *And* Freshwater has three unmarried sisters still at home. I don't at all advise you to get yourself mixed up with that family, Fanny my dear.'

Fanny looked impishly over her shoulder. 'Dear sir, you are taking exactly the wrong course! Don't you know that there is nothing more calculated to make a girl mad for a particular person than being advised against him? If you make him sound interestingly wicked instead of respectably dull, how can I help falling in love with him?'

'You talk such nonsense, Fanny,' Lucy said, but she smiled. 'But Charlotte, you are very quiet. I hope you enjoyed your first ball?'

'Oh yes, Grandmama, very much!'

'She's stupefied with tiredness, poor girl,' Danby said. 'You danced every dance, didn't you?'

'Every one,' Fanny confirmed. 'I was watching. And how did you like dancing with men after all?'

Charlotte smiled slowly, her eyes fixed on memory. 'Very much. It *is* different, isn't it? Especially in the waltz.'

Lucy looked at her closely. They had all reached the head of the stairs now, and were standing in a group on the landing, where their ways would part for their separate bedrooms. Charlotte had waltzed with Oliver Fleetwood twice, as well as dancing the two first with him; and he had taken her down to supper. It was a promising beginning. She had also danced with the other suitable match Lucy had fixed on for her, the young Earl of Preston, and he had asked her a second time, so her rather grave and shy demeanour had obviously not repulsed him. Things could be left to take their course. Charlotte's vast fortune would bring her all too many offers of marriage in the next few months; but Fleetwood and Preston were not raw boys, and could be trusted to conduct their own campaigns and know their own interest.

'I'm glad you enjoyed yourself, my dear,' she said. 'Now, off to bed with you – and Fanny, go straight to bed, don't keep Charlotte up talking. She must have her sleep.'

The two girls went off obediently down the corridor, and Lucy watched until they had turned into their rooms. Then she turned to Danby. He regarded her quizzically. 'Well? I know that look – what are you plotting?'

'Plotting? Good God, do you think I'm turning into one of those odious scheming dowagers?'

'What were you thinking, then?'

'Oh, just that Charlotte is one of those girls who shows it in her face when she does not have enough sleep,' Lucy said lightly. 'Your tall, fair girls often do. Not like Fanny – that child has the energy of a steam-engine, nothing wearies her.'

Danby reached out a hand to cup her cheek. 'And you, my bright-eyed wife? You don't look sleepy, despite having been up for twenty-two hours.'

'I feel wide awake,' she admitted, leaning into the embrace a little. 'It hardly seems worth going to bed at this hour.'

'Oh, don't say that,' Danby protested.

She smiled into his eyes. 'I suppose I could give up my morning ride, and stay late in bed. Just this once.'

BOOK TWO

The Desert Isle

Thou wast all that to me, love,
For which my soul did pine—
A green isle in the sea, love,
A fountain and a shrine,
All wreathed with fairy fruits and flowers,
And all the flowers were mine.

Edgar Allan Poe: *To One in Paradise*

CHAPTER TEN

The library at the corner of Brook Street was not the largest, but it was amongst the most fashionable, which meant that it was always thronged. Besides calling in for books, people went there to pore over the usual trumpery delights sold in libraries, to meet their friends, gossip, and drink tea; it was also known, though unofficially, to be the place for discreet assignations, having the benefit of being both crowded and respectable. If a lady and gentleman met within its precincts, who could say it was by design rather than accident?

Lady Mayhew put back the veil of her bonnet to look at a display of trinkets in the corner of the shop furthest from the door. Benedict, obeying the instructions in her note – the same note that had begged him to change hotels without introducing himself to her husband – moved over to stand beside her, and looked at her profile anxiously. 'You've grown thinner – and you look pale. Are you unwell?'

'No, not at all,' she said, speaking without looking at him, almost without moving her lips. 'I am quite well, I assure you.'

'Then you are unhappy,' he said. 'Oh Sib—!'

'Hush! Not here! I should not be doing this.'

'Not speaking to your old friend, who has known you since you were a little girl?' Benedict said impatiently.

'I wouldn't be here, except that I had to warn you about Sir Samuel. You must not seem to know me if we should pass each other in the street or at the theatre.'

'Oh, this is ridiculous!'

'I can't help it,' she said, and she turned to look at him for just one instant, an angry flash. 'I don't like it either.'

'But if I call on you openly, as an old friend, we can talk properly, can't we?'

'He would never allow it. You don't understand.'

'No, I don't.' She was silent, her face turned three-quarters away from him, fingering a lace-edged pin-cushion as if it were her heart's desire. 'Then, where can I meet you? I can't talk to you like this.'

'On Thursday he goes to a meeting at the Royal Society at two o'clock. I have said I mean to drive out to the botanical gardens. I can walk there without my maid – she suffers from hay-fever. I will meet you in the orangery at two – but understand, you must tell no-one. If he finds out—!'

'Finds out that you have talked innocently with an old friend?'

She looked at him sadly. 'In our world, a woman cannot have an innocent friendship with a man. *You* ought to know that.'

He would have argued that, but he thought of Rosalind. He said, 'I will be discreet. No-one will know.'

She walked away without another word, putting down her veil as she went. He watched her thread through the crowds, heard the shop-bell tinkle as she walked out into the street, caught a glimpse of her passing the window, a footman close at her heels. A dull rage began to glow in him, that his innocent, merry little friend had been turned into this pale prisoner – a rage pointless as it was directionless.

★　　★　　★

The Park was thronged with people of fashion driving or riding along the broad carriageway or walking along the parallel footpath, for it was the time of promenade. Not much forward progress was made by any form of motive power, for it was essential to stop every few yards to greet, exclaim over, and gossip with some friend or other, to admire and be admired. They were sad, pitiable creatures who had so small an acquaintance they could get from one gate to the next without being intercepted.

No such ignominy attended Lady Chelmsford and Miss Hobsbawn, riding side by side on an elegant bay and a peppery chestnut, followed by two very respectable and sober-faced grooms. Copper hated this form of progress, and had it not been that his mistress had had him out for two hours in Richmond Park that morning, he would have been almost beyond holding. As it was, Fanny found it impossible to keep more than two of his feet on the ground at once. His walk was a sort of slow, on-the-spot canter, and standing still seemed to have escaped his vocabulary altogether. Fanny didn't mind: she was aware that she showed to advantage on horseback, and since Copper's antics looked unseating while actually being armchair-comfortable, she was able to receive admiring compliments on her horsemanship with convincing modesty.

Within a short time of entering the Park, she and Charlotte had met and exchanged light banter with several members of their 'court', as Danby called it. Three dashing Hussar officers, in the dazzling crimson, blue and gold of the 11th, had been the first to stop: Fanny looked with favour on Captain Tooke and Captain Lord Desford, who fulfilled her primary requirement of being amusing; the more serious-minded young Colonel Bretherton was an admirer of Charlotte. Less welcome attentions came from two members of an older generation, Viscount Greyshott and his friend Viscount Cleveley. Charlotte had at first thought them merely being polite; Fanny had to warn her not to be too openly friendly because both viscounts wanted to marry her. Once she believed it, it distressed her: to be courted purely for her fortune was hard enough, but for it to happen so blatantly – because of their age, she reasoned, everyone must know, and laugh at her for her elderly admirers.

The pain was short-lived today, however, for they stopped only for a few sentences, before touching their hats and riding on.

'Thank goodness!' Fanny exclaimed. 'I do wish you would be more circumspect about choosing your lovers, Charley.'

'Oh, Fanny, don't tease,' Charlotte begged. 'How could I be rude to them?'

'No, I see you couldn't,' Fanny said solemnly. 'It would be like insulting your own uncles! Ah, now this is better – two *young* gentlemen approaching. One each for you and me, I think. Viscount Freshwater has been ordered by his papa to try to fix you, so I shall prove myself a friend to you both by keeping Mr Cavendish occupied.'

Charlotte laughed. 'You are a wicked creature. As if you didn't know Lord Freshwater had far sooner spend a minute with you than an hour with me!'

'Well, then, you can keep *him* busy and let me have Tom Cavendish to myself,' said Fanny, showing her hand. 'Oh do, Charley!'

'Is it that bad?' Charlotte asked.

Fanny laughed, but her eyes were serious. 'As bad as you and Mr Fleetwood.'

The two gentlemen reined in, made their bows and asked permission to ride along with them. The party moved off together, and Charlotte tried to concentrate on talking to Henry Freshwater animatedly enough to keep his attention from straying to Fanny, but it was hard going. His eyes evidently preferred the view to that side.

'How did you like being presented last week, Lady Chelmsford?' he asked at last, when other topics failed. 'What did you think of the Queen?'

'I liked her very much. But she's so tiny! Lord Melbourne tried to prepare me for it, but I towered over her. It was very awkward. But she didn't seem to notice it. She spoke to me so pleasantly – and she has the sweetest smile I ever saw.'

Freshwater raised an eyebrow. 'Weren't you bored to death with it all? Papa hates Court occasions – he says they are deadly.'

'I was too nervous to be bored,' Charlotte said. 'I suppose your papa was—' she was about to say 'born to it' and managed to change it at the last minute '—used to it.'

'And what did you think to the Prince?' he asked after a moment, during which he strained his ears to catch what his cousin Cavendish was saying in a low voice to Miss Hobsbawn that was making her laugh so much. 'Ain't he the world's chilliest prig?' Charlotte was shocked, and looked it. He shrugged. 'My pater says so. He don't care to have a penniless German look down his nose at him – especially when his breeches are full of English gold.'

Charlotte had not warmed to the Prince, who had greeted her politely but distantly; but she of all people knew what it was to be shy and to feel like an outsider, so she was ready to forgive him much. And she had noted his tenderness towards the Queen, who was enceinte again, and knew from what the Ashleys said that the Queen and Prince were a devoted couple, and that he was much less reserved when at home amongst friends. The Queen had spoken to her very kindly, mentioning the Ashleys as friends they had in common, and had said she hoped to see her again; she certainly was not going to join Freshwater in abusing the Prince.

Instead she said, 'Have you been at Court recently, Lord Freshwater?'

He seemed embarrassed. 'I haven't been presented yet.' He was about to add something disparaging, but remembered his father's instructions to make himself agreeable to Lady Chelmsford, and searched for a compliment. 'But now *you* may be seen there, it will be an attraction—'

He had missed his chance. Charlotte was not listening. Her gaze was fixed on the horizon. 'Isn't that Mr Fleetwood up ahead, in the blue coat?'

'Is it? Where?'

'Why, on the black, of course. Don't you know his horse?' Charlotte not only knew his horse, she would have recognised the rider's back in any crowd, at any distance. No-one else sat a horse like that, no-one else looked so perfectly at one with his mount, or so elegant, or so handsome. She tried to push down the foolish, feverish excitement she felt at the sight of him. But he was riding in the same direction as them, and therefore would not see her; and suppose he decided to trot on, or turned out at the next gate? The idea that she might miss him made her frantic. 'Shall we trot a little?' she said, trying to sound casual, as though the idea had just come to her apropos of nothing. 'Fanny, shall we trot? Ingot is fidgety.'

Ingot was patently nothing of the kind, but he obeyed the pressure of her heel, and Copper was only waiting for the chance to dash off. Fanny flashed a startled look at her for an instant, but then recognised the plea in her eyes, and understood. Copper hadn't a park trot in him, but she let him out just enough to keep him cantering alongside Ingot until they reached Fleetwood. He looked round when he heard the approaching hooves, and his face lit as he saw Charlotte. Freshwater noted the way they looked at each other, and retired without regret to take Fanny's other side. At least he could tell his father he had tried.

'I was hoping I would see you,' Oliver said when they were riding on, side by side. 'It's such a fine day, I guessed you would be out.'

'I didn't think I would see you,' Charlotte said. 'I thought you were out of Town since Tuesday morning.'

'You are an accurate journalist,' he said, with an amused lift of his eyebrow.

'Well, I haven't seen you anywhere since Monday night at the opera—'

'Dear ma'am, can it be that you have missed me? How delightful that would be!'

Charlotte felt herself blushing. 'My uncle, Tom Weston, said that you had gone to Ravendene on family business.' Ravendene was the Southport family seat in Northamptonshire. 'He heard as much from—'

'My uncle George, who has been his bosom bow these twenty years,' Fleetwood supplied easily. 'And Uncle George knew all about it because he rushed off to Ravendene on the same business, which was a sudden crisis in my grandfather's health. It was astonishing how many members of the family suddenly remembered the way to Ravendene, considering how long it was since they were last there.'

Charlotte didn't know how to respond to that. 'I am very sorry your grandfather was ill,' she said timidly. 'I do hope he is out of danger?'

He looked at her so gravely for a moment that she thought the answer must be in the negative. But then he said, 'D'you know I really think you *do* hope so.' She blushed all the more, and he smiled at her confusion, but it was a gentle smile. 'Thank you, Grandpa has rallied, and we do not have any immediate anxiety. But what a very nice person you are, Lady Chelmsford. I'm sorry if it shocks you to hear praise of yourself, but it must be said – and, yes, I can read what you are thinking. Your face is quite transparent, you know.'

'I'm sorry I'm not more sophisticated. My cousin Fanny—' she began a little stiffly, but he reached out swiftly and touched her hand, and the delightful shock silenced her.

'Don't be sorry – never be sorry for that! I love such simplicity. It is a rare quality, and should be cherished like all rare and valuable things.'

Charlotte could not speak nor even lift her eyes to look at him; she rode on beside him, aware that he was looking at her, feeling his presence at her side like the heat of a great fire. It was the most direct thing he had ever said to her. *I love such simplicity* – did that count the same as saying he loved *her*? And touching her hand – how she wished she had Fanny's experience, to be able to judge what and how much these things meant.

In the weeks she had known him, she had found herself thinking about him more and more, counting the hours until she might see him again, feeling a dreadful dullness about any social gathering he did not grace, a lethargy in facing any day which did not promise at least a chance of being in his company. But there had been few of those, and some even of those grey days had suddenly been flooded with brilliant sunshine when he had unexpectedly appeared – like the Sunday when he had attended (for the first time in memory, so Tom said) morning service at the Chapel Royal. Afterwards he had strolled across to make his leg to Grandmama and Papa Danby, and then engaged her in the light, half-serious, half-teasing conversation which she loved so much, and which he would probably have been embarrassed to know she remembered so accurately afterwards.

A natural reticence, and a fear of making a fool of herself, kept her from saying anything to Fanny about her feelings, but Fanny was not one to wait on ceremony. One night when they had been at a ball together she came bouncing through the communicating door, sat cross-legged on Charlotte's bed, and said, 'Now then, Charley, tell me about the Divine Oliver! Are you in love with him?'

Charlotte was relieved and grateful for the approach. At twenty-one she was as innocent of love as a fourteen-year-old, and badly needed advice as to how to go on. 'I don't know how you tell,' she said after a short hesitation.

'Do you think about him *all* the time?' Fanny asked promptly. 'Remember every single word he says and every single look he gives you? Feel you can hardly breathe when you know you're about to see him?' Charlotte nodded shyly. 'Dear girl, then it is love!' Fanny cried triumphantly. 'I thought it was. And I'm so glad it is someone I can admire. You have excellent taste, I must say – though it was obvious from the time of your ball that he had his eye on you.'

'Oh no, really – was it?'

'Yes, of course – but why don't you look as though you like that?' Fanny considered her. 'Is it because of your fortune?'

Charlotte nodded. 'Grandmama warned me that a lot of men would want to marry me for my fortune. I couldn't bear it if—'

'Oh, you goose! That's what's so good about Oliver Fleetwood, don't you see? He has been on the Town these ten years, and if he was going to take a bride for that reason he'd have done it long ago. But he has never shown much interest in heiresses, though there've been

217

dozens flung in his face. Besides, as soon as his grandpa pops off, he will come in for the strawberry leaves—'

'The—?'

'The dukedom, silly, and the whole Southport estate, which must make you easy on that score. No, he likes you, that's all – and why not? You are very different from the silly misses he is usually plagued with. He has the misfortune of being intelligent, you see, and can't make up his mind to settle down with a goose like other men.' She sighed hugely. 'If only he could fancy me! But then, although I'm clever enough for him, I'm rather below his touch. No, you will suit him perfectly, so you may love him with an easy mind – and my blessing!'

'I'm sure it must come to nothing,' Charlotte said. 'Fanny, I couldn't bear it if people knew, and laughed at me. You must tell me how to go on.'

Fanny grew serious, and took her hand comfortably. 'Don't worry, I only guessed because I know you. Just go on as you are. You behave beautifully, and you can have nothing to reproach yourself with, whatever happens. I must say, in all honesty, that I think it's unlikely it will come to anything with him – but he's too much of a gentleman to do anything to expose you to gossip.'

'You don't think – he can love me? Is it because of—'

'No, love, of course I don't mean that. But he is very much the man about town, you know, and famous for never falling in love. I don't think he ever means to wed – but one can hope. Only try not to be too heartbroken if it does fade away. Being in love with Oliver Fleetwood is one of those things that one has to go through, like inoculation – a little dose of fever to make your heart stronger for when the real thing comes along.'

'It feels like the real thing,' Charlotte said in a small, despondent voice.

'Of course it does, that's the joy of it – it always feels

like the real thing. And I don't mean to say you have no chance with him. Just enjoy it, that's my advice, and try not to think too far ahead.'

Since that talk Charlotte had done her best to follow both strands of Fanny's advice – to enjoy it, and not to take it too seriously – but it had been hard. She loved him more every time she saw him, and he singled her out in such a way that it was very hard to keep telling herself he meant nothing by it. She knew that it was not only her imagination, for others had noticed his attentions to her. People made way to let him take the place at her side. Little looks and whispers followed them when she danced with him, or stood talking to him at a party. She felt she *would* be talked about and pitied when it came to nothing, though she didn't know what she could have done differently.

He broke in on her thoughts, speaking quietly. 'Have I said something to offend you?'

She looked up swiftly, glad of the excuse to look at his face again. 'Oh, no! How could you think it?'

'You were so quiet and looked so grave,' he said.

She ought to say something witty, she thought, to turn the moment away, but she could not. 'You would never offend me,' she said. 'I know you could never mean to, and so I would always—'

'Give me the benefit of the doubt?' Now his eyes were laughing.

'Yes,' she said, smiling also.

'You are the kindest woman in creation, I firmly believe,' he said. 'But tell me, then, why did you look so grave? The thoughts passing through your eyes were not happy ones.'

For one mad moment she thought of telling him the truth. Then she said lightly, 'I was thinking how much I have enjoyed the last few weeks.'

'And that made you sad?'

'All good things come to an end.'

'Do they? Are you going away, ma'am?'

'No, but—' She stopped herself saying, 'But *you* will.'

'An intriguing pause,' he said when she did not go on. 'What is it about these past weeks that you believe will come to an end? Youth must, I suppose, but not yet a while. Health? But your cheeks are full of the most natural colour, your whole person glows with vigour. And the pleasures that belong to youth and health must always be available to you while you have both. So that leaves only—' He paused and looked searchingly into her eyes, and she met them steadily, though she felt herself blushing – oh, that wretched weakness of hers! 'That leaves only the particular occasions, and they are particular only by virtue of the company. Ah, I see a response! It is the people you are regretting! The particular combination of souls that you fear will never assemble again in London for any other Season.'

Now suddenly she laughed. 'You are absurd, Mr Fleetwood! How can you quiz me so?'

'No, don't recant – you are quite right. There will never be a Season quite like this again. Every one is different, of course, but this one has been – for me at least – essentially superior to any other.'

'In what way?' she asked.

He smiled. 'Well, I am glad to know there is a little of the coquette in you. I was beginning to fear you were too much of an angel for an ordinary mortal to dare admire.'

At that fascinating point they came in sight of Lord and Lady Theakston's barouche, halted at the side of the carriageway with a knot of people gathered round it. They stopped too, of course, and when they rode on their group of five had been swelled by the addition of a number of acquaintances. Conversation became general, and Charlotte was able to give it only half her attention, while the other half gnawed away at his last words. What did they mean? What did he mean her to understand? She knew it was absurd and pointless either to hope or doubt, but she couldn't seem to help doing both.

Eventually they came round to the Grosvenor Gate again, and Parslow behind her coughed discreetly to warn her that it was time to go home. While Fanny was casting off her beaux, Fleetwood took the opportunity to lean close and say, 'You will be at the Sturminsters' ball tonight, I suppose?'

'Yes,' Charlotte said. The Duchess of Sturminster's ball was a high point of the Season, and she had thought everyone would be there, but the fact that he asked seemed to suggest he wouldn't be.

He read her face with that uncanny ease which made her breathless. 'Oh no, I will be there, but I have an earlier engagement I can't break, and I'll be disgracefully late. In fact, I can't hope to get there much before supper. Will you be the soul of generosity – I know you are – and let me have the first two after supper? I wish I might ask to take you in to supper, but I dare not risk letting you down.' She was so busy thinking about his words she had not remembered to answer him, and he leaned closer to urge her. 'Do say yes! I know I am a villain to ask something so unreasonable, but I have something very particular that I want to say to you, and I must make the opportunity to say it tonight.'

Charlotte signified her assent, though she hardly knew what she said. There was something in his voice and his look – 'something particular to say' – what could that be? She tried not to let herself think about it, but there was nothing else in her mind as she rode home, as she bathed, and as she dressed for dinner.

*   *   *

Charlotte had thought her own ball grand enough, but it was a village dance compared with the Sturminsters'. Sturminster House itself floated on the darkness like a vast lighted ship, and the carriages making their way up to the door formed a queue so long it filled the streets around, and policemen had to be stationed at corners to prevent it joining up with itself and coming to a complete halt. The more important guests had been given a time to arrive, so that they should not have to wait too long in the queue; the lesser sort would have to take their chance.

As the Theakston carriage containing Lucy, Danby, Charlotte and Fanny drew up before the canopy covering the entrance, Charlotte had a moment of stepping aside from herself, and wondering that the penniless orphan of six months ago could now find herself in such an exalted position. A red carpet crossed the footway and led up to the great door; liveried and powdered footmen to either side of it held back the crowds of onlookers; as Charlotte stepped along behind Lucy and Danby, she heard her name passed amongst the spectators. Poor Charlotte Meldon, who went to her father's funeral in a badly dyed dress with worn seams, was now one of the great and famous invited to a Duchess's ball and recognised by strangers in the street. It didn't seem possible. She thought of her father, and all he had done to prevent this. Then she thought of her mother, who would not be here tonight: the Duchess of Sturminster was one of the great sticklers, and did not admit either divorced people or actresses to her house. Charlotte had wondered whether, in that case, she should accept the invitation. Surely, she had said to Lucy, they ought to show loyalty to Rosamund by refusing.

Lucy was brusque. 'Don't be a fool. Her whole concern is that you *shouldn't* share her disadvantage.'

So here she was; not only at a ball given for thousands at what was virtually a palace, but not even one of the anonymous throng. She was amongst the more important guests, was greeted personally by the Duke and Duchess, and would be sure of dancing. The Duchess – whose manner was more regal than the Queen's, Charlotte thought, and more chilly than the Prince's – even condescended to recommend a partner to her. Having stared through her lorgnon, she dragged forward a rather scrawny, red-faced and slightly spotty youth and said abruptly, 'You are not engaged for the two first, I suppose. My nephew Didcot will dance with you.'

The first was not a question, and she obviously had no idea of being refused the second. Evidently the honour of being offered the Duchess's nephew was so great that Charlotte was meant to cancel any other arrangements she had made, and be grateful for being noticed. She felt her jaw harden, and a retort form on her lips; it was only the miserable embarrassment of the nephew (who could not have been more than eighteen, she thought) that made her accept with an appearance of gratitude. It could not have been a very good pretence, though, for as they walked on Fanny pinched her arm and laughed, 'Charley, your face! I thought you were going to turn her to stone with one flash of your eyes!'

Lucy overheard and turned back. 'Fanny, behave yourself. You are not at the Manchester Assembly Rooms now.' She looked a shrug at Charlotte. 'The Duchess is a very impertinent woman. She might have spared you George Didcot. One of her sister's sons, and not even the eldest – not that it would matter, because Didcot *père* has nothing but a threadbare estate and a fistful of mortgages. You would have been within your rights to have refused to dance with him.'

My wretched fortune again, Charlotte thought: the

Duchess was after her money for her impoverished sister's son. She half wished she could give it to him – to anyone, so that she might be judged on her own merits from now on. And then her sense of humour exerted itself. My merits – what are they? And she thought of the poor, shy, spotty boy, and wondered if the Duchess hadn't got it about right!

But it was exciting all the same to be here, and she could not help feeling thrilled as she walked into the ballroom: it was vast, lofty, glittering. The orchestra, fifty-strong, was seated on a raised dais banked round with tubs of flowers, shrubs and citrus trees as though they were in a garden. Round the edge of the room beautifully dressed men and women thronged ten-deep, milling in a genteel manner for better positions where they might at least *see* the dancing, for it was obvious that for four-fifths of the guests, being there would have to be the summit of their pleasure. Charlotte began to see the despised nephew in a better light, particularly when the sets began forming for the first dance, and she was led in to the top one, which was headed by the Earl of Bridport, Sturminster's son and heir. To be sure, Charlotte and her partner were towards the bottom of the set, twenty couples below the summit; but Fanny would not even have a place in the fourth and lowest set. In acknowledgement of the honour, as well as out of simple kindness, she tried to chat pleasantly to Mr Didcot; but his nervousness was so extreme that he seemed hardly able to lift his eyes from his feet, let alone answer her commonplace remarks. His hands were sweating so much that his gloves were damp to her touch, and when he began to turn the wrong way at the top, his spots flamed like beacons. She felt desperately sorry for him: the gimlet eye and the lorgnon probably haunted his dreams.

Having been in the top set for the first dance, Charlotte

was sure of a partner for the next, and was quickly snapped up by Sir Harry Carstairs, who was an equerry to the Prince, and a very lively man. She enjoyed her dance with him very much; and was led out for the next by the Earl of Preston, whose congenital silence allowed her to look around and see who else was there. During this dance she spotted Fanny, standing in a corner near the orchestra with Tom Cavendish, their heads so close together that he seemed to be wearing her feathers. But it was the purest chance she spotted her; the crowd was so great, she thought with a sigh, that even looking out for someone, the chances were against seeing them, or they you.

At the end of the third, Colonel Lord Faversham snatched her from Preston, and in the course of the dance asked her if he might take her in to supper. He was amusing company, but Charlotte found herself saying no, she was engaged; and afterwards wondered what had possessed her. He would not come before supper – he had said he would not; and even if he did, how would he find her in such a throng? There were, Sir Harry had told her, four supper-rooms, besides the ballroom, ante-rooms and miles of corridors. Now she would have to go in to supper with Grandmama – if she could find her.

At the end of the dance, Faversham bowed to her and asked where he might leave her, but she released him on the spot, not wanting to be hampered by him, and he left her with obvious relief to secure himself against the ignominy of eating supper without a partner. Everyone was now on the move towards the supper-rooms; she drew a few curious glances as she stood hesitating, but she did not see anyone anywhere in sight whom she knew. Her foolish impulse meant she must enter the supper-room alone, or go without supper, and of the two the latter seemed preferable. But she could not stand where she was, blocking the flow. She managed to extract herself from it and stood just inside one of the ballroom doors, occupying herself with her fan and trying not to look as though she were waiting for someone while the crowd flowed past.

And then, suddenly, he was there, standing beside her, smiling down into her face; and she felt quite hollow inside.

'What's this? Have you no partner?' he asked without preamble.

'I didn't think you would be here so soon,' she said. 'You said you would not arrive before supper.' She wanted to persuade him she had not been waiting for him, but he looked at her so knowingly she began to blush.

'Not *much* before supper – those were my actual words, I believe,' he said. 'But where is Faversham? If the dog has abandoned you I will call him out and shoot him.'

'Oh, no – I told him to go. That is, I said I could not take supper with him—' Worse and worse. She rallied. 'How did you know I was dancing with Lord Faversham?'

'I saw you with him on the floor. It was the first thing I saw as I arrived.'

'You saw me in all that crowd?'

His smile changed minutely. 'If you were anywhere in the room, though there were ten thousand people in it, my eyes would always go straight to you, like a bird flying to its nest. And so, if you dismissed Faversham, who takes you in to supper?' She didn't answer. 'No-one? You weren't, by any wild chance, hoping I might arrive in time after all?'

It seemed pointless to deny it. 'I thought perhaps – as you said you wished to speak to me—'

He nodded with an expression of great satisfaction, as though she had answered some other, more important question, and offered her his arm. 'Will you walk with me? The night is very warm, and there is a private terrace which overlooks the garden. I think we might hear a nightingale. If you do not prefer to go to supper, that is?'

Charlotte laid her hand on his sleeve, and dared to look up, though she was afraid of being dazzled. 'Supper one may have any time, but I've never heard a nightingale.'

He led her through the door into the corridor, turned the opposite way from the crowds, and led her through a series of turns and doorways which left everyone behind and soon had her lost. 'How do you know your way so well?' she asked.

'Lady Sturminster and my mother are old friends – they were ladies-in-waiting together. In fact, Lady S is my godmother. I ran tame about her house from my earliest years. Her *houses*, I should say.' He looked down quickly. 'What is it? What have I said?'

'Nothing – nothing at all,' she said lightly; but she had thought how well he fitted in here, and how poorly she did. He knew this house, the duchess was his godmother, this was his stratum of society. She did not belong here. She belonged nowhere – except perhaps in Chetton Farthing. She had been a fool to indulge wild dreams of—

'Here, this is the door.' He paused with his hand on it. 'We are alone – there will be no-one else out here. You are not afraid? You don't think you do wrong?'

She shook her head. Perhaps he thought she should think so – but it was too late now. She could not have left him now if her soul depended on it.

'Trusting creature,' he said with a smile, and she saw he did not think her fast, but naïve. Well, that would have to do. He moved his supporting arm away and took hold of her hand, folding his fingers firmly round hers; gloveless, his hand felt warm and dry and powerful engulfing hers. Her heart pounding, she followed him out onto the terrace, and he closed the door behind them.

The terrace was enclosed on all sides but one, where a low stone baluster divided it from the garden below. It was more a loggia than a terrace, and completely private: even someone looking up from the garden would not be able to see into it. But there was no-one in the garden – it was still and shadowy, black bulks of trees and shrubs edged with blue light. The sky was clear, and the gibbous moon sailed serene and high in its own hazy nimbus; the air was warm and smelled of honeysuckle. He led her to the front of the terrace, and stood at the balustrade looking out. Her hand was still in his, and she was aware of the warm solidity of his body close to hers, as though it were radiating some force to which she was sensitive. It seemed to have shut down her senses; she could think of nothing but being here with him.

He turned to her now, and took her other hand as well, and stood looking down at her, his face half moonlit, half in shadow.

'How lovely you are,' he said. 'When you look at me like that, so trustingly – so transparent. Clear as glass – as crystal. Yes, crystal is right: although you are as innocent as a child, there is nothing weak about you.'

'Don't—' she said, and the sound of her own voice stopped her. She was shocked at what she had been about to say.

'Don't what?'

She took courage. 'Don't talk about me as if I weren't here – or as if I were, oh, another species. It makes me separate from you.'

'And you don't want to be separate from me?' he asked, his voice warm. She could feel it on her skin as though it touched her physically.

She looked up at him. 'You know—' Impossible to finish that.

'I wish I did. I wish I were sure. Tell me – Charlotte. Tell me, my lovely one, what you think I should know.'

'I can't,' she said helplessly; and then, impulsively, 'It isn't fair.'

He looked startled for a moment; and then he smiled. 'No, you're right, it isn't. Then I'll tell you – shall I?' He saw no unwillingness in her face. 'When I first saw you, you stood out from everyone around you as though you were rimmed with light, and I didn't know why. I couldn't see what was special about you. I have been used over the years to have the prettiest girls every Season flutter their eyes at me and offer themselves for admiration. And there *you* were, too tall, too thin, not especially pretty, dressed rather severely, without allurements, not even smiling at me. You didn't know who I was; your eyes passed over me, as over a stranger. You don't remember the meeting, do you? No, because it was no meeting. You were coming out of Lantrey's in Bond Street with your Grandmama, and you stood beside her while you waited for her carriage to draw up. I was on the other side of the street.' He smiled a sweet, secret smile. 'I stole that first meeting from you; it was all mine. I had you long before you ever had me.'

'I remember,' she said, as if out of a dream. 'I remember. A man across the road staring at me, and then I thought, no it can't be at me, I don't know him. And then the carriage came, and I forgot about it. Was that really you?'

'Yes, that was me; and if you look up at me like that, I shall not be responsible for what happens. I thought you not pretty that day; I see others make the same mistake every day, and I laugh, and wish they may go on being blind to your beauty. Yes, beauty! Don't you know I am accounted an expert in these matters? If I say you are beautiful, you may believe it.'

She only shook her head. Her eyes filled with tears. She didn't understand any of this, only knew it was too good to be true. Something bad must be coming.

'I told you,' he said in a different voice, one that shook a little, 'not to look at me like that.'

She couldn't stop looking, though; and then he had taken a step towards her, his arms sliding round her body, drawing her against him. Her hands went up to his shoulders; she could feel her heart pounding as though she were frightened. His face was just above hers, so close she could smell his skin, and the expression of his eyes made her feel faint; and then he was kissing her. It was a sensation unlike anything she could have imagined, frightening, exhilarating, like falling through the air, like dying. She felt something unlock inside her, something she had no name for, something so personal to her, so hidden away, that it terrified her to acknowledge it; but a furious sweetness seemed to pour from it, flooding her whole body, and passing in a stream of electricity through her mouth and into him. She felt his body jolt with shock; his arms tightened round her convulsively; her mouth clung to his, and his hot sweetness passed into her, his tongue was in her mouth, and every separate cell of her body seemed to swoon with ecstasy.

And then he was pulling back from her, frantically, almost roughly, disentangling delicate, fibrous filaments which had reached from one into the other in that strange, ecstatic moment, and pulling them apart agonisingly. She felt her legs weak, she almost fell, he seized her by the arms, set her on her feet, holding her up, but with a little shake, as though angry with her. She opened her eyes and stared at him, half drowned with the kissing, bruised with its ending.

230

'Oh, don't stop,' she protested faintly.

'Dear God, what have I started,' he said through his teeth. 'This was not supposed to happen.'

'What did I do?' she said, bewildered.

He smiled, but she could see he was shaken. 'The moonlight was for you, not for me. And it was only meant to persuade, not provoke Vesuvius into erupting.'

She had her balance now. Consciousness flooded her. He had kissed her – and she had kissed him back! She had done something immodest. Now he would hate her.

Her eyes widened and he looked down into their translucency, saw her confusion and shame. Something inside him clenched with a feeling he had never known before. He tried to smile reassuringly. 'Don't be afraid. I got more than I bargained for, that's all – and I think I am well served for my heartless career so far!'

'I don't understand you,' she said hesitantly. Was he making fun of her?

'Thank God for that!' he said lightly. 'But my dearest Charlotte, you must promise me you will never do that with anyone else! No,' he forestalled her, 'that is not a fair promise, as things stand. I must make sure you never do, that's all – secure you before it's too late. You still don't understand me? I will be plain, then. Lady Chelmsford, if I go to see your grandmother tomorrow morning, may I tell her that I express your wishes as well as my own?' Still she looked at him with aching incomprehension. 'I mean,' he explained gently, 'if I ask her for your hand in marriage?'

A great stillness fell over Charlotte, clear and heatless and brilliant as the moonlight from the calm sky. She seemed held in the moment, so completely there could be no moving on from it; she looked up into Fleetwood's

face, and he seemed at once perfectly clear, so magnified
she could see every detail of his delicately carved features,
and impossibly far away, at the other end of the universe,
seen through a crystal.

CHAPTER ELEVEN

In such crowds they were not missed, nor their return noted. She danced with him as she had promised that morning – was it only so recently? – and they did not speak, locked in a silence like a dream. At the end of the dance he excused himself, saying he had much to attend to, kissed her hand, and was gone.

That was a bad moment. Alone, she fell out of the dream into an aching uncertainty, sure she had not understood properly; had mistaken him, offended him; sure she would not see him again. She finished the evening in a daze which was half hope, half despair; danced once with the Earl of Preston and once with Lord Desford without remembering either of them; and when the crowds began to thin of the more important people, was found by Danby to be taken home. She dreaded the carriage-ride, expecting questions and post-mortems; but Lucy asked only if she had had a pleasant evening, and Fanny seemed preoccupied with her own thoughts. When they got home, Charlotte yawned and drooped ostentatiously, hoping Fanny would take the hint; and when they parted at their respective doors, her cousin smiled rather remotely and said she would see her in the morning. Charlotte went quickly to bed, and to her surprise fell instantly to sleep.

The rule after late nights was that they were not called, but rang when they woke. The next morning Charlotte woke when Fanny came through the communicating door and climbed up onto the bed – climbed rather than bounced, Charlotte noted, as she woke more fully. But Fanny did not seem unhappy, only wrapped in some private consciousness.

'Well?' she said, drawing a fold of the counterpane over her feet.

'Well?' Charlotte returned cautiously. She didn't want to talk about Fleetwood until she had had a chance to think about it, and discover what her memory could assure her had really happened, and been said.

But Fanny was not interested in Fleetwood. 'What a ball it was!' she said rapturously. 'Before I went, I didn't think it would be anything very great, because one hardly ever gets to dance at affairs like those. But I shall always remember it as being the best ball of my life!'

She looked so expectant that Charlotte could not disappoint her. 'Did something specially nice happen to you?'

Fanny smiled, not her usual half-wicked smile, but one so tender and innocent it was almost childlike. 'Oh Charlotte, I am in love!'

'With Tom Cavendish?'

Fanny's eyes opened. 'How did you know?'

'I didn't know, I guessed. I saw you with him, near the orchestra, talking.'

'Oh, that was before! I was not in love then, only flirting – though you know I've always liked him. But it was during the supper interval – did you wonder where I was? I hoped you would not raise a hue and cry after me when I didn't appear in the supper-room.'

'Oh, there were so many people, no-one could be sure where anyone was,' Charlotte said comfortingly.

'That's what I hoped,' Fanny said. 'But Tom asked me to go and walk with him on the terrace—'

'The terrace!'

'Don't sound so alarmed – it was not improper, I assure you. It's a vast thing which opens off the ballroom, and it was lit with lanterns and a great many people were strolling about or sitting on the benches. It was perfectly respectable.'

'I'm sorry – go on.'

'Well, at first we just chatted, and he was being very foolish as usual, and saying all manner of outrageous things to make me laugh. And then we got to the far end and turned round to come back, and there was no-one close enough to overhear us, and suddenly he grew serious. He said—' She paused to savour the moment again. 'He said that he supposed he had no chance with me, but that he had loved me since he first saw me at Batchworth House last year. He said when he saw me again with you, he thought I was too far above his touch, and then he concluded I was meaning to marry Freshwater, because he was always hanging round us – only fancy, Charley, I'm credited with your beaux!'

'Lord Freshwater was never interested in me, Fanny, I told you—'

But Fanny was not interested in Freshwater either. 'So he asked me if I had recently accepted an offer for my hand and naturally I told him that I was quite unattached, and he looked so uncertain – imagine, Tom Cavendish uncertain! – that I felt I ought just to hint that I was not entirely indifferent to him—'

'Oh Fanny!'

'But they do need encouraging, poor things. You'll find out. It's an awful step for them if they think you might reject them.' Charlotte tried to fit this information into her own experience and failed. 'And then he suddenly blurted it out, all in a rush, like a shy boy at his first ball asking someone to dance. I felt like bursting into tears, it was so touching. He said, "Dear Miss Hobsbawn, dearest

Fanny, will you marry me?" Oh Charlotte, aren't they the loveliest words in all the world?'

'Yes – yes they are,' Charlotte said. She tried to think whether Fleetwood had said them; and was pretty sure he hadn't. Her heart sank again. She had mistaken him, she must have; and his silence during their dance and his hasty departure were in disgust with her. She managed to say, 'Go on.' Better listen to Fanny than her own thoughts.

'Well, then he asked if I thought my step-papa would think him suitable, and I told him that I was of age and didn't need permission, but that of course he should ask Henry out of courtesy, and that darling Henry would naturally say yes if it was what I wanted – which he will. Not that there's anything to object to about Tom anyway. His father may have been wicked in his youth, but he's a baronet, and a distant cousin of Aunt Rosamund, and even if he does manage to go through his whole estate before he dies, it doesn't signify, because he has to leave Tom his title if he leaves nothing else, and I shall be Lady Cavendish, and I have money enough for us both.'

'You told him that?'

'Oh, he knows it anyway. He doesn't care about the money – he loves me – he only made me promise I would not let his father persuade me to pay any of his debts, which I promised right away, I can tell you! Anyway, Henry will look after my interests, he always does. And then Tom and I just walked about for the rest of the evening, arm in arm, talking and talking as if we would never stop. Oh, I am so happy!'

'Did he—'

'Did he what?'

Charlotte felt herself blushing. 'Did he kiss you?'

Fanny went a little pink herself. 'Goodness, no! There wasn't a chance, with so many people looking on. But he wanted to, I assure you – he whispered in my ear that he couldn't wait until we could be officially betrothed, and he could kiss me all he liked.'

Charlotte passed through an extreme of despair and into calm on the other side. So it was as she had feared. One did not kiss, nor was one kissed – and especially not in that way. He had thought her fast, or had treated her as if she were; and she had proved him right. She would certainly never see him again. She should not have gone with him to the loggia in the first place; what happened afterwards was a consequence of her loose behaviour.

'Well, but did you have an agreeable time?' Fanny asked at last, dragging herself from her dream of bliss.

'Yes, very pleasant,' Charlotte said with an effort.

'I saw you dancing before supper, but after that—' She smiled reminiscently. 'The Divine Oliver did not come, I collect? You seem a little blue. Poor Charley! I wish you might be as happy as me. But your turn will come.' She hugged herself. 'Didn't I tell you I was going to fall in love this Season? Well, I'm glad now it's come: I want to be married. Tom is going to write to Henry today, and as soon as his permission comes, we shall go together to Great Aunt Lucy and ask her to announce it. I expect we'll marry in the autumn – you will be a bridesmaid, won't you, darling Charlotte?'

Fanny went away at last to her own room, and Charlotte put on her wrapper and went and sat by the window, resting her hot cheek against the cold glass, looking down at the people and vehicles passing, distant and separate from her as though she were on another planet. She tried not to think of Fleetwood, but his face came back every time she tried to push it away; looking down at her, so close, his shining eyes half hooded, the way he had looked just before he kissed her . . .

Norton came in at last, saying, 'I beg your pardon, my

lady – you didn't ring, but Tibbet said Miss Fanny said you were up. Did you want to be dressed?'

Charlotte nodded, unsmiling, keeping her eyes away from Norton's kind, interested face, but feeling a little comforted by her presence anyway. At least she could trust Norton not to ask painful questions.

It was a triumph of which she was rather proud that she had persuaded Lucy to let her have Norton for her personal maid. The request had baffled Lucy. 'Norton? The sewing-woman? *My* Norton? But she is not a lady's maid. She does not understand the work.'

But Charlotte had insisted quietly that it was what she wanted.

Lucy tried to understand. 'I know you have been making do. Pauline is not right for you, of course, but she manages your hair quite nicely. And I have not been idle: I have been looking about for a dresser for you. I have put out enquiries, but these things take a little time. It's important to get the right person. Meanwhile, I think you can manage with Pauline for a few weeks longer.'

She said it as though that were all there was to be said, and her surprise was palpable when Charlotte resisted. Lucy had presented her arguments firmly, but Charlotte had simply gone on saying she wanted Norton, and would give no reason other than that she liked her. Norton could soon learn what she needed to know – she was intelligent and quick; and Charlotte did not believe it could be so difficult to take care of a person's clothes, and arrange their hair. In vain Lucy argued that it *was*, and that a countess needed a woman who knew her business; when it came to it, Charlotte was in a position to hire anyone she wanted to, and Norton was free to change employers if she wished, and they both knew it. But it would have been as unpleasant as unnecessary for things to have come to that pass. Lucy looked at the tilt of the

238

chin and the set of the mouth, and felt she had met her match; and, in justice, she remembered Docwra, who had never been a fine lady's maid, but who had always been a loyal friend.

So Norton was sent for, and the exchange was made, and if there was unpleasantness below stairs on account of it, Norton did not let Charlotte know it. Fortunately for her, Fanny's woman Tibbet took a liking to her, and most unusually a friendship was struck between the two. Tibbet introduced Norton into the rituals and skills she needed to know, and helped her with her ladyship's hair; Norton repaid her by undertaking the delicate repairs and alterations which fell to a lady's maid's lot, and which Tibbet had always hated and struggled with.

It was a strange new life for Norton, but she was already fond of her young mistress, and was growing to understand her pretty well. She had watched her falling more and more in love with Mr Fleetwood, and knowing him by repute, feared it would end in disappointment. Now it seemed, as she dressed Charlotte and arranged her hair, that the worst had happened: the tragedy in her eyes said that her dream of love had somehow been shattered.

When she had finished, she slipped quietly from the room without having exchanged a word, hoping it was just the ordinary first heartbreak of having fallen in love with someone who didn't love you back, and which would be superseded by a new and better-founded love. But her lady was not fifteen, that was the trouble; and she was not light-hearted like Fanny Hobsbawn. She took things more seriously, as at twenty-one she well might. Norton sighed, and went in search of Tibbet and a comfortable chat.

It was almost twelve, and Charlotte was still sitting by the window staring at nothing, when a knock on the door brought one of the footmen to say that her ladyship would like to speak to her in the morning-room. Charlotte rose obediently and went. She supposed Lucy simply wanted to talk to her about the day's programme, but when she entered the morning room, she saw her grandmother was in a state of agitation.

'My dear child!' Lucy crossed the room rapidly, smiling – almost beaming. 'I have had a visitor. He is just gone. An unexpected visitor – unexpected by me, that is. I think *you* know who it was.'

Charlotte started. 'No, ma'am. That is I – I can't guess.'

Lucy looked puzzled. 'How is this? Did you not know Mr Fleetwood was coming to see me this morning? He told me he had your agreement.' She tried to fathom Charlotte's unhelpful silence. 'He came to ask me, very properly, for permission to address you. He said he felt it was right to come to me rather than your mother, because I was acting as your patron, but that he would be guided by me rather than risk offending anyone, which I thought very delicate of him. He said he spoke to you last night at the ball, that you were willing for him to speak to me, and that he had gone straight from you to inform his mother of his proposals. She gave her consent, and so he came this morning, very handsomely, at the first opportunity to call on me.' She studied the averted face. 'Has he mistaken you? Come, Charlotte, look at me, give me some answer.'

Charlotte dragged her eyes up, and meeting Lucy's faint frown and steady blue eyes, took her courage in her hands and begged enlightenment. 'I don't – I am not quite sure I understand, ma'am,' she stammered. 'What is it Mr Fleetwood proposes?'

Lucy's frown deepened in perplexity. 'Why, to marry you, of course. What did you think? Child, what has happened here? Is he mistaken? Do you not like him?'

Relief flooded Charlotte's heart. 'Oh no! I mean yes! I do like him. I – I love him, Grandmama. I just wasn't sure—'

'Sure of what?'

'Whether I had understood him correctly. I didn't know how such things were said. I didn't know whether he really had—'

The frown had dissolved, and now Lucy was trying not to laugh. 'My poor girl, was it really so hard to understand? But we forget, of course, how sheltered you have been. Well, so that you shall be in no doubt, Oliver Fleetwood declared himself most handsomely, and wants to marry you as soon as possible. His mother has given her consent, and you must know mine will not be lacking. It is exactly what I wanted for you,' she added with great satisfaction. 'It's an excellent match. Considering the size of your estate, and the fact that you are a peeress in your own right, I could not have been happy with anything less. Fleetwood will be Duke of Southport whenever his grandfather dies, so you will not be stepping down in rank. And he is a very charming, personable, sensible man. He is the very person I picked out for you when you first came to us, and I could not be happier that it has all come out so well.'

Charlotte murmured something, she didn't know what. From a fog of despair she was lifted into a cloud of happiness. She wished she had seen him, though; she wished she had been present when he asked for her hand in marriage. It seemed odd that it should all be done at second hand like this, as though she were not involved. She supposed that was the way people of rank behaved. But why had he left without at least seeing her? It made him harder to believe in. Perhaps she was still in bed and dreaming, after all.

But her grandmother was still talking. 'He proposes,

and his mother agrees, that the wedding should take place as soon as possible. There is the matter of his grandfather, you see, who might die at any moment – and if he does, there can be no question of a wedding then until the period of mourning is over. You have a very ardent lover, I must say, my dear – the prospect of any delay appalls him. But I can't see why it shouldn't go ahead quickly – there's nothing to prevent it. He suggested three weeks, but I thought that smacked rather of unseemly haste. A month at the least, I said – there will be clothes, a carriage, the question of a house to arrange. At the end of June perhaps – June is a pleasant month to marry in.' She broke into that beaming smile again. 'My dear Charlotte! Your first Season not even over. It is better than I hoped!'

All other arrangements that day were cancelled, and Lucy took Charlotte immediately to pay a formal call on Oliver Fleetwood's mother, Lady Turnhouse. In the carriage on the way there she warned her not to expect a warm reception. 'She is a disappointed woman; between Southport marrying young and living so long, and Turnhouse dying untimely, and has missed her turn at being duchess. And then she waited so long for Oliver, and there was never another child. I believe it all spoiled her temper. Fleetwood was right to approach her first: she's a woman it's better to placate.'

This was not encouraging, but it proved to have been wise to warn her. The viscountess received her not exactly coldly, but civility obviously cost her an effort. Lucy, who never cared a jot for anyone's opinion, was not prepared to put herself out to make conversation all on her own, and Charlotte was too shy to speak unless spoken to, so the silences were long and hard to sit through. Oliver was not there, and no-one seemed to think Charlotte might be told where he was. When the correct length of time had been spent, Lucy rose to leave, and Lady Turnhouse rose too and did her best for her son by kissing Charlotte's cheek, and saying she would be very happy to have her for a daughter; though from the lack of warmth in her voice she might just as well have said doorstop.

Home again, and Fanny was waiting for her, bubbling with excitement, having got the news from Tibbet.

'Dear, dear Charley! How happy I am for you! But you sly thing, why didn't you say something? I was pouring my heart out this morning, and you sat there as silent as a nun. I thought you were in a reverie, and no wonder! Oliver Fleetwood of all people – absolutely the catch of the decade, you clever creature! But it's what you deserve, and so everyone will say, for you are as good as you are beautiful, and that's a rarity in these heathen days, I can tell you! Oh, darling Charlotte, wouldn't it be grand if we could have a double wedding? But you will be a duchess, and a mere baronet's lady will be too far below you. Oh, not that you would ever snub me, I know that, but your people will, you can be sure – and you will belong to them once you are married. That's a woman's fate. But you will grace your new circle, and it will be lucky to get you, and if it doesn't realise that—' The sentence ended in a choke and a very affectionate hug.

Off then, with Fanny accompanying them, to visit Rosamund and Jes. More exclamations, more congratulations. 'He's a man of sense,' Jes said. 'We shall be glad of him in the House when poor old Southport goes. You will never have to apologise for your husband's intellect, Charlotte my dear.'

My husband, she thought blankly. Is it possible?

Rosamund hugged her very tightly. 'I didn't think to lose you so soon. But it could not be for a better cause. You will be a duchess! You will be at Court –

there's one for Queen Adelaide! I dare say the Queen will make you a lady of the bedchamber – I hear from Lady Palmerston that she quite took a fancy to you when you were presented. Oh darling, I am so happy for you!'

Cavendish shook her hand briskly and solemnly, but seasoned it with the broadest of grins. 'I say, you are in luck. Of all the people you might have married! But Fleetwood is a trump. He boxed at Oxford, you know, and he rides like a centurion. I met him once at Melton, or rather I saw him out with the Quorn, and you never saw such a bruising rider – took a great black bullfinch that everyone else was funking, and never turned a hair! Even Lord Cardigan admires him, and says no-one rides straighter. To think he will be my brother! I wish you may bring him to Grasscroft, and get him to come out with our pack.'

Back home, and Papa Danby came in, having heard the news at his club. He greeted her fondly with more congratulations. 'I'm very happy for you, m'dear. Everyone thinks well of Fleetwood. And it will place you very securely: Southport ain't an old title, but the Fleetwoods are in Domesday, and Turnhouse goes back to Elizabeth. You will be as safe as houses.'

Still Oliver did not come. Benedict walked in in the evening after dinner to offer his congratulations, and to threaten Charlotte with a visit for the same purpose from Mrs Benedict in the morning. Charlotte could imagine Rosalind's delight in speaking of 'my cousin the Duchess' and how often she would bring it into conversation, whether Charlotte ever spoke to her after the wedding or not. She retired early to bed, her head spinning, her heart aching strangely, so tired she fell asleep at the dressing-table while Norton was unpinning her hair. Blessed, blessed Norton, who must have been bursting with questions, but did not say a word! She helped Charlotte to bed, and tucked her in with an air of wishing to kiss her goodnight; Charlotte would have kissed *her*, but she fell asleep before even the thought was properly formed.

The next day brought the first visits of congratulation from friends of the Theakstons and the Batchworths, who had heard the news informally – for it had not yet been in the papers. They were followed in close order by arm's-length acquaintances and vanquished rivals, who could not in etiquette own the knowledge or ask the questions, but were burning with curiosity over how the ineffable Oliver had been caught at last, and were determined to extract details by hook or crook. There was not much doubt amongst the uncharitable, and had Charlotte been less bemused, less innocent, or more interested, she would have gathered from a dozen hints that her fortune was all that interested him.

A more welcome visitor was Tom, who had been away at the races, and walked up to congratulate her as soon as he heard the news. He sat through the end of a visit from Mrs Fauncett, whose daughter had stunned the *ton* in 1815 by marrying Lord Alfred Fleetwood, another of Oliver's uncles. Lord Alfred was a weak and vicious man, who had gamed away the fortune Miss Fauncett had brought him in exchange for his title, and had died of dissipation without reproducing; but from what Mrs Fauncett said, Lady Alfred still considered it had been a good bargain. She and her daughter now lived together in straitened circumstances, and she dropped hints which Charlotte was too unworldly to understand about what she hoped Charlotte would do for them when she became Lady Alfred's niece.

When she had finally taken her leave, Tom sat down beside Charlotte on the sofa and blew a sigh of relief. 'Thank God she's gone! You will have some queer bedfellows when you marry into the Fleetwoods, Charley m'dear.' He had caught the nickname from Fanny. 'She always was a poisonous woman – you should hear Mama talk about her! I wonder she let her bother you.'

'She was called away just before Mrs Fauncett arrived,' Charlotte explained.

Tom looked at her quizzically. 'What is it? You don't look happy. I expected you to be radiant with fulfilled love.'

Charlotte looked away. 'Oh, I am tired, that's all. And some of the visitors have been—'

'Not nice,' Tom finished for her. 'But that's not it. What is it, my dear? I came to congratulate you, but I can't if you look so long-faced.'

Charlotte looked at him. 'You think it is right, then? That I should – marry him?'

'It's an excellent match,' Tom said. 'He has the rank and position, and he's a sensible, well-informed man who thinks correctly about important issues. And I'm told he is thought *shockingly* handsome and *desperately* charming by females, if that matters at all. But—'

'But?'

'But do you love him?'

Charlotte looked rather dazed, he thought. But she said, 'Oh, *yes*!' with such conviction that his fears sank to rest.

'Then all is well. You are very different from each other, and he is considerably older than you – only seven years in actual time, it's true, but he is old for his age and you are young for yours. But if you love him, that won't matter.'

'You're the only person who has asked me that,' she said. 'No-one else has mentioned love.'

'I expect they take it for granted,' he said with an easy smile. 'After all, who could fail to love Fleetwood? You've made an enemy of all womankind, love.'

She smiled a little. 'Is it – I suppose it is rather a grand thing to have been chosen by him?' she asked hesitantly.

'Very grand indeed,' he answered her solemnly. 'When every unmarried female has been dying for him since he was sixteen at least. But don't think you need to feel grateful: he is getting a good bargain. Only,' he hesitated, as if wondering whether it was wise to go on, and then continued, 'only don't forget that he is older than you. He had a life before he knew there was such a person as you. When you were a good little girl at home with Papa in Chetton Whatever-it-was, he was out in the world, a grown man. Don't forget that, will you, Charley?'

She didn't know what he was warning her against, but she knew he meant it kindly, and so she agreed solemnly that she would not forget, and he seemed content.

Yet the rest of the day brought no Oliver, and she felt increasingly restless, tired, unreal – the way one does when one has been ill, and the fever has gone, but one is still too weak for any occupation. Dinner was to be *en famille*, and late, because of all the visitors. Charlotte was silent while Norton dressed her, and Norton worried, and wondered whether to ask the question which was on her mind, but decided not to. She was finished well before the bell; and Charlotte, feeling confined, quitted her room soon afterwards to go downstairs and wait in the drawing-room. She reached the door just as Denton was coming out.

'Oh, my lady,' he began, with some message in his eyes; but she had seen past him into the drawing-room. Fleetwood was there, standing with his back to the fire, looking real, solid, substantial – not a dream after all. And as he saw her appear in the doorway, his eyes kindled in a way that dispersed her fears like mist in the sun.

He held his hands out to her, and she crossed the room like a bird flying home; and when the door closed behind

Denton, he took her in his arms. After a moment he said into her hair, 'What? What is it? In two days you have turned into a hunted deer.'

'Two days,' she said incoherently against his chest. He unclamped her gently and led her to the sofa, and sat with her. 'I haven't seen you for two days. You disappeared without a word. I thought I'd dreamt the whole thing.'

'My darling girl! Am I a dream? Look, how solid!' Both her hands were enfolded, engulfed in his; he opened one out to show her, but her hand wound round it again instantly, like bindweed. She loved the fact that his hands were large and strong enough to hold hers; she loved the fact that, tall as she was, he made her feel fragile.

'But I didn't know where you were. Why did you go away without telling me?'

'I went to see Grandpa, to tell him about you and ask his blessing. As the head of the family, he deserves all courtesy – and as he is the only member of the family who has ever cared a jot for me, I make sure he gets it. I would have been back yesterday, but he was having one of his bad days, and I didn't want to leave until I saw him better. But Mama should have told you where I was.'

'She didn't.'

'And you didn't ask.' She hung her head. 'No, of course you didn't – how could you? But you should have trusted me, after what happened at the ball.'

'I couldn't believe you really—'

He lifted her face tenderly by the chin. 'Really what? Wanted to marry you? Good God, child, the whole of bachelor London wants to marry you, you must know that.'

'But—' she looked into his eyes and took courage. 'But do you – love me?'

He met her look steadily. 'Remembering our last time together, how can you doubt it?'

'You seemed so – surprised – I was afraid I had done wrong. I thought you were shocked,' she said anxiously.

'So I was,' he said. 'I never believed I would meet such passion in one so utterly – well, anywhere, indeed,' he corrected himself. 'I thought I had seen something brooding in your eyes, some slumbering thing you were not aware of; but what woke was beyond all expectation – beyond imagining.'

She listened to the sound of his voice without really understanding the words. She was remembering now. The touch of his hand on her face and his closeness, the scent of his skin were evoking the memory of those feelings.

'That's why I have to have you as quickly as possible,' he went on. 'I can't let anyone else ever see that, let alone taste it.'

'It wouldn't be there for anyone else,' she said shyly.

Something moved in his eyes. 'If that's true,' he said huskily, 'I am the luckiest man alive. I never dreamed of meeting anyone remotely like you. And if you—' He didn't get any further, because she had lifted her face in a completely instinctive gesture, and it was beyond his control not to kiss her. He had just enough hold on himself to place his lips only gently on hers, but at once her hands lifted to his shoulders, and he felt the passion unlocking deep inside her, like the rolling back of a boulder from the mouth of a spring. The water bubbled up, pure and yet powerful, a joyful, irresistible thing; he wanted her so badly it was like death to take his mouth from hers.

'Charlotte, stop, you must stop,' he said. He pulled back his head and looked down into her eyes. She looked so disappointed he laughed shakily. 'You must not kiss me like that, my love. Not until we are married.'

'And when we are married?' she asked innocently; but with a glint of humour.

'When we are married, I will show you where such kisses lead, and I promise you will understand then exactly why you may not do it now.'

'You forbid me?' she asked, the passion growing sleepy in her eyes.

'Most sternly. Like the cruellest father you can imagine.'

She nodded, with a small, tucked smile he didn't understand, though it intrigued him. Then she said, as though it were another day, 'What are you doing here? Have you come to dinner?'

'I'm hoping to be asked now, but I did not realise when I set out to call that you would not have dined. The truth is I got back to London an hour ago, and felt I could not wait any longer without coming to see you.' He smiled. 'I think I was beginning to believe you were a dream as well – which would have been most embarrassing, now I've asked Grandpa permission to marry you.'

'What did he say?'

'That he supposes I know what I'm doing. You must come and visit him soon – he wants to see you.'

'To inspect me?'

'He will like you very much; and you will like him. He's been urging me to marry for a long time. The Fleetwoods are dying out, you know. Papa had only me, Uncle Alfred didn't have any, and Uncle George has never married. Aunt Mary has a son, of course, but he doesn't count: unlike your title, ours can't pass through the females. It's another reason I want to marry you quickly, so that Grandpa can have the satisfaction of seeing me married before he dies. You don't mind, do you?'

'If it's so important that you marry, I don't understand why you didn't marry before,' she said.

'Because I hadn't met you – is that what you wanted to hear?' he said teasingly. Charlotte shook her head. She hadn't been angling for a compliment, but voicing

250

a genuine puzzle. She had been told often enough that people of rank did not marry out of simple fancy, but for reasons unconnected with the heart; and if he had such a sense of duty towards the grandfather he loved, why had he not obeyed it?

But there was no time to probe the question further, because the door opened, and Danby came in, having been summoned from his dressing-room by Denton to cope with the new arrival.

'Ah, Fleetwood! I see you are in safe hands. I hope you will dine with us? We sit down late, as you see, but it has been rather a day!'

'Thank you, sir, I should like to very much. And it has been rather a day for me, too – two days in fact.'

Danby had seen the hastily relinquished hands when he came in, and saw Charlotte's expression as she looked up at her lover, hardly able to tear her eyes away even for long enough to greet him; and he was happy. He didn't think for a moment Charlotte could have been swayed by considerations of rank, but he was glad to be reassured; and glad to see how Fleetwood's eyes also continually strayed to her face. All would be well.

Benedict arrived early at the gardens, and walked about in sight of the orangery, trying to look as though he were interested in the plants, trying not to check his watch too ostentatiously. By half past two he convinced himself he must have missed her, and went into the orangery to look amongst its shady nooks; she was not there, but he had hardly gone round once before she came in through the end door, veiled as before, and walked slowly, without looking at him, into the most densely planted area.

When he joined her, she put back her veil and faced him. She was pale, and her eyes were angry. 'What did you mean by pacing about like that, looking at your watch? Did you mean the whole world to know you had an assignation?'

'You saw me?'

'I have been half an hour waiting for you to go in.'

'But there was no-one to see me – no-one I know, anyway,' he protested.

'You don't know who is watching. He has spies everywhere, and he knows I am coming here.'

He looked at her in helpless dismay. 'Dearest Sib, what *is* all this?'

She looked a moment longer, and then her eyes dropped, and a little colour came to her cheeks. 'Come and sit down,' she said in a more normal voice. 'I am weary with walking about.'

When they were seated on a bench in an arbour amongst the greenery, she said, 'You don't understand, you see, about Sir Samuel. He is wildly jealous – quite insanely so. Any man I speak to he suspects.'

'But *why*?'

'Because he is in love with me.'

'That isn't enough reason,' he said emphatically, and then stopped, realising where that led.

'He is old and I am young: it is enough for him. He has no reason to be jealous. I would never – betray him.' She looked at him steadily. 'I hope you understand that.'

He felt an odd warmth inside him which he did not care to investigate. 'I – I hadn't thought you would. But Sib, how did it come to this? Why did you marry him?'

She shrugged. 'One must marry. And it was what Mama wanted.'

'But there must have been dozens of young men who wanted to marry you.'

'Why should you think that?' Was there a slight emphasis on the word 'you'? He struggled for an answer.

'When I saw you at your come-out, you were the cynosure of all eyes – beautiful, vivacious, witty. What man could resist you?'

'Well, they did,' she said. 'Not that I tried for anyone. They all seemed so insipid after – I couldn't care for them, at least,' she corrected herself quickly. 'And I hadn't a large dowry, you know.'

'That isn't all that matters.'

'Perhaps not. But I am not – I was not like other girls. I didn't giggle or flirt. I spoke too straightforward, and showed too much what I thought. Callow young men like to marry fools because it flatters them to have someone more insipid than themselves to crow over.' Benedict was silent. She went on, 'So the young men were frightened by my sharp tongue and the older ones wanted far more money with their brides, and, what with one thing and another, I had my London Season without a single offer for my hand. Mama was furious. Papa thought it funny at first, but after a while he began to think like her. And when Sir Samuel saw me at a ball in Northampton – well, there was someone at least who fancied me.'

'But wasn't he repelled by your intelligence?'

'He never noticed it,' she said with indifferent frankness. 'He just thought I was a hen-witted female like all the others, but he took a fancy to me for some reason, and when he and Mama got talking, a lot of hints were exchanged, and they came at last to an understanding. He was willing to waive my dowry if she was willing to waive his age.'

Benedict was appalled. 'But your father – surely he had something to say? You were always his pet.'

'Oh, Papa wouldn't have forced me to it if I was really unwilling. But you see, he had suffered some setbacks in the last year or two, and even as small as my dowry was, it would be a hardship to have to find it: he would have had

253

to sell things he didn't want to sell, at a time when they would not fetch their true value. To be rid of the expense of me, and without capital outlay, was a blessing. And Sir Samuel has influence in circles that matter to Papa. So he asked me if I would mind it very much.'

'But surely you must have? Surely you told him you could not bear it?'

She gave him a small, sour smile. 'No, why should I? It was not comfortable at home, with Papa anxious and Mama angry with me. A woman must marry, and since I had no expectations of love, comfort must be a consideration. Sir Samuel is very rich, and promised me a fine establishment in my own country – only ten miles from home, which was an object. And he seemed kind. I was not to know then how he would be. But that can't be helped now.'

Benedict felt helpless in the face of this calm. 'Oh Sib, why didn't you wait, at least a little? Someone else would have come along. You would have fallen in love.'

'I have already been in love. I told you so.'

'Yes, I remember.' She had told him long ago that she had fallen in love with someone who didn't love her, and who was 'unsuitable'. 'But you were so young then. You will fall in love again.'

'No, never.'

'You can't know that,' he protested.

'I can; because I am still in love with him. It hasn't changed. And since I love a man I can never marry, it doesn't matter if I marry a man I can never love.'

'That sounds very neat, but you know it isn't true.'

She smiled suddenly. 'Perhaps not – but I didn't know what a misery he would make my life. Yet if I had, probably I would still have married him. To be away from Mama was a great thing. And as long as I don't speak to anyone he doesn't approve of, he can be very kind.'

Benedict was silent, the question that was in his mind being one he could not voice. But she looked at him with a secret gleam in her eyes, as if she knew what he was thinking.

'Dear Benedict! You can comfort yourself with what Papa tells himself whenever he feels guilty about my marriage: that as Sir Samuel is so very much older than me, it can't last very long. He will die and leave me a rich widow, and then I may live as I choose.'

'Does your father say that to you?' Benedict said with an unwilling smile.

'Oh, very often,' she laughed, 'when we are alone together. It is shockingly improper! Poor Papa, he blames himself very much, no matter what I say to him. But it is nobody's fault. I did it of my own free will. And now I must go.'

'No,' Benedict protested at once.

'Someone may come in. I cannot be seen here with you,' she said.

'Then – where can we meet?'

She looked at him calmly, but so sadly that it made his heart ache. 'There is no reason for us to meet again. I have answered your questions now, and you may be easy about me. Our lives lie apart. We will not meet again.'

'No, Sib,' he said, and took hold of her hand, hardly knowing he had done it. 'I can't bear never to see you again. I want—'

He stopped, puzzled by the tangle of feelings and thoughts through which he could not see clearly. He didn't know what he wanted. He thought of Rosalind, her betrayal of him, his doubts of her. He could not have her followed and spied upon as Sir Samuel Mayhew apparently did Sibella: his own pride, if nothing else, made him put a good face on it. People might think him a fool, but they would at least not call him a knave.

And yet, what sort of marriage was it for him? He did not love her, not as a wife – his care for her was more like his care for Rose, for a wayward and ignorant child whom he must keep from hurting herself, if he could. She was no companion to him – he did not think she even loved him, or ever had. He had enough money to keep her comfortably, that was all he was to her. And it was long since she had let him love her physically.

He had known all this for a long time, but had not dragged it out from the back of his mind to consider it. There was no point. There was nothing he could do about any of it. But meeting Sibella had somehow changed him; she was like the fresh wind that blows away the fog, and allows you to see what it is you have been standing next to, all unknowing, for such a long time. He wanted – he wanted – oh, just to be able to see her again, and talk to her, to talk to a woman with frank eyes and a clear mind; to look at a woman who looked at him and saw him; to hear words from a woman he could be sure were not lies.

'I don't want to make trouble for you. But can't we meet again, just as friends? I don't want to lose you entirely. And we are friends, are we not? We always were.'

She didn't say anything for a long time. Her wide, rain-coloured eyes searched his face, her hand lay in his, still but alive. He felt coming from her such a heartbreaking wave of sadness it was like darkness touching his soul, making him shiver.

And at last she said, 'Yes, we always were.' Just that. She stood up, withdrew her hand from his. 'I must go.'

He stood too. He watched her walk away. It won't always be like this, he thought. One day – but he was close to wishing Mayhew dead, and he was shocked at himself. He hurried to the door, for one last glimpse of her, saw her upright figure, straight as a wand, walking briskly along the gravel path, diminishing with distance; space swallowing her up, as time had done before. Such desolation settled over him that he wanted to fall down like a child and pummel the earth in despair. What have I done? Oh, what have I done? He had been a fool, ruined his life, ruined other people's too. Why had it taken him so long to see clearly?

'I love you,' he whispered to that retreating back.

CHAPTER TWELVE

Tom Cavendish's letter brought not just a reply from Henry Droylsden, but the man in person, to give his permission, and to hug his step-daughter and warn her that if Cavendish made her unhappy he would wring his neck. There was an engagement party at the Batchworths' house in St James's Square, with Fanny in glowing looks, and Cavendish looking rather bewildered. His parents were there, of course. Old Sir Geoffrey, creakingly corseted, heavily perfumed, his shirt collar wings fit to poke his eyes out, was elaborately courteous to everyone, and flirted ponderously with Fanny and Charlotte. Charlotte was intrigued and faintly shocked to discover, on finding herself at closer quarters to him than she liked, that he was wearing maquillage, which had been the style of his youth. It somehow had the effect of making him seem older rather than younger. Since he was in any case in his eighties, the result was positively macabre.

Lady Cavendish was much younger. She had been a Miss Edgecumbe, and had been a débutante at the same time as Rosamund. She had been an intimate friend all her life of the Miss Fauncett who was now Lady Alfred Fleetwood, soon to be Charlotte's aunt, and seemed on that account very much more interested in Charlotte's wedding plans than her own son's. Charlotte wondered whether anyone ever thought their parents-in-law quite normal; and tried very hard not to understand that Lady Cavendish's ultimate goal was to get Charlotte to agree to a double wedding with Fanny, which would bring her son nicely into the ducal circles she thought his talents fitted him for.

Henry Droylsden and Tom Cavendish were deep in talk together. They had met in Manchester when Cavendish was investigating factory conditions for the Parliamentary committee, so Henry was not being obliged to part with Fanny to a complete stranger. He was trying now to ascertain in a tactful way whether Cavendish would live with Fanny in Manchester, or insist on taking her away to live in the south. Sir Geoffrey had a small estate in Hertfordshire, which would be Tom's one day, if it did not become his creditors' first; Hobsbawn House in Manchester, where Fanny and Henry lived, was Fanny's own, and unencumbered.

Lady Cavendish, having abandoned her attempts to weasel Charlotte, was in conversation with Rosamund, trying to work out the exact degree of connection between them – Rosamund's father's mother had been a Cavendish. Rosamund had no interest in genealogies of this sort, and was growing glazed with boredom. Jes sacrificed himself nobly for his beloved by offering up his own Cavendish connection, which threw Lady Cavendish out of her orbit and sent her spinning away to far galaxies of second- and third-cousins any number of times removed.

Later, a polite little battle was entered into over where the wedding should take place. Rosamund and Jes wanted Fanny to be married at Grasscroft; Henry naturally thought she should be married from her own home; Lady Cavendish, giving up on Charlotte, was urgent for St Margaret's and all the style of a high London wedding, and Sir Geoffrey, thinking in dismay of Manchester and the trouble of getting there, supported her. Tom Cavendish laughingly suggested it would save everyone trouble if he and Fanny ran off to Scotland; but when Fanny was consulted she expressed herself modestly but firmly for London, and so it was decided. A tentative date for late September was fixed on, to be confirmed when the Dean of Westminster had been consulted.

That night, after they had gone to bed, Fanny came in and climbed onto Charlotte's bed, and sat for a while in pensive silence, rocking back and forth. 'It's a strange thing, isn't it, this wedding business?' she said at last.

'Is it? In what way?'

'I don't know exactly,' Fanny said, frowning in thought. 'But it takes over, doesn't it? And after a while you forget what it's really for. I've hardly spent an hour alone with Tom since he asked me to marry him. You do think I'm right to have said yes, don't you?'

Charlotte felt helpless before that anxious question. What did she know that Fanny didn't? Who had been brought to London to take care of whom? 'If you love him, of course you are,' she said, a formula she hoped would work.

Fanny threw the question back at her. 'But what do you mean by love? I wonder really,' she went on thoughtfully, 'whether one can know if one loves somebody until after one is married. You have to be alone with them before you can begin to find out. Perhaps that's why they do all this – to keep you apart so that you can't find out and change your mind.'

'Oh Fanny,' Charlotte said, hopeless of saying anything to help.

'Oh Charley!' Fanny responded, grinning her old impish grin. 'Just promise me one thing – that we'll always be friends, even afterwards. I know you'll be a duchess, and I'll probably be living in Manchester, but we can still write, can't we?'

'Of course,' Charlotte said. 'But I don't see why we shouldn't see each other, wherever we live.'

'It isn't the where so much as the who,' Fanny said wisely. 'But my mother and yours were friends, in spite of everything. So perhaps we can manage it, if we really try.'

'I will always try,' Charlotte promised.

Fanny flung her arms round her in a quick hug. 'So will I. And now goodnight, dear soon-to-be-duchess. You must get your sleep.' And she pattered away, leaving Charlotte to lie wakeful, a prey to the thoughts she had aroused.

The 'wedding business', as Fanny put it, did seem to have a life of its own. Once the announcement had appeared in the correct papers, a mighty machine seemed to have been set in motion, which gathered people up willy-nilly, so that Charlotte felt it would have gone on rolling even if she had disappeared in a puff of smoke. It was to be the Abbey for Charlotte, of course, and there had been urgent discussions between Lady Turnhouse and the archbishop about the date, for Lambeth Palace did not like to be hurried. Once that was settled, there were all the details of the service to be arranged – assistants, boys, decorations, music, orchestra, choir, bells, seating, red carpets, canopies, the order of carriages, the control of the crowds. These things were thrashed out between Lucy and Lady Turnhouse, on the whole amicably. The guest list was enormous, for while Lady Turnhouse knew everyone listed in Debrett's and the upper third of Crockford's, Lucy's sphere of influence covered both Houses of Parliament and the army and the navy. One glimpse of it made Charlotte feel sick with apprehension. If she were to stumble walking up the aisle, there would not be a person of any consequence in the country who would not witness it.

Her own days were spent swathed in material and stuck with pins, 'Like Saint Sebastian,' she told Fleetwood mournfully. Madame Bourdin would not do for this occasion. Three Court dressmakers were involved in making Charlotte's wardrobe. The wedding-dress itself was a miracle of ivory satin, Honiton lace (the Queen had made the home-grown article fashionable) and crystal beads, and if the splendour of it was due to Lady Turnhouse's influence, the comparative simplicity was due to Lucy's. The train was to be carried by six bridesmaids: Fanny was to be one, together with Aylesbury's daughter Lucilla and Mary Paston, daughter of Rosamund's cousin Polly. The other three were cousins of Fleetwood's.

Charlotte saw little of her fiancé, who seemed to be involved in equally time-consuming arrangements of his own. The Duke's London house in Pall Mall had to be opened up, and since it had been unused for seven years, there was a great deal to do to make it decent in time for the wedding banquet and ball. The Turnhouses had quit it after Oliver's coming-of-age celebrations, when the Duke had decided to live permanently in the country. They had rented a house in Hanover Square, and since her husband's death, Lady Turnhouse had moved into a small house in Brook Street, while Oliver had rooms in Albany.

'But Mama is really looking forward to living in Southport House again,' Oliver said to Charlotte. 'So much so that I hadn't the heart to refuse.'

'Refuse?' Charlotte enquired anxiously.

'Refuse to live with her,' he elucidated. 'It badly needs to be modernised, but with new furniture and enough servants it can be made to provide two decent suites.'

He took her to see it one day. It was only a few yards from Chelmsford House, just as big and just as neglected. Inside the decorations were splendid in the elaborate manner of the 1780s, and there was a great deal of the Egyptian and the Chinese about it. The state rooms were vast, and even on a June day struck chilly; Charlotte couldn't help wondering how they could ever be warmed, even with a fireplace at each end. A great many smoke-darkened family portraits loomed on the walls, whose eyes seemed to follow Charlotte critically, wondering if she was worthy to be treading those bare boards.

'We had the most wonderful Saponerie carpets,' Oliver said, explaining the pale gaps. 'Grandpa had them smuggled out of France in 1794, but Papa sold them when the house was shut up. I don't think Grandpa knows that.'

Upstairs the apartments were slightly smaller, the furnishings slightly less sultanesque. 'These were Grandpa's quarters. I thought we might have them done up for us.' Charlotte looked round at the dingy wallpaper, the mouse-nibbled bed-curtains, the heavy window drapes which had rotted through to the lining by the action of the sun on the dust and dirt. There were few pictures in this part of the house; the walls were lined instead with dozens of glass-fronted display-cases. 'Grandpa's collections,' Oliver said, rubbing the dust from one. Thousands of butterflies and moths, spreadeagled and pinned against grey card, their brilliant colours sadly dimmed; and in other rooms, millions of sea shells, graded by size and colour, and arranged in patterns. 'This was Grandpa's greatest pride,' Oliver said, with a wry smile, leading her up to a case in which the shells had been arranged and stuck down to make a picture, of a house in a park, with hills and sky in the background and a large tree in the foreground. 'It wasn't all his own work, I regret to say – George Stubbs helped him, in between painting Grandpa's racehorse – but he gradually forgot that as the years went by.'

Charlotte thought it looked very odd, for, given the nature of seashells, there was no green for the grass and leaves. They had been done in pink, while the tree trunks were orange. 'It's very – ingenious,' she said, struggling for the right word.

Oliver looked at her and laughed. 'You needn't be polite, my love! But Grandpa would probably count it very civil if you was to mention it when you see him. I only showed it to you because the house is Ravendene. Now, through here is Grandpa's man's room – I thought this might do for a dressing-room for you.'

Charlotte was only allowed the briefest look at the below-stairs arrangements, and what she saw reminded her of what Norton had said about grand folk who liked to make their servants' work as hard as possible. It was as black as Newgate Knocker down there, full of scuttling things, and utterly primitive in its equipment. If Charlotte so much as wanted a bath, water would have to be boiled on an open fire and carried in cans through half a mile of stairs and corridors by a succession of housemaids.

Oliver must have sensed something in her silence, for he said as they went back up the stairs, 'Don't worry, everything can be put right in time. I can't do much about it now, but when Grandpa dies it will be mine and I promise you I'll give you a free hand. You may order it just as you please, and the proceeds from Chelmsford House will pay for all the modern knick-knackery you please.'

'Chelmsford House?' she queried.

'Well, I shall sell it, of course,' he explained. 'Or lease it, if a buyer can't be found. There's no point in having two houses in Pall Mall, is there? By the by, you must tell me if there's anything by way of furniture and so on that you would like to have moved here from Chelmsford House before it's sold.'

When they reached the front hall again, where Norton

and a footman were waiting patiently, Oliver took her hands and kissed them, and said apologetically that he would have to dash away. 'I hope you'll forgive me if I put you in your carriage, and don't escort you home. I have some important business, and I've spent longer here this morning than I meant to.'

It seemed to be like that all the time. Some days she didn't see him at all, and when she did see him, they were never alone. He found time once or twice to join her when she rode in the Park, and there were evenings when they were in the same party at the theatre or the opera, or were invited to dinner at a great house; but wherever they met they were the object of every gaze, and as the eyes followed them, the heads came together and the mouths whispered. Charlotte could not get used to being talked about, and could not get it out of her head that the whispers were uncomplimentary. 'I can't understand why he's marrying her,' she imagined them saying. 'She's a nobody – brought up in a cottage – hardly knows how to hold a knife and fork.' Oliver, born to the purple, noticed the looks no more than the air he breathed, but Charlotte felt like a snail whose shell had been stolen. She wanted to shrink when those eyes touched her, but had nowhere to shrink to. How would she ever cope with being a duchess? She wished Oliver's grandfather a long, long life.

The day that Oliver took her to see Lord Southport was a delightful respite both from the eyes and the wedding preparations. They were to go by railway train, a new experience for Charlotte, and one to which she looked forward with keen anticipation and a slight nervousness. She remembered Ellen telling her how the rector of St Peter's had preached a fierce sermon against the railways when the Norwich and Yarmouth was first incorporated, and had warned that anyone wicked enough to defy nature by travelling on one would meet a horrible death.

'He said that all your blood would be sucked up into your head by the speed, miss,' Ellen had told her, round-eyed, 'and then your head would burst. Think of that! But I don't see as how it could be true, miss,' she had concluded sensibly, 'because they'd never go on building them if all their customers died horrible like that, would they?'

Charlotte was not afraid of the head-bursting theory, but she knew that the railway trains travelled at phenomenal speeds with nothing to hold them on the rails but their own momentum. Stories of horrific accidents were legion, and featured regularly in the newspapers – trains falling off the rails, colliding with each other, tumbling down embankments, having cuttings fall in on them; locomotives exploding, carriages collapsing. On the other hand, she remembered Orrock's insouciance, and his horror at the idea of being without the railway, and she would not be outdone by him, so she didn't tell Oliver she had never been on a railway before.

They went to the station in Lucy's carriage, and though Charlotte had got tolerably used to London traffic by now, the noise and chaos of the station approach was something new. She had never seen so many horses and vehicles before, every one in a tearing hurry and all apparently bent on getting in each other's way. People, luggage, packing-cases, crates of chickens, barrels of apples, screaming children, harassed servants and shoving, swearing porters all milled about wreathed in clouds of steam and sulphurous smoke, like a vision of the Inferno. But Oliver guided her through it all with such skill and ease that it seemed in retrospect he must have parted a way for them like Moses parting the Red Sea.

The train was not what she had expected: she had somehow thought it would be open to the air so that one would feel the wind rushing past one's face; but it was divided into little compartments just like carriages, and even painted on the outside to look like a series of mail-coaches all joined together. The Fleetwoods had their own private coach added to the back of the train, and when Oliver helped her in, she found herself in something like a long, narrow drawing-room, complete with carpet, red-brocade curtains, upholstered armchairs, crystal chandeliers, and little tables bolted to the floor so that they wouldn't fall over, in case one wanted to eat or drink anything. It was so comfortable and normal that she thought one wouldn't know one was travelling at all.

As it was a short journey, they hadn't brought any servants with them, so once they had moved out of the station they were quite alone and completely private. Starting off was rather a shock. She had been congratulating herself on appearing completely at ease with all aspects of railway-travel, when there was a shrill scream and a tremendous jolt, making her start and half-rise, thinking there must have been an accident. Half an instant's reflection told her it was not a human scream, and the violent jolt was followed by a series of lesser ones as the equipage started forward, and the station platform with all its indigenous life began to slip backwards out of view. She turned her head and met Oliver's amused look, and felt obliged to confess.

'It's the first time I've travelled by the railway.'

He took her hand. 'Then I'm very glad you should be sharing this momentous occasion with me. Are you afraid?'

'Oh, no! But – I like you holding my hand anyway.'

They moved at first quite slowly, and through those scenes of devastation she had seen before from the chaise. But they were less shocking from this angle, and it was obvious that new building was going on, that the truncated streets were being sealed off, like arteries being sutured, and the mangled houses were being healed over with bricks and mortar. While they were in this natural cutting of buildings, the smoke billowed around them, and she wondered what it must be like to live with the smoke and the noise under your windows the whole time. But perhaps those who had a home left at all were the lucky ones. That missing body of residents troubled her like a ghost army, appearing and disappearing in her thoughts like wraiths.

At last they plunged out into the open country, and picked up speed. The smoke was whisked away and the world was rushing past in a blur of speed. Their progress was so smooth – quite without the bumps and lurches and swayings of a road-carriage – that it made her feel perilously out of control, as though she had fallen off an immensely high cliff and was plummeting to her death, but somehow *horizontally*. She didn't notice that she was gripping Oliver's hand painfully tightly; he was watching her face with affectionate amusement, enjoying equally her reaction to the speed and her determination not to be frightened.

She had just begun to relax and enjoy the exhilaration when, with a sudden, violent bang, she found herself struck stone blind. A terrible cacophony dinned her ears and a bitter, vile smell of sulphur stung her nostrils, as though she had been plunged into hell itself. She let out a very small shriek, though the noise was too great for her to hear it; and then with another bang the noise dropped abruptly and she could see again. It had all lasted only a few seconds. She was trembling with the shock, and looked round at Oliver with such wide eyes that he couldn't help laughing.

'Oh, I'm sorry, my darling, but if you could only see your face!'

'What happened?' she managed to ask.

'We went through a tunnel, that's all. Quite a short one, but I dare say it is a blow when one is not expecting it.'

She smiled, though a little shakily. 'I shall be prepared next time. It was so sudden, I thought there'd been an accident.'

Oliver smiled. 'I know just the treatment to calm your nerves. Come here, my beloved, and kiss me. It is a very hard thing in this world of ours to get a moment alone with one's own fiancée.'

He put his arms round her and drew her close, and she lifted her face trustingly to be kissed. It *was* hard to have time alone, and she had often envied Fanny, whose wedding preparations were so much more leisurely and light, and who saw Tom alone most days, for when he called at Upper Grosvenor Street he was allowed to sit with her unchaperoned in the morning-room for half an hour at a time. She trembled now, for reasons entirely unconnected with the train, as his arms tightened about her, and his mouth touched hers. His lips were silken and firm, his breath was as sweet as apples, and the sudden awareness of him, of his wholeness and his essence, was piercing and lovely. Her blood quickened, and she yearned towards him, instinctively seeking a closer binding, though she had no idea what or how it might be. She sensed something change in him at the same moment that she felt the boulder roll from the mouth of the spring deep in herself. She yielded to it, not knowing what it was, knowing only it was what she wanted.

For a moment he yielded too, a sort of frantic desire arguing with his better wisdom. He cupped her face with his hands, and then his hands strayed to her breasts, and he felt no aversion in her, not even surprise: she moved into his embrace in a way that shocked and delighted him. He had never, never known a girl like her. They were alone, no-one could see them—

It was agony to draw back. He ached all over; her eyes opened, and he imagined how he would see that sweet, drowned look in them on their wedding night, and felt another stab of desire.

'It is a good thing, perhaps, that we don't have any time alone together,' he murmured. 'Oh my love, I have such things to show you! You and I will go on a voyage of discovery together. Every night will be a great ship to bear us away to lands you can't dream of.'

'Is this love, then?' she asked, looking earnestly into his face. 'Is this how it feels?'

'Yes, it's love,' he said, and drew her head onto his shoulder, because it was too hard to look at her.

'Does everyone feel like this?' she said wonderingly.

'I wish they might,' he said, and she accepted this enigmatic answer for an affirmative. It will be worth it, she thought. All the trials of being a duchess and being stared at and being afraid all the time of doing things wrong will be worth it for moments like these and for – whatever it is that he will show me when we are married. She was glad that the wedding would be soon. She didn't want to wait. She thought of Fanny and Tom Cavendish, and wondered how, if they felt like this, they could be content to wait until September. When Tom had suggested running away to Scotland, why hadn't Fanny said yes?

Oliver kissed her forehead, and then rested his cheek against her hair, a gesture so loving she felt her heart might break, she who had never known the caresses a child is heir to. She leaned against him in absolute trust and contentment. He said, 'Three weeks is barely enough to arrange everything, but I would not have it longer by a day.'

'Is that why I never see you – because there is so much to arrange?'

He did not answer for the beat of a second. 'Yes – more things than I can tell you. But I must have everything squared away before I take you to myself. Everything must be done and finished – no loose ends. It's hard for me – I wish I could tell you – but I will have it all done. Nothing will overshadow our life together.'

She didn't know what he meant, but she was too comfortable to ask.

Ravendene seemed oddly familiar to her, but because the colours were different she did not immediately connect it with the shell-picture. The house was tall and square, of red brick with white copings, and long windows divided into many panes – very neat and complete it looked at the first sighting from the top of a slight rise. It sat in its wide park, dotted with fine timber, and grazing sheep like fallen blossom.

'It's beautiful,' she said sincerely. He looked at her with faint surprise, not knowing that she was comparing it with the ugly, incoherent sprawl of Wolvercote, the only other great house she knew.

'It's not a bad house,' he allowed, 'but it needs a great deal doing to it, and the farms and cottages are in a poor state. Even the church is dilapidated. The land could yield much more if it were properly farmed, using modern methods. But Grandpa won't change anything. He's too old to see that what would do during the war won't do in this day and age.'

She was nervous about meeting the Duke – partly just because he was a duke, but mostly because it seemed to matter to Oliver what he thought of her. The old man's wishes were so plainly law to so many people that she thought he would be haughty and exacting. But she found that he lived in no state, other than the natural state his lifelong rank had generated about him. He was a tall, thin old man who had plainly once been vigorous; who held himself erect even now when it was obviously painful to him, and who had still the remains in his gaunt face of the beauty he had bequeathed his grandson. There was a great look of Oliver about him, she discovered, except that his eyes were dark – quite surprising in the pallor if his old, ill face.

He came forward to meet them when they were shown into the drawing-room. Oliver kissed him and then said, 'I've brought Charlotte to meet you, Grandpa.'

Charlotte curtseyed low, blushing as her mind went through a rapid inventory of all the things he might find wrong with her. But when she rose and looked bravely into his face, she saw not a great duke but an old man whom pain had come to live with, and who had made room for it with a patience and dignity that came from something inside him, a grace that was not bought with money or position. If he was a nobleman, it was not because he had inherited a title from his father. She found herself smiling at him. He took her hand between his cold and bony ones, and said, 'Thank God Oliver has chosen the right woman! I was afraid he would want to marry the sort of female his mother would like; but I see there is more of me in him than I suspected.'

'Now, Grandpa,' Oliver said, 'when have I ever disappointed you?'

The Duke didn't answer that. He was still looking into Charlotte's face. 'Does she think you awkward, plain and dull? I do hope so. It would be the best recommendation you could have to sensible people.'

'I'm afraid I do disappoint her, sir,' Charlotte said.

'Don't worry. My daughter-in-law is disappointed with everyone, especially herself. But you won't need her approval. You will make an excellent duchess. I can die happy now, knowing everything is in safe hands. How much longer before you marry?'

'Three weeks, sir.'

'Was that the quickest you could manage it, hey, boy? I suppose your mother wouldn't be satisfied without the Abbey and the Archbishop. Well, well, I shall just have to hold on a little longer. I don't want to miss seeing you turned off. And of course, if I do let go, you'll have to put the wedding off, and that wouldn't do. No, I want to see this luminous creature safely installed as my granddaughter-in-law, and then I can go in peace.'

'I hope you won't go too soon, sir,' Charlotte said. 'I never had a grandpapa.'

He laughed. 'Flattering puss! But if you knew how long the days are here, you wouldn't want to delay me. No, no, I'll see you off, and then you can see me off. Now, I should like to show you your kingdom before luncheon, if you would care to see it. Come, will you take my arm? I like to feel a woman's hand there. Yes, you can come too, Oliver, and add your penn'orth. He knows the place almost as well as me, my dear. But you must come and see my collections first, before I get too tired. I have the finest collection of minerals and semi-precious stones in the country.'

'I have seen your other collections at Southport House, sir.'

'And what did you think of 'em, hey? Ain't they fine? Oliver, the door, if you please. Forgive me, my dear, if I move too slowly for you. Young people are all for rapid movement, but it makes me dizzy. It's lucky the waltz wasn't invented in my young day. Very wicked it was thought when it first came to England. I remember Oliver's mother wouldn't do it upon a bet! But I dare say it seems quite ordinary to you?'

'Not – ordinary, sir,' she said, with a glance at Oliver which made the old man laugh.

'Yes, I imagine he uses it to his advantage. Waltz with him all you can, my dear, while you are young and well. And I pray you will never stop looking at him like that – and that he will never stop knowing how lucky he is to have you do it!'

Charlotte left Ravendene feeling much happier about the prospect of being a duchess. The old duke's indifference, almost contempt, for Lady Turnhouse and all her ways gave Charlotte confidence to suppose that her approval was not the only standard by which things could be judged.

The nearer they got to London, however, the more her new-found confidence seeped away. It was the viscountess, after all, who would be at hand; they would be living in her house, and under her eye. Oliver reached into one of her silences with an unexpected sensitivity.

'When Grandpa dies, and the estate comes to me, Mama will retire to a dower house. There are some very nice, new, handsome houses being built to the north of Oxford Street and Great Russell Street. I might buy her one of those, you know.'

'I don't like to think of your grandfather dying,' she said.

'I knew you would like him,' he said, taking her hand and bringing it back into his lap to hold. And so they travelled the last few miles in thoughtful silence.

Charlotte had grown so used to being pushed here and there like a chess piece by her grandmother and Lady Turnhouse, that it was a shock to receive a request for an urgent private audience from Mr Tarbush. The financial situation between her and Fleetwood had been something she assumed would be settled by those older and wiser than herself, for even with her limited experience she imagined the complications would be enormous.

But Tarbush's letter exuded an agitation that even survived abbreviation, and as he was also explicit that the interview must be private, she replied that she would attend him at his office. It happened that the next morning she was going to the milliner's attended only by Norton, Fanny being otherwise engaged; she said she would call on Tarbush on her way back. It was the first time she had been to Lincoln's Inn Fields since her arrival in London; and she hoped very much that she would not see Orrock there, for she had not forgotten their last encounter. But when the footman went in to announce her, it was Tarbush himself who came downstairs to escort her – proof, if it were needed, of her increased importance.

When she was seated in the high-backed chair before the fireplace – empty at this time of year except for a folded fan of paper, lightly soot-specked – Tarbush seemed at first too restless to settle opposite her, but walked back and forth a few times rubbing his hands absently, until at last she begged him to sit down and unburden himself.

'My lady, it is a matter of some delicacy,' he said, sitting at last. He looked so diffident that she thought again of Orrock and wondered if she had assumed too readily that it was financial business he wanted to discuss with her.

'Please be open with me,' she said. 'I am sure you would not embarrass me for no reason.'

'I hope not, your ladyship. The fact is, the financial settlements required upon your marriage to Mr Fleetwood are not as straightforward as one would like. You are of age and in possession of your fortune, and no part of the estate is entailed, and it ought to be the easiest thing in the world – but in this case, with a property of such magnitude – it ceases to be a question simply of dowry.'

He paused and Charlotte continued to look at him hopefully, waiting to be enlightened. Tarbush took out his handkerchief and wiped his hands with it, and seemed to take the plunge.

'You are aware, of course, that in return for his bride's dowry, a gentleman makes a settlement upon her at the time of their marriage?'

'I suppose so,' Charlotte said.

'Your husband to be,' he went on, 'inherits the dukedom of Southport on his grandfather's death, which, in view of his advanced years, cannot be long delayed. But the fact is that until that melancholy day, Mr Fleetwood has no property beyond a small competence which comes to him from his paternal grandmother. A very small competence – a matter of a few hundreds a year, and no capital which he could settle on you.'

Charlotte was puzzled. 'But he will have all my money, will not he?'

Tarbush almost smiled. 'A woman's property passes to her husband at the time of marriage, it's true, but it would be out of the question for him to make a settlement on her with her own money.'

'Then – what is to happen? I don't need anything from Oliver – Mr Fleetwood. I have quite enough for us to live on, haven't I?'

'Quite so, my lady, but there must be a settlement – one could not contemplate any other arrangement. Now, Lord Southport, as head of the family, has agreed to make an interim settlement upon you, which is in the form of real estate – land, that is, my lady. There is a small portion of the Southport estate which is not entailed and can therefore be deeded to you.'

'Well, then,' Charlotte began.

Tarbush lifted his hand. 'Your pardon, my lady. It is a very small portion, emphatically not sufficient to counter balance the huge fortune you bring to the marriage; and, moreover, the income it generates is not even sufficient for its own upkeep.'

'Mr Fleetwood said that the estate is not in good order,' Charlotte said. 'He told me the farming methods are very old-fashioned but that Lord Southport would not bear change. But I am sure he believes the estates can be made to yield very well.'

'I am afraid he did not tell you the whole story, my lady. The entire ducal estate is in very poor array. There were severe losses in the West Indies during the late war, at the same times as Lord Turnhouse – Mr Fleetwood's late father – was incurring heavy debts. He was, not to put too fine a point on it, a gamester, my lady, and a man of expensive tastes. What could be sold, was sold – all the real estate which was not entailed, apart from the property now being offered as your settlement. Much of the personal estate – valuable paintings and furnishings from Ravendene and Southport House, and much of the family plate and jewellery – was sold. And the rest of the real estate was heavily encumbered with mortgages.'

Charlotte listened blankly. 'You mean,' she said at last, 'that they have no money? That they are—' she searched for an expression she had heard – 'under the hatches?'

'Just so, my lady. Your fortune is to retrieve theirs.' He coughed. 'It is not, of course, an unusual arrangement, but in this case – given the circumstances of your upbringing and the fact that until now I have not been asked – that is to say, I was not sure, my lady, whether you had been made fully aware of the situation.'

Charlotte was thinking, hard and fast. 'Does my grandmother know?'

'I don't think Lady Theakston can be aware of the full extent of the indebtedness, though she undoubtedly does know – it is common knowledge – that the Fleetwoods are not—'

'Full of juice,' Charlotte finished for him.

'Quite so. Her ladyship, as I understand it, passed the whole matter over to the Fleetwood man of business to draft, and I have the draft here. The covering letter says Lady Theakston has seen it, but I doubt, I really doubt, whether she can have understood the purport of it. I understand her ladyship is rather unworldly when it comes to money matters. In any case, I could not be easy until I had made sure your ladyship understood what was at stake.'

'And what is at stake?' Charlotte asked. 'Will their debts entirely swallow up my fortune?'

'Oh no, my lady,' he said quickly. 'But the income of your estate is not enough by itself to clear them. Assets would have to be sold. I estimate that the income from your fortune would be reduced perhaps by a third.'

Charlotte almost laughed. 'But that is more than enough, *plenty* to live on, for both of us – and to keep Lady Turnhouse, too.'

Tarbush shook his head. 'That may be so, my lady. But it is a very great investment on your part, very great indeed. I would not recommend it. I cannot, indeed, allow you to be a party to this arrangement without protesting in the very strongest terms.'

Charlotte blinked a little at his vehemence. Her fortune seemed so large to her, she could not imagine ever being in want, even if nine tenths of it disappeared. But Tarbush was a good man, and she trusted him. 'What do you suggest, then?'

'That a portion of your estate is reserved to you, instead of passing to your husband.'

'Is that possible?'

'Oh yes, my lady. Provided all parties agree, any

financial arrangement can be set up. The capital would be held in trust, untouchable by your husband's family, the income available to you for your personal use at the discretion of your trustees.'

Charlotte thought a moment. It seemed wrong to be holding back anything from Oliver – but from Lady Turnhouse? That was an attractive idea. And Tarbush wouldn't suggest it if it was in any way wrong. 'Then, if it is what you think best, you had better do it.'

'I have your authority to speak to the Fleetwood man of business, my lady?' The relief was palpable in his voice.

'Yes,' she said. 'I am sure you know what's best. Suggest whatever you think necessary.'

CHAPTER THIRTEEN

The weather was close and sticky, the air in London – despite fewer smoking chimneys at this time of year – dark to the taste and unsatisfying to the lungs. Families were going out into the country, to the sea-side. Charlotte could now see the point of waiting until the autumn for a grand ceremonial like a wedding – if you weren't in love, that is.

If only it would thunder, deluge, and clear the air! She was sitting in the morning-room, which was slightly cooler than the drawing-room in the afternoon, writing letters. There lacked still an hour to the dressing-bell. Lucy had gone up to lie on her bed, exhausted by the heat; Fanny and Danby were not yet back from their respective afternoon activities. Charlotte sat near the open window, but not a breath of wind stirred the leaves of the plane tree outside; the air that met her face was warm and unpleasant, like a dog's lick. The sky was hazy, and the haze had a yellowish tinge – surely it would storm tonight?

She remembered storms at home (she still called it home when she wasn't thinking), where there was nothing on the horizon, no buildings, hills or trees, to hide the sky. She remembered watching from the attic window, lightning in great blue-white, fizzing arrows lancing the ground, the crack of thunder like splitting ice, and then the stealthy hiss of rain, and the cool breath that came up from the earth, like a sigh of relief. She suddenly felt homesick, for the quiet and the unpeopledness, and the vastness of sky – that most of all. In London she must take the sky in sips, instead of the glorious, satisfying gulps she had grown used to.

The door opened, and Denton announced, 'Lady Turnhouse, my lady,' and Charlotte hardly had time to rise before that dame entered.

'How do you do, ma'am? I'm afraid my grandmother has already gone up to dress.'

'It is you I have come to see,' Lady Turnhouse said grimly.

Charlotte was at a loss. At this time of day? What could it be but bad news. 'Won't you sit down, then, ma'am,' she said glumly. 'I'm afraid the stairs have tired you. Will you take a glass of wine?'

'I want nothing,' she said, planking herself down on the nearest settle. Charlotte nodded Denton away, and moved across the room to sit at a polite distance from the dowager. As soon as the door clicked closed, Lady Turnhouse said, 'I have just been informed of your impudent proposal to hold back your fortune. What can you mean by it? What can you have to say?'

Charlotte was startled. It was the last thing she had expected. 'I was following the advice of my man of business. He thought it wise in view of—' Too late, she thought she should not have said 'wise'.

Lady Turnhouse snapped it up like a trout snapping a fly. 'Wise? *Wise?* What insolence is this? Do you think, miss, that you know better than your elders – you, with your background? What can you know of high financial matters? Wise, indeed!'

Charlotte pushed down the growing rumble of anger. 'The word was not mine, ma'am, but my lawyer's. He does not propose to hold back my fortune, only a part of it. The rest will be ample to – for the purpose of – the rest will be plenty, I am assured.'

'The rest? Hold back a part?' Lady Turnhouse mottled with growing anger. 'Do you not know that a woman's fortune becomes her husband's on marriage? *All* of it – everything she has! Why should you be different? Why should you make new rules for yourself? You impertinent chit! Would you set up your own will against that of your elders – aye, and betters, betters by a very long measure, considering who and what you are!'

Still Charlotte struggled for control, though the abuse hurt her like slaps across the face. From Oliver's mother, which made it worse – how she must hate her! How could she ever live comfortably with a woman who hated her so? But she tried to speak gently.

'I regret that my lawyer's advice should not please you, ma'am, but you will admit you have not been quite frank with me. You did not tell me that the Southport estate was so encumbered that—'

'Tell *you*?' The viscountess's eyebrows climbed like skylarks. 'What in the name of goodness should you be told for?'

'Because I am one-and-twenty, and command my own fortune,' Charlotte retorted. 'I should have thought in very courtesy—'

'Don't you speak to me of courtesy, you hussy! You instructed your man of business to defy me, to countermand my orders and change my dispositions without the *courtesy* of a single word to me.'

'I thought—'

'I doubt whether you *did* think, whether you are capable of thought,' Lady Turnhouse said, plainly beside herself with rage. Her face had darkened alarmingly, and Charlotte felt she ought to placate her, but her temper was rising in spite of her efforts.

'I might be forgiven for thinking,' she said, her voice trembling with the effort to be polite, 'that my fortune was all you cared for.'

Shockingly, Lady Turnhouse laughed. 'Oh, you silly girl! Do you think my son – my only son – who will be Duke of Southport before a twelvemonth is out – do you think he would marry a creature like you for any other reason?' Charlotte went white, and Lady Turnhouse's eyes narrowed in triumph. She went on excitedly, throwing out words like repeated blows. 'Look at you! No more air or countenance than a mill-girl! And your antecedents! Who is your mother? A divorcée, not received at Court, or anywhere by decent people. Your father lived like a pauper in a forsaken hovel – God knows through what disgrace! There is bad blood in the Morlands, everyone knows it: the whole family has produced one scandal after another. And this is the blood which is to pollute the shades of Ravendene! If we had not been in desperate straits, and if your fortune had not been so large, do you think you would have been considered for an instant?'

Charlotte was silent through the tirade, too shocked even to try to interrupt. The viscountess went on, 'The alliance will give you respectability – a gift beyond price – and a position in society which even a nobly born girl would envy. The Fleetwood reputation is sufficient, thank God, to expunge the Morland shame. We are willing to do this in exchange for your fortune, because there is no other way to redeem the estate. My son knows his duty; you had better learn yours.'

Lady Turnhouse paused to draw breath, and Charlotte managed at last to speak. 'It's not true! That is not why he wants to marry me. He loves me, he loves me truly.'

The dowager curled her lip. 'What new vulgarity is this? We do not talk of love in our rank of society. Marriages of the nobility are matters of far greater import, as my son knows, and as you would know if you had been born and brought up in a noble family. I selected you for my son for family reasons, and he accepted my choice, as he is bound in duty to do. A gentleman takes his *love* quite elsewhere, I assure you,' she said with quivering scorn. 'No woman of breeding would expect sentiments of that sort from her husband.'

Charlotte struggled with shock, anger, bewilderment. 'It's not true,' she said again. They were the only words she could find.

The weakness of her voice convinced Lady Turnhouse she had won. She became almost kind. 'Of course it's true. Do you think I would speak a falsehood? Now pull yourself together, and try to think like a lady and not like a kitchen maid. A contract of marriage is a matter of business, pure and simple, as your grandmother ought to have explained to you. You suffer from a very serious ineligibility, but we are prepared to overlook it because of your fortune. What could be plainer or more simple? You are wholly the gainer: you will be a duchess, instead of an outcast. And as the estate will pass to your sons, you will not even be parting with your fortune, only handing it to those better qualified than you to manage it. But there must be no more nonsense about holding back anything. I will not have it, do you understand?' She rose, and looked down at Charlotte's bent head, savouring her triumph. 'That's better. Be a sensible girl, and do what your elders and betters advise. And let us hear no more vulgarity about love, if you please.' Charlotte did not speak or move. 'Now if you will ring the bell, I will take my leave.'

Charlotte got up automatically and went across to pull the bell. She stood where she was, looking at nothing, deep in thought, until Denton came to show the visitor out. Then she went back to her seat by the window and sat, still staring at nothing, while her thoughts worked like yeast.

It was not true, it couldn't be true. Oliver loved her. He had chosen her because he loved her.

But why hadn't he told her the estate was all to pieces?

Because she might have thought he was marrying her for her money.

But Grandmama and Papa Danby had warned her that there would be many men who wanted to marry her for her money. Why not Oliver, who needed money more than most? It was more likely, wasn't it, than that a man so desirable should love an awkward girl like her?

But then, why should he pretend to love her if he didn't – if marriage was a contract, and the balance between her fortune and his title was fair?

Because she was perhaps the only girl in London who didn't want to be a duchess. *Because he knew she would not have accepted him otherwise.*

The last thought startled her, and she took it aside to examine it. Was it true? She loved him so much that perhaps she would have accepted him anyway, just to have him.

No, she discovered after a moment's thought, she wouldn't. She had no need to marry. She had security for ever from her own fortune and family. His love was what she wanted from him – that transforming passion which was all her life lacked. She would not marry him to be wife to a man who did not care for her.

Having reached that conclusion, there was only one thing left to do. She must find Oliver, and ask him for the truth. She must ask him if he loved her, and she must do it now. She could not bear to go a moment longer without knowing.

She hurried up to her room for her mantle and bonnet, and her reticule – there wasn't time to send for the carriage, so she must take a hack. Then she ran quickly down the stairs. A footman was passing through the hall, and looked startled to see her.

'Oh, Sam, look outside and see if you can see a cab. If not, run to the corner and secure one for me.'

'A cab, my lady?'

'Yes, yes, a cab. And hurry!'

He hesitated agonisingly for a moment; but Denton was upstairs in the dining-room, and he hated to be disturbed when he was checking the laying of the table. Surely Sam's duty was to obey orders, wasn't it? And her ladyship was giving him a direct order, wasn't she?

'A cab, my lady,' he said, with a different intonation, and turned towards the door with the stately gait he had copied from Denton, in hope of eventual promotion.

'Hurry!' she snapped, and he skipped like a lamb. Fortunately there was a cabriolet putting down a few doors down the street, so he was able to run and order the driver to follow him.

'Where shall I say, my lady?' Sam asked, holding the door open for her.

'Piccadilly,' she said, from some instinct of secrecy. The cab rumbled off. When they reached Hyde Park Corner she rapped on the roof and the driver slid back his hatch. 'Drive to the Albany, if you please.'

'Albany, ma'am, aye.'

The porter at Albany was suspicious of her. A lady arriving in a hack, alone, in a state of agitation? It could hardly be respectable, and nor could she. But she spoke with such conviction, and with the expectation of being obeyed which came from being used to command servants, that he wavered. He would not let her go up, of course, but perhaps he ought to send a message, just in case it was something important. He sent a boy, and satisfied the interval by cataloguing Charlotte's attire and concluding that she certainly had money, though whether she was a lady, or in someone's keeping, was hard to determine. Her clothes were sober and she hadn't the looks or the figure to be in keeping; but then again, what would a lady be doing out in a hack without a maid and asking for a gentleman at his rooms?

'Going to be a storm, be th' look of it, ma'am,' he said conversationally, wanting to hear her voice again, to determine her accent.

'Yes,' she said absently.

You couldn't tell much from that. 'Getting as dark as Newgate Knocker out there,' he suggested; but she only nodded. 'Be welcome when it comes. Clear the air a bit,' he went on.

'Oh, where is that boy?' she cried in agitation.

Definitely a lady, the porter decided – which made it all the more of a mystery.

The boy returned. 'Mr Dinsdale says Mr Fleetwood is hout,' he announced.

'Mr Dinsdale?'

'Mr Fleetwood's man,' the porter supplied.

'Is he expected back?' Charlotte asked the boy urgently.

'No, miss, he's hout all evening.'

'Where did he go, do you know?'

'Mr Dinsdale didn't say, miss.'

'Have you no idea where he went?' She read something in the boy's eyes, and went on, trying to sound calm and authoritative. 'It's very urgent that I get a message to him. I must know where to send the message.'

The boy looked at the porter for authority, and the porter shrugged. 'Well, miss, I fitched a cab for Mr Fleetwood earlier, and I did hear him say Soho Square and then Dean's.'

'Dean's?'

'It's a restaurant, ma'am, in Shaftesbury Avenue,' the porter said, but doubtfully. He wasn't sure he ought to have given so much information. But she was a lady, surely she wouldn't go making a fuss. All the same – 'If you was to give me the message, ma'am, I could see it got to him.'

'Thank you, no, I will go home and send one of my own footmen,' she said, and saw him relax. She found a coin in her reticule for the boy, who felt himself amply repaid for eavesdropping, and went back to the waiting cab. When she was inside, she spoke to the driver through the hatch. 'Take me to Dean's, if you please.' No point in going to Soho Square, since she didn't know what number, and in any case, he would probably have left by the time she got there. He must be meeting someone there, she supposed, and going on to the restaurant with them. 'Do you know Dean's?' she asked when the driver hesitated.

'Yes, ma'am, I know it,' the driver said. 'Are you sure you want to go there, ma'am? Why not let me take you home?'

'Do as I ask, or I shall find another cab.'

The driver shrugged, closed his hatch and drove on.

Shaftesbury Avenue was very bright and cheery, with lighted windows everywhere, chop-houses and cigar-divans, ale-houses and mysterious places with open doors and closed curtains. The road was thronged with traffic and the footways with people, and there was a smell of food, hanging in greasy wreaths on the moveless, stifling air. It was not yet dark, but an unnatural, yellowish dusk had fallen, making the gaslights seem bright as stars through the windows.

The hatch slid back. 'That's Dean's up ahead, ma'am. I can't get any closer by the kerb. But hadn't you better—'

'Wait,' she said. She let down the window halfway to look out, but she was almost as doubtful as the driver about the wisdom of getting out. At closer quarters, some of the people going by looked rather strange, and she had never walked about London alone before. She did not much want to have to thrust her way through the crowds and be jostled; and Dean's looked like a private house, with lights shining behind drawn curtains and a closed door which seemed to dare her to go up and knock. What could Oliver want with eating in a place like this? She supposed it was one of those things men did together, frequenting low places – she was sure this was a low place, though she had never seen one before – for the thrill of it.

Either I must go and knock or go home, she thought. Both possibilities seemed now impossible. To disturb him at his bachelor revels was unthinkable; to go home and spend the evening and the night wondering about his state of mind even more so.

The vehicle in front of them moved off, but before her driver could move forward, another cab dashed up and snatched the space, and he gave a curse which the other cabman returned with interest. 'Best let me take you home, miss,' Charlotte's driver said through the hatch. 'This ain't the place for the likes o' you.'

Charlotte opened her mouth to answer, without a clear idea of what she was going to say; when the door of the cab in front opened and a man stepped out. She knew him even before he turned. She would have known his back anywhere; she would have known any tiny part of him that had come in her view.

'Oliver,' she breathed, her heart squeezing painfully with love at the sight of him. Oh joy, she could catch him before he went in! She fumbled with the strap to let the window down.

289

He had turned back to his own cab to help someone out. The open door obscured the figure at first, but it was not a man. Charlotte paused, her fingers enquiringly still on the leather. Oliver was helping the woman out with a solicitous tenderness. His mother? Surely he would not bring his mother to a place like this? He slammed the cab door closed, his left hand still cradling the forearm of his companion, and at the same moment she turned towards him to say something, and Charlotte saw her full-face.

It was not his mother. It was not anyone Charlotte recognised: a handsome woman, in her thirties, dressed in the height of fashion, and with diamonds glinting at her ears. She said something, smiling at Oliver, and he laughed, and looked down at her and said something in reply. Then he took her right hand and slipped it under his left arm, and turned with her towards the restaurant. She was still talking, looking up at him with a gay, warm smile; the sort of smile you give someone you know very well, someone of whom you are very fond. Then Charlotte saw him press his arm in, squeezing her hand against his side. It was a little, intimate, affectionate gesture. He had done it to her many a time when they were walking together.

'Ma'am? What do you want to do?' the driver urged.

Charlotte drew herself back from the abyss she was staring into. 'Yes, take me home,' she said.

She got to her room without speaking to anyone, though Denton had looked a grave question at her. Norton was in her room.

'Oh my lady, I was so worried about you! Why – what's wrong?' she added as she saw Charlotte's face. Charlotte shook her head, unable to speak.

Fanny came through the communicating door. 'Did I hear Charlotte's voice? Ah, there you are! Where have you been? Denton's been in such a state, thinking he was going to have to tell Great Aunt Lucy he'd lost you.' She spoke gaily, until she, like Norton, caught sight of Charlotte's expression. Then she closed the door behind her, waved Norton quickly out of the room, and taking Charlotte's hand, led her to a chair.

'What is it? What's happened?'

Charlotte felt so tired, she could not bring herself to tell the whole story from the beginning. She didn't want to tell it to anyone, not ever. She wanted to sleep. She thought if she lay down she would sleep for days. But Fanny would not leave her alone without being told something.

'I saw Oliver – with a woman,' she managed to say.

Fanny looked at her keenly. 'A woman? A relative – a cousin, or a friend of his mother's, perhaps?'

'In Shaftesbury Avenue,' Charlotte said.

'It could have been anyone,' Fanny said, trying to sound reasonable. But that numb, sleepwalker's look told her what had happened.

'It wasn't just *anyone*.' Fanny hesitated, and Charlotte felt a fresh wave of pain. 'You know who it is, don't you? Tell me!'

Fanny sighed. 'It was probably Mrs Galbraith. Oh Charley, don't look like that! Oliver's a grown man, and gentlemen have to have their – their *needs* taken care of. It's all perfectly acceptable and quite discreet. Mrs Galbraith is a very decent, quiet, respectable woman—'

'Respectable?'

Fanny flushed a little. 'It's an arrangement that's understood by everyone. No-one minds it. No-one generally even knows. I only know her name because Tom, cousin Tom Weston I mean, happened to mention it in my hearing. He knows her because she's a friend of his, um, *friend*, Mrs Routledge. They have apartments in the same house in Soho Square.'

'Why did no-one tell me?' Charlotte asked dully.

291

'Tell you?' Fanny's eyebrow rose. 'Dearest old Charley, no-one talks about that sort of thing. It isn't done to notice it, and I beg you not to repeat anything I tell you – it wouldn't be thought proper at all. And in any case, why would you even want to know? As long as a gentleman is discreet, it's his own business and no-one else's.'

Charlotte was shocked. 'How can you say that? Do you tell me that if Tom Cavendish had a – a *friend* of that sort, you wouldn't mind?'

'He probably has,' Fanny said reasonably. 'I don't know about it, and I certainly mean never to find out.'

'But if you did?' Charlotte insisted.

Fanny shrugged. 'I don't see that it matters,' she said, with evident sincerity. 'It's what men do. They're not like us.'

Charlotte shook her head. It was as if Fanny were talking a foreign language: the words made no sense to her. She felt such a weight on her eyelids, as though sorrow were drawing her inexorably into sleep; and she wanted to follow. If only she could fall asleep and never wake up again, never have to feel this pain and bewilderment again.

The communicating door opened a crack and Fanny, looking distractedly, saw Tibbet's enquiring face. She waved her away with a frown. But something had to be done. Charlotte was evidently not in a state to go down to dinner, even had she been dressed.

'Look, I must go,' she said. 'I'll tell them you have a headache and won't be coming down. It will seem perfectly reasonable, with this ghastly weather – I'm sure you *have* a headache, anyway. And as soon as we leave the table I'll come up again and talk to you.'

'I'm all right, thank you,' Charlotte said, trying to rouse herself to be civil. 'Please just leave me alone. I need to think.'

'Of course you do – but don't brood, dearest. It's absolutely nothing to be upset about, truly.'

When Fanny was gone, Charlotte went and sat by the open window, her head aching in sympathy with her heart. She had never felt so alone. Oliver did not love her as she loved him, that was plain; if he did, he would not be carrying on an affair with another woman. She had seen how they looked at each other: it was not a mere transaction. There was a world of affection in those glances. And it was a regular, long-standing thing, such that even Fanny knew the woman's name. All the time he had been kissing her and declaring love for her (such kisses! and such declarations!) he had been going off in the dark like a tom-cat to see that woman. *That* was not love – not the sort of love she wanted, anyway.

Well, if he did not love her, he must be marrying her for her money after all, as his mother had said. His professions had been lies. He would think of them, probably, as gentlemanliness; but they were lies all the same. He had cheated her – they all had. Probably the others did not think of it as cheating; but *he* knew her. He *must* have known she believed him – but he went on deceiving her all the same; because he needed the money. Oh, that wretched, corrupting money! Gladly would she have given it to him! It was nothing but a curse to her, an evil cloud that fogged every issue and confused every good feeling. She had been happier when she was living in Chetton and working as the schoolmistress. She would give him her whole fortune now and gladly, not to have to marry him, and to live that terrible lie, to be his wife and not his lover.

If only it would rain! The unnatural dark was blending into real nightfall, the sunset hidden from view behind the low bank of sticky clouds. She leaned her elbows on the windowsill, and yearned for rain. Not London rain, black with soot, leaving streaks down buildings, spoiling clothes, turning the streets into quagmires of filth – rain in London was something to be dreaded. It was country rain, home rain she longed for, clean, refreshing, sweet, rustling in the trees and filling rivers to rushing; the sort of rain pigs stood out in, enjoying its cool drumming on their backs; the sort ducks bathed in, laughing with delight.

Some time later – she didn't know how long – the door opened softly, and Norton came in, came across to her, sat down on the window-seat facing her, a large, comfortable silence of sympathy. Charlotte lifted her head from her arms and looked at her.

'I know. Tibbet told me,' Norton said. Compassion made her bold. She reached out a hand and stroked Charlotte's hair. 'I know,' she said.

A cool breath came in at the window, moving the curtains – the cool air that runs before the rain. A moment later there was a splitting flash of lightning outside, a simultaneous crack of thunder. Charlotte sat up, removing her head from Norton's soothing hand. A drop of rain hit the windowsill, fat and soft, the size of a penny. Charlotte reached out a finger to touch it. A few more drops fell, and the smell of dust rose up from the pavement outside. That cold breath again, then another flash, and suddenly the heavens opened, and the rain fell as though a vast bucket had been upended. It bounced off the windowsill, wetting them; Norton recoiled a little, but Charlotte did not move. She heard the rain hissing on the street below, gurgling in the gutters above. A fitful, cold breeze pushed the sheets of rain this way then that, and the trees, invisible in the dark, shifted and whispered.

'Come away from the window, my lady,' Norton said at last. 'The carpet's getting soaked.'

The mood was broken, the delight dissolved and the misery rushed back in to fill the space.

'What am I to do?' she said.

Norton did not answer, recognising a rhetorical question when she heard one. She guided Charlotte gently away from the window, and shut it. Immediately the noise of the rain fell to a distant drumming. Charlotte stood where Norton had left her, in the middle of the room, her head slightly bent, her brow drawn with thought.

'I can't marry him,' she said aloud. The words were a revelation to her, crystallising amorphous feelings. It was true, she thought, I can't. The dream is over. Now I am awake, I can't marry him.

Norton looked sidelong at her, unsure how to handle it. Wedding nerves, she thought – and no wonder, with the Abbey and the Archbishop and all the fal-lal to face, poor girl, and her brought up so quiet.

'Well, you don't have to,' Norton said. 'No-one can make you.' If she didn't think she was being made to, she'd rediscover how much she wanted it – that was Norton's reasoning.

'Can't they?'

'Of course not. That's the law of the land.'

Charlotte stared about her, as if looking for something, but it was just a movement generated by the rapidity of her thoughts.

'I have no need to marry,' she said. 'I have my own fortune, I am of age, I can go anywhere and do anything.'

'Just so, miss,' Norton said hopefully. 'And what do you want to do?'

Norton did not get the answer she hoped for. 'I want to go home,' Charlotte said. The rain was slackening outside. The more violent the rainstorm, the less time it lasted, she thought. Perhaps that was true of love, too. Well, she would find out!

She looked up at last and met Norton's perplexed gaze.

'I'm going to go home,' she said. 'What a good thing I insisted on keeping it! Tarbush would have had me part with it. You must pack for me, Norton – none of the grand clothes, only the simplest things. I shall go first thing in the morning. But first fetch me some paper, would you? I have letters to write.'

'Yes, my lady,' Norton said, and fled the room. The family was in at dinner, she couldn't disturb them. What was she to do? Her lady would change her mind in the morning, surely – but suppose she sent letters first, said things that would be hard to take back? Norton felt responsible for her. She had to stop her ruining her life, if she could. She hesitated about the corridor for a few moments, and then went to the drawing-room to fetch the writing-paper. By the time the letters were written, probably the family would be out of the dining-room and she could ask to speak to her ladyship.

She expected the drawing-room to be empty, but Tom Weston was there, reading the newspaper, rather damp and curly about the hair.

'Oh! I beg your pardon, sir, I didn't know there was anyone here.'

'That's all right, Norton. I wasn't expected. I just dropped in to get out of the rain. What did you want?'

'Some writing-paper for my lady,' she said.

'Carry on, then.' Norton coughed, and Tom looked up again, to meet her anxious eyes. 'What is it? Is something wrong?'

'Oh, sir,' Norton cried. 'Can I speak to you in private?'

Charlotte called, 'Come in,' rather doubtfully. Norton would not knock, therefore it could only be an unwelcome intrusion. She was astonished to see Tom Weston, could not at all account for his being there.

'You are almost as wet as me,' he said by way of greeting. 'What have you been doing?'

'How did you get here?' Charlotte asked.

'There's a nice, warm greeting! I was in this part of Town when the rain came on, so I ran for shelter. You wouldn't have me drown, would you? I thought it was time I paid my respects anyway. I haven't seen any of you for a few days.'

Charlotte's eyes narrowed through this genial chatter. 'Norton sent you,' she concluded.

'My dear child, nobody sends me anywhere. But I did meet Norton on her errand, and she said she was worried about you. May I sit down, by the by? Thank you. Norton said you were thinking of leaving us.'

'Not thinking. I am going home tomorrow.'

Tom looked at her with his head slightly cocked. 'Charley, dear, what's wrong? Tell me about it. Maybe I can make it right.'

'Not now,' she said. She hadn't meant to tell him anything, but at the thought of his perfidy it burst out of her. 'Why didn't you tell me? You of all people! I thought you – you cared for me. Like a – brother, or uncle, or something. Why didn't you tell me?'

'Tell you *what*?'

'About Mrs Galbraith.'

'Oh,' Tom said thoughtfully.

'Is that all you have to say – oh?'

'It's unfortunate you found out about her,' Tom said, 'but—'

'Unfortunate?'

'My dear, there's no need for all this grief. It's a perfectly usual arrangement.'

'Usual for you, I know. Your – *mistress* is her friend.'

'Someone has been busy,' Tom said with wry amusement. 'My dear, I did warn you, as I recollect. I warned

297

you that Fleetwood is much older than you and had a life before he ever met you—'

'*Before*, yes! If I had learned that he had known a Mrs Galbraith in the past it wouldn't have troubled me – I'm not a simpleton. But she is not in the past, she is in the present. That's a different matter.'

'But Mrs Galbraith and her like inhabit another world from yours, a world which ought not to touch yours at any point. The fact that it apparently has some-how—'

'You don't think it matters,' she said with an effort at control.

He looked at her levelly. 'No. No, it doesn't.'

'You don't understand,' she said, turning away.

'*What* don't I understand? Charlotte, answer me! Let me help you.'

'There's nothing to say or do,' she said calmly. 'I thought – silly, ignorant girl that I am – that Oliver Fleetwood wanted to marry me because he loved me. But I find that what he really wanted me for was my fortune. I suppose everyone in London realised that, except me. Well, I made a mistake – but so did he. I don't have to marry anyone, and I don't have to part with my fortune in order to be respectable.'

'Is that what he said?' Tom exclaimed in disbelief.

'Not him – his mother.'

'Oh! But she is a very rude, unpleasant woman. You mustn't mind her tongue.'

'Why not? It's what everyone is thinking. But I don't care whether I am acceptable in their world or not. Don't you see, I don't need them. I only went to all the balls and so on to please Grandmama, because she said I must. But I have enough money to keep me for the rest of my life, and if I go away from London, it won't matter that I am the child of shame.'

Tom winced. 'No-one thinks that. You're not to say so.'

She looked at him wearily. 'I don't blame my mother any more. I am very fond of her, and I would never hurt her. But I don't have to marry a man who doesn't love me, and I'm not going to, not for anyone. I'm going home.'

'To – what's it called? Chatton?'

'Chetton.'

'Chetton. Charlotte, what about Mama? All the family? We all love you.'

She gave a very small smile. 'I dare say I shall come and see them sometimes. And you can come and see me – I know you're a great traveller.'

He looked at her, perplexed. 'You really mean to cancel the wedding?'

'It is cancelled, as of this minute. I shall write the letters as soon as Norton brings me the paper. Mr Tarbush will reimburse any expenses out of my estate – no-one shall be out of pocket. I am twenty-one, Tom, and no-one can stop me, or make me do anything I don't want.'

'You'll run away and leave Mama to face all the unpleasantness?'

She winced a little at that. 'She can leave everything to Tarbush to arrange. I'm sorry if it will be unpleasant, but if she goes out of Town no-one can bother her. She always does in the summer, anyway. She told me she was only here still because of the wedding.' He went on looking disapproving, and she added defiantly, 'Not even you can expect me to marry against my will, only to prevent the scandal.'

'Is it against your will, then?' he asked quietly. 'I thought you loved Fleetwood.'

She turned away. 'I'll get over it,' she said, so low that he barely heard her. 'You can't go on loving someone who doesn't love you.'

*　　*　　*

Some time after Tom had left her, Norton came in again, looking frightened. 'You really are going, my lady?'

Charlotte sighed. 'Don't you begin! Yes, really.'

Norton twisted her hands together. 'Take me with you!' she burst out. 'Oh my lady, please let me come with you!'

'I won't need a fine lady's maid where I'm going,' Charlotte said.

'You know I'm not a fine lady's maid. But I can sew, and make all your clothes for you. I can do housework – I don't mind what I do, really I don't. I can cook a bit, too. Oh please, my lady, don't send me away. I'll serve you any way you like, if you'll only take me with you.'

Charlotte was amazed at her vehemence, touched by her loyalty. 'I won't be living like a duchess, you know – not even like a countess.'

Norton almost smiled. 'Oh miss, how can you think I'd care? Besides,' she added shrewdly, 'once you were married, they wouldn't have let you keep me as your maid anyway. Didn't you know that? Me, a duchess's dresser? They wouldn't have stood for that. They wouldn't have let you keep me.'

Charlotte looked at her in silence for a long moment, her resolve slowly stiffening. It seemed to her she had been living half asleep, not to have realised how her life was being taken away from her and used up by other people. It would be different from now on. No-one was going to make her do things, or tell her she couldn't do things, or take things away from her, or determine how she lived. From now on, she would do what *she* wanted. She would make up her own mind, and live her own life. She wondered how she had borne it so long. She wondered why she hadn't told Lady Turnhouse exactly what she thought of her.

'Of course you can come with me, if you want to,' she said at last. 'We leave tomorrow morning, as soon as I have spoken to Mr Tarbush. But it's not luxurious there like this, you know.'

'You haven't seen the sort of places I've lived in,' Norton said. 'Oh miss – my lady – thank you!'

'It's not much to thank me for, as you'll find out,' Charlotte smiled. 'And call me "miss" if it comes more easily to you. *I* don't mind.'

CHAPTER FOURTEEN

Benedict and Rosalind went home at the end of May, immediately after the announcement of the engagement. They were invited to return for the wedding, something which could be contemplated now that the journey could be made in a forenoon. The railway now reached all the way from Euston Square in London to York (and indeed, beyond York to Darlington). Benedict never approached York by railway without a quickening of excitement, and pride that he had played a part in making it possible.

He let down his window and leaned out, eager for the first view, as they steamed slowly towards the arch which had been cut in York's city walls, to allow the railway through into the city's heart. The grand new station there had been built in January of 1841, handsomely covered with a decorative canopy supported by iron pillars. The best view of it, with the Minister soaring up behind it, was from the wall-walk, and there was always a knot of people leaning on the railings and gazing down at the trains huffing in and out. There was a lady with two small boys up there now, and Benedict waved to them light-heartedly, and they waved back.

Rosalind made a restless sound of disapproval, but he shut his mind to it – she had only a few more moments of the journey to endure. These were great days for the railway, he thought. George Hudson, whose energy and determination had made the whole thing possible, had not rested on his laurels after the opening of the York and

North Midland Railway. At that time a line from Leeds to Manchester was building – the first section was ready in 1840 – and with the opening of the Hull and Selby, it was possible to see how there would soon be connections all the way from Liverpool to Hull, west coast port to east coast port. Right from the beginning, while other men dared to think no farther than a twenty-mile railway in their own neighbourhood, Hudson had envisaged a great cross of railway routes laid over the map of Britain – Liverpool to Hull, London to Edinburgh – with the pivot point York, his beloved, his native city.

The difficulty was that a vital link in the horizontal arm of the cross was the Leeds and Selby Railway (on which Benedict had worked as engineer in his bachelor days), over which Hudson had no influence. It was a rival in the neighbourhood of York which he could not tolerate. Robert Stephenson, Benedict's former employer and mentor, was called into advise, an offer was made, and in November of 1840 the Leeds and Selby was leased to the York and North Midland, with an option to purchase. At once it was closed to passenger traffic. From then on, all the traffic to Hull from any direction had to pass over the York and North Midland lines.

The next project had been to the north. The Great North of England company, which had built the line between York and Darlington, had run out of money and could not continue with the more difficult northern section to Newcastle. Hudson, again with the help and advice of Robert Stephenson, came up with a new plan, to take the railway to Gateshead by renting existing 'coal lines', which would need only a small section of new line to be built. This Darlington to Newcastle extension was to open next month – June 1844. And Benedict firmly expected soon to be approached by Hudson with a plan for taking the line across the Tyne and onwards towards Edinburgh.

Meanwhile, the York to Scarborough line, with a branch to Pickering, had been approved in November 1843, and was already under way. This project was the darling of George Stephenson, Robert's father, who had been the engineer for the line from Pickering to Whitby, and like Hudson saw Whitby and Scarborough as future seaside resorts to rival Brighton.

Benedict was essential to Hudson's plans, not only because he was a trained engineer, who had worked with both Stephensons and was regarded by them as a friend, but because he was a wealthy man – and one moreover with a passion for railways. He advised, he liaised, and he dug into his pocket. Rosalind did not approve. She had suffered in earlier years from her father's foolish speculations, which had left her without the dowry needed to secure the husband she felt she deserved. Indeed, if Benedict had not fallen in love with her, she might have been unmarried still. She had hated pinching and scraping, and now was terrified that Benedict might squander his fortune on the railways and leave her destitute.

So she sighed disapprovingly as they steamed into York station, with her husband leaning out of the window like an excited child. Benedict glanced at her, with mingled pleasure and sadness. She was pretty, and always dressed with great care and in the height of fashion, so that she was a wife any man could be proud of having on his arm – if appearance was what he valued. He knew now that her prettiness was not all natural. The artifice was cleverly applied, but just at this moment, before they passed under the canopy of the station, the sunlight was streaming in at an unflattering angle, and he could actually see the maquillage which gave her such a smooth complexion, and such dark eyelashes for one so fair.

He wondered, indeed, whether she had always used it

– he had been too green and too much in love in the beginning to notice anything. But he had married her, freely and of his own will, and it was not her fault if he had invested her with qualities she did not have. Whatever she had done, she was his wife, and he must give her his loyalty; and though he did not love her, he had a last lingering of care for her, which would sooner see her happy than unhappy.

So he said, 'What is it? Do you see my gold all around you, waltzing out of my breeches pockets to fund madcap schemes?'

She flashed a cross look at him, gathering up her belongings as the train stopped. 'Why must it always be you that pays? The railway to London is useful to us, but to Scotland, and to Scarborough? That's madness.'

'You will like to go to Scarborough,' he said.

'I hate Scarborough. I had much sooner go to Brighton,' she retorted. 'And Scotland *is* foolishness,' she insisted. 'Nobody wants to go to Scotland.'

'But the Scots may want to come here, and spend their money in York, and make us rich.' He stepped down onto the platform and turned to take her hand.

'That's not why you are doing it,' she said shrewdly as she stepped down in a billow of skirts.

'Perhaps not,' Benedict said. 'Perhaps you must put that down as a grandiose dream. But a man must have his dream, if he is to be more than the beasts.'

'Ha!' she said scornfully. Two porters ran up smartly to deal with the luggage, seeing who it was – not just Mr Morland of Morland Place, but Mr Morland the director of the company that paid their wages.

'Ah, Harris, Johnson, good day to you. We are not being met, so we will need a cab,' Benedict said.

'Very good, sir.'

'My dear?' He offered his arm to Rosalind. 'Now I will

show you why it must always be me who pays – or helps to pay, at any rate.'

They stepped outside the station into what was becoming a familiar scene to all railway-travellers, a seething mass of traffic, cabs bringing passengers, cabs waiting in the hope of picking up a fare, carts and drays of all sizes loading and unloading goods, private vehicles waiting to collect their masters and mistresses and take them home. 'What do you see?' Benedict asked his lovely wife.

She made a face at him. 'Don't be tiresome, Mr Morland. I want to go home.'

'Horses,' he said, as though she had expressed interest. 'All these horse-drawn vehicles have one thing in common – they would not be here if it were not for the railway. And where does my gold come from – at least in part? What is the main crop which I sew and reap on my ancestral lands? Horses!'

She looked at him witheringly. 'I know that,' she said.

He pressed her hand against his side. He felt suddenly inordinately cheerful: home again, after far too long in London, which he had never liked, and about to see his children. 'My brother was against the railway,' he said, 'because he thought it would kill the horse trade. How wrong he was!'

They had lost the posting-trade, of course: coach-travel was all but dead; but in every other way, the horse trade was flourishing. More and more journeys were being made, more goods were being transported, and virtually every journey, passenger or freight, must begin and end with a horse. The railways themselves required horses, for drawing carriages in and out of sidings, for working the turntables, for hauling the coal – and who should get the contract for providing those draught animals but Mr Morland of Morland Place? Finally, though by no means least, the railways were bringing new trade and prosperity to York, and prosperous people bought more horses for themselves. He had orders for carriage pairs, saddle horses and hunters for a year ahead; and his racehorses were in growing demand.

He thought of all the effort and, yes, money that his brother had put into opposing the railway, and a familiar sadness clenched his heart. Nicky had been mad at the end: he had died raving the very day the railway opened. He had left the estate in a parlous condition, and the fortune of his ward Jemima Skelwith had disappeared without trace. Benedict had felt duty bound to restore both. Jemima would have forgiven the debt, had asked only for a competence; but Benedict furnished her with a handsome pension, and the promise of a capital sum by way of dowry if she wanted to marry. He had provided for Nicky's widow, too, and these arrangements had been a drain on his fortune, so he understood why Rosalind had been so nervous of his investments in the railways. But they had paid off handsomely, in the increased profit to his York businesses, and in horses. If Nicky had had the vision to see what Benedict had seen, things might have been very different for him.

The cab journey did not take long. Almost as soon as they were out of the city, they were on Morland land. Benedict leaned forward eagerly to look out of the window, to see the condition of his wheat, to catch a glimpse of some mares in a paddock near the road, to wonder whether his new plantation had grown. He had been away too long, though almost every day had seen some communication with his steward, Haxby. He was a good man – Benedict could not have contemplated a five weeks' absence otherwise – but having a good man was not the same as being there himself.

The cab jolted over a rut, and Benedict said, 'I must

do something about this road before the winter. As soon as the wheat is got in, I'll get the men onto it.'

'Winter!' Rosalind sighed.

He reached across to take her hand. 'It's a long way off yet. And winter has its pleasures too – balls, hunting—'

She pulled her hand away from him. 'Oh, don't!'

'What is it, Mrs Morland? Aren't you glad to be home again?'

'I don't see why you couldn't have left me in London. I was having such a nice time there. If you wanted to come back and see to your silly harvests and railways, why couldn't you come alone and leave me where I was happy?'

'You couldn't stay alone in a hotel,' he said, avoiding the thought that he could not have left her alone anywhere now. She didn't answer that. 'You enjoyed your time in London, didn't you?' he said kindly.

'Oh yes,' she said. 'One meets more interesting people there. And there's always something going on.'

'I was glad you enjoyed all the galleries and exhibitions so much. I was afraid you would be bored when I was occupied with business and couldn't attend you.'

She flung him a brief, distracted look. 'Oh! I could not be bored in London,' she said.

'But there's plenty to do in York,' he coaxed. 'And everyone goes out of London in the summer anyway, to the country.'

'The country!' she moaned. 'What is there to do in the country?'

'You can ride, and walk,' he said. She didn't answer. 'Won't you be pleased to see the children?'

She made a strange, equivocal face, and he left her alone. She was evidently in a mood to be pleased by nothing, and there was no point in annoying her. And there was Morland Place at last, shining in the sun, the light reflecting off the upper windows so that they looked like polished metal. Home! His heart quickened. He had spent so much of his life in exile from it, that every homecoming was special to him. Rosalind's discontent could not spoil the moment for him, but it took a little of the shine off it – a background discomfort, like being at some special celebration and finding your collar chafed.

The cab turned in under the barbican. Here was another job he had put off, which ought to be tackled this winter: the small apartment in the barbican (what had been the old guard rooms in more violent days) had been shut up when the previous occupant had left – Nicky's steward, that wicked man Ferrars. Nicky had not only locked the apartments, but had them boarded and nailed up, and Benedict had not yet got around to doing anything about them. But as Haxby was a bachelor, the barbican would make suitable quarters for him, and it would be useful to have him closer at hand. They would probably need quite a lot of work to make them comfortable, he thought, after being empty for five years, but Haxby was worth it.

And then the thought was pushed out of his head because they had pulled up in front of the great door, and he was home, really home. Benedict jumped out, and stood for a moment looking up at the white stone panel set in the brick above the door, carved with the family device, the white running hare. Time and the effects of wind and rain had worn the date at the top – 1450 – almost smooth, but the words *Deo Gratias* at the bottom were still sharp and clear. It was what Benedict always felt when he passed under his own lintel. The hare always looked to him as though it were smiling; he smiled back, saluting it in his heart, the lucky white hare of the Morlands.

Then he turned back to help his wife down, and a small

guilty wish rose in his heart, that he could be married to someone who would feel the same way about the white hare as he did. Malton, the butler, was in the open doorway to welcome them home, and Bendy's bitch, Kai, came forward bowing and yawning her delight, tail a-swing, so full of puppies that her sides squirmed.

'So she hasn't whelped yet! I'm glad I shall be here,' Benedict said, catching her head between his hands and rubbing her ears. 'It must be any day now.' She put a paw up over his forearm and sang.

'So I understand, sir,' Malton said. 'Mr Haxby tried to keep her in the kennels, so that she shouldn't have them in the house, but she whined all day and upset the other dogs, so he brought her back.'

'She knew I was coming home – didn't you, my girl? She shall have them where she pleases, Malton. A lady in an interesting condition is not to be crossed.'

'Oh, for heaven's sake!' Rosalind snapped. 'You are perfectly spoony on that dog. It is too revolting!'

'Welcome home, ma'am,' Malton said gravely, and Benedict shot him a glance, not having suspected his butler of a sense of humour.

And then in a thunder of feet, Mary arrived. 'Daddy, Daddy, I saw the cab from the window, I knew it was you! I ran all the way down, Miss Titchell said I could. You've been gone so long! I thought you were going to miss my birthday. I can jump the brook on Bodkin now, you must see me!'

Benedict unwound her passionate arms from his waist and lifted her up to kiss her. Her long golden ringlets were ink-dabbled as usual, and there was a smudge of it on her nose. Her muslin gown was a miniature of one of Rosalind's, with its long pointed waist and lace bertha, except that it ended at calf-length, revealing the frilled cotton drawers below. Miss Titchell grumbled that a

310

stout holland pinafore over a plain cotton frock would be more suitable for common occasions, but Rosalind's influence kept Mary looking like a plate from the *Journal des Demoiselles*.

'I wouldn't have missed your birthday for all the tea in China,' he said, kissing the inky nose.

'Is that a lot?' she enquired.

'More than a lot,' he said, and, seeing Rosalind's expression, put his daughter down before there was another comment about spoons. 'Say hello to your mother.'

Mary held her skirts out and curtseyed to Rosalind, and then spoiled the effect by grinning like an urchin. 'Didn't I do it nice, Mama? Oh, you do look pretty! Is that a new gown?'

Rosalind smiled and bent to kiss Mary's cheek. 'Yes. Do you like the colour? It's called *soupir du rose*. It would suit you. I thought you might like a gown in it to wear at your birthday.'

'Oh yes *please*, that would be lovely!' Mary cried. There was a moment of palpable affection between them. Despite her phenomenal intellect, Mary loved pretty clothes: she was her mother's daughter.

And now Rose appeared, holding the hand of the governess. Five years old, solidly made, almost as big as Mary, yet as different from her as could be: Rose stumped silently across the hall until she saw Kai, when she released herself and hurried forward, hands outstretched. Kai flattened her ears and backed away – Rose could be rough – and Miss Titchell called anxiously, 'Rose, don't you see Mama and Papa are here? Curtsey nicely to Mama and Papa!'

Rose made no sign of having heard her. Mary intercepted her, catching her arm and shaking it to attract her attention. 'Rose! Rosy! Look, see, Papa's come.' Rose tried to pull her arm away, and when Mary would not let it go, aimed a fierce blow at her head with the other arm. Mary ducked it expertly, shook her again, and used the captive arm to turn her so that she was facing her parents. 'Look, Rosy, look!'

Now Rose saw the legs, her gaze travelled up; and she suddenly burst into a most flattering smile, holding her arms out sideways in the gesture that asked to be picked up. All that was missing were the words. Benedict hoisted her up, marvelling at the weight of her – Mary had come up like a bird, but Rose felt dense, like a sandbag – kissed her and received a sloppy kiss on the cheek in return. He put her back to look at her, brushed the hair away from her forehead and exclaimed, 'What's happened to her eye? And where has she this lump from?'

'She bumped into the door, Papa,' Mary offered.

Miss Titchell came forward anxiously. 'The bump on the forehead she got yesterday, sir. She hit the frame of the nursery door instead of going through it. I don't know how she came to misjudge it so.'

'But her eye!' Benedict said. Rose's left eye was slewed into the corner, giving her a drunken look. 'What happened?'

Miss Titchell's hands twisted nervously. 'I don't know, sir. She woke like it this morning.'

'Have you sent for Holland?' Holland was the children's physician.

'Yes, sir, right away, but he hasn't come yet.'

Rosalind intervened. 'Probably because he thinks we are away. He'd come fast enough if he knew we were here. That man is insolent. I don't know why you go to him, Mr Morland.'

'Because he's a good doctor,' Benedict said distractedly.

'There are plenty better. But why didn't you call him yesterday, Titchell?'

312

Miss Titchell looked miserable. 'The accident didn't seem serious, ma'am. She didn't even cry, and it only raised a bump, as you see. You don't think—?'

'You should have called him,' Rosalind snapped. 'It is not for you to say whether an accident is serious or not.'

'I'm sorry, ma'am. But children are always bumping themselves, and I thought—'

Rosalind had turned away from her to Malton. 'Send someone at once to Holland. Find him, wherever he is, and tell him he is to come at once. At once, do you understand?'

'Yes, ma'am.'

Benedict felt the bump gently with his fingers. It was red but not large, and didn't seem to bother Rose. She was preoccupied with trying to get his pin out of his cravat. The slewed eye looked dreadful. Surely they must be connected? He removed Rose's fingers from the pin, which she had almost got loose, and felt a cold weight of worry settle in his stomach. Children were so vulnerable, and Rose had always seemed especially so.

'Is Rosy sick, Papa?' Mary asked in a small voice, reading his face.

'I don't think so,' he said, trying to sound unconcerned, 'but it is best to have Dr Holland come and see her, don't you think?'

'Oh yes, because he—' As she spoke, Mary stepped backwards, and as Kai was right behind her she trod on the dog's paw. Kai let out a shrill yelp which made all of them jump. All except Rose, that was. She was staring over Benedict's shoulder at nothing in particular, and did not move or look round. A new thought took hold of Benedict.

'Rose,' he said loudly. 'Rosy!' She did not look at him. He met Miss Titchell's eyes, and remembered how Rose had not heeded her or Mary until her arm

313

was taken. 'I don't think,' he said slowly, 'that she can hear me.'

Miss Titchell's frightened eyes said that she had thought the same thing, and hidden it from herself. Rosalind drew an impatient breath. 'Oh, what nonsense, of course she can hear you! She just doesn't please to. She's always been self-willed.'

Benedict shook his head at her, and put Rose down. She looked round straight away for Kai, and started towards her. Benedict moved round behind her and called her urgently, and then clapped his hands loudly, but she paid no heed, continuing to walk towards the steadily backing Kai. Mary called her too, shrilly, and then ran after her in distress, catching her arm. 'Rosy, Rosy, you *can* hear me, you *can*!' Rose turned at the touch, and then vented one of her dreadful, shattering shrieks of rage. Mary burst into tears and ran to Benedict, Miss Titchell rushed to take hold of Rose, and Rosalind cried, 'I can't bear any more of this. I'm going to my room,' and hurried away towards the stairs.

Holland came, and examined Rose at great length, carrying out various experiments to test her sight and hearing, though it was hard, since Rose did not speak, to be sure whether her responses, or lack of them, were from inability or unwillingness.

At last, however, and reluctantly, he pronounced that she was deaf.

'Completely?' Benedict asked, the cold weight in his stomach seeming to spread outwards toward his heart.

'I think perhaps not. The exact degree is hard to determine. It is possible some faint sounds reach her, or perhaps she feels the vibration in some way. If only she could answer questions, we would know more.'

'But – can anything be done?'

He knew the answer before Holland spoke, by the expression on his face. 'There seems to be no malformation of her ears, no sign of infection, no swelling. The difficulty, I fancy, lies elsewhere.'

'Where else is there?'

Holland tapped his forehead. 'The brain. Ah, if only we knew more about it. The greatest, the most mysterious organ in the body, the seat of all man's power, perhaps of his very soul! Our knowledge is only in its infancy, but in time I fancy we will discover that everything in the body is governed by it, one way or another. We do know already that the nerves from all the sensory organs lead to the brain, and have their area of influence there, and I fancy in the case of little Rose, if we could only look into it, we would find some fault or damage there.'

'The blow on the head she received yesterday?' Benedict said.

Holland shook his head. 'That, I fancy, was an effect, rather than a cause. Her governess and nurse tell me there have been some little clumsinesses, some signs of faulty balance; and together with the strabismus – the squint – and the deafness, and given her history – that is to say, her slowness in learning, her lack of coherent speech—'

'What? Don't beat about the bush, man. Tell me what you think!'

Holland's face was as long as a dark winter. 'I am very much afraid it may be a tumour of the brain.'

Benedict was silent. His tongue felt as though it were nailed to his jaw. He could not ask what he wanted to ask. At last he managed to croak, 'How – how would she have – how did it—?'

'If my diagnosis is correct, probably the condition has been developing for a very long time, even since birth perhaps. These things vary in the rate at which they grow, sometimes slowing down, sometimes speeding up.

315

I would imagine it has been a slow growth which has suddenly accelerated. It may slow down again, or even stop. On the other hand—'

'You mean, she will die?' The words lay stark between them. He wished them unsaid, as though he had given them power.

'I'm afraid there is no effective treatment,' Holland said gently.

'How long? How soon?'

'I cannot say. I would like her to be seen by a colleague of mine, who has more expertise in the area. He can confirm my diagnosis and give a more exact prognostication. I think – a year or so at best. A few months at worst.'

'But – good God, man—!'

'It is particularly difficult to predict in the case of a child, particularly a child who cannot answer questions. But I hope my colleague will be able to be more exact.'

'She will die?' Benedict said in a dazed fashion. Solid, red-faced Rose was so very real, present and alive, it was impossible to grasp the concept. Another thought caught him off guard. 'Does it hurt? Is she in pain?'

'No – which is a point in our favour. As a tumour grows, it exerts pressure on the tissue of the brain, which causes pain – headaches which grow more severe with time. She does not seem to suffer from headaches yet, which would suggest the tumour is still small.'

Benedict grasped at that. 'Then – you may be wrong? It may be something else?'

'It may. That is why I wish her to be seen by my colleague.' But Holland's face said he didn't think he was wrong.

The household moved in a state of shock through its routines as the weeks passed: the only person unaffected was Rose herself, who adjusted to her deafness so easily

Benedict suspected it had been coming on gradually for years. Probably, he thought, that was why she had never learned to talk. She became the centre of their world; every day, every thought revolved around her; the outside world almost ceased to exist. Benedict had business to attend to, but others took most of the weight from him, out of a love he had never realised he generated in others. Haxby ran the farms and stud; Kelton, his agent, and Harry Anstey, his friend and man of business, ran the other concerns; the servants kept visitors at bay, and ran the house with a quiet efficiency that could never have been acquired for money.

Harry and his wife Celia did visit, and Rosalind, who did not much like other women, was actually glad of Celia's unobtrusive sympathy. Celia knew something of a mother's pain: she had only one child, ten-year-old Arthur; a string of miscarriages had ended her hope of ever providing him with a companion. It was by Celia's recommendation that Benedict did not cancel the planned visit of Jemima and Nicky's widow Aglaea, who was Harry's sister. Jemima and Aglaea lived together in Scarborough, having become very fond of each other in the last years of Nicky's life. Aglaea painted watercolours, and Harry believed she would be famous one day, and had for some time been planning an exhibition of her work, if he could persuade her to it – Aglaea was very retiring. They usually came to stay for some weeks in the summer, and Benedict had been for putting them off, but Celia said, 'I think it would be better for Mrs Benedict to have the company.'

'Rosalind has never liked Aglaea,' Benedict said, too worn to be tactful.

'Nevertheless,' said gentle Celia, to whom this was not news, 'it will keep her mind off things to have someone else around the house – someone to keep up appearances for. And they will both be such a help when – if things get more difficult.'

Benedict understood. Aglaea and Jemima had nursed Nicky through his last illness and madness. Nothing would throw them off balance. So they came, and he was glad of them, and he thought Rosalind was too, in so far as she noticed them at all. It was hard to think of anything but Rose. Benedict did not attend the railway opening he had looked forward to; Kai's difficult whelping did not raise a moment's qualm in him; he and Rosalind did not see his horses win at the races; Mary's birthday passed almost unmarked; the news of Charlotte's extraordinary jilting of Fleetwood barely touched them.

For after that visit by Holland things moved with a dreadful rapidity, and before June was out it was plain that Rose's short life was drawing to its conclusion. The going was not hard at first. She enjoyed the extra attention she was given, especially being taken out riding by Benedict. He would hold her in front of him on the saddle on quiet old Tonnant, while Mary trotted anxiously alongside on her pony Bodkin, and together they roamed the estate for hours. At other times he and Mary took her for walks about the gardens, to feed the swans on the moat and the carp in the fishponds; they went to see the new foals up at Twelvetrees, to look at the pigs or the calves in the barns. Rose had always liked animals better than people, and she enjoyed the new sights. She had none of her rages while they were on their expeditions, and remained well, stout and cheerful in her silent world.

Rosalind did not come with them on these occasions. Sometimes she joined them when they walked in the gardens, but otherwise she seemed almost to avoid Rose. Benedict would catch her looking at the child with an expression he could not fathom – except that it was desperately unhappy. Mary, excused her lessons, dedicated every waking moment to her sister. There was no need to tell her that time was short – she seemed to know it by instinct. She was endlessly patient and tender with Rose; and with her mother, who seemed to find comfort in looking at Mary for whatever it was she saw in Rose.

But those days did not last, and they came to look on them as the good times. The deafness was followed by gradual blindness, and as the world closed her in, Rose reacted with bewilderment and rage. Locked in her dark and silent tower, she needed to have someone touch her all the time. Nurse and Titchell took turns in sitting up with her at night, for if she woke and there was no-one there, she screamed. In the daytime Mary guided her hands to objects, tried to keep her occupied; but even so, frustration and fear often reduced her to tears.

Her balance grew more and more uncertain, and soon her control over her limbs was so poor that she had to be carried everywhere. And then the headaches started, and there were no more moments of rest and pleasure, only the painful relief when exhausted sleep ended her crying for a while.

'For God's sake,' Benedict said over and over to Holland, 'can't you do something?' He hardly left the house any more, pacing about endlessly, making a hundred useless visits a day to the nursery, where he could do nothing but stand helplessly and watch the child. In the end, Rose simply lay and screamed, shut in an unimaginable nightmare, sightless, soundless – he could only pray also thoughtless. Holland gave her opiates, which at least stopped the shrieking for a little while, but when she was awake, there was nowhere in the house where you could not hear her. Benedict felt that her cries had soaked into the walls, like stains that would never be got out. When he slept, he heard her in his dreams.

Aglaea and Jemima were patient, tireless nurses; Harry

319

and Celia called often, though there was nothing they could do. Benedict asked them to take Rosalind out in the carriage, to get her away from the house for a little while, but she would not go. When alone with her, he tried to persuade her. 'It is bad for you to be shut up here all the time. I can't bear to see you suffering.'

She looked at him across an unbridgeable gulf. 'Who else should suffer? She is *my* child.'

Terrible as that time was, it did not last long. Perhaps the opiates hastened the end – if so, Benedict could not blame Holland or himself. Before the first leaves turned colour, Rose gave up her strong grip on life, and slipped away, leaving a silence so profound that it felt as though the world had stopped with her.

'It's better so,' Aglaea said to Benedict as he stood looking down at the wasted form in the nursery bed he had slept in himself as a child. 'She's out of her pain now, and you can go on with your life.'

'I don't know if I have the strength,' he said. 'I feel so tired.'

'Of course you do, but that will pass. You have to be strong. Rosalind needs you, and Mary.'

They buried Rose in the crypt amongst the Morlands of centuries past, and Benedict had an image of their loving arms receiving her and taking her off to Paradise. Mary cried, and then began to remake her life around the space left by her sister, helped by her lessons, and by kind Celia, who took her on outings and brought Arthur to play with her. Business of all sorts claimed Benedict, things that had been waiting for him, so that he felt he had opened a door against which snow had been piled in huge drifts.

But Rosalind remained sunk in the impenetrable gloom that had descended on her that first day at Morland Place. On the day after the funeral, Benedict had found her weeping inconsolably, and it had been an agony to him, for he had never seen her cry before – not with grief. He had not supposed she cared so much for her ungainly child. He tried to comfort her, but she drove him away almost savagely. She couldn't seem to bear him near her.

But that night as he lay sleeplessly, staring up at the canopy of his bed, listening to the sounds of the house, she came into his room. Ever since they first moved into Morland Place, she had slept apart from him, taking the blue room for her own, while he used the great bedchamber where the Master of Morland Place had always slept. She came up to his bed and stood looking down at him, shivering, though it was not cold.

'I can't sleep,' she said at last.

'Nor can I.'

'I keep hearing her.'

'I know.' He pulled back the covers. 'Get in.'

She hesitated a moment, but then she climbed in, and he took her in his arms. She was trembling like an exhausted horse. He stroked her hair, and she did not pull away for once. He kissed the crown of her head, and then her forehead, and he heard her catch her breath; she grew tense in his arms, but it was not, he sensed, aversion; it was almost as if she were listening for something.

'Rosalind,' he said. He smelled her perfume, and a warmth of tenderness lapped him. She moved in to his embrace. 'Darling, we have each other, and Mary. We have so much. We can make each other happy.' It sounded more like faith than assurance; but after such a long fast, his body was reacting to her nearness as his emotions were to her vulnerability.

She sighed – oh, such a sigh, as though toiling to the top of a steep hill she had found it was only the lowest slope of a mountain – and then she lifted her face to his, and put her lips against his, and he kissed her, listening for her response, wanting her agonisingly.

But he couldn't do it. At the last his body failed him. There was too much hurt between them for comfort as simple as this. She tried to help him, and that made it worse. In the end he stopped her, and said, 'It's no good. I wish I could, but I can't.'

She lay rigid in his arms. He wished he could see her face, to judge what she was feeling. 'I'm sorry,' she said at last.

'You've nothing to be sorry for,' he said, almost in surprise; and when she started to pull away, 'Don't go. At least stay and let me hold you. I can do that, if nothing else. We can comfort each other.'

'Oh, you cannot comfort me,' she said roughly, and pulled herself out of his arms, out of his bed. She stood looking down at him for a moment. 'You don't understand,' she said; and then she was gone.

Benedict lay aching in the darkness. He thought of going to her room, but hesitated to intrude if she wanted to be alone; and then he fell asleep without having decided.

He woke early, before sunrise, aroused by the grey light seeping in. He felt heavy and unrefreshed; and for a moment was aware only of a vague sense of impending disaster, before memory caught up with him, and the weight of misery tightened his chest. Rose was dead; and Rosalind had come to him, and he had been unable to comfort her.

Even as he thought it, the door of his room opened quietly, and she was there again, in her bed-gown and wrapper, her head bare and her golden hair loose around her shoulders. She closed the door and came over to him, holding her wrapper close about her. She looked pale, worn, much older than yesterday – hardly pretty at all. He was seeing her without her artifices for the first time, he realised, and he was shocked – not at how pale and sad and old she looked, but that she let him see her like that. It seemed ominous.

He struggled onto his elbow, and reached out a hand to take hers, but she pulled away. 'Oh, don't!' she said irritably. She sat heavily on the edge of the bed, far enough back to be out of his reach.

'Rosalind, what is it?' he asked gently. 'I'm sorry about last night.'

She looked at him with such infinite weariness that he felt like a child trying to comprehend the troubles of an adult. She seemed – she looked, too – much older than him. 'You're a fool,' she said, but without heat. 'You always were. Sometimes I've tried to hate you for it, but – oh God, what am I to do?' She put her hands up to her face, and knuckled her eyes as he had seen Mary do when she was tired. There was so much of her in Mary; it was one of the reasons he went on caring for her.

'Darling, we have to put our sorrow behind us. We both loved Rose—'

She dropped her hands abruptly. 'Why did you bury my child in the crypt?' she said fiercely.

'What?' He was utterly taken aback.

'You know she's not yours. She's not a Morland. Why did you put her in there with all your relatives?'

He rallied himself, though he felt sick with pain, as though there were a blade lodged in him, and he was afraid to pull it out. 'You are my wife. Mary and Rose are my children, they are Morlands, no matter who—' Impossible to finish that sentence.

She snatched it up. 'Yes, who, that is the whole point, isn't it? You are a fool! Why do you always have to be so kind and – oh, such a *gentleman*! I'm sick of your

323

politeness! I'm sick of seeing you treat the children like your own!'

'Rosalind,' he protested feebly, helpless to ward off the blows.

'I'm pregnant,' she said.

A vast silence fell around them. Benedict could almost hear Time pattering down like endless dust; and far, far away in another world the echo of Rose, screaming. He met Rosalind's eyes, and the fear and misery and anger he saw was too strong a mixture. 'Oh God,' he said. He thought of her visit to him last night – a pathetic attempt, was it, to make him think the child was his? It was what she had done before, he remembered only too well. It was one of the memories he tried to shut away.

But for three months Rose had been ill; their whole lives had been absorbed by Rose's pitiful decline. Had she gone out during that time and—? A hideous sickness flooded him at the thought, and he turned his face from her. 'Oh God!' he said again. 'While she was dying? How could you?'

She read his thought. 'Don't be a fool!' she said fiercely. 'For God's sake, what do you take me for?'

'Then – when?'

'In London, of course.' She sighed – a short sound almost of exasperation. 'Carlton was staying in London.'

Sir Carlton Miniott, baronet, of Ledston Park – her former lover (former?) and father, in so far as nature mattered, of Mary and Rose. 'Carlton?'

'We arranged it all,' she said briskly, not quite looking at him. 'He had lodgings in Kensington. While you were busy with your railway nonsense and your family affairs—'

'You didn't go to the exhibitions, then,' he said.

A look of scorn flitted across her face, and was quickly gone. 'We meant to be careful. We tried to be. But it

324

happened just the same. I knew straight away, when we got back here, but—'

He was thinking. She must be three months pregnant at least, perhaps four. Her attempt last night was foolish in the extreme, sign of her agitation of mind, for she was always so practical as a rule. But what a three months it must have been for her, what a torment she must have been in! Almost he pitied her.

And Miniott? He thought they had parted for ever. Miniott had promised to leave her alone, had gone abroad and shut up his house. Benedict had not feared from that quarter. She had been flirting with other men, and he had thought—

'When did he come back?'

'Come back?'

'From abroad.'

'He never went,' she said. She looked embarrassed at having to make the confession, and he supposed that at least was to her credit. 'He let Ledston Park and took a house in Askham under a false name. We had to be so careful. That was why—' She looked a little defiant. 'I had to stop you suspecting, so I – pretended to be interested in—' She flushed at his expression. 'Oh, don't look at me like that! I can't help it. It's your own fault, anyway. You shouldn't be so—'

'Always Miniott,' he interrupted, hardly hearing her. He looked at her flushed, miserable face. 'You must really love him,' he said gently. 'Why didn't you marry him when you had the chance?'

'I *never* had the chance,' she cried. 'He had no money, and Papa was—' She broke off. 'Oh God! What am I to do?'

But the question was, and they both knew it, what was Benedict to do? A weight of weariness and despair was over him; he looked at the tangle and wondered how it

325

could ever be unravelled. He didn't even want to try. Rose was dead. Another baby was on the way. Maybe the son he had wanted? But not his – any more than Mary was. Mary, his darling, his daughter, whom he loved consumingly, whom he had taken to his heart. Another child – a brother or sister for Mary. But it had been Miniott all the time. The connivance, the contrivance, the endless plotting and deceit just so that they could be together! If she loved him that much, how could he keep them apart? Why should he even want to? But she was his wife. Separation – divorce – the scandal – the pain – the public humiliation and agony. And what of Mary? How could he tell her the truth? Or the new baby? Not his. Miniott all the time.

Round and round his thoughts went, and the tangle had no end to take hold of. His fists clenched in an agony of frustration. He lifted them, not seeing Rosalind flinch, thinking he meant to hit her. '*Why have you done this to me?*' he cried out. But it was not her he was addressing; it was God.

CHAPTER FIFTEEN

Charlotte was walking along one of the marsh paths about half a mile from the house when she saw Tom coming towards her. They met beside a clump of osiers.

'Your housekeeper told me I would find you here,' he said. He studied her face. 'You did say you would always be glad to see me.'

'Oh, yes! But I wondered—'

Tom shook his head. 'No, I just wanted to see this marsh of yours, which exerts such an irresistible force that it draws you away from us.' He took her arm through his and turned with her towards the house. Around them the marsh was colourless under a mute sky, on a day neither hot nor cold, with little wind to move the clouds. 'Hmm,' he said.

Now Charlotte laughed. 'It *is* good to see you! Tell me, how is everyone?'

'Mama is gone back to Town in defiance of the world. Thalia is still sulking down at Wolvercote and predicting a life of close solitude for them all.'

'Oh Tom! I am so sorry for the trouble I caused them.'

'Which is nothing. Don't blame yourself, my dear – no-one else does, except for Thalia, and nobody takes any notice of what she thinks, not even my brother.' He looked at her curiously. 'You don't repent your decision, after three months of solitude?'

'No,' she said. 'I don't believe I belonged in that world.

And—' Still too painful to talk about Oliver's affections. She hadn't yet learned to stop loving him.

'I disagree with you,' he said lightly, 'but you know best what it is you want.'

'How is he?' she asked after a short struggle.

Tom kept on walking, his eyes on the horizon, to make it easier for her. 'You heard that his grandfather died?'

'No,' she said, 'I knew that he was ill again and that – that Mr Fleetwood had gone down to Ravendene, but—'

'He and Lady Turnhouse went, almost as soon as you left Town. If it hadn't been that several people saw the messenger, I dare say their departure would have been laid to your door as well. But the call was genuine enough. The old fellow rallied again, but they stayed with him, and it's as well they did, for he was carried off at last quite unexpectedly. So Fleetwood is now a duke.'

'I'm sorry,' Charlotte said gravely. She thought of the old duke and his kindness to her. *Thank God Oliver has chosen the right woman*, he had said. She hated to think that she had disappointed him. Had she hastened his end? And now Oliver had it all, Ravendene, the farms, the cottages, the house almost opposite her own in Pall Mall. And what would he do with it all? He had needed her money to bring it back to its former glory. What would he do without that? Why, find another heiress, she told herself quickly. 'Does he – what will he—?' She found it hard to find the right question. 'Does anyone know what he will do now – the new duke?'

'I have heard,' Tom said gravely, 'that the estate is more encumbered than he thought, and that he may think of selling some of it, only to reduce the debts. I believe there is not much which is not mortgaged, but even clearing a mortgage eases what income there is.'

'Perhaps he will marry someone else,' she said in a small voice.

'I dare say he might,' Tom said easily, 'if he can find one rich enough. There are girls enough still who would like to be a duchess, but now the game is known, their papas may have something to say about it. On the other hand, he might go into the army. That would be a way out for him. He'd look well in uniform, and judging from my nephew Titus's complaints, there is little enough danger of a war to get it dirty.'

Charlotte had nothing to say to that. She tried to harden her heart to Oliver's plight, but it was a senseless organ which still pined after him like a dumb beast without understanding.

Tom drew a deep breath and let it out slowly. 'I must say, it grows on one, your marsh. The air is wonderful after London and the railway; and the horizon is so far away. It made me feel dizzy at first, but now I feel as if my eyes are growing stronger, as if I'm gazing vast distances like a hawk.'

'Yes,' she said. 'That's what I love about it!'

'And are you contented here? I won't say happy, because I see how pale and thin you've grown.'

'I like to be here,' she said. 'I like the quietness and solitude. I don't want to go back to London – I never liked the crowds and the noise all around me. But—'

'Yes?' He stopped and looked at her.

'I am lonely,' she confessed with difficulty. 'I miss my family. I miss having someone to talk to. I miss Fanny.'

'Poor Fanny! I think she took your defection the hardest of all. She did so want to be your bridesmaid.'

'I feel so guilty that I was the cause of her own wedding being put off. I think Lady Cavendish was being nonsensical, but it doesn't alter the fact that it was my fault to begin with.'

'Lady Cavendish is, was, and always will be an ass. But Tom Cavendish shouldn't have allowed it to happen. Who told you about it?'

'Fanny wrote to me from Manchester,' Charlotte said. 'Reproachfully?'

'No, it was a very forgiving letter, everything considered. She said she didn't understand me, but if it really was something I couldn't bear, it was right for me to break off my engagement.'

'And it really was something you couldn't bear?' She nodded mutely. Tom sighed. 'I think perhaps you have shown us all something we should keep in mind. But marriages in your rank of society are rarely love-matches, you know.'

'That's why I've changed my rank in society. I'm plain Miss Meldon here, and can be as romantic and nonsensical as I please.'

'I'm glad to see this hasn't knocked all the mischief out of you,' Tom smiled. 'But, to be serious a moment, if you are lonely, why don't you come back. Oh, it needn't be to London,' he added quickly, seeing her refusal forming. 'You could stay at Wolvercote – or, well, perhaps not Wolvercote! But there are lots of nice, rural places just a stone's throw from London, and you are a very wealthy woman – you could buy yourself an estate if you wanted – or just a neat, comfortable house, with room enough for your family to come and visit. Why not?'

'I need to be here just now,' Charlotte said. 'I have to think, and this is the best place for thinking.'

'You don't mean to stay here for ever, then?'

'Probably not. But I must find out what I am to do with my life. I am sure the answer will come to me, if I am quiet long enough.'

'And meanwhile, you must continue to be lonely?'

She nodded, less certainly. 'But I have Ellen and

Norton, who are very kind to me. And for intellectual company, there is always Doctor Silk.'

Tom gave her a sidelong look. 'And it's for this doctor that you jilted a dukedom? He must be quite a fellow! I should like to meet him.'

Charlotte laughed. 'You shall, if you can stay long enough. Do you mean to rush away?'

'I shall certainly stay tonight – if you can find me a bed with dry sheets! And tomorrow, if there is food refined enough for my delicate palate.'

'Oh, I think I can satisfy both requirements,' she said. 'I have returned to my father's house, but I do not feel obliged to live by his spartan rules. And Ellen is a good cook, when she has the ingredients and enough appreciation. She's teaching Norton, too. It occupies their empty hours and gives them amusement, to concoct ever more refined delicacies for me. I'm afraid I often disappoint them, but you shall make it up to them, if you please, with a man's appetite.'

Ellen and Norton were well beforehand in their conclusions, and as soon as Tom had set off from the cottage to find his niece, they had gone into a frenzy of activity. Here was a golden opportunity to set their talents before a wider audience. Norton rushed off to the nearest farm in search of fat ducks, eggs, cream, and whatever might be had in the way of fruit and vegetables, while Ellen stoked up the fire, pored through her receipt books and conjured new combinations of sauces out of the recesses of her mind.

Tom did full justice to their efforts, and for once Charlotte also ate heartily, providing the women with an excuse for significant nods and whispers about the unnaturalness of a young woman's living in such retirement.

'How are things going with your school?' Tom asked after dinner, when they had withdrawn to the fire.

'Oh, you mustn't call it mine,' Charlotte said. 'I try to interfere as little as possible, for it put Mr Lovelace's nose dreadfully out of joint to have me suddenly come back a wealthy woman, when he was used to be the local benefactor! But the school is going well enough. The young woman they found for the teacher is very nice, and her education quite good enough for what these children are likely to learn. The difficulty is in finding the children to teach. We would like to expand the numbers, but those who would most benefit from being rescued from their ignorance are those least likely to be allowed by their parents. At eight years old they are all expected to earn their living, but amongst the lowest families they put them to work at five or even younger – as soon as they can walk well enough to get to the fields.'

'Doing what?'

'Stone picking and twitching are the most common activities. They go on all year, and it's generally considered children's work, though women do it too.'

'Twitching?' Tom queried with an amused face.

'Pulling up couch grass,' Charlotte elucidated. 'In fact,' she went on, on her own track, 'I am beginning to think that if we want to do these people good, education is not the place to start. Until they can earn more money, they can't allow their children the leisure for education. I am beginning to think that Doctor Silk is right, and that it's their health we can do most about.'

'Mama would approve of your interest in medical matters. When she was a little girl she wanted to be a doctor, and was dreadfully upset when she learned that females weren't allowed to be.'

Charlotte laughed. 'Grandmama wanted to be a doctor?'

'Didn't she tell you about it? Oh, I dare say she would have if she'd had time. Yes, she caught the passion from an old horse-doctor who came regularly to Morland Place. He'd been a ship's surgeon in his youth. She used to go and visit him in his caravan and drink at the fount of his wisdom. One day he gave her his old set of surgical instruments, and Mama took that as a sign from God, disguised herself as a boy, and ran away and joined the navy.'

Charlotte simply stared. 'You are joking me!'

'Not a bit,' Tom said, enjoying himself. 'It was wartime and the navy was desperate for surgeons, and Mama certainly knew more than most by then. She'd practised on horses, you see, and her old mentor had told her that it was all much easier on humans because they could tell you where it hurt.'

Charlotte shook her head, unable to take it in. 'It sounds like a fairy story.'

'It's quite true, I assure you. That's where Mama first met my father. He guessed from the beginning that she was a girl but didn't give her away. I expect that was why she fell in love with him in the first place.'

Charlotte blushed. 'I didn't—'

'Didn't?' Tom prompted.

'Know you – she – I thought you were adopted,' she managed at last, her face hot to the eyes.

'Well, so I was,' Tom said easily, 'by Papa Danby. But Mama is my real mother. Oh dear, have I shocked you? Poor Charley, the world is very hard for you to bear, isn't it? But it rather puts your little scandal into perspective, doesn't it? Your grandmother behaved far more outrageously than you have.'

'Don't laugh at me.'

'I'm not laughing at you, dearest. But you must try to harden your shell a little, if you mean to help the poorer sort. Things are much more irregular amongst them even than amongst us.'

Charlotte knew that was true. 'Tell me about your father,' she said.

'He was a sea-officer, respectable and educated, but without means other than what he earned through his career. They met, as I mentioned, when Mama joined his ship in her ludicrous disguise. Then when she was forcibly rescued and taken home, she was married to Lord Aylesbury to cover up the scandal. Oh, there's no need to look so blue. She and Aylesbury liked each other well enough, in a brother-and-sisterly sort of way, and Mama was quite happy. Later she met my father again, and fell in love. Aylesbury knew all about it, and once she had given him his heir he didn't mind as long as they were discreet – he had his own separate life from hers. It was quite a usual arrangement. When I came along, however, circumstances made it impossible for him to acknowledge me, so Mama had to farm me out. Later when both my father and Aylesbury were dead, she brought me back to live with her; and when she married Papa Danby, he adopted me to make it all above-board. That's all there is to tell, really.'

'How did he die?' she asked, not knowing what to say about the other side of it.

'He was killed at Trafalgar – a hero's death. He left a small fortune behind him – his accumulated prize-money – which is enough to keep me respectable. My only sadness is that I never saw him, or even a likeness of him. But Mama says I am very like him in looks. *Si monumentum requiris* – in my case, look in the glass!'

Charlotte reflected for a while. 'I had begun to guess,' she said at last, 'that perhaps you were Grandmama's own – but I could not fit it together in my mind. What a world it is.'

'Do you think badly of her now?'

'Oh, no! What other people do before you know them doesn't change what they are to you, does it? I had to learn that about my own mother.'

'You are a brave girl,' Tom said.

'It's what people do after you know them that matters,' she went on. 'That's what you judge them on.'

'Yes, I suppose you do,' Tom said. 'I can't say I have ever minded much what people do.'

'But that's because you've never loved anyone very much, isn't it?'

Tom looked uncomfortable. 'Don't start being shrewd about me, or I shall have to change the subject. No-one takes me seriously, I assure you – not even me.'

'I do,' she said. 'You may joke all you like, but you came looking for me when I was lost, and I don't forget that. I wish you were happy.'

'I'm happy enough,' he said lightly.

'For you, perhaps, but not for me,' she said.

Before he left, Tom met the doctor, and they took an instant liking to each other, and came to a secret understanding that Doctor Silk would contact Tom if ever Charlotte were in trouble or unhappy in any way that Tom could remedy. Tom went away privately convinced that a few more weeks of solitude would have her packing her bags and returning to civilisation – particularly after Silk described to him what winter was like on the marsh. Charlotte parted with him reluctantly, and in the immediate reaction to his absence came close to proving him right. But he had not taken into his calculation the fact that she had lived many years in this place, and was used to the quietness. And he could not be aware, because even Charlotte was not, how great a shock to her system her time in London and its abrupt ending had been. She

335

was still enough of a convalescent not to need much in the way of diversion.

Shortly after Tom left, something occurred to give her enough to think about to keep her mind from fretting after what might have been. Charlotte had been aware of the agricultural gangs only as something that the servants talked about in hushed voices. She heard that the mixed gangs were notorious for their unlicensed behaviour, that the men were unlettered and violent, the women coarse and as foul-mouthed as the men; that all were steeped in immorality and immodesty, and moved from place to place like gypsies as the work demanded, descending on a village from nowhere, throwing the respectable housewives into a tizzy, and disappearing again when the work was done.

But now the phenomenon was brought to her closer attention. A large, neglected farm at the edge of the village changed hands on the death of its owner, and the new incumbent, a vigorous young man, threw himself into making the land bear a profit. The railways were coming: the line from Norwich to Yarmouth had been opened in April of that year, and next year, 1845, the line connecting Norwich to London was due to be finished. The railway would open up new markets, particularly for seasonal foodstuffs. Instead of just the traditional taties, carrots, and mangold wurzels, this remarkable new owner meant to grow peas, beans, strawberries, currants – even asparagus and raspberries, if reports were true.

The first job, however, was to clear the land, and he got in a large gang to do the work. Charlotte, on one of her walks, passed round the margin of one of his fields, and saw a flock of them picking stones and weeds. It was a misnomer for Ellen to have called them gypsies, she thought, for in the stories and songs gypsies were always dashing, beautiful and gay, so much so that high-born ladies and gentlemen fell in love and ran away with them. These draggled, dirty creatures were not beautiful or gay. Their clothes were coarse and muddied, their faces lined, weather-worn, toothless, ugly. The younger ones seemed strong and vigorous, but the older ones were like scarecrows, and the children in the field tugged her heart with pity: they worked bent double, their faces to the earth, never looking up, no speech or laughter or play about them, aged before their time, apathetic.

As she passed, one or two of the women looked up from their work. One was a youngish woman near the field edge, straddling with her feet bare in the earth, her skirt tucked up to expose her legs up to the thighs, the great swelling of her pregnant belly hanging down between her and her work. She met Charlotte's eye boldly, and Charlotte blushed with shame and pity that a woman in such a condition should have to work like that; but her blush seemed to amuse the woman, and she straightened her back, holding one hand to it, and shouted something to her companions. The accent was too broad for Charlotte to understand it, and by the cackles it prompted, its meaning was probably too broad as well.

Later she called on Doctor Silk, and mentioned the gang, in particular the woman who was so very pregnant.

'It is a problem,' he acknowledged. 'If they don't work, they don't eat, so they cannot stay away when they're big with child.'

'But won't their men take care of them?' Charlotte asked. 'Surely her husband should work to keep her until she's delivered?'

Doctor Silk looked at her doubtfully, wondering what it was proper to say; but he respected intellect above all things, and if Charlotte cared enough to ask the question, he felt she deserved an honest answer.

'She probably isn't married. She may not even know who the father is,' he said, and seeing that Charlotte was more interested than shocked, he went on. 'The gang you saw is an itinerant one. They are the worst sort. The gangmaster gets together a band of men and women, with their children, and walks them from contract to contract. They have no permanent homes. They sleep wherever the work is – in a barn or shed in the winter, but in the summer sometimes wherever they can get shelter – a haystack or ditch. So of course the kind of people he employs are the lowest and most hopeless. And shut up all together in a barn at night, the inevitable happens.'

Charlotte said, 'I'd heard that the gangers were im- moral—'

Silk interrupted her with a shake of the head. 'Ah, you mustn't mind what the pious say of agricultural workers. Most of them are decent enough creatures, doing as well in their circumstances as anyone could. The fact is that some respectable housewife of the middling sort sees a woman in the fields with her skirt tucked up, and assumes that anyone so immodest as to bare her legs must have no morals at all. And again, when they are working out in these big fields from dawn to dusk, they have to answer the call of nature when it comes upon them, and frequently there is no cover, no hedge or even a meagre bush. Your respectable housewife can't imagine herself doing what must be done in an open field, so concludes that they are lost to all decency.'

'I see.'

'Do you?'

'Yes, of course. If I were working in a muddy field and had no way of washing my clothes, I would tuck up my skirts to try and keep them clean.'

'God bless you for your imagination,' Silk said with a smile.

'But that woman I saw—?'

'Well, as I said, that sort of gang is different. They work, live and sleep all together, and the women have little protection against the men, especially the gangmaster – who is generally a man of bad character, or he would get some other employment. Women like the one you saw come to regard pregnancy as an inevitable nuisance, like rheumatism or blisters. Having children is a trouble to them. They avoid it when they can, and put up with it when they can't. Few of their babies survive,' he added non-committally. 'It's a scandal; but perhaps it's just as well.'

After this conversation, Charlotte took more interest in the gangs. The local gangers usually worked in much smaller groups than the itinerants. They lived at home, and walked to whatever work their gangmaster could get them in the vicinity. This might mean a walk of anything up to eight miles each way, a dreadful addition to a day's hard labour; but in this sparsely populated part of the world settlements were far apart. Living at home, and therefore limited as to the area they could cover, these gangers could not be sure of continuous employment, though even in the depth of winter there was generally some work: stone-picking and twitching went on all year round, and once the root crops were in there was 'trimming' to be had – scraping and cutting the earth and fibres from the roots before they were stored. In the area of Chetton there was also reed-cutting and carrying; and when the hard weather came ice formed on the dykes and pools, which was cut in thin sheets and sold to the smacksmen of Yarmouth and Lowestoft.

The local gangers kept up a kind of respectability, for all the bare legs and squatting in the open to relieve themselves might suggest to the prudish. But the itinerant gang was the one by which the others were judged, fairly or unfairly. Charlotte's next contact with a member of it happened about a month later. She was walking home when she saw a ganger woman kneeling by a clump of gorse a little way from the path. Thinking the woman might be ill, she approached quietly, and when she got nearer, she heard the thin, faint wail of a crying baby.

'What's the matter? Can I help you?' she asked.

The woman started violently and leaped to her feet. 'Lord Jesus!' she gasped, staring at Charlotte wide-eyed. 'You frit me.'

'I'm sorry, I didn't mean to startle you. I thought you must be ill,' Charlotte said.

The woman made some muttered reply, looking away over her shoulder as though seeking escape. She was a strong-looking creature, though gaunt and unkempt, and distressingly lacking in teeth; barefoot, dressed in a gown of thick brown cloth, much muddied about the hem, and a heavy shawl fastened crosswise over her upper body. Charlotte saw that the wailing came from a baby wrapped in a piece of cloth that was lying amongst the roots under the gorse. 'Don't be afraid,' she said. 'I want to help you. Is your baby ill? It sounds it, poor little thing.'

The woman looked at her a moment, and then down at the infant, and then at Charlotte again. She seemed to be calculating – whether or not to trust her, Charlotte supposed. 'That woant eat, miss,' she said at last. 'Not whatever. Tes as sick's a cat, poor beggar.'

'But then you must take it to a doctor,' Charlotte said.

The woman cocked her head slightly. 'Hent got no money f'ra doctor,' she said, fixing her eyes on Charlotte's face. 'Doctors cost dear, miss.' Her hand crept slightly outwards, turning at the wrist almost of its own accord, so that the palm was uppermost.

Charlotte didn't notice the hand. The baby's crying was

thin and desperate, not the lusty cry of a healthy infant, and she found it hard to bear. 'I have a friend who is a doctor,' she said, frowning. 'If you come with me, I'll take you to him. It isn't far. There will be no charge to you, I promise you. He is a good, gentle man, and he will see what can be done for your baby.'

The woman looked strangely disappointed. 'Can't do northin' for un,' she said almost sulkily, putting out her bare, dirty foot and stirring the baby ungently with it.

'Yes, yes he will know what to do for it,' Charlotte said. 'He is very clever, I assure you. Oh, do pick it up, poor little thing! It must be cold lying on the ground like that.'

Reluctantly the woman stooped and picked up the baby and tucked it under her arm, and followed Charlotte along the path towards the village. She seemed inclined to trail behind, and Charlotte had continually to look back and encourage her. She was afraid of being a nuisance, Charlotte thought; or perhaps afraid that this contact with the 'gentry-folk' would rebound against her, cost her money or get her clapped in gaol.

When they got to the doctor's gate, the woman shrank back and planted her feet in the mud of the street, looking very determined. 'I can't go in there, miss.'

Charlotte said gently, 'Don't be afraid, the doctor is very kind. I promise he won't be angry with you. He'll be very glad to help the poor baby.'

The woman thrust it abruptly forward. '*You* take un, then, miss.' And seeing Charlotte look doubtful, she added, 'Lord, I can't go in there. I hent fit f'ra gentry-house.'

Charlotte could not argue with her there. She shrugged and held out her hands. 'Very well, then. Tell me exactly what is wrong with it.'

'Sick, that's all. Woant eat. Tried it with everthun, but

341

that woant,' the woman said, passing the bundle quickly, as if afraid Charlotte would change her mind. Charlotte took it. It seemed very light, wrapped in a dirty piece of green cloth, and it wailed faintly and wearily, staring up at her with milky, unseeing eyes out of a face as shrivelled as an old apple. Given the rankness of its mother, she had thought it would smell, but it didn't.

'Wait here then,' she said. 'I shan't be long.' And she walked up the path and rang at the doorbell. In a moment she was past the surprised Martha and in the doctor's front parlour, and the doctor himself was rising from his chair by the fire, putting aside his book.

'What have you there, my dear? Where did you find it?'

Charlotte handed over the baby, grateful for his calm intelligence. She explained the situation in a few words. 'The mother was so worried, I knew you wouldn't mind if I brought it here. I hope you will be able to help it. She's waiting outside.'

Doctor Silk unwrapped the piece of cloth and laid the baby – a girl – on the table. He examined it carefully and palpated its abdomen. 'You say the mother's outside?'

'Yes. She wouldn't come in because she's so rough and dirty. Do you know what's wrong with it?'

'I think I do,' he said, with a sour expression. 'Come with me to the kitchen, will you?' He folded the cloth round the grizzling infant and led the way. 'Martha,' he said, 'just put a little milk in a cup and add a spoonful of hot water, will you?'

Martha, her eyes and back eloquent, obeyed him in silence. The doctor took the cup and sat with the baby on his lap, dipped two fingers into the milk, and put them to the baby's lips. The baby seized them avidly, and even from where she was standing Charlotte could hear the frantic sucking. The doctor extricated his fingers, dipped, offered them again.

'It's hungry,' Charlotte said, surprised.

'That's right,' said Silk.

Martha sighed disapprovingly. 'Best let me do that, sir.' Silk handed over the job without demur, and watched her in silence for a moment.

'But she said it wouldn't eat,' Charlotte said. 'Do you mean there is nothing wrong with it but hunger?'

'Just that,' Silk said. 'Its stomach and intestines are quite empty.' He put a hand on Charlotte's shoulder and guided her out into the hallway. 'Shall we call the woman in?'

Charlotte opened the front door and looked out. The road beyond the gate was empty. 'She's gone.'

'Yes, I rather thought she might be,' Silk said. 'Do you remember, my dear, that I told you these women look upon pregnancy and childbirth as a nuisance? When they find themselves with child, they try to bring about a miscarriage, if they can—'

'How?' Charlotte asked bluntly.

'Oh, there are ways. Slippery elm is a favourite remedy. But I don't think I should discuss that with you. Of course, more often than not they fail – nature is a great survivor – but when they *are* obliged to bring a living child into the world, the child stands a very poor chance. Infanticide is regarded as a sin and a crime amongst people of our rank; to these women it is a shrugging matter.'

'Infanticide?' Charlotte was shocked now.

He nodded gravely. 'Sometimes they smother them; sometimes expose them – that's a quick end in the winter. But most often they just don't feed them. In any case, the women rarely have any milk, working as they do and generally undernourished themselves. What was the woman doing when you first saw her?'

343

'She was crouched down by a gorse clump. I thought she was sheltering with the baby,' Charlotte said. 'You think—?'

'Yes,' said Silk. 'Probably she was abandoning it.'

Charlotte was silent for a moment, as shocked by the circumstances that could drive a woman to such heartlessness, as about the heartlessness itself. 'What will happen now?' she asked.

'We must try and find the woman, I suppose,' Silk said with a sigh at the thought of so much effort. 'Would you know her again, do you suppose?'

'Yes, I think so,' Charlotte said. 'I'm sure I would.'

'But?'

'But – I was thinking, if we make her take the baby back, won't she do the same thing again?'

'I dare say she will. If not in this parish, in the next, or on the road in between. I'm afraid that particular infant has a small chance of survival.' He looked at her, concealing a faint smile, able to follow her thoughts without difficulty. 'You would like another solution?'

'Could not a home be found for it?'

'For a ganger's brat? Who would take it in? Who would want it?' He shook his head. 'No, it would have to go to the workhouse – and there would be an end in no time. Better for the child, perhaps, if you had not come along when you did.'

'Oh, no, don't say that,' Charlotte said. 'My coming along must have been intended. It wasn't meant to die under a bush.'

'My dear, one must be practical. It's an unwanted baby. It was unwanted from the moment it was conceived. If its mother doesn't take it back, it must go to the workhouse.'

Charlotte thought of what Norton had told her about the workhouse. Well, she had survived it, and had grown

344

up to lead a happy and useful life. All the same, it was not the home she would willingly send anyone to, and she felt a sort of attachment to this infant, as if they were connected in some essential way. 'Suppose I take it in?' she said at last.

Silk burst out laughing. 'Oh my dear!'

She felt her jaw harden. 'What is so very funny about that? I have money enough. Why shouldn't I give it a home? *Her*, I should say. We must stop calling her "it".'

'I think you would do well to consult your domestics before you introduce a ganger's bastard into their midst! I'd love to be present when you brought it in and placed it in their laps! Well, well,' he said, his laughter subsiding, 'I suppose it might be possible to find a cottage family to take it in, if they were paid well. Certainly no-one will do it for nothing.'

Charlotte had to admit that seemed like a better solution. 'How much do you think they would want?'

'A shilling or eighteenpence a week would do it,' Silk said. 'That would be enough to make a great difference to a poor family. And they had better be pretty poor. You would do the child no service by trying to raise it out of its native stratum.'

'But I want her to be well-treated.'

'I think you can safely leave it to me. I will find a suitable family for you. Eighteenpence a week, let's say, and a sum of money in cash – ten pounds, say – when the child reaches ten years old. That will be an inducement to them to take good care of it.'

Charlotte saw the sense of that. 'I should like to approve them myself before it is all settled. And I shall want to see the child from time to time. And you can tell them that I will give them a gift of money every year – at Christmas, say – if she seems well and happy.'

Silk looked amused. 'If you mean to get so involved in

the business, you will thrill the neighbourhood beyond measure.'

'Why so?'

'You left London with great suddenness and secluded yourself down here. Can't you imagine what will be said if you now produce a mysterious baby and display a deep concern for its welfare? It will be too good a titbit of news for anyone to keep to herself. Before you know where you are, her ladyship's baby will be the talk of London.'

'Oh,' said Charlotte, discomposed. She thought of the gossip and speculation; she thought of Oliver. Then she straightened her shoulders. 'I can't help it. I must do what I think right, and the world must construe as it will.'

'It will certainly do that. Very well, my dear, you shall be as involved as you like. I'll look for a suitable family, and Martha shall keep it in the mean time. I can only hope she doesn't give me notice. But I must advise you not to go rescuing any more brats. Once the ganger-women discovered a market for them, I fear you would be rather encouraging immorality than otherwise.'

They had, of course, first to look for the ganger woman, but no trace was found of her, and none of the other gangers seemed to know who they were talking about. Doctor Silk suspected a natural closing of ranks against the gentry, whose interference they perceived as always causing them trouble. The gangmaster denied employing any woman who had recently given birth, and assured them that all his employees were present and correct, and Charlotte could only suppose that the woman had put as much road as possible between herself and her unwanted infant, and gone to join another gang somewhere else. She hoped she had not unwittingly caused her hardship; though it was shocking to abandon a baby, and the woman had appeared to show no remorse, she couldn't condemn her, her imagination telling her she might not have done any better in the same circumstances.

A family in Earl Chetton, five miles away on the other side of the marsh, was found to take in the baby – Doctor Silk thought it was better to place it at a little distance, rather than where Charlotte was so well known as in Chetton Farthing or Chetton St Peter. Their name was Boggis. The father was a labourer who did field work from March to September, and, like many others in the area, went off after the harvest to Lowestoft or Yarmouth to take employment on the fishing boats. The herring season lasted from Michaelmas to December, and most of the herring crews were farm labourers. This year, however, Boggis had missed being taken on to the boats because of ill health, and was now eking out the year with whatever piece work he could get, ditching, reed-cutting and cutting wood for the smoke-houses.

They had three small children of their own, two boys and a girl, and would be glad of a regular income of any sort, even a few pence for looking after a baby, which they could depend on week in and week out. Charlotte judged, therefore, that they would take very good care of the baby that was to generate this income.

Despite Doctor Silk's advice, she insisted she must see where the baby was placed, so he took her along there one day in his trap. It was a very low place, and Charlotte, who had been imagining something much more agreeable, would have demurred, had Silk not pointed out to her that it was still a great step up for a ganger's abandoned bastard. But she liked the Boggises, who seemed honest and anxious to do right, despite their hideous embarrassment at finding a lady in their hovel (though Silk introduced her as Miss Meldon, feeling her title would do no-one any good in the circumstances). Charlotte decided eighteenpence was too little, and promised them

347

two shillings a week, with a review when the child was older and more expensive, besides an immediate present of five pounds to provide necessities by way of a cot and clothing and a Christening for the baby. The latter sum almost overwhelmed the couple, and Mrs Boggis wept with gratitude, and promised nothing should ever hurt miss's baby, if she had to lay down her life for it.

'You will thank me in the best way possible if you treat the child kindly and bring her up a Christian,' Charlotte said.

'We will, miss, we will,' Boggis assured her fervently. As they were leaving, he called out to her, 'Oh, by the by, miss, if we are to have her kirsted, what name should it be by?'

Charlotte hadn't thought of that, and was startled. For a moment her mind was blank. 'What are your other children called?'

'James, George and Mary, miss.'

Good regal names, Charlotte thought. What other queens had there been in England? Matilda? Victoria? No, perhaps not. 'Call her Elizabeth,' she said.

CHAPTER SIXTEEN

The morning was as clear and limpidly sunny as June under a sky like polished crystal, and the trees were still green; but the air was sharp, and there was a smell of melancholy which belonged to October. The grass was heavy with a dew as cold as melt water; in the distance it refracted the low sunlight dazzlingly, so that a whole meadow was sewn with gold discs and sequins, a length of fabric fit for a gypsy princess. The bushes which grew alongside the path were thick with the webs of those large, soft spiders who take up residence in autumn, and the webs were hung too with pearls of the dew. It was a fresh, chilly, beautiful, sorrowful sort of morning.

Benedict had gone out early, meaning to walk up to the Bachelor Hill paddock and look at some mares who were running there, but the sad enchantment of the day had distracted him, and he was idling along like a boy on holiday, with Kai, glad to be free of those troublesome puppies, questing nose-down now in front, now far behind him. He picked a blackberry and put it in his mouth, but spat it out again. The Devil spits on them in October, his father used to say. He paused for a moment to notice the bizarre beauty of a hogweed's seed head, stuck up starkly above the bushes and draped in cobweb like spindrift. Further on, here was a flattish stone by the path, on which fragments of snail shell lay like the remnants of a sacrifice. Thrush's altar, he thought. It was supposed to be unlucky to disturb them – thrushes,

349

like hares, were witch-people. The elders had been almost stripped of their berries: it would be a cold winter, he fancied.

The path turned away from the bushes and started uphill a little. He knew why he was noticing everything so sharply this morning: it was his mind's attempt to avoid what it ought to be thinking about. But he could not delay any longer. The problem would have to be faced, the decision made. Rosalind's pregnancy had not been announced, but the servants must know about it by now, and what the servants knew was soon common knowledge. He had begun, without realising it, to avoid going into York, in case anyone should accost him and offer congratulations. He had no mind for society anyway, and poor Rose's death prevented anyone's issuing invitations or making calls. Harry had come once, without Celia, on business, and Benedict had seen him alone in the steward's room, where his state of abstraction had needed no explanation to his friend. Jemima and Aglaea had gone back to Scarborough taking Mary with them for a change of air and scene. There was nothing to distract him but his unwillingness to face his own thoughts.

He came to a junction in the path, where the track joined it that led away over the moor to Askham. Kai had gone on towards Bachelor Hill, knowing perfectly well where they were heading, but Benedict paused to look down the track, wondering painfully how often Rosalind had ridden that way; and as if on cue he saw a horseman in the distance, coming towards him. He did not recognise the horse, but he knew who wore that greyish beaver with the rather old-fashioned curve to the crown. A moment's steely rage was followed all too quickly by a feeling of sick dread. The problem he had avoided thinking about had come to meet him. He could run, but it would only follow

350

him. No, he must get it over with. There was nothing else for it.

He stood his ground, watching the horse grow larger. Kai came running back to look up at him questioningly; then her ears sharpened as she saw the horseman too, and she stared long and hard, and set up a warning rattle in her throat. 'Still,' said Benedict, and she desisted, but continued to watch, and now and then gave a little throaty grunt which was as close as she ever got to barking. The horse was a big-boned brown hunter which dished its off-foreleg as it trotted – a bad habit which would have been corrected in a Morland horse before it was sold. But this was not a Morland horse, of course. For the last few yards its rider pulled it down from a trot to a walk. And then it was halted just before him; he smelled its clean warmth, heard the jingle of the bit as it stretched its neck and mouthed, the creak of the saddle as it shifted its forefeet and stamped against a fly.

Miniott swung out of the saddle and slipped the reins over the brown's head, and at once it dropped its nose to the grass. Kai growled again, but softly. Now Benedict had no choice but to look at the man who had wronged him. Miniott removed his hat, and Benedict's unwilling eyes went to his face.

Miniott looked older, he thought; much older – old enough to be Rosalind's father. His hair was greying, not at the temples, as men like it to grey, but all over, badger-spackled; and his face was lined with worry and perhaps sleeplessness. But he was handsome still, in a way Benedict had never been handsome, in a lean, distinguished, statesmanlike way. He met Benedict's eyes gravely, and waited for him to speak; even when the silence extended itself, he waited.

At last Benedict said, 'You know, then? She's been to see you.' He had hardly seen her since that morning

351

confession, only at meals sometimes, when they avoided each other's eyes. What she did in the daytime he did not know, but it would not have surprised him if she had fled to her lover for advice and comfort. He was so numbed with it all, he hardly cared.

'No,' Miniott said quickly, as though it mattered. 'She wrote to me.'

Benedict made a throwing-away gesture with his hand. What did it signify now? 'You had better say what you came to say.'

Miniott looked at him consideringly for a moment. 'I came to ask what you mean to do,' he said at last.

'You think that is your business, do you?'

'It shouldn't be, I know. God knows, I have made your life hell, Morland, and I wish it were otherwise. I would not add to your pain, but—'

'Oh, spare me your sympathy!' Benedict said harshly. 'No hypocrisy!'

Miniott flushed a little. 'I deserve everything you can throw at me,' he said quietly, 'but there are things that must be decided.'

Benedict searched his mind for some clue as to what he might decide, and found nothing. He seemed to have fallen into a pit where no movement of any kind was possible. He looked at Miniott out of that black emptiness, and Miniott almost flinched. 'Have you come here with some proposition?' Benedict asked.

'I wish I were in a position to do so,' Miniott said.

'And what does that mean?'

Miniott said abruptly, 'Morland, do you mean to acknowledge the child?'

'No, by God!' It was startled out of him; and staring in surprise at his own words, he discovered at least one truth. He adored Mary, he had loved Rose; but he had believed them his own children, and learned the truth only after he had loved them too much and too long to take it back. But the child that was coming had no such dispensation. He would never be able to pretend, never be able to accept its smiles without thinking of this man. 'No, I will not own your bastard.'

'Then, what is to be done?' Miniott asked patiently.

Benedict looked at him with weary resentment. 'Why did you do it? Why didn't you go away when you said you would?'

'I meant to. I swear to you, Morland, that I meant to. But she begged me, and I was weak. I love her, you see. I know I should not say so, but I want to be honest with you. When she begged me, I couldn't leave her. I have hated this business. I want to be a man of honour. I have hated deceiving you, putting myself outside decent society, living in hiding. It has been a terrible punishment to me, if that is any consolation to you.'

'No, I don't think it is.' Benedict looked into the future. 'She won't leave you alone,' he said, admitting the painful truth, 'unless you put yourself beyond her reach. But how can I go on living with her, knowing that is how she feels?'

'You mean to cast her off, then?'

A long silence. Whatever the pain and shame of separation, it would be better than the private agony of living with a woman who wished herself elsewhere, and who would betray him again without hesitation or compunction if the opportunity arose. He didn't love her, and pity was a poor substitute. Let her go, then, to someone who did love her; and let him at least keep the last tatters of his self-respect.

'You have her,' he said at last, 'since you seem to want her.'

A complicated set of emotions seemed to flit across Miniott's face, including, intriguingly, dismay.

'I do want her. I love her – and I think that I could keep her respectable. She heeds me – God knows why. And the child—' A naked look from which Benedict drew back, not wanting to feel anything towards this man. 'I would cherish the child.'

'But?' Benedict said. Incredibly, there seemed to be a 'but'.

Miniott spread his hands. 'I have very little money – enough to keep me in a bachelor condition, but not enough for an establishment such as Rosalind would need, not enough to support a wife and child. She might be persuaded to give up some of the luxuries with which you provide her, but I cannot expect her to live like a cottager.' He looked an appeal. 'Can you imagine her cooking her own food, mending her own clothes?'

Benedict could, just for a moment, and it was a vicious satisfaction. But in reality, he could not condemn his wife to such unhappiness, nor would he have respected the man who could. 'Then what do you suggest?'

'If you will not acknowledge the child, I suppose it must be put out somewhere. And then—'

'And then the problem will continue. We seem to have a snag in our smooth-running line. You want her and the child, but you can't afford them. I am not prepared to keep her and the child and let her continue running to you every day. So it seems to me the only way out is for me to cut the knot; for you to take her, and for me to pay you a pension for as long as you keep her.' Miniott was silent. 'Well, isn't that what you came here to ask for?'

'No!' Miniott said, aggrieved. 'I expected nothing. I couldn't see any way out.'

'Except the one you weren't prepared to take – to leave my wife alone.'

'As you have pointed out, that wouldn't change the way she feels,' Miniott said.

'By God, I should—!'

'Knock me down? Do, if it will relieve your feelings.'

But it wouldn't. Things had gone beyond that now.

'So I am to pay to support my wife in another man's arms, am I?' Benedict smiled a sour little smile. 'I shall have a splendid pair of ass's ears to add to my cuckold's horns! No, don't say anything. Who should suffer for my folly but myself? Well, I dare say she will cost me less that way, first and last.'

'Will you – divorce her?' Miniott asked carefully.

'Perhaps. I don't know. Do you want to marry her, then?'

'I should like her to be respectable. And there is the child.'

'Ah yes, the child. How you do like to rub it in! I think you had better go now, Miniott. I don't think I can bear you any longer. I will consult my man of business, and he will communicate the details to you. It had better all be settled as soon as possible, considering her condition. But you will have to go away somewhere, the pair of you. I will decide where – and the pension will be dependent upon your staying there, do you understand? I won't have you flaunting yourselves on my doorstep.'

'I'll take her abroad, if you wish. One can live more cheaply abroad,' Miniott offered. 'One more thing – will you let her take Mary with her?'

'No, by God,' Benedict said. His golden child to live with that corrupt pair? 'You had better be satisfied with my wife. You shan't have my daughter.'

Miniott didn't say what he might have said then. He nodded and turned away, pulled up his horse's head and mounted. When he was settled in the saddle he said, 'You have behaved very generously. No-one will think you a fool for acting like a man of honour. I wish I might come out of this half as well. But I will take care of her, I promise you, and try to make her happy – if that is something you can still care about.' Benedict kept a stony-faced silence. Miniott gathered up the reins. 'As for me,' he went on, with the ghost of a shrug, 'I think she will go on being my punishment.'

He turned the brown and rode away, and Benedict stood where he was and resisted the temptation to fall to the ground and bawl like a child with misery. Kai stood looking up at him, waving her tail, hoping to be off. And when the wave of despair had passed, Benedict found a small patch of lightness in the black of his personal sky, for a decision had been made, and that was better than the agony of indecision. And when he looked more closely, he could see that there might be happiness beyond the immediate pain, a happiness in being without Rosalind at last. He did not feel it yet, but he could see that it might come. It was not a patch of clear sky yet, but the clouds were just a little thinner.

He spent the whole morning closeted with Harry Anstey, telling him the miserable tale. Much of it was shocking to Harry, some of it suspected if not absolutely guessed at; all of it painful to both of them. At the end of the recital, Harry got up and went across the room for the decanter and glasses, and poured them both a stiffener.

Benedict swallowed half of his, and sat staring at the amber residuum, which glowed in the light from the window – it was still sunny outside. 'I have not been a good guardian for Morland Place,' he said. 'My mother would be so shocked. Nicky and I – why should we both have gone so wrong?'

'You mustn't blame yourself,' Harry began automatically, but Benedict interrupted him with a grim smile.

'Oh yes I must. I left home to pursue my own interests, because it was easier than staying and trying to establish the truth. I abandoned Morland Place, I left my mother grieving, and when it came to choosing a wife, I used all the judgement of a blind blockhead. There's no-one else to blame, Harry. Now I must do what I can to make things right again.'

'And what have you decided?' Harry asked.

Benedict told him what he had agreed with Sir Carlton Miniott, and the lawyer in Harry frowned over it, even while the man rejoiced.

'Are you sure?' he asked at the end of it. 'It is a radical step, and an expensive one. A divorce, if you mean to get one, is a lengthy business, and will cost thousands, and to tie yourself to a pension as well—'

'I thought a pension was usual in these cases,' Benedict said lightly.

'In place of the dowry which is not returned, yes. But Mrs Benedict brought you no dowry.'

Benedict turned his head away a little. 'I can't be paltry, Hal. Let her have her pension, enough to keep her in comfort rather than in luxury; but let it be paid to Miniott. She hasn't the slightest idea of how to manage – she'd run herself into debt in a month. As to divorce – I can't decide about that now. There's no need, is there?'

'You will want to marry again,' Harry said. 'You will need an heir. Unless you mean Mary to inherit.'

'I don't know,' Benedict said painfully. 'I love her, and I shall not allow anything to make any difference to her. She shan't suffer for her mother's sins. But when it comes to Morland Place, I'm not sure I could leave it all to her. There are four hundred years of Morland history at stake, and I am not sure I would be justified in passing it all to someone who has no Morland blood. I'm afraid my ancestors would haunt me.'

Harry nodded sympathetically. 'The question of divorce can wait,' he said, 'as long as you bear in mind the length of time it will take. If you fall in love, don't come running to me expecting to be freed in a fortnight.'

'I won't,' Benedict promised with a faint smile.

'Well, if you're sure this is what you want to do,' Harry said, drawing paper towards him, 'we had better discuss the details, and start drafting a contract. You will want everything settled as quickly as possible, before the news of the pregnancy becomes common knowledge. Has she decided where she wants to go?'

'Oh, I haven't told her anything about this yet. I spoke to Miniott only this morning, and came straight to you.'

Harry put down his pen. 'Hadn't you better discuss it with her?'

'No,' said Benedict, and Harry had never seen him look so grim. 'I will discuss nothing with her. I shall tell her what will happen, that's all. You seem to forget, she is not leaving me – I am sending her away.'

'Yes, of course,' Harry said hastily. 'And where are you sending her?'

A strange smile played over Benedict's lips. 'Scarborough,' he said.

Rosalind was shocked at the speed with which things had moved, and angry that she had not been consulted, but she took her sentence quietly enough, even accepting the choice of Scarborough as her prison, until it transpired that she was not to have Mary with her. Then she demurred. To be deprived of her child was cruel, inhuman, not to be borne! Benedict could not do it, she would not let him! Mary was not even his child! At this tactless reminder her husband's face grew so grim that she was frightened out of her anger and into tears; and her misery was so great that in the end Benedict, desperate

358

to quiet her, said that he might allow Mary to visit her, though in his heart he thought he would die sooner.

After that she made no more noise, and even seemed to brighten up a little, as though looking forward to a treat. He allowed her to pack all her clothes, and some of the jewels he had bought her since their marriage, though the family pieces stayed, of course, along with the more expensive items which he could not feel justified in letting go. Harry Anstey moved quickly, and spurred Miniott into a sense of urgency. Temporary lodgings were found in the quiet end of the town, to serve until a suitable house for rent was chosen, which would be more conveniently done once the last of the summer visitors had left at the end of the month. This reminder of the winter coming – a winter when she would be living in lodgings in a half-empty seaside town – brought on one last plea from Rosalind, but Benedict was deaf to it. He wanted only for it to be over now.

Within a week of his meeting with Miniott, she was packed and gone. A carriage was sent for Mary, to fetch her away before her mother could enter the town. Perhaps they passed on the road, but if so, Mary did not know it. She returned to Morland Place to find her mother gone, and when her father explained that she was gone for ever, nothing would console her. It was the hardest part of it all for Benedict; but children adapt as adults cannot. Mary's mother was gone, but though she had idolised her, she had never had much to do with her; Rose had been the greater loss, but Rose had been gone for weeks now. Morland Place was the same, and her father was there at breakfast every day, and Miss Titchell was still her daily companion. Lessons resumed opened ever new horizons to her hungry mind, and for her body's recreation what could equal a pony and a large estate to scramble over? Especially as Papa had promised to take her hunting this winter for the first time. And to fill the hole in her affections that Rose had left, Benedict gave her one of Kai's puppies, and promised to help her train it.

Mary settled down into the new pattern of her life, and Benedict, though he sometimes looked at her sadly, never loved her less. He could not regret his decision, even though all of York was talking about it, and he could not go into town without eyes following him, and heads inclining together to whisper about him on every street corner. Harry and Celia made a point of inviting him to their house, and brought Arthur over to play with Mary, and through them, Benedict learned what people were saying. There were those who blamed him, who thought he had treated Rosalind harshly; those who felt he should have put a good face on it and pretended nothing was wrong. There were those who thought him a fool for not being able to control his own wife, those who thought him a fool for putting up with it for so long, and many more who thought him a fool for paying another man to cuckold him. The latter would have favoured casting her out barefoot and penniless, and only regretted that whipping at the cart's tail had gone out of fashion.

But while everyone had an opinion as to what he should or should not have done, no-one, he was relieved to know, had supposed other than that Mary was his daughter. He had told no-one but Harry, and had made Harry promise not even to tell Celia. That part of it was all right. And he was surprised and touched to discover that he had many friends in York whom he had hardly known about, many who were pleased that he was free of Rosalind, who while not necessarily suspecting her of wrong had never liked her, and had been distant with Benedict on that account. Now they could invite him without her, they invited him warmly, and he could have dined out every evening that autumn and winter if he had wanted. No, he could not regret his decision, nor blame himself for making it. But alone in bed at night, and in the day when occupation left his mind for a moment empty, he mourned. His wife, whom he had loved for many years, lay night after night in another man's arms, and would soon be bearing him a child – a son, perhaps. Benedict was thirty-two years old, and he had no wife and no child. He was lonely.

Benedict and Mary spent Christmas with the Ansteys. To spend it alone at Morland Place would have been too sad, and when Benedict invited Aglaea and Jemima to stay, he discovered they had already accepted invitations to Anstey House. Ansteys always tried to get home for family celebrations, of course; but Benedict couldn't help thinking he had been manoeuvred into accepting the invitation which came immediately afterwards to join them all there.

He was glad of it, though. He knew all the Ansteys from childhood; and to secure Mary some companions of her own age was an object. The old mansion seethed with Ansteys of various generations, and hordes of children ran up and down stairs and in and out of rooms shrieking with pleasure all day long, except when vast meals rendered them temporarily comatose.

It was a happy few days, and Benedict managed to forget Rosalind entirely, except for one brief exchange with Jemima. He found himself alone with her in the breakfast room one morning before anyone else was down, and felt suddenly guilty about having foisted Rosalind and Miniott unceremoniously on her by banishing them to Scarborough. He asked, diffidently, if it made things unpleasant for her and Aglaea.

'Why, no,' Jemima said. 'I've only seen her twice to my knowledge, and that was at a distance. They live in a different part of town from us, and I don't think they go out very much, on account of her condition. In any case, we have our own circle of friends, and keep very much to ourselves.'

'I should not like you to be made uneasy – you or Aglaea.'

Jemima smiled. 'Aglaea doesn't notice anything when she is out of doors but the sea and the sky. Our own friends have to catch her arm and shake her before she notices them! If there should ever be any unpleasantness, I will let you know, but I can't conceive there will be. Scarborough is a large enough town, and *they* are bound to be discreet, don't you think?'

The cold winter Benedict had expected held off until the end of January – to the benefit of the hunting at least, though Haxby gloomily predicted plagues of insects and ruined crops next summer if they did not get some hard weather soon. He need not have worried. The last day of January saw the wind come round to the northeast, and a low bank of cloud unrolled itself over the sky. Through the day it got steadily colder. The sheep grew nervous and huddled in the shelter of hedges. Haxby and Benedict stood to the north of the Whin and sniffed the air, and agreed that the in-foal mares should be brought down to the closest paddocks just in case. The first day of February broke slate-grey and bitter cold, and all morning tiny separated fragments of snow fell like a warning. Then at noon it began to snow in earnest, and by the time the early dusk set in, it was settling on the hardening earth.

It went on snowing for four days, and there was work for everyone hauling food out for the animals, and bringing the mares nearest their time into the stables. The sheep had brought themselves down from the higher ground, but fodder had to be carried for them, too, and hurdles put up to give them some shelter. Benedict, sweating as he tried to drive a stake into the frozen ground, wondered how anyone could think snow cold stuff. He paused to rest his arm, and noticed someone at a little distance, who had just dragged a bale of hay into the corner of a hedge and was preparing to cut the string with a large knife he had taken out of his belt. There was something familiar about the movements, though he could not see who it was, bundled up in shapeless, countryman's clothes.

And then he dropped the mallet and was running clumsily through the snow, his mouth open in a shout that never reached the air. His hands closed over the bulkily padded arm, and the man turned his head and smiled.

'Is it you?' Benedict said in astonishment. 'What are you doing here?'

'I am earning my keep,' Father Moineau said calmly, 'anticipating that you will invite me to dine with you.'

'I was only thinking about you yesterday, wishing I knew where you were, longing for the chance to talk to you,' Benedict babbled, scanning the face almost frantically, as though he feared Moineau might disappear again as inexplicably as he had appeared. 'Where have you been? How do you come here?'

'Both long stories,' Moineau said, 'which would be better told indoors by a good fire. Shall we finish what we have to do here first?'

Benedict nodded, but said, 'I have been in such trouble—'

'I know, my boy, I know. You shall tell me everything – over a large dinner, I hope?'

Divested of some of the layers of clothing, Moineau seemed so familiar to Benedict that he swore he had not changed a bit, despite the years which had fallen between them. But Moineau, his eyes twinkling, patted his stomach and his bare pate. 'Less here, and less here, I assure you. Hard living has made me leaner in both places.'

Father Sparrow, as Benedict called him, had been the Morland Place chaplain and Benedict's tutor besides. He had taught Nicky and Harry Anstey too, but Benedict had been his special protégé. Many was the beating he had saved him, many the fascinating avenue of learning he had opened to him, and Benedict had loved him, and in all his troubles had longed to be able to open his heart and his conscience to his old mentor, and receive comfort and advice. But Moineau had left Morland Place when Benedict's mother died, and had not been heard of since.

Moineau looked around him keenly as he re-entered the house for the first time in twelve years, but he said nothing, except about the welcomeness of the fire, and the pleasure a glass of wine could bring. Mary was fascinated with him, stood at a little distance at first, interested but wary; but when Kai and her puppy, Dog, went at once to him, to put their heads into his hands and swing their tails and sing to him, she knew he must be a good person, and before he was halfway down his first glass of wine, she was sitting on his knee and leaning back at ease against him as if he were her personal throne.

'I thought you had gone back to France,' Benedict said.

'Not a bit. England is my home now. I felt I had enjoyed a long period of more luxury than was good for me at Morland Place, so I took myself off on my two feet to see what work God might send my way. Oh, how they complained – my feet, I mean. But the work was there in plenty, just waiting for me; and it pleased me that I was able to hear of you from time to time, because it reminded me of happy days gone by.'

364

'You heard of me?'

Moineau nodded. 'You have made quite a name for yourself on the railroads. When I think of that first trip we made to the coalfields, and how fascinated you were by the tramways and trucks, I little thought then what would come of it. And now they talk of you up there on the banks of the Tyne, not only as an engineer but as an undertaker, a man whose investment makes things possible.'

'Is that where you have been, up in Newcastle?'

'Just lately, yes – but before that, here, there and everywhere. I have had a mission, you see, to minister to the godless navvies of the railway workings. Ever since I left Morland Place, I have been travelling with them, living with them, listening to them, helping them when they would let me, which wasn't often, and praying with them. I've shared their joys and sorrows, heard their confessions, bound their broken heads, splinted their limbs, buried a good few of them, and married some – though not as many as ought to have been married. It's a hard life – as *you* know – but I have some tales to tell, and a great many good memories to keep me warm in my old age. The wonder is we have never happened to be on the same workings at the same time, but God has His own reasons for everything.'

His bright, quick gaze, which suited his name so well, seemed to penetrate Benedict's outer shell and look directly into his heart.

'I have so much to tell you,' Benedict said in response to it.

Moineau nodded. 'Yes, and I have a great many questions to ask, but they will keep for now. That will be for later, when we have eaten, and the fire is red in the heart, and our little friend here is sleeping the sleep of the innocent.' He gave Mary a little hug, and her arms, folded over his, pressed him back. 'For now, we will talk about railways, and I will tell you some of the things I have seen and done. But I hope dinner will not be long? I talk much better when my mouth has competition.'

Benedict laughed. 'Yes, it will be very soon. And you will stay the night, of course. I have ordered a room made ready for you. In fact, I hope you will stay a long time – unless you have urgent business elsewhere. Though even that will have to give way to the snow. From the sound of that wind, you won't be going anywhere for a day or two.'

'Oh, I'm in no hurry,' Moineau said, as the wind gusted and banged the shutters hard against the window frame. 'I'll stay as long as you like.'

'Good. But you haven't told me yet what brings you here,' Benedict said.

'I have been idling my way south since the Tyneside workings were finished. I thought of looking at the Scarborough workings – an easy line, I'm told, and it would be pleasant to be on an easy line for once. But then, when I was halfway down, I felt most strongly that I had to come here. It's a feeling I have learned not to ignore. I thought I had finished with Morland Place, but there is something left to do here, I don't know what. But God wanted me here, and He wanted me here *now*.'

'To advise me, perhaps,' Benedict said a little wanly.

'Perhaps,' Moineau said non-committally.

Moineau had always been a good trencherman, and Benedict enjoyed his simple enthusiasm for food so much that he ate with more gusto than he had done of late. During the meal the priest regaled Benedict with railway stories. Benedict reciprocated – Moineau was particularly interested in the Kilsby Tunnel – and a satisfying discussion ensued about past works and how the future of the railways might be shaped.

Outside the storm blew, and grew stronger, and after dinner, beside a fire that glowed red as Moineau had predicted, Benedict began to tell him his own story. It was the beginning of a conversation which, like the storm, lasted for days on and off. There was so much to tell, so much in which Moineau himself had a close interest. Moineau could tell Benedict about his mother's death, which had happened while Benedict was from home; Benedict told him about Nicky's end, and the painful things that had preceded it. And he told about his marriage and betrayal, about Mary, and Rose, and the present situation. Pain and rage and guilt and sadness seeped slowly out of him, carried by his words, so that they soaked like poisoned water into the endless annihilating sands of Moineau's attention.

And at the end, Benedict felt empty, but restored, as though a fever had finally broken. Moineau said, 'God will show you what to do. Be quiet, listen for God's voice; do nothing in haste, or spite, or anger. Do what is right, always, and God will guide your steps.' It was only what Benedict might have told himself, but he had not had the quietness within to do it; and coming from Moineau, it seemed to have an authority of continuity. Moineau had guided him as a child, and now he needed him again, he was here.

But when the storm ended, even when the tracks were cleared again and departure was possible, Moineau didn't go. Benedict might secretly, and with an affectionate smile, think that the old priest was enjoying soft beds and well-cooked food for a change, but Moineau said that God had brought him here to take care of some unfinished business, and until he knew what it was, he could not leave. Benedict was glad of his company. And also, as the time approached when Rosalind's baby was due, he thought he would better be able to bear the news of it with Moineau at hand.

The storm had proved one thing to Benedict, that it was time and well past that he did something about the apartment in the barbican which he had thought would be suitable for Haxby. While the snow was down, he and his steward had been at an inconvenient distance from each other, and actually out of touch for two days. 'I need you closer at hand,' he said. 'If I make the barbican comfortable, would you like to live there?'

Haxby jumped at the chance, especially as it would mean eating at Morland Place – his present landlady was no great cook. So as soon as the snow was cleared, Benedict summoned the estate carpenter, and with an interested audience of Haxby and Father Moineau and several of the grooms who had temporarily escaped the eye of the head man, he set him to work on removing the boarding from the barbican door.

It had been thoroughly done, and it took some time to prise off the boards; and then the door was found to be locked, and the key missing from the collection in the butler's room. A long delay ensued while a locksmith was sent for, for the lock was massive and ancient, and, like the door, part of the original fabric of the house: Benedict did not want to destroy either. By the time the lock was at last dismantled, the sun was off the yard and it had begun to feel very cold. Standing about with frozen feet was dismal, shivery work, and everyone, including Haxby, had found other things to do. But Father Moineau remained, patient as a rock, keeping his hands warm by pushing them up his sleeves so that he looked like a baggy-trousered monk.

At last the door swung open, revealing the stone stairs behind, worn by generations of feet into so many shallow dishes. It was cold inside, but not as cold as out in the yard, and the air smelled quite dry – no hint of damp.

'It's a good place, you see,' he commented to Moineau. 'It will make a pleasant home.'

Moineau said nothing, only gestured to Benedict to go up. There was another door at the top of the stairs, and Benedict thought with a sinking heart that it would also be locked, and there would be another delay. But the handle turned and the door gave, only to stop after the fraction of an inch.

'What now?' Benedict asked. The carpenter wriggled past him and tried it, and said, 'There's something stopping it, sir. T'ain't locked. Shall I give it a shove?'

'Yes, do, or we'll be here all night.' He shivered, though in here out of the wind it was not too cold. But it was dark, and he wanted to get back to his fire. The carpenter put his shoulder against the door and shoved hard, and the door gave, and then slithered open, while something behind it could be heard rubbing over the floorboards as the door pushed it back. It was lighter inside, of course, because of the windows, and Benedict stepped in, seeing the furnishings as the previous occupant had left them, a table and chairs, a rug on the floor, an armchair by the fire and a kettle on a trivet pushed to one side. Clothes hanging on the back of a further door opposite him gave him a start for a moment, for they looked like a headless man standing in the shadows. The rug by the fireplace was rucked and out of its place, as though it had been dragged away, but otherwise everything was tidy.

'He left it in good order, anyway,' Benedict commented, and stepped round the door to see what it was that had been holding them up.

The shock jarred his heart so hard it actually hurt him, and he felt his hair rise so violently that the cold air touched the skin of his scalp. A man lay there in the

369

shadows behind the door; a man with the hideous face of a death's-head, pit-nostrilled, grinning at him and reaching hooked, skeletal fingers towards him. Benedict thought he had screamed, but in fact he made no sound except the sharp intake of breath, but he stepped backwards so hastily that he hit the table, lurched sideways, knocked over a chair, and almost fell.

'Dear God alive, maister, what is it?' the carpenter cried out, and he too went backwards away from the horror, his hand flying to his throat in terror.

It was left to Moineau to bend over the thing. It was the body of a man, perfectly mummified. The face had shrivelled like a stored apple, the brown, creased skin pulling back as it shrank, giving it that death's-head appearance. The flesh had shrunk away everywhere, so that inside its clothes it was bones covered in that same brown, toughened skin; light as a bundle of twigs. The room was perfectly dry, almost warm after the chill outside, and there was a strange, dry, almost sweet smell on the air, which was not dust.

Benedict's shocked mind was trying to function. 'It must be Ferrars. He didn't go away after all. But what—?' Ferrars had disappeared some months before Nicky's death, seven or eight months before; and Nicky had had the apartment nailed and boarded up. But if Ferrars had been here all the time, how did Nicky come to think he had gone?

Moineau was examining the rug which lay halfway between the fire and the door. 'This stain is blood, I think.' He straightened and looked around. 'Yes, he fell here, and then dragged himself to the door. His hands are crooked – there are scratches down here at the foot of the door. I think he was trying to pull himself up, or perhaps trying to attract attention.'

'But – but I don't understand. Why did—?'

Moineau looked at him gravely. The carpenter was kneeling, perhaps involuntarily, and murmuring shocked prayers to himself. Moineau said quietly, 'He knew, Benedict. Nicky *knew*.'

Benedict shook his head, still not understanding. 'He could have broken the window and called for help. Even if he was locked in, he didn't need to die.'

'He did not die of starvation. There is blood on that rug, and a wound here, under this torn clothing. He was shot, do you understand me? He died because he was shot with a pistol.'

Benedict stared, rigid with horror. Moineau turned away and began to say a prayer over the grinning, store-apple corpse. Six years it had been lying here, waiting for this moment. Now Moineau knew why he had had to come. There was exorcism needed, and a burial, and many, many prayers to be offered; and Benedict would need him, more than ever. Nicholas had murdered the man, and boarded up his crime, and lived for eight months with the knowledge locked away like a festering foreign body lodged in his mind before he had died, mad and unforgiven. And the unquiet spirit of the victim had hovered about Morland Place, creating who knew what mischief. Yes, there was work for Moineau here, and he exchanged a nod of understanding with his God, even while he wondered how long it had taken Ferrars to die, how long he had scratched at that solid oak door for deliverance which did not come.

A reliable servant was left on guard with orders that no-one should enter the apartment; another was sent with all haste to fetch Harry Anstey. He would know what must be done to satisfy the law. In the drawing-room, Benedict sat close to the fire with a large glass of brandy in his hands, shivering, though he was not really cold. His mind

371

jumped and twitched like the hide of a horse tormented by flies, as images came together and flew apart, sequences of events possible and impossible suggested themselves to him.

Moineau said at last, 'He must be buried in the crypt.'

Benedict's head flew up. 'No!'

'It is necessary,' Moineau said. 'It is what I was brought here for – to perform the ceremony, and end the episode.'

'That evil man?'

'He gave his life for the House, in his own way. He belongs to it now.'

Benedict shivered more violently. All around him he could hear the house rustling and creaking like an uneasy sleeper. He thought of Ferrars' bones lying beneath the chapel floor with those of his ancestors for ever and ever, and that hideous, abhuman face jumped at him again out of the shadows of his mind. 'It would bring bad luck,' he cried desperately.

'No, no,' said Moineau surely. 'He was part of a long piece of evil that got hold of the house, but it is all worked out now. He and Nicky have paid for it between them. Now that the truth is known, it will be the end of it; he will lie quietly, I promise you.'

'I wish I could believe you,' Benedict said. 'But I can feel it all around me, like a cloud of evil.'

Moineau felt it too, the restlessness, and it puzzled him a little; but he said, 'It is just the house stirring. Once he is laid in the crypt and the stone put back, it will all be over. The house will be at rest, and there will be a new beginning.'

'I wish we could do it now,' Benedict said. 'Why is Harry so long coming?' The wind in the chimney moaned, and the panelling of the walls made a thin crying noise, as if all the unhappinesses of the past had soaked into the walls. The house was like a live thing, a beast that devoured blood and demanded sacrifice. How could he ever have felt he loved it? He didn't own it – it owned him; and had Nicky felt like that all his life? Was that what had driven him mad? Nicky, and Ferrars – how much evil had they done between them that would never be known? Which, after all, was the victim?

At last the door opened and Harry was there, hurrying across the room toward Benedict, his hands outstretched, his face grave, though the servant who had been sent for him had known nothing, had simply been bidden to fetch him. 'Bendy, I'm so very sorry! It must be a dreadful shock for you. I don't know what to say. You know you have my deepest sympathy.'

The words seemed to Benedict somehow slightly out of kilter, but he accepted them as kindly meant. 'How did you know?' he wondered.

'Aglaea told me,' Harry said.

'Aglaea?

'I had a letter from her this morning. She said she had written to you, too. How did you hear?'

Benedict screwed up his face in an effort to understand. 'Hear what?'

Father Moineau stepped in. 'Let us be quite clear, my children. What is it, Harry, that you have learnt from your sister?'

Now it was Harry's turn to be surprised. He had not seen Moineau, sitting in the depths of an armchair; now he turned, stared, doubted his eyes. Could it be? Where had he come from? What was going on?

Moineau nodded calmly. 'Yes, it is I. All will be explained to you in due course. But first tell us, *what is it you have heard from your sister?*'

'Why, about Rosalind – Mrs Benedict Morland, that

is. Isn't that what you sent for me about? Aglaea wrote to tell me. She heard it from an acquaintance. You mean you didn't know?' His kind face crumpled in dismay. 'Oh my God, I am a clumsy fool! I'm so sorry, Bendy. Mrs Benedict was brought to bed of a son yesterday, but she suffered a haemorrhage shortly afterwards. By the time the surgeon arrived—'

'She's dead?' Benedict heard himself ask.

'Yes, she's dead.'

Benedict bowed his head. A great silence seemed to fall, in which the soft, domestic sounds of the fire and the clock could be heard for the first time. Moineau tilted his head and listened. Far away, almost below hearing, the house sighed as it settled back into its customary sleep. Now he understood. The last debt of blood was paid. It was all done now, all over.

CHAPTER SEVENTEEN

In the August of 1845, Charlotte went to stay with her mother at Grasscroft. She went there from Manchester, where she had spent six weeks with Fanny and Henry Droylsden – they would be joining the Grasscroft party in a day or two, when they had fulfilled some social engagements.

'How is Fanny looking?' Rosamund asked her daughter as they strolled about her favourite walk in the shrubbery.

'She tries to be gay, but she's looking a little peaked. I feel so guilty about it all,' Charlotte added

'I thought she and Tom Cavendish parted by mutual agreement?'

'That's what Fanny says, but I think she's just putting a good face on it. From something Mr Droylsden said, I gather that Tom Cavendish asked to be released, and Fanny had the choice of pretending she wanted to be released too or being pitied for being jilted.'

'If that was the case, I can see that Fanny wouldn't want to appear the victim. But Charlotte dear, if Tom Cavendish was so shallow that he would give Fanny up for such a pitiful reason, then Fanny is well out of it.'

'That's what Fanny says,' Charlotte said with a wan smile. 'She says he only wanted to marry her because she would have been the cousin of a duchess, and that she's glad to have him exposed before it was too late. She says I've done her a good turn. But if that's *really* why he wanted to marry her, it's even more mortifying.'

'I dare say her money had a good deal to do with it,' Rosamund said drily. 'The Cavendishes are only just above water.'

'She was awfully in love with him,' Charlotte finished sadly.

'Fanny will get over it. You mustn't blame yourself. You did what you felt you had to do, and you couldn't be expected to foresee that it would affect Fanny's prospects.'

'And even if I had—'

'Precisely.'

Charlotte was silent a moment. 'Do you think I did the right thing?'

'It doesn't matter what I think. Do *you* think you did the right thing?'

'Yes. But I seem to be the only person who does.'

'Perhaps you were a little harsh on Fleetwood – Southport, I should call him now. The arrangement was quite a usual one – your money for his title. But you weren't to know that, I suppose. The situation was a little unusual. And if you thought the marriage would make you unhappy, you were quite right to call it off. God knows I wouldn't wish an unhappy marriage on you.'

'Were you very unhappy with Papa?' she asked in a small voice.

'Oh, no,' Rosamund said lightly. 'We got by pretty well for the most part. But any mother who had enjoyed the happiness I have with Jes would want her daughter to have the same.'

They walked in silence for a while. Then Rosamund asked, 'Have you decided what you mean to do?'

'Not precisely. I see the general direction now, but not the specific,' Charlotte said.

'Is that what you've been doing all this time, tucked away in that village of yours – deciding the direction?'

She nodded. 'I've been talking to Doctor Silk, and helping him in his work – visiting the poor and sick, helping him to treat them. I've learned so much. As he says, there is so much that needs doing – and I have the money and the freedom to do it. And the will.'

'Helping the poor? Well, it's Christian work.'

Charlotte looked at her sidelong. 'You sound as though you don't approve.'

'How could one not approve? If you are quite sure it's what you want.'

'Oh, yes! I want to—' She paused, searching for the words. 'I want to make a difference to more lives than just my own. All that vast fortune – it must have been given me for a purpose. I can't just spend my life riding about in carriages and eating fine dinners.'

'Poor darling, did you hate it so much, then, your Season?' Rosamund asked, faintly amused.

'No, of course I didn't hate it. Some of it was – delightful. But I didn't fit in, you know. I was never one of them. They looked at me and whispered about me. I felt as though my upbringing was a bad smell that hung about me, and even having all that money didn't wash it off.' She thought of Lady Turnhouse's scorn – *do you think he would marry a creature like you for any other reason?* – and blushed at the memory.

Rosamund saw the blush. 'It is my fault,' she said. 'I did that to you.'

Charlotte turned to her like a flame leaping up. 'Oh, no!' she cried eagerly. 'I didn't mean that! But I couldn't judge a person in that way – not for what they were good for, but for where and how they were born; and I don't belong with people who can. I don't *want* to be part of that society. And if my fortune isn't for that –

377

for making me part of it – then it must be for something else.'

'You make me feel guilty for being content with – what did you say? – riding in carriages and eating fine dinners.'

'I didn't mean to. You and he—' She always had difficulty in knowing what to call Jes – 'you do a great deal of good in your own ways, on the estate and in the factories. And of course—' She was puzzled how to express the feeling she had, that being married to the man you loved and having his child was somehow a part of the natural order, and its own justification. 'It's different for you,' she finished a little lamely; but Rosamund understood what she meant.

'I want you to be happy,' she said. 'I can't give you anything, or do anything for you. I was never given the chance to. And now all I can do is pray for you, and hope, and wish. And try to understand why it is that you are so different.'

'Am I different? How?'

'Grave, I think, is the word. You want to be good, rather than happy.'

'I want to be happy too,' she said, looking at the ground, 'but I have to find the right way. As for being good—' She smiled suddenly. 'Grandmama says *you* are good. She says it with such an air of puzzlement it makes me laugh.'

'It might well puzzle her to find an instance of my goodness,' Rosamund said, smiling too. 'Well, go on about your plans. Do you mean to go back to Chetton?'

'No. I would much sooner live in the country, but my work must be in the town, I think.'

'Because you want to mortify yourself?'

Charlotte burst out laughing. 'Oh, do you think me such a martyr? I hope I don't take myself so seriously!'

'I hope not too. Then why?'

'Because it is so much worse there, and I feel I must help where it can do most good. While I was staying with Fanny, I went about Manchester and saw some of the conditions the poorest sort live in. Quite dreadful! In the country there is terrible poverty, but somehow things are never so hopeless. There is always some beauty somewhere, and clean air, and the sense of things renewing themselves. But in the town the ugliness is so – unrelenting.'

Rosamund brightened. 'If you do your good works in Manchester, you can live with us at Batchworth House, and here at Grasscroft.'

'Is that all you care about, where I should live?'

'My darling, I don't pretend to be a saint. I thought I had lost you for ever, and now I have got you back, I want to see as much of you as possible.'

'And you would be much happier if I were to get myself sensibly married and produce some grandchildren for you, wouldn't you?'

'Much,' Rosamund said equably, and Charlotte laughed.

They had reached the place where the walk crossed the main gravel path, and stopped as they saw two horses approaching – Jes and Cavendish back from their early ride.

'There you are!' Jes greeted them with enormous satisfaction, thinking how elegant and beautiful they looked walking side by side.

'You've been gone a long time,' Rosamund said. 'I hope you haven't gone too far and exhausted yourselves. Charlotte and I will be expecting an escort later when we take our ride.'

'No, we didn't go so very far. We stopped for a long time to watch the buzzards.'

'And then Papa showed me some cavalry manoeuvres,' Cavendish said eagerly. 'On that piece of flat ground by the river, where the three pines grow. If we go that way this afternoon, Charlotte, I'll show you.'

'Cavalry manoeuvres?' Rosamund said sternly.

Jes looked from his son's hopeful face to his wife's disapproving one, and laughed. 'It's no good, my love, it will be a military career for him or nothing. You will never get him to stay home and do embroidery.'

'As if I ever meant to. Didn't I agree he should go to Eton this Michaelmas?' It was not for anyone else to know the long, long talks that had been needed for Jes to persuade her. Her father had been at Eton, and she remembered his stories; and Cavendish had always been delicate. But Jes had told her it was different there now, and that it would be much easier for Cavendish, going in as an older boy, to hold his own.

'He is much stronger these days,' Rosamund had agreed doubtfully. 'He's outgrown so many of his old weaknesses. But still, Jes—'

'It will do him good to be with other boys his own age. He is too much isolated with us. And I survived, don't forget.'

'You weren't your mother's only son,' Rosamund said; but she had agreed to it, with a reluctance that was tempered, she didn't quite understand why, by the fact that she had Charlotte now. But a military career was a different matter. Cavendish had been mad for it ever since he saw a cavalry review in Hyde Park; and since Jes had been a soldier, he saw it as quite natural that his son should want to follow his own trade.

Now she met her son's bright, pleading eyes, and said, 'There's the estate to manage, and the factories. I think a man ought to learn how to run his own businesses, before he puts them into the charge of someone else.'

'I can do that too, Mama,' Cavendish said. 'I can learn all that in my vacations from school. After all, I can't go into the cavalry for another four years. There's plenty of time.'

Plenty of time to stop this nonsense, Rosamund thought, and her thought was plain on her face at least to one of the three observers. Jes jumped down and gave his rein to Cavendish, asking him to take his horse to the stable, and Charlotte, seeing a private conversation was imminent, said she'd walk there with her brother. Jes took his wife's arm through his, and as they walked away, Charlotte heard him say, 'It's not so very dangerous, you know. We've had thirty years of peace, haven't we? It's not as if he's likely to have to go into battle . . .'

When Fanny arrived at Grasscroft, it was without her stepfather. 'Some trouble at the mill, with a piece of machinery,' she explained. 'Henry says we ought to replace them and start again, but it would mean shutting down for weeks and weeks, so he tinkers them up and hopes for the best. You should think yourself lucky,' she told Cavendish, 'that your papa overhauled Ordsall Mills so completely when he inherited them. It's a thing you must do at the beginning or not at all, for you never have the courage to shut down.'

'What would happen to your workers if you did?' Charlotte asked, and Fanny shrugged.

'I don't know. If they don't work, they don't eat, that's for sure, so I suppose you can be glad about it on their account.'

Fanny did seem rather out of sorts, but a few days of fresh air and riding out on the moors with Cavendish and Charlotte soon improved her colour and her temper. The two girls spent a lot of time alone together, walking and talking, and in the peace of the countryside, their old intimacy was restored. Fanny told Charlotte, with amusement, about 'Henry's widow', as she called her.

Henry Droylsden had recently begun to show an interest in the widow of an old friend of his. Mrs Worsley had begun life as Lisbeth Audenshaw, daughter of a factory master whose eldest son had been a close friend of Henry's. Audenshaw had had five ravishingly pretty blonde daughters who had been the dancing-partners of Henry's contemporaries. Lisbeth had done well for herself by marrying Adrian Worsley, an only son who inherited his father's entire fortune. There had been no children of the match, so now the widowed Mrs Worsley was a mill-owner of some consequence. 'Not that her fortune's anything like mine,' Fanny said, 'but Henry would be making himself comfortable, and who can blame him?'

'Oh Fanny, surely that isn't why he wants to marry her – if he does want to,' Charlotte said.

'He takes her to concerts and meetings, and she takes him up in her carriage whenever she passes him in the town,' Fanny said. 'And one of the reasons he is delaying coming here is that she has invited him to a supper party. I'm sure I don't know what so much interest betokens if it's not marriage.'

'I don't know him as well as you must do,' Charlotte said, 'but I do know he is a warm-hearted man, and if he's interested in Mrs Worsley, I'm sure it isn't because she's wealthy. He must be lonely without your mother.'

Fanny's defiant look broke. 'Oh, I know that, really. Henry is the nicest man in the world, and I wish him happy. But everybody has someone except me. Oh Charley, what's to become of me?'

Charlotte was distressed. 'I'm so sorry Tom Cavendish cried off. It's my fault, I know—'

'Oh, don't! I don't care about hateful Tom any more! But I'm twenty-three now, and I'm starting to think I may end up on the shelf.'

'Nonsense! You're prettier now than when I first saw you, besides witty and charming and clever.'

'Hmm. Perhaps that's the difficulty,' Fanny said, making a face. 'No man wants a wife cleverer than himself, and there aren't many brilliant men for me to choose from.'

'Oh Fanny! But I'm sure you will meet the right person at last. You don't want to marry just *anyone*.'

'True. And that *is* your fault. You've made me particular. If you can turn down the handsomest duke in the country—! But until I do meet the right person, what am I to do with myself? Dancing and flirting are pleasant enough, but they don't satisfy as they used to.'

Charlotte found the answer promptly enough. 'Use your money and influence to do some good amongst the poor, as I mean to.'

Fanny wrinkled her nose. 'Dull,' she said. 'And besides, it would make me very unpopular in Manchester to be interfering with other people's employees, besides causing trouble for poor Henry. I shouldn't like to be the cause of his widow's throwing him aside.'

'Then come to London with me,' Charlotte said.

'Is that where you mean to do your good works?'

'Yes. I had almost decided, and now I'm sure. I saw such things when I was there – just glimpses of them, and the whole picture must be so much worse! Oh do come with me and help me! I should so much like us to be together! And it would make it more respectable – for I have to tell you, I don't mean to live with Grandmama.'

Fanny opened her eyes wide, pretending shock. 'You don't mean to live alone? An unmarried girl!'

'I know I shall have to have a chaperone. That's a problem to be solved. But we're not girls in our first Season, and if we are together, it will cause much less comment – after the first surprise of it.' Fanny looked unconvinced. 'We could do so much good, Fanny!' And then she added, 'And you would be far more likely to meet your brilliant man in London than in Manchester.'

'Oh, is that how you mean to bait your trap? Dear Charley, you know I haven't a philanthropic bone in my body! But I must say I am tempted – as long as we don't have to wear ugly clothes and do good deeds all the time. If you promise me there will be *some* dancing and fun, I might think about it.'

'Of course there will be,' Charlotte said. 'And don't you see how it will intrigue the men – two beautiful, *rich* females engaged in noble works. They won't be able to resist. You'll be besieged with offers from handsome, eligible men. Probably cavalry officers,' she added temptingly, 'with glorious side-whiskers.'

'Wicked girl – you are much too young to be so cynical! Very well, I will talk to Henry about it, and as long as he sees no objection, I will come and be your lady-companion, and you can do philanthropic works for the good of your soul, and I'll do them to make myself appealing to cavalry officers.' She grinned impishly. 'Great Aunt Lucy will hate it of anything! She hates do-goods.'

'She's one herself – what she dislikes is people who make a parade of it. But in any case, cousin Tom has shown me how to enlist Grandmama. She is fascinated by anything to do with medicine. Once we get her interested in the medical problems, she'll be completely won over.'

Fanny looked at her a little askance. 'And I thought you so innocent and helpless! You are turning into a veritable schemer.'

'I like to have my own way, as much as anyone does,' Charlotte said.

'Or perhaps just a little more?' Fanny suggested, and then they both laughed.

There was less opposition to overcome than Charlotte

had expected. To be sure, no-one could actually stop two women, both of age and in possession of their own fortunes, from setting up house wherever they pleased, but Charlotte had expected resistance, on Fanny's account if not her own. But it seemed that as long as they were respectably chaperoned, it would be generally viewed as a harmless romp, with a few charitable visits justifying a residence in London which would inevitably end in marriage.

The two girls were invited most cordially to stay with Lucy and Danby, while Mr Tarbush was making enquiries after a suitable house – Charlotte having rejected Chelmsford House as much too large – and Lucy was looking for a suitable chaperone for them. There was no shortage of volunteers, for Lucy's first husband, Charlotte's grandfather, had had a large family of poor relations, any of whom would have given their hair for the chance to live expense-free in London. The difficulty was to find one who would add anything to the girls' credit. The house was found before the chaperone, and Fanny and Charlotte had visited and approved it – a pretty, three-storeyed building at the top of Berkeley Street – and gone a long way towards furnishing it before there was any likelihood of their being able to take possession of it.

But their stay at Upper Grosvenor Street was not uneventful or dull. Lucy had found last Season very flat, without a young woman in the house, and now that she had two, she was making the most of it. They never sat down to a dinner en famille if she could help it, and there was a continuous programme of entertainments to divert them – visits to the theatre, dancing, parties, routs. Now that Lucy did not have the responsibility of finding Charlotte a husband, she could have her own friends about her, and introduce the girls amongst her own circle, and Charlotte found it much more to her liking than the world of fashion. Statesmen, thinkers, men of letters – they might have sounded dull to Fanny, but Charlotte wanted to learn, and that winter presented her with ample opportunity.

There was also a strong military presence in Grandmama's drawing-room, for Lord Theakston had been a cavalry officer, and with Fanny in mind, he invited a number of younger officers as well as his old friends. The Theakstons stayed in Town for Christmas, and those young officers who could not get home were glad of an invitation to such a gay house and such lavish entertainment. But though they were happy to pay homage to Fanny's prettiness, it was Cavendish who welcomed them with the most excitement. He had come from Eton to spend the Christmas vacation with the Theakstons, and being amongst military men was bliss to him. He bombarded them with questions, and began to model his comportment and vocabulary on theirs, much to Charlotte's amusement. Alone in his room he spent much time in front of the looking-glass staring anxiously at his lip and chin, willing the hair to grow; and spent half his pocket money on patent nostrums solemnly guaranteed to produce luxuriant whiskers from the most rudimentary down.

Fanny danced and flirted with the officers, but it was with a distracted air which, though she didn't know it, added to her charms. Her thoughts were elsewhere. She had expected to find Lucy's circle dull, and curled her lip at the idea of spending the winter amongst such company as the Palmerstons and the Ashleys. But it was at a ball given for the New Year by Lady Palmerston that she met what she thought of for a very long time afterwards as the perfect man – and he was not in uniform. He was as brilliant as he was beautiful: tall, graceful, almost ridiculously handsome with dark eyes and thick, waving chestnut hair; witty, charming, erudite – 'horrid clever', as Fanny put it with a sigh – and wealthy to boot, being the heir to the Earl of Pembroke. He danced twice with Fanny at the ball, and was charming to her; she was ready, even eager to fall in love. She soon discovered he had his eye on someone else entirely; but it was a lesson to her.

'His views were so serious, but somehow they didn't seem dull at all when he talked about them,' she told Charlotte. 'It has proved to me that an intellectual lover is what I want. No more merry rattles for Miss Hobsbawn! I must have a man of sense.'

'Poor Fanny!' said Charlotte. Mr Herbert was practically betrothed.

'Never mind,' Fanny said briskly. 'If there is one, there must be another.'

Lucy was roughly sympathetic. 'Sidney Herbert would never have done for you, Fanny. He's a good man, I don't deny, and very clever, but there's something insipid about him. Too much milk in his veins and not enough fire. And too religious by half, like so many of these philanthropists.'

'Oh Grandmama, how can anyone be too religious?' Charlotte said with mild reproach.

'You'll find out,' Lucy said. 'Simple piety is all very well, but when it's mixed with sentiment and sighing and self-abasement and false humility, it slips and slithers into something quite different that I've no taste for. Religion and sentimentality need to be kept well apart, especially if you're going to have to do with the sick and the poor.'

One evening after dinner, when Charlotte was doing the honours of the tea-table, Lord Ashley lingered by her after she had filled his cup, and said, 'I understand that you have had some experience of teaching poor children?'

'Just for a few weeks,' Charlotte said, and explained the circumstances. 'I still have an interest in the little school, but it is confined to financial support now.'

'Not to be decried,' Ashley said. 'But I wonder if I could enlist both your financial and your active support in a scheme which is dear to my heart – the Ragged Schools.'

Charlotte had heard the term, but didn't know much about them. Ashley explained. The missionaries of the London City Mission had started the movement some years ago, providing free teaching on Thursday and Sunday evenings for children and adults too ragged to be accepted in regular schools. 'The difference it makes to these people's lives is remarkable,' Ashley said. 'To lift them even a little out of the black despair of ignorance in which they live – well, I'm sure I don't need to tell *you* what a revelation it is to them, and how grateful they are. It is the work of the greatest importance, and all carried out by volunteers. Last year they formed themselves into a Union of Ragged Schools, and asked me to be their chairman, and so it is something I have always in my view. If I could interest you—' he paused hopefully.

'I should be glad to help,' she said.

He smiled, and it transformed his face. He was tall and rather grim-looking, with his beaky nose and deepset, dark eyes, but his smile was very sweet. 'Thank you. Your grandmother told me that you were looking for a way to be useful.'

'You need only name the sum,' Charlotte said.

'You are most generous, and money is always needed, always welcome. But with your previous experience, I wonder if I could persuade you to teach at one of our schools as well? We are so short of teachers, and there are always more poor people eager for the benefit than we can accommodate. Every minute of your time would be well spent.'

'If you think me capable, I will do it willingly,' Charlotte said at once. 'Had you somewhere specific in mind?'

'There is a school newly set up in the rookeries of Westminster,' Ashley said eagerly.

Lord Theakston, who had wandered over to see what it was they were discussing so earnestly, heard the last words and said, 'The rookeries of Westminster? Our national disgrace, eh, Ashley? That such a place should exist right under the walls of Parliament, and the Abbey, and Buckingham Palace! Conyngham was telling me there was another intruder the other day, climbed over the wall into the palace grounds. Wouldn't be tolerated in another country.'

'In another country they would burn down the rookeries,' Ashley said, 'and the people would be driven elsewhere. I hope we have better feelings in this country. I was telling Lady Chelmsford about the Ragged School just being set up in Blue Boar Alley, and enlisting her services to teach there.'

Danby frowned at that. 'Blue Boar Alley? Come now, Ashley, you don't mean her ladyship to go walking into that den of thieves?'

'I assure you, sir, I wouldn't suggest it if I thought there was any danger. It's true that the poor wretched inhabitants have resented attempts to improve them, and that visitors have been attacked, but they were ill-advised people without the slightest sympathy, who wanted to preach morality without understanding the problems or trying to alleviate them. I assure you I have always been gently treated, and I have walked through the worst alleys and courts. They come to me to tell me their needs, and they speak with a natural courtesy which would do them credit if they were living with every comfort, but which coming from people in the direst of want simply makes me—' He stopped and shook his head, his eyes full of tears.

Lord Ashley did weep a lot, as Charlotte was to discover,

but his help was nevertheless always practical, and he did not stint the time and effort he gave to those who enlisted his pity. Danby went on being doubtful about the wisdom of Charlotte's venturing into such a dreadful place, and Lucy, when appealed to, thought it pointless to teach people without first addressing their physical needs, but when Charlotte showed herself eager to be a teacher, and Lord Ashley promised to take her to the school himself and guarantee her safety, they made no further objection.

That night, Charlotte told Norton about the scheme, and Norton, taking the pins out of her hair and watching her covertly in the looking-glass, saw that opposition would be useless, and merely added in a matter-of-fact way, 'You had better take me with you, my lady. I know these people and their ways. I could be useful to you.'

'Do you really want to come?' Charlotte said. 'I would be very glad to have you with me, but I thought it might distress you, so I wouldn't suggest it.'

'Oh, it won't trouble me, my lady,' Norton said. She did not think it necessary to repeat the terse but heartfelt conversation she had had with Lady Theakston on the stairs on her way up.

The Devil's Acre, as the bad area of Westminster was sometimes known, did not come as such a terrible shock to Charlotte as some had supposed it would. She had heard plenty about such places from Norton, and she had seen something of them herself while in Manchester. It was typical of the low places which were growing up around the old centres of expanding towns, when wealthy people moved away to more airy districts, and poor people crowded in.

First of all the good-sized old houses, once inhabited by the rich, were divided up: they had plenty of rooms on several storeys, and cellars and attics besides, and with division and sub-division soon resembled a rats' maze of human nests and burrows. Around these were lesser houses, smaller, more simple dwellings originally intended to shelter the working families who served the rich. Subdivision turned these into lodging houses for the poor, sometimes merely crowded, sometimes filthy and vile. And finally the gardens, yards and other spaces in between were filled in, with buildings of flimsy construction, low cottages, wooden sheds, pigsties, rickety lean-tos, which became shelters of unspeakable squalor.

Thus the creation of the rookery was completed; and the people, vermin and waste matter accumulated in the foetid spaces of what were coming to be called 'back-slums'. It was a term Charlotte now grew acquainted with. From Norton she had learned that 'slum' was a cant word meaning simply one's living-place; 'back-slum' had meant the living-place of the poorest sort who inhabited the spaces behind the main thoroughfares, but now it was coming to connote the whole area of a rookery, like the Devil's Acre or the Nichol.

Ashley was right to say that Charlotte would come to no harm. She entered the Devil's Acre for the first time in his company, and on foot, and saw for herself how he was already known and liked, how people greeted him respectfully, and on his stopping to talk to them, crowded round him eagerly to tell him their troubles. He introduced Charlotte to them, and they inspected her carefully and then, when they had seen that she did not shrink from them with horror or stare at them as though they were freaks, greeted her, too, with politeness. Charlotte said little, listened attentively, learning what aspects of their deprivation troubled them most; and wondered at their cheerfulness in spite of all their wretchedness, which even spilled over into humour. To joke in the face of such adversity seemed to Charlotte a special kind of grace, and alone of all the things she heard and saw brought her close to shedding a tear.

The Ragged School, when they were finally able to get to it, was a disused stable which had been scrubbed out and patched up and furnished with some trestles and benches. Slates, slate pencils and some copies of the Bible had been provided by charitable individuals; the minds of the volunteer teachers furnished the rest. Charlotte took up her duties with a good will, and found that, as Ashley had said, there were more potential pupils than teachers to teach them or space to accommodate them. Long before the appointed hour people began gathering around the school in the hope of being taken on, or at least of overhearing what was being said to the lucky few. There was never any difficulty, as there had been in Chetton, of finding people willing to be taught. If any pupil disappeared or failed to arrive, there was a throng waiting to take his place.

There was no lack of enthusiasm amongst the pupils – even the children wanted to learn, and applied themselves to the best of their abilities; though there were times when she wondered whether their motives for learning were as pure as the teachers believed them to be. Some of the filthy, barefooted, verminous children admitted cheerfully to her that they lived by thieving, and one imp told her that he wanted to learn to read and write so that he could 'go on the screeving lay' – become a forger – which would be more lucrative and less risky than pickpocketing or housebreaking. She suspected there was more than one who hoped to move himself up the criminal hierarchy by learning a new skill, and was hard put to it to blame them. She was even approached by a prostitute who wanted to be taught to talk 'like a swell' so that she could attract a better class of customer – though as the woman was indescribably filthy and had a large number of sores on her face, Charlotte doubted a change of accent would help her.

Charlotte did not enjoy the teaching; often it was frustrating and sometimes seemed hopeless; but she was glad to be doing something to help, and felt that anything that lightened the fog of ignorance that prevailed was useful. Naturally the people who came forward wanting to be taught were the more vigorous, less hopeless ones. She was aware, both from the exercise of logic and from her own observations, that there was a mass of people in far worse case, either more debilitated, more hopeless, or more depraved, whom this little exercise could not and did not touch. But there were occasional moments which made it worth while, when someone who had been struggling suddenly broke through the invisible barrier to their understanding, and the loveliness of enlightenment shone in their eyes; and the gratitude of those she taught was expressed daily in many ways.

Once she was settled into the work, she persuaded Fanny to help. Fanny came very reluctantly; she hated the sights and smells she was exposed to; but she was a tough little person, and once she had resigned herself to it, she did well as a teacher. She was better with the adults than the children, and as far as possible Charlotte saw to it that she was given the brighter and less filthy pupils. She was not doing it for the mortification and ultimate salvation of her soul, as were the missionaries and the evangelical volunteers, and Charlotte saw no reason why she should be tried as they were.

Meanwhile, Lucy's quest for a chaperone for them had yielded at last a distant cousin's widow, a Mrs Pemberton Manvers. This lady scored highly with Lucy by not presenting herself but having to be sought out, and for at least seeming reluctant to give up her humble independent establishment for the fatter pastures of dependency. Lucy invited her to come down from her village in Northamptonshire and be interviewed, approved her, and introduced her to Charlotte. Charlotte took to her at once. She seemed sensible, good-tempered, and without the slightest interest in fashionable society or titles or who was related to whom. She was a woman of some education with a passion for the history of ancient civilisations, and Charlotte was able to persuade her to the position of chaperone largely because living in London would give her access to the libraries and collections, and the public lectures at University College and the Museum. She and Charlotte came to an agreement that she would come and live with Fanny and Charlotte in the house in Berkeley Street for a trial period of one year; though after a month or so it was obvious that it was working so well, there was no question but that the arrangement would continue.

The final arrangements were made, and Fanny and Charlotte took up residence in Berkeley Street at the end of May, 1846. Charlotte was delighted with the freedom of having her own establishment at last, and the value of having money was keenly appreciated by her, both for making it possible, and for making them all comfortable. The house was fitted up with all the latest conveniences; and every sensible luxury, in the way of lighting, heating, baths, books and pianofortes, had been provided. Nor had Charlotte forgotten the servants: Norton's advice had been sought, considerable rebuilding had been carried out, modern appliances and arrangements installed. If the matter of the stairs – which in every London house were necessarily numerous – could be overlooked, it was certain that Lady Chelmsford's servants would have nothing to plague them, and no reason ever to want to leave.

BOOK THREE

The Harbour

Go from me. Yet I feel that I shall stand
Henceforward in thy shadow. Nevermore
Alone upon the threshold of my door
Of individual life I shall command
The uses of my soul, nor lift my hand
Serenely in the sunshine as before,
Without the sense of that which I forbore—
Thy touch upon the palm.

Elizabeth Barrett Browning:
Sonnet from the Portuguese

CHAPTER EIGHTEEN

Benedict didn't think he could have coped without Father Sparrow. The one shock to some extent cancelled out the other, like a toothache giving relief from a stomach ache, but between the two there was no rest; and there was so much to do.

There was no hope of keeping the news of the discovery of Ferrars' body secret. The carpenter could not have been silenced, short of killing him too, and the story lost nothing in the telling. Father Moineau heard many versions featuring rotting corpses, grinning skeletons, headless ghosts, oceans of blood and rivers of horror – the reality was decorous in comparison. But as easily as he and Benedict could reconstruct the story, so could everyone else. There were enough people who knew that Nicholas Morland had not only ordered but had personally supervised the nailing up of the door. As to why he had murdered his steward, no-one knew, probably no-one would ever know – but that didn't stop everyone having a theory.

There had to be an inquest, of course, and though it was held at Morland Place, it stirred the story into a county-wide talking-point. The verdict was returned as murder by person or persons unknown, but the county knew better. There were some who resolved to cut Benedict from then on, and never to buy another Morland horse as long as they lived, but on the whole the story was taken as more interesting than scandalous, and Benedict was well enough liked to be pitied rather than shunned.

Father Moineau carried his point and buried Ferrars in the crypt, and Benedict furnished a handsome coffin, which the county took as a generous gesture and much to his credit. And the stone was put back, and that ought to have been the end of it, as Moineau had promised. But it wasn't, of course. The barbican apartment was full of Ferrars' things, which had to be gone through. Moineau volunteered for the task. The clothes and personal bits and pieces were bundled into sacks to be taken away and burned, but there were papers there too, which proved interesting reading.

'You know where the money is?' Benedict said in astonishment.

Father Moineau, toasting his behind at the fire – it had been a cold day up there in the barbican rooms – nodded calmly. 'The odd thing is that the man was a good steward in his way. And the reason the house accounts were so badly kept is that he had no interest in them and no time for them. Everything is recorded exactly and in great detail in his own private account books. If you want a full history of the period, you have only to graft his pages into the household records.'

'All the money?' Benedict persisted, not interested in written history at this juncture. 'Jemima's too?'

Again the priest nodded. 'He kept the accounts quite separately.'

That was a relief to Benedict, who had been unable properly to compensate Jemima without knowing what had been stolen from her. 'And where is the money? The actual gold?'

'In a bank in London,' Moineau said. 'There is correspondence about it.'

'In a bank?' Benedict said in astonishment. 'In all these years they never sent to enquire? Never wrote to him?'

'What for? He made deposits at irregular intervals, and

unless he asked for a withdrawal, what was there to tell him?' He smiled to himself. 'Young Harry Anstey will have a pretty problem, establishing rightful ownership to the funds. You had better not count on having the money soon.'

Moineau was right about that, at any rate. The business dragged on and on, and Benedict's only comfort was that Jemima expressed herself resolutely uninterested in the outcome. 'I have enough for my needs. You have been very generous with me, and Papa's business brings me an income. Why should I want more?'

But the money side of it was the least troublesome to Benedict. The worst thing was contemplating the awful fact of what must have happened, and not knowing the details. Had there been a quarrel? Why had Nicky gone up there, and whose was the gun? Had he meant to kill him, or did it happen by accident? He hoped the latter – he hoped that nailing up the door was the reaction of panic to having accidentally killed him – but he feared the former. What had been the relationship between them, why had Nicky kept him on, why had he finally turned against him? These were questions he plagued himself with, as he played the scenes over and over in his mind, first one way and then another; he dreamed them at night, through uneasy, prowling sleep, and woke sometimes crying out and sweating as the brown, grinning face with the black gaping nostrils sprang out of the corners of his memory, or when the thing with the hooked fingers shuffled towards him with murderous intent and he found his feet turned to lead.

He wondered sometimes how much Aglaea knew. He thought of her withdrawal from the world into a place of her own, where nothing existed but the sea and the sky; thought of her sitting endlessly painting, hardly aware even of Jemima sitting beside her. He wondered how much she must have suspected, and did not want to ask her. Her life here as Nicky's wife must have been hellish, and whatever peace she had found for herself, he would not disturb. Jemima he was sure had known nothing: she was too normal and contented to be harbouring dark secret knowledge.

And when thinking about the horrors of that became too much for him, there was a counterbalancing pain in thinking about Rosalind. Aglaea's first letter had told him only what Harry had blurted out – that Rosalind had been brought to bed of a boy and had died of a haemorrhage. More details came later, from Aglaea at his request, and from Sir Carlton. Such haemorrhages were not uncommon – were one of the most frequent causes of death in childbirth; the midwife had done all she could; the doctor had been sent for, but was out with another patient and could not be found in time. No-one was really to blame.

His wife was dead. Benedict was a widower. There were many things to think about there. One of them was that there would not now have to be a divorce. He could not help thinking that he could have saved all the agony of the separation and the consequent exposure of his cuckoldry. If he had kept her by him – ah, but if he had kept her by him, she might not have died. Had there not been some neglect? Why was the doctor not on hand? Why was he not sent for as soon as she went into labour? Was her death, in short, not Benedict's fault?

He put on mourning. He told Mary that her mother was dead, and Mary wept a little, but she had lost her mother once already, and Father Moineau was teaching her French songs. And he thought about the funeral. Miniott wrote to ask him, as was proper, whether he wanted to bury Rosalind at Morland Place. She had died his wife, though apart from him; the decision was rightfully his. Benedict thought about it, and for once he did not ask Father Moineau's advice. Rosalind had never liked Morland Place, and it had never liked her. Her childhood home he had sold, and there wasn't another place she really belonged – except, perhaps, he thought in a spirit of irony, at Ledston Park. No, let Scarborough have her. Miniott might as well bury her, since he had loved her. He wrote back to Sir Carlton telling him to make what arrangements he liked, and send the bill to Harry Anstey. Aglaea offered to represent him at the funeral, and he accepted guiltily, wanting nothing but to forget as soon as possible.

But at the last moment he found he could not be so indifferent so soon. When it came to it, he had to go to say goodbye. It was a tiresome journey in winter, by carriage. The railway was building fast, but it would not be opening until July, another five months. He would have been glad of it then. He suddenly remembered telling Rosalind how she would like to go to Scarborough by railway, and was suddenly in tears, the tears that had eluded him so long. He wept for her and for himself, for the children she had borne, and his own children unborn, and for the waste of it all. Jolting along in a stuffy, chilly coach on a dark February day, he put his face down into his hands and wept.

Scarborough was bitter: a northeasterly wind with Siberian ice in its breath did not seem to have lost anything from its crossing of the north sea. If the wind had dropped, Aglaea assured him, he would have found it much warmer than in York – as witness the fact that the funeral was taking place at all, for in York they would not yet have been able to get a spade in the ground. The little churchyard on the top of the cliff overlooked the sea, separated from it, it seemed, by nothing more than a railing fence and a row of stunted, windbent thorns. In summer it would have been a lovely place, when the sea was blue and sparkling; today it was tormented by the wind, which was so full of spray it was salt on the lips. The sea was grey and tossed under a grey sky, and gulls whirled about restlessly, crying like lost souls.

Rosalind was attended to her grave by Benedict, Aglaea, her maid, and the landlady of the lodgings where she had died. The priest hurried through the service, shivering in his billowing surplice. Aglaea stood gravely, her head bent, a spray of winter jasmine in her hand. Benedict wept again as the coffin was lowered, and thought that he should have brought her home after all. She was his wife, he owed her that. But it was too late now.

The priest hurried away as soon as the last words were said and the sexton and his lad stepped forward to start shovelling. Aglaea threw the spray of flowers down, and they gleamed a moment like a spark of sunshine in the gloom, before the first clod struck, scattering into dark crumbs over the blossoms. Then she and Benedict turned away. The cold, salty wind dried the tears on his cheeks. He held open the wicket gate for her, and she said, 'Well, that's the end of it.'

But it wasn't, of course. Miniott had had the decency not to come to the graveyard, but driven by his own concerns he accosted Benedict in the town, after he had parted from Aglaea and was heading back for his own lodgings.

'What do you want?' Benedict said, more weary than affronted.

'I'm sorry,' Miniott said, 'but I have to speak to you.'

He looked so miserable, so pinched with cold, blue of cheek and red of eye – above all so *old*, that Benedict, absurdly, took pity on him. They were near the Clarendon. 'Step in here, then,' he said, 'out of this accursed wind.'

Inside the hotel Benedict found a quiet corner and sent the waiter for whisky – nothing else, he thought, would ever warm his bones again. When it came, he sipped, but Miniott drank his straight down, as if to give him courage.

'I wish I could tell you, Morland, how sorry I am,' he began.

'If that's all you want to say,' Benedict began, but Miniott shook his head, lifting a hand as if to stay him.

'No, it's something important. You've been very generous. The pension you gave her was generous, more than anyone could have expected. She spoke warmly of you—' He raised his eyes cautiously, but Benedict's face was grim. 'I thought you would want to know that. Also that there was no neglect. It all happened very suddenly – there was no time, no chance to save her. The midwife said it was the uterine artery. It was over in minutes.'

Benedict turned his face away, feeling sick. 'Well?' he said. 'And is that all?'

Miniott hesitated. 'The child – her child. It's a boy. Healthy. He's a stout, lively baby, the midwife says. She found a wet-nurse for him—'

'Why should you think I want to hear this? In God's name, what is it you want?'

'I have so little money,' Miniott said starkly. 'The child is bonny, he deserves a chance of life. I wondered if you would consider continuing the pension for the child – for Rosalind's sake.'

Benedict stared at him incredulously. He had never seen a man look so miserable. In an instant of sympathy he saw what the loss of Rosalind meant for Miniott, and how little he felt himself equal to the task of bringing up a son alone, when he ought to be enjoying his grandchildren. Benedict wanted to laugh, though he knew it was the impulse of hysteria, and resisted it. 'You – want me – to pay you a pension – to keep your son?'

403

'Rosalind's child,' Miniott urged. 'If she had lived you would have done so.'

'*Your* child. The one you killed her for,' Benedict said, and then was sorry. Miniott's face grew visibly greyer.

'For God's sake, don't you think I've thought that?' he said in a low voice. 'Have a little pity—'

'And what pity did you ever have on me? You or her? Well, it's finished now. I never want to see you again, Miniott – you or your son.'

He stood up to go. Miniott stood with him, reached out an urgent hand, actually laid it on his sleeve in his desperation.

'You *must* help me. For the child's sake. He's Mary's brother, don't forget—'

And now Benedict did what he had always restrained himself from; but this time the thing was simply surprised out of him by anger on Mary's behalf. He hit Miniott. At the last instant, in deference to Miniott's age and misery he managed to open his hand and turn it from a blow with a fist to a slap with the palm, but it was hard enough to knock the man off his feet. He sat down hard in the chair he had just vacated, his hand flying to his injured face. Benedict stood a moment looking down at him, his hand stinging, feeling satisfaction and a queer twist of regret.

'I never want to see you again,' he repeated softly. Miniott said nothing, looking up at him from behind his hand, and he turned and went away. But that look stayed with Benedict long after he had forgotten any that Rosalind had ever given him; and he knew that the thought of Miniott's boy, Mary's brother, would haunt him all the rest of his life.

Work was his salvation, and there was plenty of it. Morland Place and all its concerns, the home farm, the tenant farms, the sheep, the wool and the weavers; and the horses, most of all the horses, kept him busy from morning till night and from day to day. He had good men under him, and he could have hired more and done less, contented himself with supervising, but it was not what he wanted then. He needed to find a purpose for everything that had happened, a meaning for his life, and if it wasn't Morland Place it was hard to see what it was.

Haxby came asking about the apartment over the barbican – when would it be possible for him to move in? 'You still want to live there?' Benedict said in astonishment.

'It's a good place,' Haxby said solidly. 'Good rooms, and I should like my independence, and to be handier for the house.'

'But – after what's happened there—'

'There can't be many old places that haven't got their secrets,' Haxby said. 'And I'm not afeared of ghosts, Mr Morland.'

'It's yours as soon as you want it,' Benedict said, almost babbling with gratitude. 'Throw out anything you don't like the look of. I'll furnish it new if you like.'

'No need, sir. What's there is stoutly made, and my needs are simple.'

'Thank you, Haxby,' Benedict said, feeling the shadow of Ferrars' death lighten a little.

'Thank *you*, maister,' Haxby returned, as if it were a mere exchange of courtesies.

Father Moineau helped him, too. Benedict kept expecting him to announce one morning that he was off, but he did not seem to be in any hurry. He was enjoying having his old chapel back, and Benedict was glad to have it occupied again, and the daily services he had grown up with resumed, the candles lit and the smell of fresh incense always thrumming about that corner of the staircase hall. Worshipping in there every day with the old familiar words and responses made it seem less and less important that

405

Ferrars' bones were under the floor. There were so many bones down there; you couldn't start minding about bones if you lived in a house with its own chapel and crypt. And Father Moineau had promised he would lie quietly. The lamp on the Lady altar was lit again, and burned its soft pale light day and night, as though She had returned to watch over them. It was almost like having his mother back. He brought flowers one day to put on her altar, and found someone had been before him: a bunch of daffodils and catkin sprays had been put in Her silver vase.

When he asked Moineau about it, the old man smiled. 'It's Mary. Her governess complains that I'm turning her into a "papist heretic", but I promise you it is her own idea completely. She has a natural piety, that's all.'

When Benedict asked Mary about it, she just said that she wanted to make the Lady's place look pretty. 'I like it in the chapel, now Father Sparrow's come. He makes it jolly there, and lets me take Dog in, and never makes me hush or look solemn, or tells me I mustn't laugh. He says God likes us to be happy, and doesn't care to have glum faces around Him. But Miss Titchell says it's bad to laugh in church and she says Father Sparrow's wicked and a Roman – and something else about a haw and babbling, I think she said, but I don't know what that means.' She looked up into her father's face, her own shining like a flame in the silver lamp of her hair. She looked so like her mother, it made him quake; but – was it imagination, or was there something of him in that face, too? Didn't she resemble him, just a little? Was it possible for a child to grow like someone they weren't related to by blood?

'You like Father Sparrow, don't you, puss?'

'Oh yes,' Mary said with enormous enthusiasm. 'I *love* him. And he tells me such interesting things – not just about God and the Lady, but about France and Bonaparte and railways and flowers and birds and – *everything*! I wish he could always stay here.'

'So do I,' Benedict said. He watched Moineau more carefully after that, trying to judge what his intentions were. There was sometimes a wicked glint in the old man's eyes, as if he knew he was being watched, and Benedict began to have the feeling that if he would only leave well alone and *not* ask Moineau what his plans were, everything would be all right. The priest liked being here, felt he was at home, enjoyed the comfort and the good food, was fond of Benedict himself, and, most of all, was fascinated by Mary. They spent more and more time together, walking and talking, or heads together over a book, or romping and laughing in a way that Miss Titchell deeply disapproved of. As spring wore into summer, it was plain that one or other of them was going to have to give up dominion over Mary. He would have done without Miss Titchell altogether, if it was not that he felt Mary needed a female influence. The visiting tutors still taught her – Maitland music and dancing and Crofton mathematics and astronomy – so Benedict thought he had better regularise the situation and show Miss Titchell she must put up with Father Sparrow by making him her official tutor for French, German and religious instruction.

After that, things settled down. Miss Titchell saw she was not going to get her way, and since the alternative was to leave, and she really loved Mary, she put up with it, and did her best to counter Moineau's papish influence with a strain of her own. But since Moineau saw religion as something delightful and pleasurable and Miss Titchell saw it as a a stern and rather gloomy duty, she hadn't much hope of succeeding. Benedict had the satisfaction of seeing Mary bloom between the ministrations of the two, and of knowing that now Moineau couldn't leave.

*   *   *

Benedict would have called it an accident, although Father Moineau would probably have said God had his reasons for it, that he found himself in the vicinity of Moresby Manor at hay-time, when he was feeling a little melancholy. There was a small outlying tenant farm near Acaster Malbis where he had gone to see the harvest; riding back on his young horse, with Kai running ahead of him, inspecting the hedges, he had passed a field belonging to Lord Howick of Moresby Manor where they were still getting in. It was natural to stop and look on – what farmer wouldn't?

It was a lovely sight, the rhythm of man, beast, and ripening earth, all working together for the same good. But haying always made him feel a wistful kind of sadness, for it was a time of youthful joys, and every harvest drew one further from it. And somewhere working on this same land was the only son of his body, Thomas, little Tommy, whom he had given up for his own good when his mother had married Joe Thompson. If Benedict had known how things would turn out, he would probably not have parted so easily from his own flesh and blood. He had not seen Tommy since the wedding – had thought it was fairer on the boy and his mother to take himself out of their lives altogether. It was so ironic to think of the children scattered about who had at one time or another had a claim on him – Mary at Morland Place, Rosalind's son in Scarborough, Thomas at Moresby Park – and only the last was of his blood. He had no son to inherit Morland Place. A sudden desire was on him to see the lad again; just to see him, and how he had turned out. He would not admit to himself that there lay carefully concealed under that the faint and shapeless idea that perhaps he could take Tommy to Morland Place in some capacity . . .

A labourer who was tedding close to the hedge stopped

to forearm the sweat from his brow, and nodded courteously to the gentleman on horseback.

'Looks like a good one,' Benedict said in response.

'Yes, sir, 'bundant. Thank the Lord,' the man said.

'You're late though.'

'That's right, sir. But the weather's holding. They're still cutting over to Copmanthorpe as well. Two days behind us, they are.'

'Is Mr Turner about?' Benedict asked casually. Turner was the land agent for Lord Howick, responsible for the estate workers.

'Yessir. He's over yonder far side, by the cart. Shall I call him for you?'

'No, don't you trouble,' Benedict said. There was a gate a little further along. 'I'll tie my horse to the gate and walk over. I just want a friendly word with him, as I'm passing.'

He tied up his horse, climbed over the gate, and stepped down into a world he knew so well, which was filled with memories, overlapping each other as one hay-harvest merged into another in his memory. It was a world of enclosed heat, and the smell of hay, like the smell of new bread coming out of the oven; of sore hands and parched throats, dust in the eyes, and scratchy wisps inside the clothing; of the smell of hot horses and man-sweat, of the silvery hissing of the scythes, and the rustling of the hay forever just under the level of hearing; of swallows swooping back and forth almost underfoot, and swifts far up in heaven, shrieking to God; of the white shimmer of sunlight and the cool juicy delight of the grass under the hedges. He remembered stone jugs brought out of stream or well and sweating coldness under the June sun – lemonade sharp enough to cut a hay-thirst, and the queer, flat taste of buttermilk. Bread and cheese and onions or meat pasties eaten under the shade of the

409

cart, staring out between the spokes at the colours of the hot world, the uncut hay like the rough blonde hair of a country girl, scarlet poppies and deep blue cornflowers her summer finery, and the sky overhead like a great bowl of creamy blue, with clouds so white you could hardly look at them.

Hay-harvest was a world you entered as a boy and never really left; it claimed you, a natural place of joy and endeavour, where work could not be other than holy, and laughter rose up from the hot earth like steam from a pot. Your innocent gladness lived there for ever, to be revisited sometimes, if you were lucky; the rest of you came away to get on as best it could without. Benedict walked across the field, feeling his loneliness come with him, but as his shadow did, attached to him, but not troubling him just now in this shadowless place. Kai ran ahead, running up to the harvesters and startling them by jabbing her cold nose suddenly into their hands, or whipping their legs with her hard tail. Some boys called to her, and she ran to them, frisking like a foolish puppy, bowing and grinning and inviting them to drop their rakes and play with her.

Benedict altered his course just slightly to head for them. It was a boy's time, hay-harvest, and he wanted to see their pleasure. Kai was frisking round a stocky lad with baling-string round his trouser legs (to stop mice running up them of course – gullible boys since time began had been warned about the danger of mice in the trousers at hay-time!). Benedict came strolling up, Kai bounced over to him, the boy turned, and Benedict found himself looking into his own face.

He was big for twelve, Benedict thought distantly, through the shock. He had not known that he knew how old the boy was until that moment. Thirteen in November. He was almost as tall as Benedict himself, and hard work and good farm food had built him solidly, strong bones and good muscles, like a young stirk. He had dark curly hair, curly as a ram's fleece, with two corkscrew bits that stuck up like embryo horns, so that he looked like a young devil, or a Hereford bull, one or the other. Solemn dark eyes stared out of a brown face, through which the healthy red of the cheeks still showed – red and brown – brown as a berry, as the saying was.

'Izzat your bitch, maister?' the lad said, breaking the bubble that had formed round Benedict. He spoke like a country boy. He *was* a country boy, after all.

'Yes – yes it is. Her name's Kai.'

'She's right comely,' the boy said appreciatively, hunkering down and holding out his hands. Kai came to him and he caught her head and she tussled with him, putting a paw over his forearm and pretending to bite him. 'We 'ad a dog like this when I were a bairn. They're right cunning, are these – aren' ya, ma lass?'

That was Fand, Benedict thought – the dog of Tommy's youth. His own dog, Fand, who had been his father's before him. And Kai was Fand's – well, no, he had to give up the calculation, but they were kin all the same. Tommy remembered the dog, but didn't remember *him* – and that was how he had designed it. He had taken himself away to give Joe Thompson a fair chance at being Tommy's father, and he couldn't go back on that now.

'You're Thomas Thompson, aren't you?' he heard himself say.

The boy looked up, and then stood up, and Kai pawed his leg for the game to be resumed. 'That's right, sir,' he said, the question in his eyes.

'I – I knew your uncle,' Benedict said. Liza's brother Dandy Dick, the horse-boy on the railways whom he had befriended, was now bailey to Lord Lambert of Balderswick, and doing well, his railway days long forgotten, his language now steeped in the vocabulary of the land, as once it had been with the language of the cuttings and the tunnels. 'Have you had any news of him recently?'

'No, sir. I don't know, sir,' the boy said, obviously sorry to be disappointing the gentleman. 'He writes to me mam, sometimes, but I don't know if he's wrote recent. Me dad's over there, though, sir. He'd know – likely,' he added, with a desire to be perfectly honest.

Benedict glanced in the direction the boy indicated, and saw the unmistakable giant frame and blonde head of Joe Thompson. All his children would be blonde too, Benedict thought distractedly. What did people make of this dark, horned Pan in his brood?

'How many brothers and sisters have you now, Tommy?' Benedict asked suddenly.

'Four, sir, two of each. But me mam's—' He hesitated, not knowing if it was polite to mention it to a gentleman, or what would be the most suitable words. 'Hopeful again,' he finished.

Hopeful. Yes, that was the right word, Benedict thought. He had no business here, or with the boy's family, dispersing the hope and clouding the issue.

'I won't disturb your father. It doesn't matter,' Benedict said.

'He'd be pleased to speak to you, maister,' the lad said eagerly. It was plain he thought talking to his father was a pleasure, and one he would share with all the world.

'I must be off now, in any case,' Benedict said. The boy looked disappointed, and he said without thinking, 'Give my regards to your mother.'

'Yessir. What name shall I say, sir?'

Benedict thought of Liza, hopeful again. It would only upset her to hear his name. 'No, on second thoughts, don't say anything. It was your uncle I knew, properly speaking. I don't suppose she'd remember me.' And he

412

nodded a farewell, called to Kai, and walked back towards the gate. All the way across the hayfield he felt the boy's eyes on him, and longed insanely to turn back, tell him the whole story, and invite him to come home with him to Morland Place. But he was not his son any longer, he was Joe Thompson's boy – and what would a berry-brown country boy do at Morland Place? So he went on walking, with Kai trotting anxiously beside him, looking up into his face. The sun was still shining down with all its might, but the colour seemed to have gone out of the day, and even the poppies around the field edge seemed faded.

One day in March 1846, Father Moineau said to Benedict, 'You can take off your mourning now.'

Benedict looked down at the bands on his sleeves. 'I'd forgotten I had them on.'

'Very good,' Moineau nodded. 'You have reached the end of mourning. Life can begin again.'

'But in which direction?' Benedict said.

'God will guide you,' was the answer Benedict could perhaps have predicted. It seemed, in the immediate aftermath of having the bands removed from his sleeves, that everybody else in York was prepared to guide him. Invitations began to arrive to public meetings and private functions – particularly the latter – along with requests for him to interest himself in this or that scheme of charity or civic benefit. The number and urgency of the demands on his attention suggested they had been accumulating while his eye was off them like spiders in a corner. But he was a sociable man, and, sorting the wheat from the chaff, was glad to be visiting his friends again, and taking pleasure as well as work. He thought it might do everyone good if he indulged in a little entertaining at Morland Place too. Mary would certainly enjoy it, and it would ginger up the

413

servants, and though he hadn't a hostess, there was always some Anstey or other who could be borrowed to fill the position.

One fine Sunday he drove in to York with Mary to the service at the Minster. He wore a rather jolly striped waistcoat under his jacket, and tied his neckcloth with care; his hair was rather long because he hadn't got around to having it cut recently, but longer hair was becoming fashionable, so he thought he would pass. Mary came down into the hall all ready, looking like something out of a story-book, with her multilayered, bunchy skirts, her lace-edged drawers, and her long golden ringlets drawing attention to her perfect pink-and-white face.

'You look nice, Papa,' she said. 'It is a special occasion?'

'I think it is, rather,' he said. 'You look nice too – as if you were entirely made of sugar.'

'Then I should melt in the rain,' she objected practically.

'It won't rain today. Will you drive with me in my curricle, princess?'

Her face lit. She loved the curricle, and the speed of four horses. 'Oh yes! And will you let me drive?'

'Certainly not,' he laughed. 'But I will teach you to drive – in a phaeton. We'll drag your grandmother's out and see if it's still fit to go.'

'Two horses?' she said hopefully.

'One to begin with. Then a pair. And when your hands are big enough, I'll teach to to drive a team – that's a promise.'

It satisfied her for now. He wondered if she remembered the tiny child-size carriage he had had made for her first birthday. He didn't mention it now, because it brought back memories of her mother, and he had almost managed to eliminate Rosalind from his thoughts. They walked out into the yard together, where the curricle was

414

waiting, and after a short tussle when it became clear he wasn't taking the dogs, they set off.

It didn't surprise him to find all eyes drawn to them as he drove through the narrow streets of York: his curricle was a smart one, and his team splendid, and a man accompanied by a ravishingly pretty little girl must always attract attention. He touched his hat and smiled and nodded, and Mary sat up straighter and waved more proudly moment by moment. As they drew up before the Minster and the groom jumped down to run to the horses' heads, a lady nearby on the footpath stepped up to the vehicle.

'Good morning, Mr Morland! What a fine day, is it not? It does one's heart good to see such a pleasant morning, not too hot and not too cold.'

Benedict removed his hat. 'Good morning, Mrs Crompton. Yes, it's very fine.' He could not jump down because she was standing just where he would land. Unless he turned his back on her and got down on the other side, he was trapped.

'You are come to the service, of course. The bishop is come so we are assured of a fine sermon today. I suppose that is what has tempted you away from your splendid house, for you have your own chaplain, as everyone knows. What a comfort that must be! And so this is your little girl! Do you know, I don't think I have ever happened to see her before. I don't know how that is. How do you do, my dear? What a pretty little love! I am sure if I had been so fortunate as to meet you before, we would have been great friends by now. I am excessively fond of children, Mr Morland. It was the greatest sorrow to me that Mr Crompton and I did not happen to have any before he passed on, for I always thought motherhood a woman's finest calling. But of course Mr Crompton was a great deal older than me.'

Fortunately the footpath was growing very crowded,

and the lady was forced at last by the sheer pressure of the current to move on, and Benedict heaved a sigh of relief as he jumped down and turned back to lift Mary out.

She had been following the progress of Mrs Crompton's hat from her vantage point, and now asked, interested but puzzled, 'What did that lady want?'

Benedict smiled a little grimly. 'I think she wanted to be your mother,' he said.

'How could she be?' Mary demanded.

'By marrying me.'

'Oh.' Mary frowned up at him. 'Are you going to marry her?'

'Certainly not.'

'Good,' said Mary. 'I thought she was very silly.'

'I agree with you, but it isn't polite to say so.' And Mrs Crompton was a well-known trap, who had married a confectioner forty years her senior and, disappointed in the fortune he obligingly left her after a very brief union, had been looking to augment it ever since. Benedict took Mary's hand and began to walk with her towards the Minster doors. 'Would you like a new mother?' he asked her.

Mary considered. 'I might. If she was nice.'

That day in York showed Benedict that Mrs Crompton was not the only unattached female with her eye on him, though she was the boldest. But the interest shown in him and in Mary by the distaff side of York's population made him feel like a large beefsteak at a civic banquet. He had not expected the interest to be so intense or so immediate – though, without conceit, he had known that as a wealthy widower with a handsome property, he would generally be considered an eligible match. He returned from the service in a thoughtful mood; and after a long conversation with Father Moineau, he sent Malton up to pack for him. When Mary came down from her lessons, he told her that he would be going away for a few days.

'You remember you said you might like a new mother? Well, I think I know of a nice one.'

'Are you going to fetch her?' Mary asked.

'It isn't as easy as that, chick. I have to find her first, and then I have to ask her if she'll come. It may take time. You must wish me luck.'

'I'll sit on my handkerchief,' Mary said. 'Aunt Celia says that brings good luck. What's her name – the nice lady?'

'I'll tell you that when I get back – if I'm successful,' Benedict said.

Because of the necessity for discretion, it took him a week to discover that the Mayhews were in Bath, but only a few hours to follow them there. Not for the first time, he was grateful for the railways. He was also glad that Bath was beginning to fill up, for a few weeks earlier he would have been very conspicuous, the resident population of the city being now rather elderly. The Mayhews, he understood, were staying at The York House, so he took a room at a small hotel at the other end of town, and prepared to hang around the Pump Room as his best chance of encountering his quarry. Everyone came sooner or later to the Pump Room, whether or not they were in Bath to drink the waters – though in view of Sir Samuel's age, he had a good hope that the waters and the baths were his object, rather than the social round.

At the most crowded hour of the following morning, his vigil was rewarded. He had placed himself between the tea urns and the pump, shielded, he hoped, from view by a large tub of ferns; feeling ridiculous and nervous by turns. And at twenty after eleven o'clock he saw them enter: Sir Samuel, red of face and blue of nose, in a wheelchair pushed by an elderly servant, Sibella walking just to the side. She was wearing a dark-green redingote and a tubular bonnet trimmed with black marabou, and looked so neat and smart that several pairs of eyes turned as she passed. Benedict felt his palms grow damp and his pulse quicken at the sight of her, though in fear of being seen by Sir Samuel he drew back a little behind the fern. Whether the movement caught her eye, or whether it was some deeper instinct he hardly dared think about, but she turned her head and looked directly at him. For an instant her face was blank, as if not understanding what she saw. Then her eyes flashed wide. He saw her turn pale and flush in rapid succession, and she shook her head in warning before she passed on.

The chair was wheeled directly to the pump, where Sir Samuel took his glass of water and drank it down with a grim expression. Benedict wondered about the chair, desperately trying not to hope it betokened some serious decline in health. He watched Sibella bend over him tenderly to take back the glass and hand him a handkerchief to dab his lips. When the ceremony was complete they turned away and moved to a table at the side of the room, where a chair was found for Sibella, tea was ordered from the waiter, and Sir Samuel opened his newspaper. He seemed to have no acquaintance, for no-one stopped to speak to him; nor did he speak to Sibella during that time. She sat with her hands folded in her lap, silent, looking at nothing, apparently absorbed in her own thoughts. After half an hour the newspaper was folded up, and the party left by the far door. Sibella did not look again in Benedict's direction. He tried to follow them discreetly, but lost them at the busy crossing at the corner of York Street. He supposed they were going back to the hotel, and since he could not present himself there without being conspicuous, he was forced to let it go.

For the rest of the day he mouched about the town, feeling frustrated, foolish, and doubting the wisdom of his being there at all. He ate an indifferent dinner and went early to bed, to toss and turn all night, thinking of Sibella, sleeping in unrefreshing snatches, and dreaming guiltily of being caught out by Sir Samuel, who bore in his dreams a strong resemblance to Father Moineau.

The next morning he presented himself at the Pump Room again with better hope, for water-takers were generally methodical in their self-inflicted suffering, and now that Sibella knew he was here, he hoped she might find the opportunity to separate herself from her companions. The party arrived at a quarter to twelve, and followed the same routine. When they were seated and the tea had been brought, Sibella looked directly at Benedict and shook her head again, and his heart sank. He remained at his post, however, in the hope of something happening, and it was well that he did. When Sir Samuel folded his newspaper and the party prepared to leave, Sibella hung behind just a little, looked again towards Benedict, and slipped a piece of paper under her empty cup and saucer before hurrying after her husband.

Benedict waited until they had left the room, and then made his way, as casually as possible, towards the table they had vacated. He was a little too casual – the waiter had come with a tray to clear the table before he reached it, and Benedict saw the piece of paper swept with the crumbs onto an empty plate and carried away. It was a time for desperate measures. He flung himself across the waiter's path and tripped him, sending the man and the tray crashing to the floor. In the general consternation he was able to secure the piece of paper and thrust it, a little tea-stained, into his pocket, and then was forced to endure the waiter's resentful apologies and a post-mortem by the manager under the curious eyes of a score of onlookers before he could remove himself to a private place to read his precious note.

It was very brief. '3pm. Library, Gay Street.'

His heart sang.

It was nearer four when she came, heavily veiled, to browse among the bookshelves. He drifted over to stand beside her. She was to the point, speaking without looking at him. 'He sleeps in the afternoon, but I must be back when he wakes. I will go into the gardens opposite. If it is safe to talk, I will hold my parasol in my left hand. Otherwise don't come near me.'

She left, and he waited a few moments before following, strolling casually, as if enjoying the fine day. She was walking slowly along the gravel path, looking about her. He walked behind her; saw her switch her parasol to her left hand and turn off onto a side path, and increased his pace, trying not to look too purposeful, feeling ashamed at so much subterfuge.

When he reached her she put up her veil and turned to look at him. She looked drawn and older than her years; her grey eyes were troubled, and her freckles stood out like scars against the pallor of her skin. Benedict remembered how full of spirit she had been, and mourned the loss of her bright youthful joy. Had that old man done this to her? A low rage burned in him.

'It is not safe,' she said without preamble. 'I am watched constantly. Why have you come here?' She scanned his face eagerly even while she reproved him and he wanted to snatch her up onto his saddle and gallop off with her. But she had gone to the dragon of her own free will, he reminded himself.

'I had to see you. I needed to talk to you.'

'The time for that was long ago,' she said with bitter humour.

'I know,' he said. 'I understand that now. I was a fool – I'm sorry.'

'So you should be,' she said. 'You have ruined both our lives. You should have married *me*.'

'You were so young. I didn't know. Was it – was it me you spoke about, when you said you loved a man who was unsuitable?'

'Of course. Has it taken you until now to find it out? I always loved you, from the time I first met you, when I was fourteen years old. But it's no use now. I should not speak of it at all, but – oh, this life is intolerable!' The last words burst out of her, as though against her will.

'The wheelchair,' Benedict said quickly. 'Is he ill?'

'His health is failing. The doctor says it is his liver – drinking bad port in his youth. He only drinks good port now, but the damage is done, according to the doctor. He sent him here, to take the water, and to go to the baths. I don't know if it will do any good – the doctor didn't seem very sanguine about it. I think he sent him just to be rid of him for a while. His complaint makes him bad-tempered, you see.'

'Poor Sib – does he take it out on you?'

She said calmly. 'I am used to it now, and it's not so bad. He would never strike me. But he is so suspicious – and unjust.' She raised her eyes to him again. 'Why have you come here to torment me? It only makes it worse. I get by very well if I don't think of you.'

'I didn't come to torment you, but to tell you—' There was no choice of words. 'Rosalind is dead. I am a widower. I am free, Sibella, and I came to tell you that I have come to my senses. I love you – I think I always have, but I was too much of a fool to realise it.'

She said nothing for a moment, staring at him desperately, as if straining to read his soul through his face. 'You're free?' she said at last. She stopped walking and turned towards him. He nodded, and took her hand, and it rested in his, small and quiet, but somehow more alive

421

than anything else in the whole world. 'But it's no use,' she said at last, hopelessly. 'I cannot break my vows.'

'I wouldn't ask you to,' he said. 'I know what it's like to be a deceived husband; I have been sickened by lies and subterfuge. I want nothing for us that is not open and honest and wholesome. I want you, dearest Sibella, but I want to claim you before the whole world.' She said nothing. 'He is an old man,' he went on, 'and you say he is failing—'

'I won't wish him dead!' she cried out suddenly. 'Don't make me think it.'

'No, no. Hush, darling. I don't mean that. I don't want anything to overshadow our time, when it comes. I only want you to know that it *will* come. I will wait for you, however long it takes.'

'Wait for me?' she said, sounding almost dazed.

'If you will have me.' He smiled a little. 'I am being presumptuous. When that day comes that you are free as well, will you marry me?'

'Yes,' she said simply.

'Then everything is all right,' he said with satisfaction. 'It's only a matter of time.'

When he got back to Morland Place, Mary came running to meet him, with the dogs frisking like puppies around her.

'Did you find her, Daddy?' was her first question.

'Yes,' he said, sweeping her up into his arms – something that was getting harder to do. 'Good God, I think you've grown two inches since I've been away, and I haven't been gone a fortnight.'

'Don't be silly,' Mary said, sweeping all that aside for the important matter. 'Did you ask the lady? Will she come?'

'Yes,' he said again. 'Not now, but one day.' He thought of the wheelchair, and the not-sanguine doctor, and Sir Samuel's congested face. 'One day soon.'

422

CHAPTER NINETEEN

Teaching in the school was not enough to satisfy Charlotte's energy or her curiosity. It was impossible for her to spend hours trying to coax the relationship between the written symbols and the spoken word into the mind of a ragged, bare-footed, and permanently hungry individual, without wanting to know more about his life, without wanting to help him in other ways. She began, on her way to and from the school, to take circuitous routes, and investigate the lesser streets and alleys and courts. Perhaps because she did not expect it, she never received any insult. Some shrank from her, some gave her resentful looks, some simply slid inside their dwellings and shut the door, like lizards disappearing down cracks when a shadow falls over them.

But others came up to her to speak to her, and finding her easy and affable, told her their troubles. Many begged from her or tried to cozen her, and though native caution warned her not to carry large sums of money with her when she walked about the back-slums, what she did have she always parted with before she reached home again. But what she found she was most often asked for was advice, particularly medical advice, and it was not long before she found herself agreeing with Lucy, who had told her from the beginning that it was little use to minister to the minds of people who could barely keep their bodies alive.

'The ills of these people stem largely from their poor

health,' she had said, 'and their poor health stems largely from their poor housing.'

Though Doctor Silk had said much the same thing to her, Charlotte had thought this too simple a summing-up at first, especially as Lord Ashley seemed so certain that education would have such a huge effect on the lives of these people. Educate the mind, she had thought, and it would lead the body out of the mire. But the debility of the body, in so many cases, made it difficult for the poor people to learn. And as, week by week, she penetrated further into the rookeries, she saw that it was impossible to live a healthy life in conditions of such filth and overcrowding.

She had an answer, at last, to the question of where people went when their dwellings were destroyed to make way for the railway: they simply crowded into someone else's. Many of the people she met had been displaced at least once, some several times. They had few possessions: one of the things she learned was that even the decent, hard-working individuals amongst these very poor lived from day to day, never able to get far enough ahead to plan or save or settle down. What money was earned each day was spent each day on food and rent. When she visited a family, she never found any food in the room, except perhaps a bit of bread left over from dinner which was being saved for breakfast. When the wage earner came home, someone, often a child, would be dispatched to the nearest shop or cookhouse to buy what the available money would get. Because of this, the food was often less nourishing, more adulterated, and always more expensive than for people higher up the social scale. And when the wage-earner fell sick, or was out of work, there was nothing to fall back on. They begged, stole, borrowed – or starved.

Because they had nothing in reserve, even a little bad

luck, she learned, could set an individual or a family whirling down a spiral of degradation. A young couple, both in work, could live decently, pay for a lodging which gave them perhaps a room to themselves, keep their shoes and clothes mended, have enough to eat. But as children appeared, the money grew less and had to go further, life became more precarious. And once on that downward spiral, it was hard to stop the descent. And for the children of ill-fortune there was no chance at all.

Charlotte had Norton's own story always in the back of her mind. Norton had hoped to stay with her prentice-master and be taken on as a mature worker, but it was not to be. Mr Pertwee died, and his widow had had to retrench. With a good character from her, Norton got work making-up for a clothier in the Whitechapel Road. 'Trousers paid better than most, but you can't live by piecework,' Norton said, with the bitterness of one who has tried. 'I had a miserable little room over a fletter's, which I shared with four other girls – oh, the smell of those pelts and the boiling meat! And you work morning till night until your eyes give out and your fingers bleed, but still you can't get ahead. Three shillings a week clear on average earned, and two shillings rent to be found out of that. Tuppence a day for food and you were out on your rent – and tuppence a day doesn't even fill your stomach. You were always running behind, you could never catch up. Eat or pay your rent. Eat or buy a bit of soap. Eat or get your shoes mended. The only good thing about it was you worked such long hours you were often too tired to eat – but if you fell into bed without eating, you were even more tired the next day.'

But she had been young and hopeful; and she fell in love with a 'Club Row swell', a barrow-boy with money in his pocket who took her to an ale house for a 'sixpenny tightener' of sausages, potatoes and suet pudding, and promised with a head-turning air of condescension to get her into a better job with a 'business acquaintance' of his. This tight-trousered, sleek-haired, mighty-whiskered young man got her to work with a 'translator' – making over second-hand clothes to be sold again. The shop, with the workshop below in the basement, was at the upper end of the trade, making over silks and velvets into cheap finery for the flashier members of the community, and paid correspondingly better; and since the youth had persuaded her on a promise of marriage to come and live with him, she was saving the cost of her lodgings. Suddenly things were looking up: she had enough to eat, a new dress, she felt pretty and full of life and hope. It had been a shock to her to discover that the clothes she was making over were stolen, and that the man she was hoping to marry was one of those who stole them, breaking into 'toff kens' and ransacking their wardrobes. But she was too far in by then to help herself, especially as she discovered she was pregnant, and still Jimmy, her flash lover, put off the wedding day.

But prigging clothes was not the summit of his ambitions – he wanted to be a cracksman. One evening he went out promising her a fine gown if his luck held; the next day he was in custody, and facing a severe sentence. He and his confederate had been surprised by a watchman; the confederate had made a run for it, but Jimmy had lost his head and bludgeoned the man, and then ran straight into the arms of the police.

'Once the jacks came sniffing round, I had to look sharp and get out,' Norton told Charlotte. 'It would only be a matter of time before they twigged the translator's lay, and then I'd be for it.' She was out of work, without a roof over her head, and pregnant. She had fallen into a nightmare world then, moving from bad lodging to worse, doing whatever piecework she could get hold of, dodging officialdom – terrified for her life, because the watchman had died, and the word on the street was that Jimmy was to be hanged. But in the end he 'got the boat' – was transported – and Norton was at least saved the private shame of giving birth to the child of a hanged man.

After the baby was born, she changed her name, called herself a widow, got a room in a low beer house, and took in sewing to try to keep herself and the child. 'Shirtmaking,' she said to Charlotte bitterly. 'Collar and wristbands stitched, six buttonholes, four rows of stitching down the front – all for twopence-halfpenny a piece, and find your own thread. You can't live on that. And I had no milk for the baby. The mot that ran the beer house told me I should go on the buzzing lay – she had half a dozen kids who prigged food and clothes and silk handkerchiefs, which she sold to her customers – but I'd seen where that led. Besides, I was brought up to be honest, and it went against the grain. Then she said I should go the bad way to live.' By this Charlotte understood she meant prostitution. 'She said she'd mind the baby while I worked, and would even let me use my room if I paid her. I didn't want to do that – though I dare say I might have had to in the end. Lots of the pieceworkers did it, and those I met said I was a fool not to – especially with a kinchin to feed.'

But she resisted; and then the baby died. Of congenital debility, the certificate said, a polite expression for malnutrition. 'I thank God now he died, for what sort of a life would it have been for the poor little mite?' She ate nothing for three days to pay back the money she borrowed from her landlady to give the baby a burial; and then she left her lodging and just walked. She tramped the streets in a daze of grief and hunger, not knowing what she was doing, thinking she would probably die, and welcoming the idea; until at last she collapsed from cold and starvation outside the railings of St James's Church in Piccadilly. She was taken to a missionary house – 'The first piece of luck I'd had since I left Mrs Pertwee's.' There they fed her, gave her a bed, and when she had recovered enough to speak, questioned her as to her circumstances and abilities. She said nothing about Jimmy or the baby; told them she had been prentice to Mr Pertwee, and had since been trying to earn her living as a seamstress. One of the missionaries was a lady whose good work was placing deserving females in domestic service, and she was widely acquainted with the best London families and knew what vacancies there were. She was impressed by Norton, and sent her to Upper Grosvenor Street, where Lady Theakston was known to be looking for a skilled sewing-maid.

'I was given some work to do by way of a test,' Norton said, 'and oh, how my hands shook with nervousness, for fear I should mess it up! And your grandmama came in and questioned me pretty sharp, and looked close at my stitching, and I thought I was done for. But then she said, "What is your name?" and I said, "Norton, ma'am," and she said, "Can you read and write?" and I said, "Thank God, I can, ma'am," and she laughed a bit at that, and said, "Thank Him by all means, for it has got you a position. You may start at once, but you must call me *my lady*." So now you see why I was so grateful,' Norton finished. 'Your grandmama is a great lady, but in all the years I worked for her, I never knew her to take on a servant without seeing them herself – and a good many come from the St James's Mission, too.'

From Norton Charlotte learned a good deal of the rookery cant without which she would have found it difficult to understand much of what was said to her. And with Norton mounting a stout and knowing guard over her, she saw for herself the sort of conditions that led to the desolation she witnessed. A room in a house, furnished with a bed or at least a mattress, might cost from two shillings to ten shillings a week, depending on the size of it; but for that the landlord's responsibilities were limited to the most basic of repairs, and since collecting the rent was often difficult and sometimes dangerous, most landlords did only enough simply to stop the building collapsing into the road. The houses were therefore in very poor condition, damp, leaking, verminous, with crumbling plaster, rotting wood, windows open to the air or blocked with rags. And since anything could constitute a room, passages and landings were often sealed off, large cupboards colonised, and low, earth-floored cellars without any light or ventilation at all subdivided to house a family or two.

Moreover, in the rookeries like the Devil's Acre, the regular tenants often made their living by sharing their room with a number of sub-tenants at tuppence or fourpence a head per day, which paid their rent and gave them a cash profit, and quite often provided them with a share of the lodgers' food too. So a house with eight rooms might have a hundred or more people sleeping in it every night – not counting the children. For these people the sanitary arrangements were of the most primitive – a single privy in the back yard if they were lucky, or a couple of buckets or a hole over a cess-pit if they were not. When the buckets were full, or sometimes just for the sake of privacy, some lodgers would make use of the stairs and passages instead.

But even these were not the worst places. For those without a permanent home, there were the netherkens or paddingkens ('ken' was simply the cant word for a house) where lodging was had by the night, and a fee of tuppence or threepence entitled a person for shelter up to eleven o'clock in the evening, after which a further fee was paid, or swift eviction followed. The accommodation in one of these consisted of a large kitchen, in which a fire burned night and day, winter and summer, before which the lodgers could warm themselves, dry their clothes, and toast their food, if they had any. Some of them also had a single gas-jet which was lit during the hours of darkness. Around the walls would be a running bench and a series of wooden tables, at which the lodgers sat, ate, and sometimes slept. The sleeping-rooms, if there were any, were generally windowless (to prevent anyone sneaking in at night) and would contain filthy, verminous palliasses, laid on the floor edge to edge, and sometimes a few unspeakable blankets. Here the lodgers lay, both sexes, young and old, to shiver and scratch the night away – or in summer to stifle and scratch. Charlotte put her head round the doorway of one of the sleeping-rooms once, and withdrew it again sharply as the smell clawed at her throat and made her eyes water. When the netherken was crowded, which seemed to be the rule rather than the exception, the overflow would sleep at the kitchen tables or on the kitchen floor, or wherever they could find a space to lie down, and on the whole, Charlotte thought that would have been preferable to the sleeping-rooms.

Sanitary arrangements for lodgers of this sort seemed to be the street, or a corner of a yard, or a dungheap, or an open sewer; water came from a common pump, often shared between a number of houses or a whole street, and in summer often failed altogether.

And even this, Charlotte learned, was not the worst. The vagrancy laws – and a simple desire to be out of the weather – made the poorest people desperate for any kind of shelter. The casual ward of the workhouse, to prevent permanent settlement, allowed only one or at most two nights lodging to any person, so all that was left was the 'pack' – a bare room, shed or cellar where for the price of a penny or even a ha'penny, the lodger had the right to lie on the floor for the night, if he could find room amongst all the other bodies. She had one pack pointed out to her – it was on the other side of the back yard of a netherken she visited. The yard was small, and contained nothing but two privies, long since overflowed, since entrance to the yard had been built over and the night cart could no longer get into it. The pack was nothing but an outbuilding which had once been a workshop of some kind. It was a lean-to with a sloping roof and a clearance inside of five feet four inches at the highest, five feet at the lowest. The depth of the room was four feet six inches, it was nine feet long, and every night it sheltered eight people. The floor of this pack was bare earth, but since it was at the lower end of the slight slope of the yard, it was always damp, and in wet weather sometimes awash with the overspill of the privy. When it was really wet the landlord put down woodshavings to soak up the worst of it. There was never any shortage of applicants for the spaces.

With these sorts of conditions, it was no wonder that sickness haunted and early death took the rookery dwellers. As Lucy said when Charlotte discussed her experiences with her, 'It isn't by chance that we have had these outbreaks of cholera in recent years. Health and sanitation are related, and I think we are going to find out as time goes on what close cousins they are.'

'If everyone thought like you, Grandmama, these awful back-slums wouldn't exist right on the doorsteps of some of the wealthiest people in the land.'

'Oh, I don't pretend to be more interested in the lower orders than the next person,' Lucy said, 'but with the poor crowding into the towns, tens of thousands of them living in spaces designed for hundreds, the questions of health

431

they pose are going to be questions for everyone before long. I must give you some things to read. You can start on Chadwick's reports – I have copies of them upstairs. Though I think they will not tell you anything you don't know by now.'

She gave Charlotte the report to Edmund Chadwick and the Poor Law Commissioners of 1838 on the causes of destitution and death in London, and the report of 1842 on the 'Sanitary Conditions of the Labouring Classes'; and the following day acquired for her the 1844 report of Peel's Royal Commission into 'The State of Large Towns and Populous Districts'. Charlotte read these with appalled attention, finding a horrible confirmation that what she had seen in the back courts and alleys was to be found in every city and large town. She became fascinated by the whole question of sanitation, and set her grandmother's house in uproar by trying to find out where the various waste-pipes went. Having soothed the ruffled feathers of the servants Lucy told her rather tartly that she ought to talk to Prince Albert, who had a thoroughly Germanic interest in plumbing, and was in a perpetual state of outrage about the drains at Buckingham Palace.

But Lucy was a source of information and encouragement whenever, as became increasingly common, Charlotte had medical problems brought to her attention. She had read scores of books, and on her visits with Doctor Silk in Chetton had learned the rudiments of treatment of common ailments. Now she was having to put them into practice, for in a place where few medical men would venture and none could have afforded them if they had, Charlotte's small expertise was often all there was to turn to. Hopefully they brought her their sicknesses to be cured – not just the dysentery and fever endemic in the rookeries, but the results of accidents and assaults, wounds, broken limbs, and the endless succession of infections which drained the strength from already debilitated bodies.

Lucy's interest in the poor was perfunctory, but with all matters medical she had a lifelong fascination, and she shared her knowledge and experience willingly. 'Nothing you can learn of medicine will be wasted,' she told Charlotte, while she demonstrated on a resentful servant the best way to bandage various parts of the body. 'Servants are always cutting and bruising and scalding themselves, and you cannot be sending for a doctor every time, especially if you live in the country.' She instructed her granddaughter, too, in the elements of sick-nursing and assisting at childbirths, and provided her with books to read on the subject. 'You too, Fanny. You mean to marry one day, I suppose. Leaving these things to menials is exposing yourself and your loved ones to unnecessary risk. *Your* grandmother, for instance, would have died if I hadn't been on hand to stop a bungling doctor from pulling her to pieces.'

Fanny looked away from the illustrative diagrams in the books and denounced them as 'too horrid'. 'I shall make sure I can always afford the best doctors,' she said.

'And suppose there are no doctors available?' Lucy said sternly. 'One day while driving down to Wolvercote we came upon an overturned stagecoach, and I splinted fourteen broken bones and stitched a very nasty gash with an embroidery needle and thread out of Docwra's reticule. And during the Waterloo campaign, I set up a hospital in the house I'd rented in Brussels, and we tended the battle-wounded and the typhoid victims.'

'You must know as much as a doctor,' Charlotte said, to stop Fanny arguing with her.

'More than most,' Lucy said shortly. 'Much of it is common sense, and that's a thing most doctors are short

433

of. It's a great pity the profession isn't open to women, but these things are becoming less liberal as years go by, rather than more. I'm afraid if I were beginning now, I would be doomed to terrible frustration.'

'Well, I don't want to be a doctor,' Charlotte said, 'but I do think that if I had skills like yours, I could do a great deal more good than just by teaching them to read and write.'

'I don't know how you can even think about it,' Fanny said. 'Or how you can go into those filthy places. Having to teach them is bad enough, for they smell so dreadful. You must be terribly brave.'

Charlotte smiled. 'Not at all – it's you who are brave. You hate it all much more than I do, but you go on helping all the same – *that's* real courage.'

As her skills developed, Charlotte gradually gave up the teaching in favour of the other, more direct help she could give – basic medical treatment, advice on childcare and sick-nursing, and exhortations on the subject of hygiene. Despite Fanny's horrors and Mrs Manvers' mild disapproval, she found the work so interesting that she managed to ignore the smells and squalor. She gave financial help, too, where she identified an immediate want she could remedy. Many of the back-slum landlords were themselves hardly better off than their lodgers, and where she saw it would not be money thrown away, she arranged, through a growing band of agents and workmen of various kinds, for repairs to a roof, to have windows glazed, to clear a yard of ordure, to provide a set of cooking-pots for communal use.

But it was slow and piecemeal work, and anything she could do barely scratched the surface of the vast misery. There were so many of them, and so few to help them; and many of the well-meaning missionaries and slum-visitors imposed too-strict rules, which excluded the most needy,

434

or obliged the recipients of the charity to endure such an uncomfortable course of moral improvement that they preferred physical hardship to the mental discomfort. There was already a model lodging-house in the Devil's Acre, owned by a philanthropic lord, but its insistence on an early curfew meant that the street-sellers, hawkers, road-sweepers and so on, whose best trade was at night from theatre crowds and other well-to-do pleasure seekers, could not use it.

Fanny, with the co-operation and encouragement of Rosamund, made sure that Charlotte did not give her whole life to the rookeries, and insisted on a regular diet of pleasure and society. When she had been thoroughly scrubbed and doused with perfume (Fanny had a morbid fear that people would smell the back-slums on her), Charlotte would be dressed in her finery and become for an evening one of the glittering people she was beginning to see from the other side, from the shadows, as they passed along the wide and well-lit thoroughfares. She went to the theatre and the opera and to concerts, to dinners and parties, exhibitions and routs, picnic rides and Venetian breakfasts. All too often she fell asleep during the play or the concert, and was likely to break away on the steps of some great house to address some poor lounger on the fringes of the onlooking crowd; but at least she went, and gave Fanny the excuse to go too. And in her other life, her daytime life, Lady Chelmsford was becoming as well-known a figure as Lord Ashley.

On New Year's Day, 1847, Charlotte put into practice something which she had been planning for some time, and which, while it did not make any lasting difference to their lives, greatly cheered the hearts of a group of the rookery dwellers. Jobley's Ken was one of the netherkens she had taken under her wing. Jobley himself had started life as an educated man, but a fatal weakness for drink had brought him low. He had gone on the screeving lay, been caught and sent to prison, and coming out more hopeless than he went in, had married a lodging-house keeper who had taken a fancy to him and had hoped he would raise her class of clientele. It hadn't happened – in fact, his weakness for a hard-luck story as much as for the lush had gone a long way to ruining her, and she died poorer than when she met him, and with her lodging-house in much worse condition.

But Jobley was essentially a kindly man, though self-indulgent to his and others' ruination. Charlotte decided the filthy conditions there could be improved without fear that the landlord would take advantage of her, and had the roof repaired, the kitchen chimney mended, the walls limewashed, and provided a set of cooking utensils and crockery to be used on the premises. The sanitary arrangements puzzled even her to improve much – four buckets in the yard, and no way to dig any kind of pit that had a hope of draining in that low-lying area – but after some lengthy questioning and negotiating, she found a man willing to empty them twice a week. The man, a filthy, one-eyed outcast who hitherto had made a living collecting dog faeces for tanners, was delighted with the commission; and when he discovered that she would find out and withhold the payment if he ignored his duty, even carried it out. Charlotte had no idea what he did with the contents and did not ask. She was rather afraid he took them into someone else's yard and emptied them there, but 'sufficient unto the day', as Norton said when she confided her fears to her. 'Can't worry about everything at once, my lady.'

When this part of the operation was established, Charlotte brought in her tame carpenter and had him build a square shelter with four compartments, each with a half-door, to house the four buckets. This sudden access of privacy enchanted some of the lodgers who, once they found they were not to be charged extra to use them, desisted from fouling the yard all around and became quite dainty. There were others who thought it a waste of money and an imposition, and others who simply couldn't get the hang of it, but the yard was still a great deal better than it had been.

Charlotte also replaced all Jobley's palliasses, and paid a man to cart the old ones away and burn them. Again she had a suspicion that he was going to sell them to someone even less particular than Jobley's customers, but she was growing quite philosophical about the amount of good she could do. The new mattresses were soon infested again, but there wasn't much to be done about that, unless Jobley refused to take in verminous clientele, which would negate the object of the exercise by excluding those who needed help most.

On this New Year's Day she planned to brighten the lives of Jobley's lodgers by giving them a 'tightener' she meant them never to forget. All those who had paid their tuppence and were in the lodging after eleven o'clock the previous night were to be eligible for the dinner which would be served at noon. There were forty-five names taken (Jobley wrote them down) and one of Charlotte's trusted agents went to the nearest market and ordered the ingredients, and negotiated with the cookshop on the corner to cook it for them – under supervision, or Charlotte had no doubt a great deal of it would disappear. There was a vast cauldron of beef stew, another of pease pudding, a mountain of boiled potatoes, and huge suet puddings with raisins in them, which wrapped in their cloths looked like pale cannon balls and, thought Charlotte, would probably weight the stomach in much the same way.

This was one piece of philanthropic work Fanny would not miss, especially as Charlotte had ensured Jobley's smelled so much less vile than before. She offered quite cheerfully to help hand out the feast, and cousin Tom offered his services as escort too. He had been urged to do so by Rosamund, who was worried about her strange daughter's stranger predilections, but he was curious to see himself what went on.

Charlotte inspected him before they left, and said, 'You are too fine, Tom, with that ticker sticking out of your garret, and that fogle up your sleeve. If you don't go to my feast out of twig, you'll be a target for every flimp in the Acre.'

Tom smiled at her ironically. 'I'm happy to say I didn't understand a word of that – as no doubt you intended! Do I gather you object to my watch and handkerchief?'

'*I* don't object to them, and neither will the pickpockets,' Charlotte said pleasantly. 'I only warn you – you may do as you please, of course.'

Tom removed the offending objects. 'I thought you had tamed these people. Don't tell me we are going to feed a grand dinner to the *un*deserving poor?'

'I leave the question of *deserts* to others,' Charlotte said. 'It's pudding for all at my table.'

When they arrived at Jobley's, they found a large crowd gathered around the door, and Jobley, red in the face, arguing with the front line of it.

'What's going on, Jobley?' Charlotte called. Tom noted for his sister's benefit the immediate and respectful silence that fell, and the way the crowd parted to let her through.

'There's far more people here, my lady, than the forty-five we took the names of. I've sorted 'em out as far as I can. The paid-up are mostly inside, but as you see the word has spread, and there must be thirty more out here wanting to join in.'

The man nearest her knuckled his forehead and said, 'If there's summink going, mum, an' it ent paid for speshul by them inside – which this 'ere cove says it ent – well, mum, and not meanin' no disrespeck, but I'm as 'ungry as the next man, an' why carn I 'ave a bit?'

There was a murmur of agreement from those around him, and Charlotte thought he was being unduly modest – he was plainly much hungrier than most. His eyes were deeply sunken, his cheeks hollow, his neck a collection of strings, his upper ribs, visible through the torn neck of his shirt, like well-picked soup bones. There was a glitter of famine in his eyes, something which she had come to recognise by now. His clothes were pitifully inadequate, even though it had not yet been a very cold winter – torn, and black with greasy dirt. On his feet he wore a pair of child's boots so much too small for him that he had had to cut away the toecaps to get them on, and his black toes stuck through the gap, innocent of any shred of stocking.

Charlotte turned to Jobley and spoke in a low voice. 'Go in, tell those whose names you took what has happened—'

'Oh, they know, my lady.'

'Very well. Ask them, then, whether they will have it all, or whether they will share with these people. Let them vote by a show of hands. The majority shall carry it. Hurry, the food will be here at any moment.'

The crowd stood silent all around, not knowing what was going on, but awaiting her pleasure. It was like having a well-trained dog sitting quietly by your dinner table but watching every mouthful. Jobley was not gone long. Sooner than she had expected him, he was back, looking almost dazed.

'They say they will share, my lady. Not one dissenting. I had hardly put the question before they were giving me the answer.'

439

'God bless them!' Charlotte said. She looked at Tom and Fanny, and for once she felt close to tears. 'The less people have, the more willing they are to share. God bless them all! Tell these people the news, Jobley – I see the cookhouse men coming.'

A huge cheer went up, both to the news of the vote, and the approach of the feast. There were plenty of willing hands ready to carry the containers into Jobley's kitchen, and plenty of helpers to dish up and pass plates. The extra guests crowded into the back yard, to have plates passed out of the window to them. There wasn't enough crockery for all, and half of them had to wait until empty platters could be sent back for them. But Charlotte had provided so lavishly that there was a big plateful for everyone, as near to a tightener as made no difference; and a pot-scraping left for some scrawny urchins who had come sniffing round like pi-dogs at the unexpected smell of food.

Charlotte found a surprising lot of gentry-folk appearing too – word of the New Year feast seemed to have spread amongst the philanthropists and missionaries, and they had come along to see the fun and, in some cases, to improve the hour with a homily or two to anyone who would listen. But the replete lodgers had got the spirit up for some music: a couple of penny whistles and someone's precious fiddle (though it had only three strings) had appeared, and a jolly was on the make, with several people cutting a jig, an impromptu hornpipe from a couple of out-of-work boatmen, and an urchin turning somersets and walking on his hands – to the consternation of one of the pi-dogs. What with the music, singing, laughing, talking and barking, there was not much chance of a sermon getting itself established.

Charlotte didn't remember when she had enjoyed herself more. She had got separated from Tom and Fanny, but hadn't the slightest apprehension, though from the expressions on the faces of some of the gentry-folk, it was plain they thought she ought to have. With her hands deep in her muff – it was beginning to turn cold – she watched the fun and tapped her toe to the squeaky music. And then a voice at her ear said, 'I understand all this is your doing, Miss Meldon – or is it Lady Chelmsford?'

She turned, and found herself looking into the grey-blue eyes of Doctor Anthony. 'Both,' she said, too surprised at seeing him to find more words.

'You must be very proud,' he said.

'It makes me happy,' she said cautiously, not sure if he was being ironic – for there was some strain in his voice she could not account for. 'But it distresses me that I can do so little, when there is so much to be done.'

'I remember saying to you that a place I had just come from was more dreadful than anything you would ever know.'

'Drover's Rents,' she remembered.

'So it was. I had forgotten. There have been so many.' He waved that away as unimportant. 'But it seems I should apologise to you. I hear your name on every side as one who does not just think good thoughts but puts them into action.'

'You don't need to apologise to me,' she said, puzzled.

'I misjudged you. You do great good wherever you go.'

She studied him, wondering why his sensitive face was so stern, his blue eyes so grave. 'Even so, it doesn't seem to please you very much,' she concluded. 'What have I done to earn your disapproval?'

He blushed suddenly and painfully, his eyes moving away from hers. 'You speak very roundly, ma'am,' he said.

'I'm sorry,' she said, blushing herself at his reproof. 'It

441

is a habit I have got into – a very bad habit, I know. Females are not supposed to be so bold, or say what is in their minds. But since you find me here where no gently bred female ought to be anyway, pray do me the honour of a round answer. What have I done?'

'It is not for me to—' he began stiffly, but she interrupted.

'Oh *pray*,' she begged, 'don't freeze me. I have so few friends, I cannot bear to lose such an old one for want of an explanation.'

He looked quizzical. 'You regard me as an old friend?'

'Should I not?'

'But I was acquainted with a Miss Meldon, who I understand no longer exists. You are Lady Chelmsford.'

'Oh, is *that* it?' she was enlightened at last. 'But I could not help it, indeed I could not! I did not mean to deceive anyone. And I am Miss Meldon inside. I always will be.'

'I doubt that,' he said, but he was smiling now.

'What brings you here, though? Is this not a long way from your usual haunts?'

'Oh, not so very far. I was at the Middlesex Hospital earlier today, and heard a pros—a street woman talking about your feast, so I thought when I had finished I would stroll along and see what was happening. Imagine my surprise when I saw that the mysterious and beneficent Lady Chelmsford was none other than Miss Meldon.'

'I hope the journey was worth your while,' Charlotte said. 'Do tell me how everyone is! Though I knew you for such a short time, I promise you I have thought of you all very often.'

'Come now, you must not gammon me, as they say hereabouts.'

'Indeed, it is true! Why don't you believe me?'

'You are titled and wealthy, a great lady – why should

you care about half a dozen plain people you met once three years ago?'

'You were the first people I had ever sat down to dine with,' she said gravely. 'And you were kind to me. I was alone and very frightened that evening, and you all – but especially you, Doctor Anthony – made me feel a little warmth in my poor cold heart. Why should I not remember you? And as to being a fine lady – you see here what a fine lady I am, and where my interests lie.'

'I have been wronging you again,' he said, smiling, 'and now I must beg you to forgive my stupid pride. I thought you had hoaxed me and was angry, when I had no right. Will you forgive me?'

'Readily. Shake hands,' she said. He blinked at her directness, but did so heartily. 'And now will you tell me how my old friends are?'

'I would do so gladly, but it would take too long, and I must hurry away. But I can do better than tell you – I can show you, if you will come and take supper with us. I know I can issue the invitation on Mrs Welland's behalf. Would you – oh, that is if—' He pulled himself up, frowning doubtfully. 'I had forgotten. I imagine it would be out of your power to—'

'Now don't begin all over again,' Charlotte laughed. 'I should be delighted to come and sup with you all. Just tell me when.'

'Tomorrow? Or is that too soon?'

'Tomorrow it is,' she said. She had a dinner engagement which she would have to cancel – but Anthony was so sensitive, she was afraid he would not be able to bear it if she said tomorrow was not convenient.

CHAPTER TWENTY

'Lamb's Conduit Street!' Rosamund said, with a mixture of perplexity and exasperation. 'What can be the attraction of Lamb's Conduit Street?'

Tom smiled. 'I fancy it is not the what, but the who.'

Rosamund sat down. 'I suppose I should not be offended, but when she talks about this Mrs Welland as being so motherly and kind—!'

'No, you should not. It's hardly surprising that she doesn't view you as being motherly, dearest. That doesn't mean that you don't mean more to her than a thousand Mrs Wellands.'

'Do you think so?' Rosamund was ready to be comforted, but the hard fact that could never be got over was that she had not been Charlotte's mother in the motherly sense, and nothing could alter that now. And if she could have had the time back again, would she even have known how? Her own mother had never been motherly. It was not done in their class – or had not been in her day, she amended, thinking of how Lady Ashley was with her children. She changed tack. 'I wonder Mrs Welland and her lodgers are not overwhelmed out of any pleasure, to be entertaining the Countess of Chelmsford under their humble roof.'

'She is not Lady Chelmsford to them. When she goes there, she is Miss Meldon again. I fancy,' he added with a private smile, 'that she feels easier in that twig.'

'Twig?'

'Guise,' Tom translated.

'Don't you start talking cant,' Rosamund said irritably. 'It's bad enough when she does it at the dinner table and everyone falls silent and stares. It's so embarrassing.'

'She only did it once,' Tom said. 'Don't exaggerate, love. You know she manages very well, passing from one world to the other and back, and hardly ever putting a foot wrong.'

'It's true,' Rosamund acknowledged. 'She does it very skilfully.'

'Then what?' Tom asked.

'I'm afraid it means she does not really belong in either. I do so want her to be happy, and I'm afraid the way she lives—'

'Means that she can't be? Or is proof that she isn't? Do you think she does good works *because* she feels she doesn't fit in to our world?'

Rosamund looked defiant. 'Yes, I do think just that.'

Tom was thoughtful. 'Well, you may be right.' He had always been an outsider himself. He had said 'our world', but it was Rosamund's really, and his only under tolerance. And not being part of any world was a lonely thing; but there were compensations. Being an outsider meant you saw more and felt more, even if you also suffered more. And if you were an outsider, there was nothing in the world you could do about it. You could not change it by any means, and therefore could only make the best of it. Rosamund had done that to her child when she began the affair with Jesmond Farraline, and though it had not been her wish or her intention, it was none the less for that her responsibility. Removed from the nest in the way she was, Charlotte could never again be part of the flock. They all, Charlotte most of all, had to come to terms with it.

But there was no point in saying any of that to Rosamund, even if he could have found the words for it. So he said, 'But I think she is happy in her own way. The good works may take her to places you would find revolting, but they satisfy her, and she really loves the people she helps. And she *does* help them, so we should not begrudge her to them.' Rosamund did not answer. He added, 'And she does give us her time, doesn't she? She went up to Grasscroft in the summer for Henry Droylsden's wedding, and stayed almost a month. And she comes to dinner and the theatre, and even dances sometimes.'

Rosamund laughed. 'You knew I wouldn't understand! And yes, she does those things. But she is getting so – eccentric. Or at least, people are beginning to see her as eccentric. Even people like the Ashleys and the Herberts—'

'And you think *them* odd enough!'

'But at least they don't go visiting lodging-houses in Lamb's Conduit Street for their social pleasure. I'm afraid if she goes on like this she will never get married.'

Tom thought he ought to ease her mind a little. 'There is a man in the case,' he said casually.

'A man? Not a son of this Mrs Welland, I hope?'

'Of course not,' Tom laughed. 'By our reckoning, a son of Mrs Welland's would be Charlotte's brother, wouldn't he? No, it is the doctor, I fancy, who is the great attraction in that house.'

'This Doctor What's His Name—'

'Anthony. Philip Anthony. I've met him, and he's devilish handsome.'

'*Is* he?'

'Oh yes, a man to swoon over. Fair hair and skin, blue eyes you could drown in, the sort of fine-boned, delicate, porcelain features some women find irresistible.' He said it with the generously puzzled air of a man who has none of those attributes.

Rosamund narrowed her eyes. 'You've been digging, haven't you? Come, tell!'

'Of course I have. Do you think I would let my favourite niece entangle herself with a man I knew nothing about? I'm getting to be quite a skilled detective, I can tell you. And he's perfectly respectable, dearest. His father's a clergyman, rector of a wealthy parish in some remote place in the north of Norfolk – very devout, in a Puseyite sort of way, and independently wealthy – *his* mother was the heiress of a local landowner, so there's a very nice property coming the doctor's way when his father is finally called above.'

'Brothers and sisters?'

'Has he none. There was an older half-brother from a previous marriage, who went into the Church and would have inherited everything, including the living, but he died untimely. Philip is the son of the second wife, apparently a ravishingly pretty thing and a great deal younger than her husband; but she's dead too. The air around the Wash is evidently strong stuff. She died when our doctor was nine or ten – a bad time for a boy to lose his mother – and he was brought up from then on by the father, a rather stern cove and full of piety. That may account for his reserve.'

Rosamund considered this, and did not think it sounded too dangerous. 'So he is a gentleman – and will be wealthy?'

'Quite adequately wealthy. And gentlemanly enough for any company. He's very well educated, too. Studied medicine at Edinburgh, passed everything with full honours, and walked his wards at Guy's, under Astley Cooper and Robert Liston.'

Rosamund looked relieved. 'Well, Cooper at least is a gentleman.'

'Because he has a wealthy wife?' Tom smiled.

'It helps,' Rosamund said shortly. Tom left her to make the connections of logic herself, and after a moment it was proved that she must have because she said, 'Perhaps we ought to invite this doctor to dinner and—'

'Inspect him?'

'Get to know him. Do you think Charlotte would like that?'

'I'm not sure he would come. He doesn't seem to eat anywhere but at Mrs Welland's. But I expect Fanny could persuade him,' he added after a thought. 'I never expect to meet the man Fanny can't persuade.'

'Does Fanny know him too?' Rosamund looked puzzled.

'Oh yes, Fanny knows him. She's even been to Mrs Welland's,' Tom said, and added enigmatically, 'I rather fancy he is what has reconciled Fanny to philanthropy at last.'

He was glad Rosamund did not think to ask what had reconciled *him*, for he was feeling rather vulnerable on that point. His decision to go along with Charlotte on the day of Jobley's Feast had been an idle one, and he had not expected it to lead to a programme of good works, much less a regular attendance at a Mission House where the poor were fed, exhorted to lead a better life, and given a bed for the night. Tom did his part in handing out food and clothing, and occasionally helping to break up a fight or eject a violent drunk, and all the while stood back and watched himself doing these things with astonishment.

It was not his soul or his conscience which had led him there, but an altogether more worldly organ. The fact was that at the Jobley's Feast he had fallen into conversation with one of the mission volunteers who had come along to see if help were required. Several of them had come from the Mason's Yard Mission, which was just off Jermyn Street in the heart of St James's and alternately annoyed the exalted residents of the area by its simple existence, and aroused their gratitude by removing certain unsightly persons from their doorsteps. It was in fact not much more than a long stone's throw from Rosamund's house in St James's Square, which caused Tom some amusement, and his own rooms in Little Ryder Street, which made it convenient. Quite often when leaving Lady Batchworth's house he would decide just to drop in on the mission (never forgetting, of course, to remove his ticker, the gold fawney from his signet finger, and the diamond-headed pin from his silk kingsman, and to stow them, wrapped in his fogle, in a pick-proof pocket) in case she was there.

The 'she' in the case was a Miss Thorn – the name always caused him amusement as being the most inappropriate possible for such a round little person. Emily Thorn could just about claim title to five feet but not a fraction more, and since she was also plump, the full-skirted fashion of the day made her look almost as broad as she was tall. She had a round face, smooth, rich brown hair, and laughing brown eyes which were the only beauty amongst her undistinguished features. She moved so quickly and lightly on her invisible feet that she seemed almost to glide as though on wheels; her quick hands were always busy, and though she was brisk and practical with everyone she met, her voice was sweet and seemed full of music, as though at any moment she might burst into song. She was, indeed, so small and quick and brown and round and tuneful that he had an image of her in his mind as having been turned into a human being by a sorcerer, having started life as a wren, and being always on the brink of turning back again. When he told her that once, she laughed and said she had been called many things in her time, but never that. 'An interfering old hen, perhaps, but never a jenny wren!'

He was absolutely at a loss as to why she so enchanted

449

him. It had happened on the instant. He had found himself standing next to – in that crush, to be frank, almost on top of – a little person in a brown mantle and elderly grey beaver bonnet decorated with black pompoms which looked, from his position of vantage, distinctly home-made. He had moved to allow her a little more room, out of courtesy using his body to brace back some others and make a space around her. 'I'm afraid you are at a disadvantage in such a crush,' he said. 'I hope I didn't jostle you?'

And she had looked up, tilting back the bonnet and giving him the full benefit of her smiling, dancing eyes. 'Oh, I don't mind a bit of jostling in a good cause,' she said. 'I'm so glad to see the poor things enjoying themselves.' It was at that precise moment – he was perfectly well aware of it – that he was lost, transfixed by the most inexplicable desire never to be out of her company again. 'And what brings you here?' she went on while he was still inwardly gasping like a landed fish. 'For I see you are a gentleman.'

'Even when I expressly took off my – my ticker!' he complained, remembering the term at the last moment.

She laughed energetically. 'Now, who's been teaching you to talk flash?'

'My niece,' he replied.

'Is Lady Chelmsford your niece? I guess you must have come with her, for there's no-one else of your class here. And taking off your budge doesn't change your whole air, you know. You are a gentleman to your toes.'

'Then I may as well own up – I am Tom Weston, and yes, Lady Chelmsford is my niece.'

'Tom Weston – the Member of Parliament? Lord Aylesbury's brother? Well, I am in luck!'

'You've heard of me?'

'It's our business to know all those who might be in a

450

way to help us,' she said. 'We knock on many doors when
we go collecting. You live in Ryder Street and have a very
proper manservant called – called – Billingsgate!'

'Billington,' Tom corrected, laughing.

'Ah well, he always looks as though he has the smell
of fish under his nose!' she said. 'But I'm sure he is a
good man for all that. We can't help how we look, can
we? If prayer would help, I might ask God for another
few inches of height – not for vanity, you know, but so
that I could reach into the stewpot at the mission without
having to stand on a box.'

'Oh, but you are perfect as you are now. Pray don't ask
Him to change you in any particular,' Tom said. He said
it with such obvious sincerity that her smile was replaced
by a puzzled look.

'You must be gammoning me, Mr Weston. We aren't
even acquaint.'

'I have done my part towards it,' he said in a wounded
tone. 'Is it my fault you did not reciprocate?'

And she blushed rosily – it remained almost the only
time he ever saw her do so – and said, 'It is not proper
at all, but since we are both on God's work – I am Emily
Thorn, and I am here with my Mama and Papa, who are
missioners too.'

Tom offered his hand solemnly, and she placed her
small, woollen-gloved one in his with a hesitant and
puzzled air he found utterly enchanting. But then he
found everything about her enchanting. He didn't understand it, and he couldn't resist it, and it certainly put
him to a great deal of inconvenience, for the only way
he could be with her was to help at the mission or to
accompany her (always with a group of fellow volunteers
or her parents) about 'God's work'. This meant going into
disagreeable places and smelling bad smells and handing
out food and tracts and listening to sermons – all things

he would previously rather have had a headcold than have to do – but he had to be near her. If he was out of her company for any length of time he began to grow restless and miserable. And when he was with her, often all he could do was to stand and gaze at her. 'You look like a wasp in a jug of lemonade,' she told him once, and he thought it was apposite. He was drowning, but nothing in the world would make him get out.

The whole thing was absurd. He had met her parents – decent people of limited education and decidedly limited outlook, whose entire lives revolved around the mission, and who saw Tom, when they made his acquaintance, as merely another recruit to the army of volunteers, an extra pair of hands, with a possibly useful connection to Parliament. Mr Thorn had retired from actively running his successful cabinet-making business, leaving it to a manager, and lived comfortably enough on the profits while he and Mrs Thorn pursued God's work amongst the poor. They did not invite Tom to their house – why should they? They entertained little enough amongst their own friends, and him they regarded as decidedly outside their circle and their class. They even lived on the wrong side of the river, Tom told himself sometimes, with a kind of helpless exasperation – in a new house on the south side of Westminster Bridge. He could not go there uninvited. He could not visit Miss Thorn. He had no entrée into their lives – he, who was accepted in the drawing-rooms of the highest in the land, was ineligible for the parlour of the Thorns. He could see Miss Thorn only in the course of her good works, and in company; that was all she wanted him for.

As for what he wanted her for – it puzzled him to know. Was he in love with her? Did he want to marry her? The idea seemed absurd, given that she plainly had no interest in him other than as a fellow-worker. She was over thirty, the Thorns' only daughter, had never married, had always lived at home with Mama and Papa. Had she ever been in love? he wondered. Had she ever wanted to marry, or had she regarded herself as fit only for missionary labour? Might she now, if he could get her alone and in the right environment, fall in love with him? Would she be susceptible, or would she just laugh at him, as she so often did when he proved himself awkward or inept at some task she did without thinking. She did not laugh unkindly – it was almost affectionate – but it was galling for a man in love, a man with such extensive practice in making ladies sigh with pleasure, to arouse nothing but amusement in the woman he adored.

And if she did fall in love with him, what then? Could he marry her, carry her away to the right side of the river, and – and – spend the rest of his life a-missioning?

No, no, the whole thing was absurd. Much better remain as he was, and simply go along and see her when the wanting grew too much for him.

But he dreamed of her at night, and in his dreams she lay in his arms, her rich brown hair with its gold lights spread like a pool of autumn about her head, her dark eyes gazing up at him not in derision, but melting with passion. In his dreams they walked in gardens, beside streams, through meadows of flowers and dappled woods, talking, talking, soul to soul and heart to heart; and never, in his dreams, did she yearn for the teeming and filthy yards of the back-slums, or the airless tedium of the mission.

Charlotte and Norton, large baskets on their arms, were making one of their regular rounds. She had just been to see a couple who had taken in a baby she had found abandoned on a pile of rubbish in a court behind a paddingken. She had placed several foundlings by now, as well as little Miss Boggis, and she felt obliged to visit

453

them all, just to make sure all was well and the money sent with them for their keep not being misapplied. The condition of the children in the rookeries was desperate, and it was something she tried not to involve herself with, for it was a whole separate task, and would have taken up all her time and energies if she had let it. Abandoned and semi-abandoned children ran wild and barefoot about the back-slums, sleeping wherever they could find a scrap of shelter, snatching food or begging it, defecating in the street like animals, and, if they lived so long, gradually easing themselves into a life of crime to support themselves in adulthood. These unattached urchins were supposed to be taken into custody – the workhouse or the house of correction – but even if they did not manage to evade Authority, Authority was often pleased – or even bribed – to turn a blind eye to them. An urchin in the Union was another charge on the rate-payer, and the rate-payer would sooner he looked after himself.

Many of them attached themselves to certain low lodging-houses, where the proprietor was a 'kidsman' – the organiser of a gang of child thieves. Here, in return for what they brought back, they were given food and shelter. Sometimes the kidsmen even gave special training in housebreaking and pickpocketing. At the other end of the scale there were the casual landlords who might accept a silk handkerchief or some stolen food in place of the lodging-fee. Few of the children stayed in one place for very long. They drifted from one lodging to another, one kidsman to another; dirty, hungry, victims of casual brutality and sometimes more calculated abuse, they wandered until adolescence or disease claimed them, until they disappeared into adulthood, the Millbank Penitentiary, or death.

But many of them, of course, did not live to urchinhood.

Babies were abandoned, very young children simply turned out of doors, some smothered or drowned like unwanted kittens by the parents who could not or would not feed them. Others were placed with baby-farmers, and while in some sections of the community there might be honest and kindly baby-farmers, in the rookeries the unwanted babies were unlikely to receive any tenderness. The pretty ones might be kept until they were of an age to be sold; the others were just let to die, so that the insurance could be claimed. Burial clubs and insurance societies abounded in London, and as the payment for a dead infant was about £1 on average, most of them were worth more dead than alive.

All this Charlotte knew, and kept resolutely out of her mind. There was so much to do, so much; and a person could too easily be overwhelmed, and by trying to care about everything, achieve nothing. It was necessary to narrow the focus: she had seen enough by now to know that the most effective help came from those who might appear to outsiders to be callous. Sentiment, weeping, and sighs and scattered shillings did no good to anyone. So when an abandoned baby positively thrust itself on her notice, she did her best for it, and put out the word for a family prepared to take it in in return for payment; otherwise, she left the whole juvenile problem alone, and tried to keep her eyes away from rubbish heaps and dark corners.

Now she and Norton were going to a house in Apple Tree Yard – a wild misnomer, for though there might once have been a tree there, it had been very long since it bore any higher form of vegetation than moss. The yard had probably once been part of the garden of a large house – over the roofs it was possible to see the Dutch gables of a once-grand Carolean house, now a cracked and crumbling rookery. The four cottages which formed Apple Tree Yard were about eighty years old, with stone walls and tiled roofs, rather more sturdy than many in the area. Each contained two rooms downstairs and two upstairs, but there were probably close on a hundred people who could have given Apple Tree Yard as their direction at any one time.

Their present quarry was a prostitute who called herself Mrs Saville. Charlotte rather liked her – when she was in the right mood, she could be very amusing, and also informative, though Norton had warned Charlotte not to believe any of her stories. She had the smallest upstairs room of the smallest house, a space of about five feet by eight, and shared it with another woman, a seamstress – and also, probably, a prostitute, though not a declared one. Today they found Mrs Saville alone, lying on her mattress smoking a large cigar, which she tried with a hasty movement to hide when they came in.

'Be careful, you'll set the bed alight,' Charlotte said quickly. Mrs Saville brought it out again, gave them a quick look from under her eyelids, and decided on defiance. She took a deep drag and puffed the smoke in their direction. It was at least better than any other smell in the vicinity, but Charlotte, who knew something of her habits, said sternly, 'Where did you get that? You went out again last night, didn't you?'

'Only for a walk, to get a bit o' fresh air, like you're always telling me.'

'You were supposed to keep off that leg,' Charlotte said sternly. 'How will it ever heal if you keep putting weight on it? You were working, weren't you?'

'No, I swearter God,' Mrs Saville said earnestly, 'I met this flat, see. I was standing on the corner o' Haymarket with this other judy o' my acquaintance, just blabbing, and this toff comes out o' the theatre, and walking by he tips me a wink and then slaps me on the nancy. Well, this friend o' mine, she cries out right away, "Oh that'll cost you dear, my lad, assaulting of an honest woman," and makes out to call for the constable. This flat – he don't look more'n a kid, and lushy into the bargain – he starts a-blubbering and a-blustering as how he didn't mean no harm, and after a bit she says it'll cost him a bull apiece f'r us to forget about it. Well, he's keen enough and he gets out his pogue, and picks out four half-bulls. And I see thiseer judy's eyes gleaming, seein' as how his pogue is as fat as a pig, and notes in there as well as coins. So she says to me – puckering, like, so he can't understand – as how we ought to get him down the alley back o' the theatre and clean him down. Well, I ain't a bug-hunter, I'm an honest woman, but I can see he's for it if I leaves him to her mercy. So I tells her, being as how I can't run with this leg o'mine, I proposition to take him round the back meself while she keeps crow, then I'll neddy him with a brick or a bottle or summink, and come back to her with the swag. Only when I gets him down the alley, y'see, I takes him the other way, tells him he's a lucky boy and to watch his step another time, and lets him go. And he was so grateful, he give me thiseer cigar.'

Charlotte followed this story with difficulty, not because of the 'flash talk', in which she was fairly fluent now, but because Mrs Saville had very few teeth. At the end of it, she said, 'I don't believe a word of it. You were turning the trick, weren't you?'

Mrs Saville grinned wetly. 'Had to have some reason for luring him down the alley, didn't I? Anyway, I didn't forget what you told me about resting – I did it standing on one leg.'

'Don't talk so shocking!' Norton gasped, but Charlotte had to turn her face away to hide her smile. The irrepressible side of the people she tried to help was a tribute to their courage, she always thought. While Mrs Saville was

457

talking, Charlotte had been unwinding the bandage from her leg. It had been put on quite expertly, but Charlotte knew it was not as *she* bandaged; and the leg underneath was filthy.

'You've taken this bandage off again,' she said in exasperation. 'How often have I told you you must keep the wound covered? I'm tired of picking maggots out of it.'

'Been on the scaldrum dodge, have you?' Norton said scathingly. That was begging by displaying wounds and deformities.

'I ain't that low,' Mrs Saville said sulkily. Charlotte flashed Norton a look, and by patient questioning got the truth – or what sounded like the truth – out of the woman. She had been 'working' every night since Charlotte last saw her, and the bandage was a handicap. At night, in the dark, and especially in the unlit places Mrs Saville conducted her business, no-one saw the condition of her leg; but the bulk of a bandage could be felt, and then questions were asked. It put people off, she said; but she always put the bandage back on when she finished for the night.

'I got to pay me rent, ain't I? I got to eat, same as any toff,' she cried at last.

'But I gave you money last time,' Charlotte pointed out. 'Enough for your rent and food, so that you didn't have to work.'

This elicited another long rigmarole, but the truth of the matter, as she finally discovered, was that the money had gone the first day on one good 'randy' for Mrs Saville and the friend she shared the room with, and various other ne'er-do-wells they had picked up on the way to the public house.

'I can't help you if you won't help yourself,' Charlotte said at last. 'This leg won't heal unless you rest it and

458

keep it covered. Do you want to end up being taken to the hospital?' This was usually a good threat – they all dreaded the hospital. 'Do you want to end up having it cut off?'

Mrs Saville began to blubber and plead.

'Very well, I'll do what I can for it, and I'll give you enough money for your rent and—'

'No, miss, don't do that,' she said quickly, coming out of her howling with suspicious speed. 'Don't give me no rhino. I ain't to be trusted. I won't gammon you no more. You're a real lady, you are. Listen to me now, while I'm talking straight. In two minutes I'll be lying like a trooper and trying to fleece you again. You get out of here now, and leave me be. I ain't no good, and if you give me money, I'll only blow it on lush. There now, I've give you your chance, swelp me God I have. You just git out, miss, while you can, and leave me to it.'

Charlotte finished bandaging the leg and tied her usual neat knot, which could not be undone without being detectable. 'There now,' she said. 'You must keep that on, and since you've been honest with me, I'll do you the credit of believing you, that you can't be trusted. Do you know the cookhouse at the corner of Terrier Street, just down from Jobley's Ken?'

'Yes, miss.'

'I will tell them to expect you. You can call there for your dinner every day, and take it along to Jobley's to eat it, and sit by the fire there. And I'll give you a piece of paper to give your landlord. If he takes it to Jobley, it will be redeemed for your rent. But mind – he must take it himself. That will stop you using the note as currency.'

'You're a sharp one, miss, and no mistake,' Mrs Saville said, not entirely with gratitude.

'And one more thing. If you rest up and don't go out working, I shall tell Jobley to give you a glass of

459

gin to help you sleep – one every night, if you haven't worked.'

Mrs Saville eyed her with an ancient and knowing look. 'How will he know if I ain't worked?'

'Because you will tell him.'

Mrs Saville seemed puzzled by this. 'But – what's to stop me saying I ain't when I 'ave?'

'Nothing at all,' Charlotte said. She looked at Mrs Saville and Mrs Saville looked at her.

'You're a queer one,' Mrs Saville said at last in a restless tone; and so they parted.

'You don't really think she'll tell the truth, do you?' Norton asked Charlotte a little crossly as they went out into the yard.

'I don't know. Probably not. But perhaps she will. She might decide to try it for the sheer novelty,' said Charlotte lightly.

'She was right about one thing, my lady,' Norton said. 'You are a queer one.'

'In a mad world, the merely queer man is king,' Charlotte said. 'Or in this case—'

'Out of pocket,' Norton finished for her.

They had almost reached the main road when Norton made an indeterminate noise of warning and tried to interpose herself between Charlotte and something that came at them from a narrow alley to the side. And instant later they could see that no protection was necessary, as a woman staggered, held out her hands beseechingly, and collapsed at their feet. She was dressed in a coarse brown skirt and a chemise which was not only badly torn but stained with blood. Huge bruises were apparent on her thin arms; the side of her face was swelling even as they looked; her hair, coming out of its pins, was sticky with blood.

Charlotte made at once to go to her, but Norton tugged her arm, looking about her nervously. 'Leave well alone, my lady. There's mischief afoot here.'

'Of course there is. Let me go! She's been assaulted.'

'Yes, and they'll assault you too if you interfere.'

Charlotte wrenched her arm free and went to the huddled figure. Through the blood and hair it was impossible to see how bad the head wound was; and from the splotchy marks on the back of the chemise it looked as though she might have been stabbed as well. This was beyond her meagre skills. She looked up, to see a small crowd gathering cautiously and at a distance. She picked out the most intelligent faces.

'We must get her to the hospital. You, run out into the street and get a cab – quickly now! And you, find something to carry her on – a plank of wood will do if you can't find better. No, don't you go, Norton. I need you. I must have something to wrap round her head. What can we contrive?'

'That's Lizzie Parker,' someone said. 'Who's done that to her?'

'She came from there,' Charlotte indicated the alley. She wondered briefly about the assailant, but her concern was with the victim.

'It'll be Ned knocked her about,' someone else said.

'Is that her husband?' Charlotte asked.

'No, miss,' said her informant with a short laugh. 'She ain't married – she's gay.' This was cant for a prostitute. 'Ned's her fancy-man. Likely she tried to chouse him out of his money. He's got a short temper wi' tails that chouse.'

Her helper came back with a handcart. Charlotte persuaded two reluctant men to lift the woman onto it, and wheel her down to the main road. An interested band now followed, chatting eagerly about the

461

incident. 'Where they takin' 'er?' Charlotte heard some-one ask.

''Orspittle.'

'That's the end of 'er, then. Someone better tell Ned.'

The cabman was reluctant to take the fare, when he saw the tattered mob and the bleeding woman, but Charlotte fixed him with a stern eye and a half-crown, and her accent and the quality of her mantle convinced him that she was a likely source of compensation for spoiled upholstery. The woman was lifted in, Norton and Charlotte followed, and the cab set off at a brisk trot. In the confines of the cab, the smell of the woman became apparent; and she also began to groan. Charlotte tried asking her questions, but she didn't seem to be conscious enough to understand, only to moan feebly and mutter. The jolting of the cab was throwing them all about, and it was all Charlotte could do to stop the woman being tipped onto the floor.

When they reached the hospital, Norton went in to fetch two orderlies to carry the woman in. They looked like retired prize-fighters. One had a broken nose, the other a patch and a puckered scar down the side of his face.

'Her name is Lizzie Parker,' Charlotte told them as they manoeuvred the limp body out of the cab. 'She has been beaten – hit on the head, and stabbed, I think.'

'Don't you worry, miss,' said scarface indistinctly – he evidently had no teeth on the wounded side of his head. 'We'll take care of her.'

'Be careful! Her head is badly broken. She may have a fractured skull.'

'That's all right, miss. The doctors'll know all about it.'

Charlotte paid the cab driver, to Norton's surprise, and then hurried after the two orderlies, who were carrying the woman easily between them, but with as much tenderness

462

as they might move a sack of grain from one side of a loft to the other. 'My lady, you can't go in there!' Norton said urgently as she caught her mistress up.

Charlotte looked surprised. 'Of course I can. I must see that she's taken care of. And I want to speak to the doctor about her.'

'No, my lady, really,' Norton said, evidently distressed. 'I've come with you most places, and said nothing, but not a hospital! You don't want to go into a hospital! It's – it's not decent!'

Charlotte stared at her. 'Well, you don't have to come, if you are so delicate.' And she hurried on after the orderlies. They also seemed surprised, but shrugged it off as not their business. Norton, her face twisted in despair, followed a few steps behind, her feet dragging with reluctance, but unable to let her mistress out of her sight.

Charlotte had thought herself inured by now to squalor and smells, but nothing she had yet encountered prepared her for the hospital ward she found herself in. It was a large, long, gloomy room, with a bare wooden floor and bare plaster walls. There was a fireplace at one end, and windows along one wall, which were high and narrow and shut tight; and along both sides of the room were the beds, crammed together, with no more than two feet of space between them – fifty or sixty, she supposed, each with its occupant. Many of them looked old, all were poor, all were dirty; many were covered with sores or swollen with infections; some moaned and cried, some lay in desperate silence, some were plainly drunk.

But what was most noticeable about this desolate place was the stench. Charlotte felt her stomach rise in protest, and fumbled desperately for her handkerchief. Norton already had hers over her face. The reason for the smell was perfectly obvious. Without even approaching, Charlotte could see that the beds were as dirty as the patients, the sheets grey with use and stained with various kinds of matter, which must have soaked into the mattresses too. It had evidently soaked into the floor, for even underfoot the boards were spongy; and the walls were made of common, porous plaster which, as the fire was alight and the windows shut, glistened with condensation. She glanced at the wall just to the side of her, and saw that there was something blackish green growing on it, flourishing in the sodden plaster and adding, she supposed, its own element to the miasma.

Lizzie Parker was being put into a bed by the orderlies under the direction of a woman who, because she was wearing an apron, Charlotte assumed must be the nurse. She was filthy too, and her apron was encrusted with stains too horrible to wonder about. Two other nurses were sitting by the fire and toasting scraps of food, chatting, and drinking in turns from a small bottle they passed between them. Even as she looked, one slattern pulled up her skirt to scratch herself, exposing a blue-white, mottled thigh with as little concern as if she had been the only person left in the world. Charlotte turned her head away again. They had taken off Lizzie Parker's skirt and boots, and were putting her into the bed in her shift.

'Aren't you going to change the sheets?' Charlotte said. She could see the condition they were in. No-one paid her any attention. She darted forward, handkerchief tight over her face, and pulled back the corner to see the mattress. It was a flock mattress with a woollen cover, and she did not need to touch it to know it was sodden with whatever fluids the previous occupants had emitted. Patiently the nurse pulled the sheet back over the corner of the mattress, and then, as Lizzie Parker was lowered onto it, pulled the top sheet and single blanket over her and turned to Charlotte.

'Doctor'll come and see her prenly, miss. You go 'ome. This ain't no place for you.' She was toothless, raddled, and plainly also lushy – the smell of gin was almost stronger than the smell of her body.

'But – *will* she be taken care of? As I brought her here, I feel responsible for her.'

Behind the nurse an altercation of some kind was growing between two adjacent patients. ''Course she will, miss,' the nurse said urgently but distractedly. 'You rub off now – if you please. You done all you can.'

Norton was positively tugging at her arm in her anxiety to be gone, and the smell was overpowering anything her handkerchief could do. She nodded and turned away. It was absolutely true that this was 'no place for her' and she was almost in a panic to breathe fresh air; but she could not help thinking this was no place for *anyone*. No wonder the rookery-folk dreaded being taken to hospital. She had expected it to be bad, but it worse than anything she could have imagined. She wondered whether anyone ever recovered, and almost regretted taking the woman there.

They hurried out onto the landing – Charlotte had a time only to glance at a large wooden cage between the door of this ward and the next, in which some women were sleeping on mattresses on the floor – and down the stairs, and in a moment were out into the blessed daylight. Charlotte lowered her handkerchief and breathed in the usual manure-and-sulphur mix of London air as though it were the perfumes of the Orient – though it took a few breaths before even that got through the hospital stink, which seemed to have coated the inside of her nose and throat. Norton had her lips tight closed and was very pale, and Charlotte knew she must be looking that way too.

'Very well,' she said after a moment, 'we'll go home now.' Norton threw her a look of abject gratitude. 'But there must be a better way,' she added. 'There *must* be.'

CHAPTER TWENTY-ONE

'You went to the hospital? You went into a ward?' Anthony said in shocked tones.

'What else could I do?' Charlotte was a little nettled. 'I couldn't leave the poor woman where she fell.'

'Poor woman! A prostitute, you say.'

'Her – *profession* did not make her any less wounded.'

'I applaud your desire to help, but you needn't have gone yourself. You could have placed her in the cab and paid the cabman to deliver her.'

Like a sack of grain, Charlotte thought, remembering the way the orderlies had lifted her. 'I couldn't abandon the responsibility I had taken up, until I'd seen her safe inside. Though I wonder,' she added, 'whether that's the right word. What safety could she have in such a dreadful place?'

'Exactly my point,' Anthony said. 'It is not a place for a lady.'

'You have ladies on the board of trustees,' she pointed out.

'They contribute to the funds, but they do not visit the hospital. None of them, I am sure, has ever set foot inside it, and no-one would wish them to. It is entirely unsuitable for anyone of gentle birth – for a female of any rank – to go into a hospital ward.'

'And this is the place you do so much of your work,' she said wonderingly. 'I had not expected it to be so bad.'

'I am used to it.'

'But *why* must it be so bad?' Charlotte asked. 'That woman – all the poor – have no choice but to go there. *Must* they be exposed to such horrors?'

'Depend upon it, they don't mind it as you would mind it.'

'But must it be so filthy? Surely it cannot help recovery for the patients to be lying in such filth and breathing such a stench?'

'If you *will* talk about it,' Anthony said with a shrug. 'I've done my best to turn the subject, but I see you are unturnable.'

'It would be treating me like a friend to satisfy my desire for information,' she said coaxingly.

'Your desire for information seems insatiable,' he said, 'but as I hope always to be regarded as your friend—' He was looking into her eyes and smiling as he said it, and it was a moment she would have liked to have prolonged; but he went on, 'Very well. I am of the belief that the filthy conditions do cause harm. The death rate in hospitals is shockingly high, and the fear of the poor, that if they go in to hospital they will not come out alive, is not unfounded. But there is nothing to be done about it.'

'Isn't there? The woman I brought in, for instance, was put between sheets still filthy from the last patient.'

'I dare say she was filthy herself.'

Charlotte remembered the smell. 'She could have been washed.'

'Washed?' He laugh mirthlessly. 'It would probably be the first time since the midwife did it. And who would wash her?'

'The nurses, I suppose,' Charlotte said doubtfully.

He looked at her consideringly for a moment. 'You must understand that this is a problem incapable of solution. If anything could be done, I would gladly do it. You must have seen the nurses.'

'I saw them, yes. The one I spoke to was drunk.'

'They all drink. I never met a nurse who didn't,' he said with a shrug. 'And who can blame them? It's the only way they can tolerate their work. They live on the ward, you know – it is their only home. They sit there, cook their food over the ward fire, sleep there—'

'The wooden cage on the landing?' Charlotte said, enlightened.

'To protect them from the patients while they sleep – though in some cases it may serve to protect the patients from the nurses,' he added. 'Unsupervised as they are, and generally in liquor, the patients are at their mercy. But those patients who have any friends or any money generally manage to get hold of drink as well.' He shook his head. 'Even I would not willingly go into a hospital ward at night.'

'But why must it be so?'

'You have to understand that no-one else would take the work. No decent woman would even step inside a hospital. Therefore only women of low character become nurses – dirty, immoral, immodest, and drunken – thieves and prostitutes – the very lowest of creatures who have nowhere else to go. There is nothing you can threaten a woman like that with. The best you can hope for is that they will watch the patients and stop them falling out of bed or setting fire to themselves. More than that—' he shrugged. 'I have never seen a nurse wash a patient. And as for washing the sheets—!'

Charlotte shook her head. 'It is wrong. It must be wrong.'

'Perhaps. But there is nothing to be done about it. You had much better forget about it. I hope – indeed I advise very strongly that you should never go to any hospital again. It is not proper, and it is not safe.' He lowered his voice. 'I know I have no right, but as a *friend* I am concerned about your safety. I am sure you will forgive me for that.'

Charlotte's heart tripped a little, and she found she was not too old yet to blush. 'I am glad of your concern,' she said. 'And to be truthful, I have no desire to go to a hospital ever again, if there's nothing I can do to help.'

'There is nothing. They are all the same.'

'Then it will be of more use for me to go where I can do some good.'

'You are so very practical,' he said. 'I wish all philanthropists were as practical.'

This conversation took place at Mrs Welland's, and was interrupted at that point by a general inclination for a round game. They all sat down round the table for Conundrums, one side of the table against the other. Charlotte noticed happily that Doctor Anthony took care to secure the place at her side. The other team began with a conundrum from Mr Snoddy: *Where did Charles I's executioner dine, and what did he take?* which Doctor Anthony got very quickly.

'He took a chop at the King's Head,' he said, and lowering his voice whispered to Charlotte, 'That is such an old chestnut! If that is to be their standard, we shall beat too easily!' It was new to Charlotte, and she hoped privately that she would not prove too much of a drag on her team.

Anthony presented the other team with: *Why did the Queen's accession throw a greater damp over us than King William's death?* It seemed to puzzle them greatly.

Charlotte murmured to her companion, 'I think I have it. Is it that the King was missed, but the Queen reigns?'

'Of course. I knew *you* would find it out,' he whispered back.

Mrs Welland, watching them across the table, said indulgently, 'Another time we shall have to keep you

469

two apart – must we not, Miss Hobsbawn? It is not fair to be putting them in the one team. Come, Mr Gaits, can't you think what it must be? Miss Hobsbawn, you must have an idea.'

'Something about "reigning" and "raining", you know,' Fanny said almost absently, her eyes still on Charlotte and Doctor Anthony opposite her.

'Just so,' Mrs Welland said. 'But what can the other part be?'

Charlotte didn't mind if they never got it. Doctor Anthony's forearm, resting on the table, had touched hers as he leaned towards her to whisper, and though he had straightened up, he had not removed it.

Charlotte felt half ashamed to be feeding on such crumbs; but in the carriage going home she told herself as long as it was all kept inside her head, it did no harm. She had not intended to fall in love again, after Mr Fleetwood; she had decided then that her life would be organised rationally and used for the greatest benefit of the greatest number. Love and marriage obviously had no place in that. And indeed, she was not sure now that falling in love was what she was doing. She only knew that Doctor Anthony was the most beautiful and agreeable man in the world, besides being intelligent and good, and that any little sign, however slight, that he preferred her, made her tingle in the most absurd way.

Well, she told herself defiantly, there was no harm in admiring him. He was very admirable. His life was not spent in idle and vacuous pleasure. He had been born with natural abilities which he had trained and was now applying to the greater good of mankind. He hadn't a thought for himself; he wore himself out in the service of the poor and the sick. Who would not admire him? And if – *if* – in the remote possibility that he preferred her

– if anything should come of it – was that not rational? Would he not be the perfect husband for her, and she the perfect wife for him? Both united in the same purpose and working for the same good, what could be more convenient than to be married?

She felt that he did admire her. He had often commented on her work, on the fact that she did not spend her days thinking about clothes and social events, on her practical nature and the way she could face the horrors of poverty without squeamishness. 'You are not like other females,' he had said more than once. And today he had shown a warm interest in her safety, had almost begged her not to be going into hospitals any more. She smiled to herself, and saw the reflection of her lips move in the dark glass beside her.

'Did you have an agreeable evening?' Fanny asked her, breaking a long silence.

'Yes, very. Did you?'

'Yes indeed,' Fanny said, but she sounded a little low.

Charlotte turned to look at her, but she had turned her head away. They were just going into Piccadilly, and on both sides there were handsome shops, glovers, milliners, perfumiers, confectioners, dedicated to the comforts of the rich. The smartest and most exclusive shops in London were in Piccadilly, Bond Street, Jermyn Street, the Burlington Arcade. Charlotte smiled. 'I can never look at these fashionable shops, so full of elegant, expensive articles, without thinking of what Mrs Saville told me, about the rooms upstairs.' Many a glittering shop-front, she had been told, concealed quite another trade. Here a smartly dressed young woman, discreetly veiled, and accompanied by a man she had perhaps only just met, might enter the shop like any other customer, but give the pass by word or sign and lead the way to a room upstairs. It amused Charlotte to think what activities might have been going on over their very heads when her grandmother took her to buy a new bonnet. She thought of the milliner innocently tying her ribbons, with the paphian's guinea still hot in her pocket, and it made her want to laugh.

Fanny saw the smile, and sighed. 'Oh Charlotte, how can you? It's bad enough having to have to do with these creatures, without your finding it all so amusing.'

'Oh dear, poor Fanny! Is it very hard for you, this life?'

'I can't pretend to enjoy visiting back-slums,' Fanny said. 'I wish there was some more pleasant way of doing good.'

'Well, you don't have to come with me, you know. I think it's very brave of you to do all you do, when you hate it so much. If you want to stay home and amuse yourself, I shan't be in the least offended.'

'Oh no,' Fanny said. 'I must do something to help. I only wish it weren't all so dirty and depressing.'

'I don't suppose it need be. There must be things you might do that don't involve going into the rookeries. I'll ask Doctor Anthony if he—'

'No, don't,' Fanny said quickly. Charlotte glanced at her. 'Don't trouble the doctor. I'm sure he has enough to think about.'

'It won't hurt just to ask him,' Charlotte reasoned. 'If anyone knows what opportunities there are, it must be him.'

Fanny bit her lip. 'I don't want him to think—'

'Think what?'

'That I am half-hearted about helping.'

'Dear Fanny, I'm sure he knows the goodness of your heart.'

'I would sooner you didn't ask him, all the same,' Fanny said quietly, and Charlotte could not argue any further.

Besides, something had caught her eye. 'Oh look,' she

said, 'coming out of Bab Mae's Street – it's Tom Weston!' She reached up and knocked on the roof of the carriage; Tom had seen them, and walked to the kerb to meet them. Charlotte let down the window. 'I have just been saying to Fanny that for all this looks a respectable area, there is a great deal going on that we don't see.'

'You may be sure of that,' Tom said. 'Are you just come back from Lamb's Conduit Street?'

'How did you guess?'

'Too smart for philanthropising, not smart enough to have been dining anywhere else.'

'But it would be unkind and inappropriate to be going to Mrs Welland's in full fig.'

'Oh, I don't criticise. I applaud your tact.' He glanced around. 'We're holding up the traffic. Will you let me drive the last few yards home with you?' He climbed in, the carriage moved off again, and he settled himself opposite them and said, 'I dined in St James's Square this evening. You were spoken of.'

'It's a week since I was there,' Charlotte said. 'I must call tomorrow morning.'

'If you call early enough, you will save a footman a walk. Your mother intends to invite you and Fanny to dinner on Friday. And she proposes to ask Doctor Anthony as well.'

Both women looked at him. 'Why Doctor Anthony?'

Tom concealed a smile. 'She can't help being interested in someone she hears so much about. And Batchworth, you know, is on the Public Health Committee and the Sewers Committee – he will value Anthony's views on conditions in St Giles's.'

'Oh, not drains again!' Fanny wailed. 'If we are to spend the whole evening talking about stinks and sewage I shall go mad! You can't imagine what it's like at home, cousin. Sometimes I think I'd give anything for one of the old, dull kind of evenings, where everyone talked about hats and weddings and what Lady This said about Lady That.'

Tom laughed. 'Poor Fanny! But you know, we all firmly expected *you* to reform Charlotte. You were always so strong-minded and self-willed. How is it you let Charlotte bully you?'

Fanny looked gloomy. 'If it's strong-will you want, Charlotte has so much there's none left for anyone else. There's no budging her an inch. When I think what a meek, shy little soul she was when I first met her – afraid of everything and thinking everyone knew better than she did – I wonder what happened to that nice girl?'

'Am I not a nice girl now?' Charlotte asked her, amused.

'Hardly,' Fanny said.

'Poor Fanny! Well, I'll tell you what we'll do. We'll have a whole weekend devoted to pleasure. We'll dine with my mother on Friday, and ride in the Park on Saturday, and go to the theatre, or dance if we can find out a ball, and do something else on Sunday.'

'What about a picnic ride on Sunday?' Tom suggested. 'You could ramble about Richmond Park and have a good gallop, and eat al fresco. The weather's still warm enough, if it doesn't change.'

'Oh yes! We haven't ridden for such ages,' Fanny said.

She turned such a yearning face on Charlotte that she felt quite guilty. 'Whatever you like. Yes, of course, I'd like to ride too. Do you think Grandmama and Papa Danby would come?'

'I wonder if Doctor Anthony rides,' Fanny said. 'Perhaps he might care to join us. I'm sure Uncle Jes would lend him something if he did.'

'We must ask him,' Charlotte said, thinking how handsome the doctor would look on a horse. 'And you'll come, won't you, Tom?'

'Not I,' Tom said. 'You know I never get on a horse if I can help it. No, I have quite another amusement in mind for Sunday.'

Charlotte enjoyed the dinner party quite as much as Fanny – perhaps more, and certainly more than Mrs Manvers, who had a catalogue of the new discoveries from the Valley of the Kings to pore over and would sooner have stayed home with something on a tray. But despite what both those ladies thought of her tastes, it was a delight to Charlotte not to be going to the back-slums. She spent all of Friday getting herself ready for the dinner engagement, much of it spent in the bath, for Fanny's nagging had given her the morbid notion that the smell of the Devil's Acre had seeped into her skin. Norton scrubbed her with a good will and washed her hair for her and rinsed it with camomile, and then she had a whole fresh lot of water brought and poured Otto of Roses into it, and Charlotte submerged herself in that for half an hour.

It was after all rather delightful to be choosing a fine silk gown, to be putting on lace-edged petticoats, to have her shoulders powdered and her hair curled, and fresh flowers pinned in her hair and at her bosom. She liked the feeling of fine clothes, she liked to be clean and sweet-smelling, she liked to look in the glass and see her hair hanging in glossy ringlets like dark burnished gold. *He* had never seen her like this, she thought; and she could not help a small, instantly thrust-away thought that it might be the turning-point in their relationship. He had only ever seen Miss Meldon; now he would see Lady Chelmsford. She did not mean to dazzle him: she put on no jewels, except a simple, very pretty cameo her mother had given her last birthday, which she wore on a black velvet riband about her throat. But he would see her dressed with feminine elegance, and she hoped that she might quicken his pulse a little.

At all events, it proved to her that she had developed, all unknowing, a taste for the finer things in life. Her mother's dinners were first-rate, Lord Batchworth's cellar small but excellently chosen. Tonight she would move about lovely rooms, eat off damask, fine porcelain, crystal and silver, hear gently modulated voices, smell delicately scented skin and clean linen. She would not like, no she would not like, to go back to being poor. She did not any longer even want to live in Chetton. London was her place now, now that she had it on her own terms. And she realised suddenly how very lucky she was, to be able to have everything she wanted, just for the asking.

Well, almost everything.

Poor Fanny, she thought, without wondering what the connection was. She must do something to make Fanny happy.

'Well, and what do you think of the doctor now?' Lord Batchworth asked his wife as she sat before her glass taking out her pins.

'Oh, he was perfectly presentable,' she said.

'Presentable?' Jes raised an eyebrow at such cool praise. 'Wouldn't you say charming?'

'Yes; yes, he was; certainly.' Rosamund frowned thoughtfully at her reflection. 'I must say I was a little surprised. After what Tom said about his perhaps not liking to come, I thought there would be some awkwardness or gaucherie, or some deliberate coolness. But he seemed as willing as anyone could want to be entertained. I certainly saw no reluctance for good society there.'

Jes smiled, and took up the hairbrush. He loved the occasions when he was allowed to brush out his wife's hair. He drew the bristles through the shining copper length, and turned the tress over his hand at the end, and Rosamund leaned to the stroke like a good horse being groomed. 'So he has your approval, does he? Charlotte has your permission to think of him?'

'My approval? Ah no! I am not going to be an officious mama. There is nothing but trouble that way. Charlotte is old enough to know her own mind. She can choose a husband for herself without my help.'

'But?'

'But what?'

'There seemed to be a but in that sentence.'

Rosamund sighed a little. 'I am just a little surprised at her liking him so much.'

'You said he was charming.'

'But what else? He doesn't seem to have much to offer a young woman in her position.'

'I didn't have much to offer a young woman in your position when you fell in love with me,' he pointed out with a smile. 'A younger son with nothing to inherit, no money, no position—'

'A war hero,' Rosamund said.

'Anthony is a peace-time hero. And frankly, I'd sooner face cannon fire than do what he does day by day.'

'Oh well.' Rosamund shrugged. 'But then you were *so* handsome.'

'I should have thought Anthony was handsome.'

'He is well enough, for anyone who can't have you, my darling.'

'Spoony!'

'But all the same, I can't help thinking of Fleetwood.'

'Thinking *what* of Fleetwood?'

'Wondering about Fleetwood. It is rather odd, don't you think, that he has so completely disappeared since – well, since it all happened.'

'Since his grandfather died, don't forget, and since he

inherited the title,' Jes amended. 'I think he found the estate a great deal more encumbered than he expected. I imagine he is retrenching down in the country, and trying to put things in order. I see him occasionally at the House,' he added, 'and he isn't hollow-cheeked and wasted with grief, if that's what you're thinking.'

Rosamund was not convinced. 'But he never goes anywhere else. One never sees him anywhere—'

'We never did keep the same company.'

'—and Lady Turnhouse doesn't come to Town either, and she always hated the country. Why should she stay away unless he makes her?'

'I imagine Lady Turnhouse stays away for the same reason as her son – lack of funds. Her income depended entirely on the estate, you know. Old Southport let her run up bills, but if Fleetwood is retrenching, he'd have to cut her off too.' Rosamund looked disappointed. 'What fiction were you concocting in this sleek head, my lovely one?'

'Just that he did love Charlotte after all, and was heartbroken when she jilted him.' Jes laughed heartily at that. 'Oh well, if Charlotte really wants this doctor of hers, I suppose we shall have to make the best of it. At least he is sociable and presentable, and from what Tom says, he may well be brilliant. With her money behind him, he may become famous. The Queen will give him a knighthood, and then he'll come up with some miraculous new cure, or discover a disease, and she'll ennoble him, and it will all work out very happily.'

'What makes you think that Charlotte wants any of that? Her present habits rather suggest she prefers obscurity.'

'She likes the good, comfortable things money and position provide. Just at present she may be inclined to undervalue them, but offer to take them away, and I think she would be forced to know her own mind.'

'You seem very sure of her opinions.'

'She's my daughter, for all I didn't bring her up.'

Fanny and Charlotte rode in the Park on Saturday, and it was almost like old times, for they no sooner turned in through the gate than they were surrounded by courtiers. Charlotte was glad to see Fanny brighten and grow animated under the attention. She felt she had been being selfish, and not taking Fanny's wishes enough into consideration, and vowed that would change from now on. As for herself, she enjoyed the vivacity and foolishness of the young men much more now that she didn't feel threatened by it. No-one could expect her to marry any of them, or suspect her of wanting to, and so she could relax and enjoy them as she would have enjoyed the gambolling of a litter of puppies; equally, when she had had enough of them, she could send them away with a kindly but authoritative nod.

Older sisterly, she thought; Fanny, however, said that it was 'like riding with one's aunt'.

'You frighten the poor creatures to death, Charley,' she said. 'I see them peering at you sidelong to see if it's all right to be frivolous with me in your presence.'

'Oh dear, am I spoiling things for you?'

'Not a bit. I begin to seem much younger than my years by comparison with you, which can only be to the good. But how do you come to be immune to their charms? You've been laid siege to by the handsomest men in London, and all you do is smile at them sadly and shake your head *so*, as though wondering at the folly of the children.'

'Oh Fanny, I don't look like that!'

'But you do!'

'Well, they are very silly,' Charlotte said, with a sudden laugh. 'When one has been used to conversing with sensible people—'

'Ah, yes, then,' Fanny agreed gravely. 'Especially people both sensible and good.' She stopped abruptly. Charlotte thought of Sidney Herbert and did not enquire further; but she thought she had the clue to what Fanny was missing, and began forming plans in her mind as to how she might reintroduce it to Fanny's life.

They were embarking on a second circuit when there was a sound of hurrying hooves behind them, and they were joined by Cavendish astride Lord Batchworth's young horse, a rangy bay, which was throwing its head up and down in a manner hazardous to the rider's handsome features. Charlotte and Fanny pulled up as Cavendish circled the youngster round them in the vain attempt to make it stand.

'You should have him in a martingale,' Charlotte said severely.

'There's a nice sisterly greeting,' Cavendish panted as the bay *passaged* across the tan and back.

'Hello, Cavendish, how lovely to see you,' Charlotte said ironically. 'You should have that animal in a martingale – he's getting away from the bit.'

'Oh hush! I'll have him a minute.' The bay decided to join the party, stopped sidling and began nuzzling the neck of Fanny's mount, who resented the rôle of surrogate mother, laid her ears back and bared her teeth. 'Let's walk on,' Cavendish said hastily. 'I told you I could manage him.'

Charlotte smiled to herself and let it pass. 'You arrived this morning, I suppose? It's a pity you missed dinner last night.'

'Yes, I should have liked to meet your doctor friend. Papa says he is a very decent fellow. But I dare say there'll be other opportunities.'

'Aren't you coming on the picnic ride with us tomorrow?'

'No, worst luck, I have to be back. This is the most flying of flying visits.'

'I'm flattered you're giving so much of it to me, then,' Charlotte said. She studied her brother as he rode the bay, quiet for the moment, on a loose rein. When she had first met him he had been small and thin for his age, with a look of fragility. Now at sixteen he had grown and filled out, but despite his cherished whiskers – still so fine they looked as though they had been painted on by a water-colourist – he was still not what one would have described as robust-looking. He had a delicacy of line and colouring that would not have shamed a girl, and though Charlotte thought he would be tall, there was never an ounce of spare flesh on him. Yet he had been very healthy in recent years, had a splendid appetite and was full of energy and enthusiasm. She thought his mother need not fret too much about him – though doubtless she would. He would be handsome, too – was already, in fact—

'Have you done staring at me?' he enquired, breaking into her thoughts.

'I was just thinking that you need nothing more than a Hussar's uniform to be a regular heartbreaker,' Charlotte said.

'Oh, gammon!' he cried, the high blood showing under his fine skin. 'Don't make a muffin of me!'

'Goodness,' Charlotte said, 'if you can't accept a compliment from a sister, how will you be able to bear the admiration of unrelated females?'

Fanny laughed. 'Poor Cav! The truth is, Charley has her blood up these days, and there's no holding her – with or without a martingale! The woman who walks alone in Devil's Acre is beyond anyone's control.'

'All this medical stuff,' Cavendish said, wrinkling his nose. 'It ain't the thing, you know, not for females. The fellows at school say – oh well, it don't signify what they think,' he corrected himself hastily. 'The thing is, Charley, that I wanted to enlist your help with Mama. She listens to you more than anyone else. She thinks you're dashed clever, and if *you* tell her to let me be a cavalryman—'

'Oh Cav, she won't take any notice of my opinion!'

'But she will!' he said earnestly. 'You see, everyone tried to make you do what you didn't want, and you broke away and now you're doing what *you* want, and they've all accepted it and even think it's probably for the best. And Mama wants me to go to Oxford and then stand for Parliament, and I'd simply die of boredom. But I'll be old enough next year to get my colours, and if only Mama can be persuaded, I'm sure Papa will buy them for me. And there's no point in my staying on at school when I could be getting on in my career, is there?'

'Is that really what you want to do?' Charlotte asked with a little wondering shake of the head. She couldn't imagine anything more dull than life as an officer in a fashionable regiment – parades, reviews, and endless social engagements.

'Yes, it is,' he said, blushing a little. 'I know it the same way you knew what you wanted to do. But I'm not independent like you. Oh do say you'll speak to Mama for me!'

'I can't persuade her against her will,' Charlotte said. 'That would be wrong, even if it were possible.'

'But you could tell her you don't think it's dangerous. She's afraid I'll be killed, but I'm no more likely to be killed as a Hussar than out hunting, and she doesn't stop me doing that.'

'That's true,' Charlotte said. 'Well, my dear, I'll tell her I don't think it is particularly dangerous, if you think it will help, but I won't try to persuade her. That wouldn't be fair.'

482

Everyone should be allowed to follow the career of their choice, she thought, if it was at all possible. Cavendish was now chatting to Fanny, telling her about some rag or other he and his schoolfriends had got up to. Fanny listened, smiling, but Charlotte knew she was not happy. She must do something for Fanny, and if she couldn't get her Sidney Herbert, she must at least put her in the way of meeting some more intelligent and good men.

The weather stayed fine and remarkably warm for the Sunday expedition to Richmond Park. Doctor Anthony, to Charlotte's secret surprise, accepted the invitation to borrow Jes's second horse, and he looked even more handsome astride it than Charlotte had anticipated.

'It is a great pleasure to be on horseback again,' he said as they jogged into the wide open spaces of the park, the horses catching excitement from each other. 'It is something which, living as I do, I have little chance of, but at home, as a boy, I was never out of the saddle.' He addressed the remark equally to Charlotte and Fanny, who were riding one either side of him.

'Let's have a gallop, to settle them down,' Rosamund said.

'Come on, Charlotte, I'll beat you to that crooked tree,' Cavendish cried, clapping his legs to his horse's side, and Charlotte took off after him.

The other horses threw their heads about, wanting to race, and Doctor Anthony said to Fanny in a low voice, 'Your cousin has a great deal of energy. I wouldn't be surprised if she beat her brother, even though he has a start on her.'

'She is a very good rider,' Fanny said generously, 'particularly when you consider that she didn't learn it as a child. She rides as well as me, or better, though I was put on a pony when I was four years old.'

483

'She rides very differently from you,' Anthony said enigmatically, and Fanny, stealing a glance at him, saw him watching Charlotte's progress with a faint frown. He is worried for her safety, she thought with an inward sigh; and took what comfort she could from the fact that he was too much a gentleman to leave her side when they all cantered off.

They rambled pleasantly about the park for several hours before making a rendezvous with the brake in which the servants had brought the picnic lunch. This was spread out in a dry spot, a deer-lawn under a clump of birch trees. In the general movement amongst the group, Charlotte took the opportunity to make good her promise to Cavendish, and sitting down by her mother, opened the subject.

Rosamund looked at her wryly. 'Has that naughty boy been pestering you to come and pester me?'

'I told him I wouldn't try to persuade you,' Charlotte began, and seeing the set of her mother's mouth, she laughed. 'As if I could! Fanny thinks me stubborn, but if I am, I know where it comes from.'

'Oh dear, it's a very unladylike trait,' Rosamund said ruefully. 'If you have it from me, I've given you the worst of me.'

'I don't think so,' Charlotte said. 'In my position, it would be pitiful to have no mind, and be swayed this way and that by every new person one met.'

'But one ought not to take it to extremes,' Rosamund said, and then gave herself away. 'At least until one is married.'

'Oh, are we there again?' Charlotte said, laughing. 'I came to talk to you about Cavendish.'

'Well, we shall if you like. But indulge me a little first. Have you no idea of marrying?'

Charlotte phrased her answer carefully. 'I am not averse

484

to the state itself. It's a matter of finding the right person – and of the right person making the offer, of course.'

'And *have* you met the right person?'

Charlotte looked down at her fingers, twisting a blade of grass. 'The rightness must depend on his feelings too.'

Rosamund smiled at the heightened colour. 'I thought so! I'm glad, my dearest. I like him very much.'

Charlotte looked up, startled. 'Have you guessed? Am I so obvious?'

'No, no, don't be afraid. Call it a mother's penetration, if you like. You behave just as you should. And he obviously admires you. I see him looking at you all the time; and when he talks to you, it is with such ease, as if to an equal, or an old friend.'

'You want me so much to be married, don't you?' Charlotte said wonderingly. 'Is it so important?'

'I want you to be happy as *I* am happy. Yes, it is important. I don't like to see you letting your youth pass untasted, your days taken up with such serious concerns, always looking at misery and trouble. There's enough of that in life without seeking it out. This is the time when you should be laughing and enjoying yourself.'

'I can't ignore the misery,' Charlotte began, but her mother caught up her words.

'No, of course not, but need you put yourself so much in the way of it? There are other ways to help, besides binding the wounds with your own hands. Perhaps better ways, which would help more people. You are growing quite middle-aged, my darling – and it's affecting Fanny, too.'

'Yes, poor Fanny – I must do something for her. But now, first, I must fulfil my promise to Cav. He so much wants to be a cavalry man, and I promised I would tell you that I don't think it is such a dangerous occupation. It's not as though there were a Bonaparte rampaging about the continent. We're not likely to go to war.'

Rosamund shook her head. 'Europe is very unsettled. You could hardly name the country which isn't rumbling on the brink of revolution. And when they erupt, there's no knowing how our position might change.'

'Is that what makes you reluctant, then – the prospect of war?'

'I was in Brussels all through the Waterloo campaign,' Rosamund said. 'I saw those boys – the Hyde Park Cavalry, people called them – boys like Cavendish; laughing, full of spirits, parading themselves like peacocks in their gaudy uniforms, dancing and making love and talking about the battle to come as if it were just another romp. And I saw them afterwards.' She shook her head. 'I dare say their mothers tried to tell them beforehand, but they wouldn't believe, any more than Cav will believe me, that war is not like a day's hunting.'

Charlotte was silent, never having heard her mother speak so strongly. She was sorry now that she had brought the subject up.

Then Rosamund said more lightly, 'But his father saw all that, and more, and he doesn't object to Cav taking colours, and so I suppose in the end I will have to agree. And,' she added with a wry smile, 'when I think back, your father and his cousin Bobbie both yearned to be soldiers. Marcus got his colours and Bobbie was kept out of uniform by his doting mother, but it was Bobbie who died.'

Charlotte put her hand on her mother's, surprising herself, since she had never learned to touch for comfort. Rosamund squeezed it briefly, and said cheerfully, 'We must hope he marries early and sets up a family – and after all, there is nothing more conducive to matrimony than a Hussar uniform!'

While the rest of his family was enjoying the delights

of Richmond Park, Tom was taking pleasure in quite a different way, rowing a little boat on the Serpentine River. He was surprised at himself. It had taken him a very long time to decide to ask, and he had been convinced that he would be denied. But though Miss Thorn's parents had looked doubtful, Miss Thorn had dealt with them firmly. *She* hadn't seemed surprised by the approach, and she told them it was a perfectly respectable way of taking the air; and at her age, and in a public place, there was no need whatever of a chaperone. Morning service having been duly attended, Mr Weston might call for her at any time he nominated.

So here they were, in one of the hired boats, with a picnic basket, put up by the resolutely silent Billington, between their feet. Tom rowed in silence at first, simply trying to come to terms with his own ambivalence – his soaring heart and his astonished mind vying for supremacy. Miss Thorn looked bewitching in a muslin gown and a light mantle of lavender wool decorated with black braid and a matching bonnet with very gay striped ribbons. Her hair was curled in quite a different way, and she looked younger than she did in her missioneering suits of hardwearing black and brown, but still when the sunlight fell full on her face, he could see that she was neither young nor pretty by the world's standards; yet he felt an invisible hand squeeze his heart.

She was looking at him quizzically, and when he raised an enquiring eyebrow, she said, 'I was wondering when you were going to tell me what all this is about.'

'All this?'

'Why you have brought me here.'

'I didn't think you'd come,' he said.

'Is that why you asked?' she said, and laughed. 'What a poor compliment! And I thought you were a man of the world, Mr Weston.'

'I don't feel like one when I'm with you. I feel like an awkward boy.'

'You do seem a bit tongue-tied,' she acknowledged. 'Well, never mind it. I'm quite happy just sitting here looking about me. It's a very pleasant motion, isn't it? I don't think I've ever been on a boat before. You row uncommon well, I must say – looking at some of the others on this pond.'

'My father was a sea-captain, a hero of Trafalgar, so the least I could do, seeing I bear his name, was to learn to row properly.'

'Have you ever been to sea?'

'Only in the Channel packet,' he said with a grin.

'Well, that's more than I have. I've only ever seen the sea once, when Father took us to Southend for a treat.'

'Didn't you go down on the steamer? Then you have been on a boat before.'

'Oh, I meant a little boat like this. I've never been so close to the water – on the Southend steamer you might as well have been on dry land for all you felt it.' She grinned. 'Mother was sick, all the same – or said she was. I think she thought it was expected of her.'

'And you? I imagine you don't often care to do what's expected of you.'

'Now, why d'you say that, I wonder? Don't you see me as a dutiful daughter?'

'Hmph! Not quite. I can't imagine you ever doing anything you didn't like.'

'I don't *like* going to rich people's doors and asking for money,' she said severely, 'but I do it because it's my duty.'

Tom was unrepentant. 'My point exactly. You *like* doing your duty.'

She burst out laughing. 'There's no arguing with you! So now, won't you tell me why you asked me here today?'

'If you tell me why you accepted the invitation,' Tom smiled.

'Oh, that's easy. It sounded enjoyable, and I like to enjoy myself. And it was something I'd not done before, and I like new experiences. And you didn't ask Mother and Father, and I hardly ever do anything without them. And I was curious about you.'

'Were you?'

'Oh, that pleases you, doesn't it?' she teased. 'Men are such vain creatures, you can always fix them by talking about them. Yes, of course I was curious about you. I want to know why you come so often to the mission when it isn't your kind of thing at all. You dislike the work, and you disapprove of the way we do it – yes you do! I see you look so exasperated sometimes at the preachers that I'm afraid I won't be able to keep my countenance. I have to bite my cheeks so as not to laugh, to see you fidget and frown and stuff your fists in your pockets as you were like to split them! So if you hate it so much, Mr Thomas Weston MP, what I want to know is – why do you keep coming?'

He looked at her for a minute in silence, and she cocked her head a little, like a bird, as though she expected him to gammon her. And so he said at last, 'I come because of you.'

Her eyes became very still, almost wary, but she said in a light, teasing tone, 'Because of me, forsooth! And what do I do that's so fascinating?'

'It's not what you do, it's what you are.' He drew a quick breath, like a man who has just slipped into the water. Well, he had begun now; now he must strike out for the depths. 'Ever since the first moment I saw you, I have been drawn to you in a way I can't explain. I like to see you, and listen to you, and be with you. To tell you the truth—' He heard his own voice tremble alarmingly, and gripped the oars tighter from sheer nervousness over what he might be going to say. 'To tell you the truth, I'm only really happy when I'm with you. When I'm out of your company, all I can think about is when I will see you again.'

He stopped, and his words seemed to echo on in the silence, drawing attention to themselves, making a fool of him.

She looked at him gravely for a while, to see if he would say more, and then she said, 'I see.'

'I see? Is that all you have to say?'

'What did you expect?' she said, sounding nettled. 'Am I to thank you for making me an object of – of—'

'Of what?'

'*I* don't know. Whatever it is! Your fancy or curiosity or whatever it might be! Now, Mr Weston, I think you are a good man at heart, and I absolve you from wanting to make a fool of me, but if you are expecting me to be grateful for your notice—'

'Grateful!' Tom exploded. 'To hell with gratitude!'

'Aye, if you like,' she said. 'But what then?'

'I don't know,' he said miserably.

'Oh, very well then,' she said; and then she laughed. 'Don't look so blue! I don't know what it is that's got into your head, and I dare say you don't either, but I am nothing special, so don't try to make out I am. Jenny wren you called me, and that was fanciful enough, but—'

'I love you,' Tom said – in a low, half-frightened voice that seemed forced out of him without his volition. She looked at him as surprised and troubled as he had sounded, and it was that which broke through his self-consciousness. He had brought her here to have pleasure, and here he was making her anxious and doubtful, and he couldn't bear to see her lovely face without its smile. 'I'm sorry, I didn't meant that to sound so reluctant. I love you, Miss Thorn! Let me say it with all the joy I feel in my heart: I love you, I have loved you from the moment I first set eyes on you.'

She didn't smile. Her expression was troubled, but there were evidently thoughts and calculations rushing through her busy mind. 'What do you want from me?' she said at last.

'That would take all day to tell you!' he said, light now with the relief of confession. 'But to begin with, you might tell me whether you care for me at all.'

'That's beside the point,' she said, waving it away.

'I should have thought it was very much the point.'

She looked at him almost narrowly, an expression he felt did not suit her. 'I'm not a fool, Mr Weston. I am quite well aware that I am not of your station in life. I have nothing that might attract you – not fortune or looks or birth. I'm an ordinary woman, not even in my first youth. And you suddenly tell me you love me, as if that answers all questions. But it doesn't – it puts more questions than before. I can't believe – no, I *can't*,' she added, as though she had seriously considered it, 'that you mean to ruin me; you don't seem to be trying to make a fool of me; and you can't want to marry me; so what *do* you want?'

What did he want? The question floored Tom. Love usually meant marriage, unless it were platonic love – and as he looked into her eyes he felt the quiver of desire run through him again. But how could they marry? His income was comfortable for a bachelor, but he had no establishment, and the cost of one was beyond him to calculate. Besides, where and how could this round, brown jenny wren of a woman fit into his world? He thought of her a society hostess, he thought of her in the drawing-rooms he frequented, he thought of Billington's delicately flared nostrils this morning as he laid out Tom's trousers, he thought of giving up his comfortable rooms and his accustomed routine and his complete lack of accountability to anyone.

He desired her, he wanted to lie with her in his arms for ever, but he would not harm her, never, never. So, if he didn't want to marry her – what?

'To be with you,' he said at last, helplessly. 'Not just at the mission, but like this. To spend time in your company, as a friend.'

'A friend, is it?' she said, and there was a hint of irony in her voice that provoked him.

'Isn't it possible for us to be friends? To talk, to enjoy each other's company? We could go for drives, for walks – to the theatre. I could take you to see all the new exhibitions. There's so much to do. Wouldn't you like that?'

'Oh yes,' she said unemphatically, and lapsed into a disconcerting silence.

'I'm sorry,' he said, 'I shouldn't have said I loved you. It – was surprised out of me. Could we pretend it not said, and then be friends?'

'Was it true?' she asked abruptly.

'Yes,' he said.

'Then you were right to say it. One must always declare the truth.' There was a gleam of humour in her eyes that he took for encouragement.

'Do you—' he began tentatively.

'Love you?' she anticipated. He nodded, tense with anticipation. Yes, there was definitely a gleam in her eyes. 'That is more than you need to know, Mr Weston,' she said. She thought a moment. 'Very well, we shall be friends,' she said; and there was that in her tone which suggested the words, 'and we'll see who weakens first.'

CHAPTER TWENTY-TWO

Unexpectedly, it was Mrs Manvers who suggested a new interest for Fanny. Charlotte had mentioned the matter to her in a general way, not supposing that Mrs Manvers had any interest closer than Cairo. But one day in February 1848, when they were alone at breakfast together – Fanny was often later down than either of them – Mrs Manvers said, 'I have something to say to you about Fanny. I was glad that you came round to seeing that your sort of charity work does not at all suit her, and I have been thinking what she might occupy herself with. Her talents lie in the drawing-room – and, perhaps, the committee room. I'm sure she would be a wonderful manager if she was given the chance.'

'Grandmama thinks so. She thinks Fanny ought to be managing a household,' Charlotte said. 'But Fanny is so adamant that she must do good works – heaven knows why!'

'You really don't know why?' Mrs Manvers asked, looking up over the top of her spectacles. She had received a programme from the Egyptian Hall in the morning's post, which was promising a new exhibition, and had been reading it with her buttered toast.

'I assure you I don't press her into it,' Charlotte defended herself.

'I know that. Well, we must each conjecture according to our wits. But now, as to Fanny, I think I have the very outlet for her energies. A young friend of mine has recently

493

come to live permanently in London, for her husband's sake – he is a great deal older than her, and in poor health, and needs special treatment which can only be got at Guy's. So they have settled in a nice little house in Sackville Street, and Lady Mayhew having a great deal of time on her hands—'

'Lady Mayhew?' Charlotte interrupted. 'I'm sure I've heard the name.'

'Have you, my dear? Well I don't know why not. She is a charming young woman, just Fanny's age. I knew her when she was a girl in Northampton. She was a Miss Leytham. I knew her mother, Lady Mary – we were at school together for a year – and my late husband had business dealings with Sir John Leytham, her father. They were a numerous family, but Sibella was always a favourite of mine – a very lively, clever sort of girl. Her marriage to Sir Samuel Mayhew was something of a shock.' She paused, frowning.

Charlotte remembered now where she had heard the name. It was back in the year forty-four, before her come-out, when Fanny had pointed out, in a shop or some-such, the young woman so scandalously married to the elderly man. Charlotte had a vague memory of a slim, smartly dressed figure.

Mrs Manvers continued. 'Well, as I said, Lady Mayhew – Sibella – has a great deal of time on her hands, and too much energy to do nothing with it, so she has interested herself in a charity school just round the corner in Boyle Street. She was got into it by Lady Vigo, who is a neighbour, and a trustee of the school.'

'And what does this school do?' Charlotte asked.

'Oh, the usual thing – it's a boarding school for the daughters of poor people in the parish. It takes them away from the influences of poverty, teaches them to read, write and work, and to know the Catechism and the Bible and so on, and then finds them positions as domestic servants to respectable families. Thoroughly good work, but the school is desperately short of money and, to be frank, in need of reorganisation. Sibella is trying to interest people in making donations, but what the school needs as much as money is someone vigorous and right-thinking to shake it up and set it to rights. It has got into rather a state, according to Sibella. Now don't you think, my dear, that with her experience, Fanny would be just the person?'

'It sounds so, indeed. But what do you propose?'

'That she should interest herself in it, become a patron, perhaps even a trustee – there is a vacancy on the board now the Archdeacon has died. And Sibella would make an excellent friend for Fanny, which she needs now you are so much occupied. Together they could visit people and arouse interest and hold meetings and raise funds and – generally be useful to the school and the children, without—' She hesitated delicately.

'Without having to mix with low people who smell disagreeable?' Charlotte supplied solemnly.

Mrs Manvers eyed her askance. 'Well, dear, not everyone shares your taste for the *macabre*.' Charlotte laughed at the choice of word. 'Dear Fanny wants to meet charitable people, and we want her to meet people of rank and fortune, and, well, this seems calculated to do both.'

'I think it's an excellent idea, ma'am,' Charlotte said. 'I think you should put it to Fanny, and I will support you. I might interest myself in the school, too – after all, it is a close neighbour, and charity ought to begin at home.'

Charlotte met Lady Mayhew alone to begin with, calling on her in Sackville Street with a card of introduction from Mrs Manvers. But it proved unnecessary.

'We have an acquaintance in common, besides Mrs Manvers,' Sibella said. 'An acquaintance on my side, but your cousin, I believe – Mr Benedict Morland. He used to come often to our house when I lived at home with Papa and Mama. I hope he is well?'

'I haven't very recent news of him,' Charlotte said, 'but he writes to my grandmother, and the last I heard he was well.' She hesitated, not knowing the degree of acquaintance, but Lady Mayhew was watching her with expectant eyes, so she added, 'I don't know if you heard that he was sadly widowed three years ago.'

'Yes, I did hear,' Sibella said. 'He is still—? That is, I suppose – does he think of marrying again?'

'He is still unmarried,' Charlotte said. 'What he plans I can't pretend to know.'

Sibella nodded and changed the subject quite abruptly to the latest news from France, where there had been another revolution, and the king, Louis-Philippe, and all his family had been forced to flee. It had all happened suddenly and unexpectedly, though Charlotte remembered what her mother had said that day in Richmond Park, about Europe being in a state of unrest. The word now was that the king of France had landed in England to seek asylum, and no-one quite knew what that would mean, or whether England would recognise the new government; though Sibella and Charlotte agreed that the whole idea of revolutions and deposing monarchs seemed oddly anachronistic, something left over from the last century and not suited to these modern times of railways and telegraphs. Certainly it was nothing to do with them.

Charlotte liked Sibella. She seemed a sensible, intelligent young woman, though obviously bowed down with care for her elderly husband. Charlotte tried to remember what Fanny had told her about Mayhew, and could not, except that there was supposed to have been some element of coercion on Sibella; but when she spoke of her husband it was with anxious concern, and Charlotte could not think that she would look so worn if she hated him or had been forced to marry him. It was, of course, emphatically not her business, but as she came to know Sibella better and liked her more and more, she often wished there were something she could do to ease her burden.

The meeting between Sibella and Fanny was successful, and Fanny was happy to interest herself in the charity school. It proved that Sir Samuel and Sibella were both acquainted with Doctor Anthony, which strengthened the connection between them. Fanny had feared Anthony would think her weak for wanting to give up teaching at the Ragged Schools, but he seemed thoroughly to approve, and said that administration and organisation of charitable work was far more suitable to a lady's nature and talents than back-slum visiting. The drawing-room at Berkeley Street now regularly housed meetings of philanthropic-minded people, and Doctor Anthony often dropped in on them, so Charlotte was as happy with the change of Fanny's occupation as Fanny was.

During that spring, Lord Ashley was frequently to be found at Berkeley Street too, accompanied by his eldest son Accy, Cavendish's friend. Accy was a cheerful boy but without any great talent, and Lord Ashley had decided that Eton would not do him any good, and had sent him instead to Rugby. He hadn't done well there, either, and now the plan was to send him to sea. Whenever Cavendish could get leave to come to London, Charlotte's drawing-room made a convenient place for the friends to meet: Accy was to sail soon for Australia, and they might not meet again for years. Cavendish was all envy that his friend had been allowed to leave school and go off on such an adventure, and made many pointed remarks to Charlotte, hoping she could encourage their mother to see the similarity of the cases.

Lord Ashley's main concern that spring, apart from

his family, was the Public Health Bill which was being steered through Parliament by Lord Batchworth and his old friend Viscount Morpeth. Lady Chelmsford's drawing-room became a useful unofficial meeting-place for those interested in public health and the question of sewerage, and Mr Chadwick and Doctor Southwood Smith as well as Ashley, Morpeth and Batchworth were often to be found there arguing about bores and the replacement of wooden pipes and how many votes could be garnered in which quarter to get the Bill through. Anthony could not but be drawn into these discussions, and Fanny, who had nothing to say about drains, would sit in sad silence observing that Charlotte was as knowledgeable as the rest and could discuss the matter on equal terms with them, especially with Doctor Anthony, who addressed her sometimes as though she were another man.

Fanny's charity school was ultimately benefited by these meetings. The drainage system and water supply to the school were both improved, a laundry-room set up in the basement (Charlotte could not forget the filthy sheets in the hospital ward), and the children were to have a warm bath once a week, and to take walking exercise in the Park every morning to give them fresh air. A new and improved diet was also worked out for the children, including a good ration of vegetables – something the lower orders tended to regard with suspicion, but which Lord Ashley and Doctor Anthony both agreed was beneficial to health. All these improvements were put to the credit of the Trustees, but it was the meeting of minds in the drawing-room at Berkeley Street which gave rise to them, and Charlotte's purse which largely paid for them.

In April these charitable deliberations were interrupted by fears of revolution. A monster meeting of Chartists was to be held on Kennington Green on the 10th of April, followed by a march on Parliament to present a petition. Half a million men were expected to be assembling, and bearing in mind the recent events in France, London high society feared a Paris-style Terror would follow, and that they would soon find themselves swinging from the lampposts. Many families fled to the country; others more resolute stayed, boarding up their windows and arming their servants in preparation for a siege.

Lady Theakston pooh-poohed the panic, and said it would all come to nothing. 'A revolution needs co-operation, and the English are too stubborn to co-operate – and too self-conscious to demonstrate. All that will happen is that it will come on to rain, and everyone will slip away looking sheepish.' Charlotte laughed, and Lucy went on, 'Mark my words! It was the same in the year seventeen, the Pentrich Rebellion – the whole of the north was supposed to rise and overthrow the government, and it ended up with forty-six wet, miserable peasants being cornered in a muddy field.'

'So you don't think Fanny and I should to go out of Town?' Charlotte said.

'Not at all. Why should you?'

'Lots of people who visit us have gone. Mrs Manvers thought it might be wise, and Doctor Anthony seems very concerned for our safety.'

'Does he, indeed? Well, far be it from me to counter the opinion of the doctor,' Lucy said. But later that day Charlotte was visited by the Duke of Wellington himself, who had called at Lucy's request to clarify the situation.

'Not at all, not at all,' the Duke said when Charlotte thanked him for his kindness. 'Took you in on my way. Thank you, no, nothing; I dine with Russell at an early hour today. I can stay a moment only. Your grandmama was anxious that I should allay your fears about this monster meeting. I can't say I am as sanguine as she pretends to be, as to the numbers and intentions of these damned Chartists, but I can promise you there will be no trouble. Mayne and I have it all under control. They won't get past me, I assure you.'

'So there's no need to leave London?' Charlotte asked, with a glance at Mrs Manvers.

'I would not dissuade you, if it makes you feel safer. But I anticipate no inconvenience to those who stay.'

'I heard a rumour that the Queen was to leave,' Mrs Manvers said.

'Ah yes,' said the Duke, taking a turn up and down the carpet, evidence of stronger than usual emotion. 'I've just come from the Palace. It was Russell's idea – put up to it by the Prince, I fancy. Her Majesty being so recently delivered, the Prince is naturally anxious as any husband and father would be—' He paused, rubbed the side of his nose thoughtfully, and said, 'Thing is, of course, the Prince don't exactly understand the national character. But Russell would just as soon have them all out of the way, and as they usually take a vacation at Osborne at this time of year, he has recommended they go a few days early.'

'So there is some danger?' Charlotte asked.

'One can never be absolutely certain about these things. There *may* be trouble – but I shall have nine or ten thousand of infantry, concealed about the town. And Mayne will have sworn in a hundred thousand special constables by the day. No soldiers on the street, that's my plan, until and unless trouble starts. Do nothing to inflame passions – police only on view. But I will have the bridges and the telegraph secured before it begins, just to be on the safe side. So upon the whole I would say that you would be quite safe in staying.'

Charlotte hardly knew whether to be comforted or alarmed by all these preparations. Cavendish, coming to visit her the next morning, was in no doubt that the whole thing had been put on for his personal amusement. 'Ain't it a lark?' he cried. 'I'm a special constable. I took the oath this morning. Every gentleman in Town is swearing in.'

'Does our mother know?' Charlotte asked sternly.

'Papa does – I shall leave it to him to sweeten Mama. I met Lord Ashley on the way here – he's sworn in too, and he's quite sure there's going to be a revolution. He says the whole of Europe is going up in flames, and that now the Irish Nationalists have joined with the Chartists, we shall have a bloodbath.'

'Oh, don't talk such nonsense,' Charlotte said, seeing Fanny and Mrs Manvers both looking nervous. 'Bloodbath indeed! What sort of language is that?'

'Oh, well, I don't suppose it will come to that,' Cavendish said apologetically. 'But we ought to have a splendid scrap at least. Ashley is paired with Prince Louis Bonaparte to guard Fleet Street, and he says I ought to come with them so that he can keep an eye on me for Mama, but I shall take good care to be as far away from him as possible. The Prince is a prime fellow, but Ashley fusses so, and I mean to have some sport.'

By the time the day dawned, Charlotte's apprehensions had taken up a position halfway between her grandmother and Lord Ashley. It was a cool spring morning, the air damp, the sun pale; the streets were unnaturally quiet, with half the families having left, and the others, like Charlotte's household, staying indoors with the downstairs shutters closed. The servants were very nervous, somehow taking into their heads that Charlotte's activities in the Devil's Acre made her particularly vulnerable to attack, no matter how much she argued that the opposite must be true. They wanted the upstairs shutters closed too, and the fires put out, to make the house seem deserted, but Charlotte refused to sit all day in the dark without a fire. She thought there might be bricks thrown, and minor damage to property as the marchers surged past, but to begin with they would be eager to get to their destination of Parliament. Afterwards, depending on their reception, there might be rioting, but it would be time enough to close all the shutters then.

The day wore on, and the quiet got on everyone's nerves. At about eleven o'clock there was a flurry of activity in the street, sounds of running feet and wheels, and everyone braced themselves; but quiet fell again. Soon afterwards it began to rain, and the sky gradually darkened until by midday it was teeming down. At one o'clock Charlotte looked out of the window and saw people walking by under umbrellas, and a cab going round the corner at a normal pace. The town's activities seemed to be resuming.

'I think it is all over,' she said.

At half past two Cavendish arrived and was admitted to the drawing-room, looking very bedraggled and disappointed. 'What a choker!' he said. 'We didn't see a bit of sport! We stood about all day and no-one came. And then a runner came with the word that it was all over and we could stand down.'

'Didn't you see any rioters at all, poor Cav?' Charlotte asked.

'Not one. There were a lot of spectators waiting to see the march come past, but they drifted off when the rain came on. The most excitement we had was when some workmen ran past, hurrying to get out of the rain, and one old fellow who fancied himself a wag shouted, "There's the revolution, gents, just turning down Fetter Lane!"'

'Never mind, come to the fire and get dry.'

'Grandmama was right all along, wasn't she,' Cavendish said despondently. 'I'm *never* going to get into a scrap unless we have a war abroad.'

Shortly afterwards Lord Batchworth arrived. 'Ah, I thought I'd find my brat here,' he said cheerfully. 'You had better go home and show your mother a whole skin, my boy. You should have gone there first, you know.' He turned to the ladies. 'I just came to tell you what happened, and then I must go to the House.'

'The rain did the trick, I suppose?' Charlotte said.

'Oh, it was pure burlesque from beginning to end,' Jes said. 'To begin with, only ten thousand or so assembled on the common, nothing like the half-million the Chartists boasted. There were some half-hearted speeches, and then the waggon carrying the petition and Fergus O'Connor started off towards Westminster. But before they got to the bridge they were stopped by a constable who asked O'Connor very politely if he would step into the public house just by the road and speak to Lord John Russell. And there was Mayne warming his tails by the fire and Russell with a glass of hot whisky – it was raining like the dickens by now and damned cold outside. They told O'Connor no-one would disturb the meeting, but for reasons of public order it would not be allowed to cross the river. And then Russell, very courteous-like, offered to call O'Connor a cab to take the petition to Parliament.'

Cavendish laughed. 'Talk about taking the wind out of their sails!'

'Oh, they played it just right,' Batchworth said. 'O'Connor must have been feeling pretty fed up by then – I dare say he would dearly have liked to sit down for a warm and a glass of something himself. But he thanked them kindly and went out again to tell his rabble they had better go home; only by the time he got back to them, they'd taken the chance and rubbed off already. Nothing like steady, cold rain to dampen the fires of insurrection! We simply haven't the climate for revolution.'

Lord Ashley, when he called a few days later, agreed

that the rain had helped disperse the assembled protesters, but assigned the credit for the lack of sympathetic rising in the capital to the work which had been going on for the last ten years in the back-slums.

'The influence of the word of God has saved the realm from suffering the same fate as Europe,' he said. 'Missionaries and clergy and people like you,' he bowed towards Charlotte and Fanny, 'have brought a gentleness and good bearing even to our poorest and most wretched classes. They know that we care for them and want to help them; and they know what our Redeemer teaches about patience and obedience. Ten years ago, this event might have had a very different outcome.'

Charlotte remembered what Grandmama had said about the Pentrich Rebellion; but she could not argue with such a man as Ashley. 'I do believe,' she said, 'that our people have a very good disposition on the whole. In all the visits I've made to the rookeries, I have never been offered the slightest insult.'

'Exactly so! Exactly!' Ashley said, leaning forward eagerly. 'But we must do more. We must move more quickly. It's a miracle that our people are as good as they are, considering the conditions they live in. And, I have to say, I am coming more and more to feel that it is useless to try to Evangelise them without first alleviating their misery. How can a man lead a moral life when he and his wife share a room, even a bed, with twelve strangers, and have no sanitary arrangements but the kennel in the public street?'

The Home Secretary and the exiled French prime minister both agreed with Ashley's evaluation, and the result was that the Queen summoned Ashley to Osborne to discuss the matter, and to ask how she and the Prince could help relieve the working classes. Ashley proposed various schemes to do with rebuilding the rookeries and improving sanitation, and the patronage of the crown did help to bring matters more to public notice. It also made what Charlotte did more respectable, and she found to her amusement that she was nodded to and greeted in public by some Society people who had hitherto been cold towards her, or ignored her altogether. She was asked to patronise several societies, some old and some newly formed, and to address ladies' meetings and sit on committees for various charitable works.

These things tended to draw her away from her direct work in the rookeries, which pleased everyone except her. Anthony approved so vigorously that she almost felt reconciled to giving up that side of it; she wondered sometimes if it was that which had prevented him so far from making her an offer of marriage. In her own mind she was sure that eventually they would marry, and carry on their work together. He was the rational choice of husband for her, and she was sure that he cared about her: his constant presence in her drawing-room, the closeness of his interest in their lives, his acceptance of social engagements simply because they would be present – there were so many little clues. But he had made it very clear he disapproved of females being exposed to the degradation and vice of the back-slums. Perhaps if she went less often to Devil's Acre, his last scruples would be done away with and he would propose. She longed for it now. She wanted to be married. She wanted to taste again the warmth and excitement of intimacy – but this time, with the added satisfaction of knowing it was the genuine article, intimacy with a truly good and devout man.

But even for Anthony she could not abandon all her creatures. Committees and campaigns and donations were very well, and she appreciated the wider good they could do; but there was also the immediate and individual good which she could do with her own hands and voice and presence. She felt that it would be all too easy away from the back-slums to forget the individuals, to see suffering humanity as a mass and forget that each of them had his own intense and personal suffering. She was afraid that pity might become mechanical and cold if it was divorced from the sight and sound and smell of the pitied. So she went less often, but still she went, though she tried not to draw attention to it, or speak of it when Anthony was present.

As a result of Ashley's visit to Osborne, Charlotte was summoned to dine at Buckingham Palace, and give the Queen her own views on what should be done. Fanny was asked, too, which cheered her enormously, and repaid her for all the disagreeable things she had had to do. The dinner was rather formal, and Charlotte felt it gave little opportunity for any sort of useful discussion; but it proved to have been only a testing-ground. She was asked next day to a private luncheon, which was a very different affair. For the first time Charlotte saw the royal couple in their informal mode, and with their children, and she liked them very much better. The Prince in particular she had always thought rather cold and distant, but that day he was like a different person, warm and charming, with a disposition to laugh and a chuckle that was irresistible. He played with his children in a way she had not supposed any father would play, romping without regard to his dignity, and spoke to the Queen with such tenderness that Charlotte could quite see why Her Majesty had fallen in love with him.

When he sat down to talk with Charlotte about the problems of the poor, he showed himself very sensible and concerned. Charlotte remembered her grandmother's jibes about his interest in sanitation. She did not find it a ridiculous preoccupation, of course, and they had a long and interesting talk about sewers and drains, about which he was very knowledgeable. He told her that the newly formed Metropolitan Commission of Sewers was facing severe opposition to its plan for building a main drainage system for London, but that interim plans were being made at least for covering the hundreds of open sewers, and for flushing them regularly into the river, to prevent overflow and seepage into houses. Charlotte was impressed by the fact that he had actually gone into the back-slums himself, and had walked about and seen the conditions in the courts and houses.

'I haf heard of your similar activities, Lady Chelmsford,' he said. 'You are to be complimented. Not many ladies would have the courage to do such things.'

'I'm afraid, sir, that most people think I am to be condemned for it, rather than praised. It is usually seen as immodest in me to confront squalor.'

'It is never immodest to do God's vork,' he said; and his blue eyes twinkled. 'And I haf seen enough of you to suspect that you do not care this,' he snapped his fingers, 'for what foolish people tsink.'

Charlotte laughed. 'In my heart, I don't. But I am obliged to care a little, for my family's sake. However, now your Highness has shown the way, I shall be able to hold up my head more boldly!'

Later, when he had spoken with the other guests, he came back to her.

'Your brother, so I understand, is very anxious to join the light cavalry?'

'How did you know that, sir?' Charlotte said, much surprised.

'Oh, the Duke told me, of course.' The Duke of Wellington had been made Commander-in-Chief of the army for life in 1842. 'We talk of this and that, and he happened to mention that he had met your brother again at St James's Square, and vas charmed with his enthusiasm.'

'My brother yearns for his colours, sir,' Charlotte said with a smile. 'And as he is a very fine horseman, it would make it logical for him to join the light cavalry, if he is to be a soldier at all.'

'Vell now, I tsink I may be able to help him,' the Prince said. 'You know, of course, that I retain my interest in the Eleventh Hussars, even though it was thought wise for me to resign my colonelcy?'

The 11th had been the regiment chosen to meet Prince Albert at Dover in February 1840 and escort him to London for his marriage to the Queen. As a result the regiment had changed its name from the 11th Light Dragoons to the 11th Hussars, with the additional title of Prince Albert's Own. The Prince had become Colonel-in-Chief, and with the aid of the regiment's commander, Lord Cardigan, had redesigned the uniform. Now the 11th wore tight overalls of cherry-red, short jackets of royal blue encrusted with gold lace and bullion braid, fur-trimmed pelisses, and high fur caps with glorious waving plumes. The Earl of Cardigan increased out of his own pocket the government allowance for both uniforms and horses, with the result that the 11th were the most gorgeous and gaudy of the whole army, and the best mounted.

He and the Prince had taken a keen interest in training the regiment, so that at drills and manoeuvres it was as polished as its appearance on parade. Unfortunately Cardigan, who was hot-headed and quick-tempered, had been in so many scandals that Peel had finally insisted that the Prince give up his position as Colonel-in-Chief; but it was well known that both the Queen and Prince Albert had a great affection for Cardigan, and still thought that the 11th was the model for a light cavalry regiment.

'I inspected the Eleventh in the company of the Duke last week,' the Prince went on, 'and I happen to know that there is a cornetcy vacant. Now, Lady Chelmsford, if you can persuade Lord Batchworth to it, I might very well use my influence with Lord Cardigan to see that the commission goes to your brother.'

Charlotte hardly knew what to say. She stammered her thanks.

The Prince nodded. 'The smartest regiment in the army, you know, which every young man would wish to join if he had his chance. And if he does not take this opportunity, who knows when he might get another? In a year or two years, he might have to settle for a lesser regiment, you see?'

Charlotte had no doubt what Cavendish would say to the chance of becoming a Cherrypicker; and he certainly would look glorious in the uniform. The Prince and Lord Cardigan would no doubt be equally eager to have Cavendish, scion of a wealthy and titled family, well-looking, and a fine horseman to boot. It would be a marriage made in heaven, she thought with a smile; and Cav would be able to parade about on horseback in the most brilliant and fashionable guise and be the cynosure of every unmarried female's eye in London. He would grow his whiskers, affect a cavalry drawl, and probably be married and breeding within two years – which would please their mother.

'He will be very grateful to you, sir,' Charlotte said. 'And I'm sure Lord Batchworth will be glad to take up the offer.'

'I thought that you would like to have the pleasure of conveying the news yourself,' the Prince added. 'I know you are very fond of your brother – as you should be. He is a fine young man, and will be a credit to the regiment.'

It was not likely that Jes would refuse the patronage of the Prince, or that Rosamund would long resist it.

Hussars, Jes said, spent most of their waking lives thinking about their clothes and their horses, and Rosamund laughed and said it would be nice to have Cavendish in London where she could see more of him. It would, besides, be very tactless to refuse the Prince's offer of intervention, especially as the Queen was rather tender about anything that looked like a snub of the Prince or any of her personal pets, of whom Cardigan, for God-knew-what reason, was one.

Cavendish, of course, asked if he would like to leave Eton at once and take up his colours, could hardly answer for excitement. It was an expensive business: the colours cost nine hundred pounds to begin with, which Jes thought reasonable for the time; but then there was the uniform and all the accoutrements to buy, to say nothing of two horses, their extra rations, and his mess charges. But Cavendish was in a daze of bliss, and when they first gathered in the drawing-room at St James's Square to see him dressed in his uniform for the first time, it would have been a hard-hearted person who would have wanted to deny it to him. And when they saw him in all his glory at his first review, even Rosamund said that it was worthwhile.

'If only we could see you as happily settled,' she said to Charlotte, and Charlotte looked surprised.

'I am settled,' she said.

The hot weather came and people were going out of London. Fanny had been planning a seaside visit with her friend Lady Mayhew, but that had to be cancelled when Sir Samuel's not-unexpected death took place at the end of June. Sibella accompanied his body home to his estate in Northampton where the funeral would take place; Charlotte, making a formal call of condolence in the brief time before she left, thought Lady Mayhew looked dignified and handsome in her blacks, and also strangely younger. 'I hope you will be coming back when your mourning period is over,' she said. 'We will miss you very much.'

'Thank you,' Sibella said, and added rather hesitantly, 'I am not sure what I shall do. My plans depend on – they are not settled, in fact. I do hope I shall see you again. Indeed, I am sure I shall. That is – we will always be friends, I hope, whatever happens.'

'Of course,' Charlotte said, mystified.

Fanny decided instead to visit her stepfather and his bride of one year, and departed by train for Manchester. Rosamund and Jes were going to Grasscroft and then on to Scotland and invited Charlotte too. Mrs Manvers gave herself amenable to any plan; but Doctor Anthony was not leaving London, and Charlotte said she wanted to stay too.

'Someone has to keep an eye on Cavendish,' she said.

'Well, don't stay in Town to be ill,' Rosamund said. 'If it gets too hot, you should go down to Wolvercote. Aylesbury will be there all summer; Mother and Papa Danby are going down later – and the Ashleys will be visiting at some point, if that makes a difference to you.'

'Don't worry about me,' Charlotte said, smiling. 'I have plenty to do. And I hope to have some news for you when you come back – news you will like.'

Doctor Anthony had asked her if she was going out of Town, and when she said not, he had said perhaps they ought to have some riding expeditions to Hampstead and Finchley and Harrow and such places, for the sake of the fresh air. Charlotte thought that was a very good sign, and that alone on horseback with a beautiful view before them, he would at last find the courage to ask her to marry him.

CHAPTER TWENTY-THREE

Harrow-on-the-Hill was wonderful after London, leafy and quiet, and with a breeze blowing which smelled as air should smell. London had been increasingly difficult to bear in the last few weeks, as the Sewers Commission's flushing plan got to work: unfortunately all the sewers were designed to empty into the Thames, and with the lower flow-rate of the river in summer, the effluvia lingered between the banks.

Since all the family was away there were no horses to borrow, and Anthony had to hire one, which was a pity – Charlotte was tender of involving him in expense. But he made nothing of it, nor of ordering an early luncheon for them both in a charming little inn in the village. And now they had ridden out to a field on the hilltop where they could look out over the rolling foothills of the Chilterns, and the dense woods and wide hayfields of Middlesex.

They had talked a little at first of the usual things, and had had a friendly argument about Lord Ashley's new scheme to send children from the Ragged Schools to the colonies, to give them a new start in life.

'It must be good to take them away from the influences of the back-slums,' Anthony said. 'What can be the use of teaching them better ways for two hours a week, when they go straight from the schoolroom to sleep on rubbish heaps, and to keep themselves alive by stealing, or worse?'

'It is very hard,' she acknowledged, 'to make a difference, to outweigh the influence of their environment—'

'Impossible, I should say.'

'Not impossible, but difficult. And yet to be taking them from their parents, those that have them, and every familiar thing, and transporting them to the other side of the world—'

'I don't suppose they are unwilling,' Anthony said. 'I'll wager Ashley never has to scratch around for candidates.'

'No, I don't expect he will,' she said. 'I'm sure it is a good scheme, but I wonder what will happen to the children when they get to Australia or New Zealand. They will be so vulnerable to exploitation.'

'As they are not at present?' Anthony asked shrewdly.

'Yes, that's true. Only here we can see it and try to stop it.'

He smiled. 'You are a good creature. There is no arguing with your concern. But I think they will be better off.'

They fell silent, gazing out at the beautiful country, each following the thread of their own thoughts; until he seemed to come to a snag in his, and gave a deep sigh. She asked quietly, 'Is something troubling you? Can I help you in any way?'

'I have a problem,' he admitted, and lapsed again into silence. She waited. At last he said, 'I would like to consult you – to ask your opinion – if you would not think it an imposition. May I – or do I ask too much – may I confide in you?'

'Of course,' she said. She felt a flutter in her stomach at the seriousness of his voice. The moment, she was sure, was approaching. She stole a glance at him. He was staring away towards the distant hills, a slight frown between his brows; even so, he looked as beautiful as an angel to her. 'Ask me anything. I hope I am your friend.'

He smiled suddenly. 'Yes – yes, always that! Well then.'

He seemed to have difficulty in beginning. 'Well then, a question for you, if you would be so kind as to give me your opinion. Do you think that a woman who remains unwed, although one knows she has certainly had offers, perhaps many of them – who reaches, say, her middle twenties and is still unwed – do you think such a woman necessarily has an aversion to marriage?'

Charlotte waited until she could speak without a tell-tale quiver in her voice. 'No,' she said. 'Not *necessarily*. Perhaps she may not have found the man she likes, in spite of the many offers. Or perhaps she may have found him, but be waiting for him to ask her.'

'Do you think so?' he said thoughtfully.

She thought he needed a little encouragement. 'Do you think of marrying, Doctor Anthony?' she asked bravely.

'It has not been something I have considered before,' he said hesitantly. 'My work was always important to me, and since it left me very little time for society, I have hardly met any females except for my patients. And besides—' He stopped again, and cleared his throat awkwardly. 'Do you favour matrimony, Lady Chelmsford?'

'I think the state itself is the best arrangement for both sexes,' she said. 'With the right partner, I think it cannot but enhance every aspect of a person's life.'

'Ah yes, the right partner,' he said, and lapsed again into silence. She wished she knew what his difficulty was, so that she could help him on, but a woman was always at a disadvantage in these matters, being obliged to wait as if she did not know what was coming. The horses sighed and stamped against the flies. At last he said, 'May I put a case to you? There is a man who finds himself very attracted to a woman. Not to put too fine a point on it, he finds himself very much in love.'

'Is this a hypothetical case, or a real one?' she asked, faintly amused at his diffidence.

He looked at her, and then away again, and his ivory cheeks seemed a little warmer than usual. 'Let us say – a friend of mine, whose concerns are very dear to me.'

'Very well. Please go on.'

'Like me, my friend has never considered marriage before. Now that he does think of it, the problem arises that his estate is not large. He is not indigent by any means, but the woman he loves – he has not yet declared himself, you understand – this lady has greater means than his. It is a delicate matter. She is, in fact, independently wealthy. Could he be justified in thinking of her?'

So that was his trouble! Charlotte wished she could have laughed aloud and told him not to be so foolish; but she knew something by now of a man's pride, and forced herself to answer gravely, as if disinterested. 'If the lady is independent as well as wealthy, I can see no barrier to making her an offer. She is surely capable of making up her own mind on the subject closest to her happiness.'

He bit his lip. 'But might not others misunderstand, and despise him? Would not the world think him base, a mere fortune-hunter?'

'It is a possibility, but that is something your friend must weigh up in his own heart. If he finds that the bad opinion of a few shallow fools and idle gossips matters more to him than securing the affections of the woman he loves—' She shrugged.

He smiled faintly. 'Is that how you see it?'

'What other way is there to see it?'

'I salute you for your unworldliness. But it is a man's duty to provide for his wife and family. In this case he – my friend – could not provide everything that the woman already enjoys. Can he be justified in asking her, in effect, to provide her own establishment?'

'That is a matter for *her* to weight in her heart. I repeat,

515

if she is independent, she can surely choose for herself.'
He was silent, and she added with a little urgency, 'Think
how unfair it would be – suppose the lady in question loves
your friend as he loves her – to deny her the opportunity
of making the choice. Women are helpless in this matter,
for they must always wait for the man to make the offer.
Now, if she is wealthy, and only men richer than her
may propose to her, she will have a very limited field
of choice – and perhaps, you know, that is why she
is still unmarried. If your friend would not consider
himself barred from marrying a woman with *less* money
than himself – which I suppose he would not – is it fair to
deny the same freedom to the woman whose happiness is
an object with him?'

Now he looked at her, and smiled openly, with a
gladness in his eyes that made her palms suddenly damp
and her breath quicken.

'Thank you,' he said with simple warmth. 'You are
very good.'

'Does – does your friend really love this lady?' she asked
faintly.

'To distraction,' he said. He laughed with sheer pleasure. 'He never thought he would meet a woman who is
lovely, feminine, graceful, modest, gentle – everything
that woman should be – and yet also vigorously inclined
to good. So many women only *think* of good, but here
is one determined also to *do* good, however great the
inconvenience to herself. Is not such a woman worthy
of the highest praise? Could any man *not* love such a
woman? Yes, my dear Lady Chelmsford, he loves her –
almost more than he can bear.'

She waited, trembling inwardly, smiling at him in
expectation; but after a moment, he looked away again,
surveying the view and whistling soundlessly like a happy
boy on the first day of holiday. She felt a jolt of puzzled

dismay, of expectation denied, as though she had trodden up a step too many on a staircase.

'Then why does he hesitate?' she said. 'Let him ask her at once. Why postpone the happiness that could be theirs – united in God's work—'

'Yes, yes, you are right!' he interrupted, almost impatiently, but did not go on to say the words she was waiting for. She felt it would be indelicate to say more, to appear to press him further, and remained in a puzzled silence, while the lovely view before them seemed somewhat dimmed. She didn't understand why he still hesitated. She had indicated her willingness, got over his difficulties for him. Perhaps he was still not convinced that her money was not a barrier – though he had seemed so. Perhaps he merely thought horseback not the right place to propose. He was rather reserved and formal by nature, and might perhaps wish everything to be done in form. He might even think he ought to consult her grandmother, or his father, or both, before making an offer. Yes, on the whole, she was inclined to think that the likeliest explanation; and when a little while later he supposed that they should be starting back, she agreed calmly, and managed to carry on a comfortable enough conversation with him as they rode back down the hill.

Fanny was glad to be home again. Hobsbawn House, where she had been born and raised, was an old-fashioned house and now, with the spread of the town, was no longer in the most select part of Manchester. The wealthy people were moving farther out from the town's centre, but Fanny loved the house because it was home. Henry found it convenient to be near the mills, and his new wife was a placid creature who would live wherever her husband bid her.

517

Since the time she became betrothed to Tom Cavendish, Fanny had not thought much about Hobsbawn House, firstly because she supposed she and Tom would not spend much time there, and latterly because she had been living in London and hoping – however wistfully – for something else. But on that visit home in 1848, she began to feel that her future must after all lie in Manchester, and that if it did, serious thought must be given to the location of the house she meant to go on sharing with her step-papa. For it was a warm summer, and the air in the centre of the town was none too pleasant: Hobsbawn House was too near to the rookeries.

'I didn't use to think much about the back-slums,' she said to Henry one day, 'but now I've seen conditions for myself, I know the dangers. The cholera is bound to come back, and we are vulnerable here. And besides, the smells are getting worse all the time.'

'I've been thinking the same,' Henry said, 'but of course I wasn't in a position to do anything. I'm only grateful you have let me live here all these years.'

'Oh fudge!' Fanny said. 'Grateful indeed! Who looks after the business? Who took care of me?'

'And still would, if you'd let me,' he said gently. 'What happened in London, Fan? You don't seem happy, not like my merry, wicked little girl any more.'

'I don't feel wicked,' she sighed.

'Nor merry either. Too much do-good work, not enough dancing, that's my judgement. You were never meant for a missionary.'

'I wouldn't have thought so either,' she said, 'but I find I miss it. There's a sense of purpose that I didn't have when I did nothing but dance and flirt. At least, I didn't feel so then, but I do now. And if I am not to marry—'

'*Aren't* you? Don't tell me that Cavendish fellow broke your heart?'

She laughed, but it was rather a pale laugh. 'Oh no, not him! I am well out of that, and though my pride was hurt at the time, I don't think my heart was more than a little bruised.'

'So who has got hold of it this time, Fan? I think I know you well enough by now. Don't he fancy you, the villain?'

'Not a bit,' she said with a wry smile. 'He is an angel on earth, and I adore him, but he will never care for me. I am not good enough for him. I think – I am almost sure – he loves Charlotte, though it's hard to tell. He is so reserved, and high-minded, and so very virtuous—'

'He sounds an intolerable monkey!' Henry said vigorously. 'Too good for my Fanny? Nonsense! How did you ever come to favour this pious parson?'

'Oh, he isn't like that, not priggish or parsonical, just grave and good, very devout, and given entirely to charity. He and Charlotte suit each other very well, and I suppose, if he marries at all, he will marry her.'

'And that's why you decided to come home – to get away from the horrid sight of the lovers?'

'And to see you, of course, dearest Henry.' She flung her arms round his neck as she used to when she was young, and he wrapped his arms round her and held her close. It was *such* a comfort, she thought; and wondered why she hadn't sought it before. 'I'm so glad *you* are happy, at any rate. I like your widow exceedingly.'

'Woah! Hold hard, miss – she's not my widow yet!'

'Well, but you know what I mean. And to go back to where we started, I think we ought to build a new house in a better area, away from the stinks, and settle down and be happy together – we three.'

'It must be as you choose, Fan, it being your house entirely. But you know, you don't have to live in Manchester, not for my sake. Lizbeth has plenty of money, and if you want to sell this house or pull it down and live somewhere else, we can find a place of our own. You mustn't worry about us, or restrict your choice to what you think suits us.'

'Where else would I live but with you?' Fanny said lightly.

He grew serious. 'You mustn't give up hope of marrying. Your parson is not the only man in the world, nor, probably, the best one for you. You are too lively and too full of feeling not to marry someone. It would be a shocking waste. Put him out of your mind and go and dance your slippers through every night until you find a man who values you as you ought to be valued.'

'Darling Henry, you're such a comfort! Well, I have to go back to London to begin with, because I can't just desert Charlotte; but I fancy she will soon be announcing her engagement. He surely can't delay much longer. And then I shall be free to come home.' She sighed again, without being aware of it. 'I suppose the poor in Manchester are just as deserving as anywhere else, for I must have my good works, you know. But I don't think I'll ever marry now. When one has had a taste of the best in mankind, one cannot settle for less.'

'Tastes change,' Henry said, and left it at that.

Tom went out of Town at the end of June, spent a little time with his brother at Wolvercote, and then went off to visit friends. He had meant to be away three months – he was a popular guest and had many invitations – culminating with some shooting on Greyshott's estate in Northumberland. But he found himself restless and out of sorts, and the pleasures of a gentleman at leisure didn't fulfil him as they had used to. He got as far north as Yorkshire, where he spent a few days with Benedict at Morland Place. He found his cousin's womanless household oddly unsatisfying and Benedict himself also distracted, as if he had something on his mind. Tom enjoyed seeing Mary again – at eleven she was quite a little woman, and so knowledgeable and sensible her conversation was like a grown person's – and had some pleasant riding with her and Benedict, trying out new horses and galloping over the moors.

But instead of going on from there to Ravensknowe, as he had planned, he turned south again, heading for London with a sort of guilty eagerness, and turned aside at the last moment to detour via Wolvercote, where his mother was staying. He found her indoors and furiously sulking, because she had had a fall from a horse and was too stiff and bruised to ride. She had not been placated by the physician's telling her she was lucky at her age to have got away with contusions, and that if she had any sense she would give up riding altogether and buy herself a donkey-phaeton.

Tom sympathised with her, and tried not to smile. 'But there's nothing wrong with a phaeton, Mama. Do you remember that dashing one Aunt Héloïse had, with the matching cream ponies?'

'Héloïse was never much of a rider,' Lucy snorted. The truth was she was in some pain, and not a little frightened by the fall – and most frightened of all simply of being afraid. She had had more falls in her life than she could count, and had never turned a hair, simply remounted and carried on. But this time as she had flown through the air and seen the ground rushing towards her, she had known a moment of terror, had heard in imagination her bones snapping. Now she was wondering whether, when the stiffness was sufficiently eased for her to ride again, she would approach her horse with the same confidence as before. She remembered guiltily how often she had bullied Parslow for not taking care of himself and

521

reminded him of his age; and she wondered whether the times Danby had not accompanied her, but had preferred to remain indoors by the fire, he had been suffering not from laziness but the aches and pains of age.

She didn't want to grow old; she was afraid of growing old. She couldn't do it gracefully as Danby did with his gentle jokes about his departing hair; she railed against it.

It was a relief to talk to Tom and take her mind off herself. 'What are you doing here?' she asked abruptly. 'I thought you were going to shoot with Greyshott?'

'I changed my mind. Somehow I just hadn't the taste for it.'

'I'm not surprised. A boring sport, I always thought.'

'Anything that doesn't involve horses is boring to you,' Tom teased.

She veered away from the subject of horses. 'How was Benedict? He didn't write to me this month as he usually does. He was well?'

'In health, yes. He seemed to have something on his mind, though.'

'A woman, I suppose. Well, it is time. He's been widowed long enough, and only one daughter. He ought to marry again. It's his duty to the family and Morland Place.'

'Isn't a daughter enough?' Tom asked. 'Morland Place has always fared well under its women. Your mother, for instance.'

'Times were different then. It is much more a man's world now than ever it was. I don't say he couldn't leave it all to Mary, but a son would be better. And one child, of whatever sex, is not enough. Suppose she dies? No, he must marry again. I hope he has someone in mind – he is not so young as he was.'

'What about me?' Tom said diffidently. 'Have I a duty to marry too? I am even less young than Bendy.'

Lucy moved restlessly. She didn't want to be reminded of how old Tom was, because it reminded her of her own age. 'It's different for you. You haven't an estate.'

'Thank you for reminding me.'

'And in any case, you have nephews and nieces to leave your fortune to. A large family like Aylesbury's needs unmarried uncles and aunts – preferably rich ones.'

'I am not rich. I am damnably poor, in fact.'

'Nonsense – you have a very comfortable life.'

'For a bachelor.'

There was a silence, and Lucy looked at him sharply. 'What do you mean? Do you tell me you are thinking of marriage?'

'Is it so unthinkable?'

In one way it was. Tom was her baby, her last-born and dearest, and she had always been glad he had never had any inclination to marry, because she didn't want to share him with another woman. But she said only, 'You have never thought about it before. At your age, it is absurd to change.'

Tom sighed. 'Mama, I want to ask your opinion. It is something very important to me. Will you be kind?'

'There is a woman,' Lucy concluded flatly. 'Well, and what's wrong with her?'

'Nothing! Why should there be?' Tom said in wounded tones.

'Because you are not running straight, and you have a guilty look on your face, like a hound that's been cur-dog hunting.'

Tom laughed uncomfortably at the expression. 'Mama, there is nothing wrong with her, I swear to you. She is a dear, good creature. But she is – people will think she is—' He shook his head, unable to phrase the objection.

'Unsuitable?' Lucy suggested. Tom nodded. She looked at his bent head and longed to touch it, to stroke his hair, to hold him in her arms as she did little Maurice and Clement. Her heart opened to him; she put away sharpness and self-concern. 'Is it money? I suppose you would have to live in a pretty small way, but if that puts her off, she is not the woman for you.'

'I think she could manage on a great deal less than I ever could,' he said wryly.

Lucy drew a sharp breath. 'Tom, what have you done? You haven't got a servant into trouble?'

Tom burst into laughter, both relieving and annoying his mother. 'No, Mama, she isn't a servant; but you are on the right track. Her father was a tradesman, though he no longer works with his hands. She is not of our class, as people would say.'

'But you love her?'

'Yes.'

'Then damn the people,' Lucy said decidedly.

'Would you damn them?'

'Of course.'

'Well, so would I. But suppose they snubbed her, or pitied her, or laughed at her? I wouldn't put her in that position. I wouldn't lay that burden on her.'

'My dear Tom, is she simple-minded?'

'No!' he said indignantly.

'Then she can decide for herself whether she finds you worth the risk or not. Ask her.'

He picked up her hand and kissed it. 'Thank you, Mama. You give very sensible advice when you put your mind to it. I thought you would be against my marrying at all.'

'I didn't say I wasn't,' she said, but she smiled to take the sting out of it.

Cold Ashby was the name of the place where Sir Samuel Mayhew had had his estate. The property was not large,

524

but it was old, though he had not inherited it. He had bought it in his middle years with the profits of his business, the original family having died out. It consisted of a yellowstone house and a deer park, some fine stands of trees, a good trout river, and half a dozen houses in the village. Despite its name, it was in pretty country. But all the way down to Rugby, Benedict heard the train wheels reciting Cold Ashby, Cold Ashby as they rattled over the lines, and it had a glum sound, like cold ashes.

In Rugby he hired himself a gig and a good horse and set out for Crick. He had stayed there during his engineering days when he was working on the Kilsby Tunnel. He had ridden all over this part of the country, and it looked pleasantly familiar, comforting. At Crick he asked directions for Cold Ashby, and set off again. It was a warm day; the harvests were all in, and the birds were gleaning in the stubble fields. The air was full of little black flies, attracted by the horse's warmth; above him, swifts and martins wheeled and swooped in a high, pale September sky.

Was he mad to be doing this? he wondered. Would it cause a scandal? Well, he hardly cared about that. It had been a scandal for that horrible old man to marry such a luminous young woman in the first place. But he did not want to distress her. She had been widowed less than three months; and the fact that she had not written to him to tell him of Mayhew's death suggested that she was observing strict mourning. Perhaps he ought to have waited until she *did* write to him; but when Tom had mentioned it so casually, just in passing, not thinking it would mean anything to him other than that Fanny's friend had suffered a bereavement – well, it had driven him mad. He didn't know how he had managed to go on playing the host with his mind so far absent; and then estate business had kept him tied up a fortnight longer;

and then as he had been preparing to depart Mary had come down with a summer cold which had had alarming symptoms of the throat. It had turned out not to be septic, thank God, but by the time he had felt secure enough to leave her, September was well advanced, and still Sibella hadn't written. He couldn't bear the inaction of waiting any longer. He had to find out what she was thinking and feeling.

Cold Ashby was only five miles from Crick across the fields, but nearer ten by the winding country road, and by the time he reached the village, the horse needed a bait. There was a decent-looking inn, the White Horse, so he stopped there, asked them to feed and stable the animal, and strolled into the parlour for a quart of old ale and a plate of eggs and ham. The innkeeper was of a chatty disposition, and it was not difficult to work him round to the Mayhews.

'Ah, he wasn't well-liked here abouts – God rest his soul – wasn't Sir Sam'l. The old family, you see, the Berrymans, had been here since the Conqueror, and the old Squire was a real gentleman, open-handed as you like, and a fine man over timber. Four sons he had, and you'd have thought that'd be enough. But one died in the Peninsula and one of diphtheria at Oxford, and the eldest fell at Waterloo – a cruel blow that was. It just about finished old Squire. But young Squire, the second son, was a good man, and we was all glad to see him inherit. Killed in a hunting accident,' he concluded, with a mournful shake of the head, 'before he could so much as wed. God moves in a mysterious way, sir.'

'He does indeed,' Benedict concurred.

'Well, then the old place was to be sold, and there was a lot of gentlemen come to look at it, but it was too old-fashioned for 'em, and the stables wasn't good enough for the hunting gentlemen. And then Sir Sam'l came along and took it, wanting an estate, like, him not having been born to property, as you might say.' He gave a significant nod. 'But he's never spent any money in the village or hereabouts, gets everything sent in from Northampton or Leicester, and that don't endear a man to a place. Didn't hunt nor shoot, and hardly never went to church. So he wasn't well liked. And then he married that pretty young Miss Leytham, not even half his age – a proper scandal, that was.'

'Miss Leytham?'

'From over Kilsby way. Her mother was one of Lord Pulborough's daughters, and her father—'

'Yes, I knew the Leythams, Sir John and Lady Mary.'

'Then you'll likely know Miss Sibella, as became Lady Mayhew,' the innkeeper said, looking pleased.

'Indeed I do. I knew her as a child.'

'Well, sir, now there's a coincidence! Poor lady, she's up there at the house now, all alone. I dare say she'd take it very kind if you was to find time to call and pay your condolences, you being an old friend, seeing as you're in the district.'

'Is the house far from here?'

'About a mile and a half by the road, but no more than half a mile by the footpath over the stile, if you was of a mind to walk. Very melancholy the poor lady's been, shut up all alone in the house ever since the fruneral. Some trouble about the Will, I heard said, but I don't know about that. The attorney was a man from Northampton, so we only learned what his groom would let drop to our ostler, which wasn't much. Oh, you will go, then, sir? I'm sure her la'ship will be very pleased. I can keep your horse for you, o' course, sir. No trouble at all.'

The walk was pleasant, over a stile behind the church, across a field, through a wicket gate into the deer park

527

itself, and then the house was in view. Benedict walked slowly up to the front door, feeling as uncertain as a boy. The house looked forbidding, with its lower windows shuttered, and the others glaring in the afternoon sunlight. It had an air of being deserted. The great door was shut fast, and he pulled the bell and imagined it ringing unheeded in some distant, echoing kitchen inhabited only by mice and spiders.

The afternoon sun on his back was making him sleepy, as was the soothing sound of a wood-pigeon somewhere, and the occasional chack-chacking of jackdaws – the only sounds in the still afternoon. And then suddenly there was a sound behind the door, some fumbling and scraping, then the thud of heavy bolts being drawn, and at last the door swung back, to reveal the same manservant he had seen with the Mayhews in Bath – a gaunt, stern-looking individual, who glowered unwelcomingly at him.

Benedict proffered his card, and enquired if Lady Mayhew was at home.

The servant did not move to take it. 'This is a house of mourning, sir,' he said forbiddingly.

'So I am aware,' Benedict said pleasantly. 'But I am an old friend of her ladyship's. Is she within?'

'Her ladyship sees no-one,' the man said, and, incredibly, made as if to begin closing the door again.

Benedict took half a step forward and held out his card again, his nostrils flaring with suppressed anger. 'Kindly take my card to Lady Mayhew and enquire if she will see me.' The man still seemed to hesitate, but Benedict stared him down, and at last, reluctantly, the servant admitted Benedict to the hall, indicated a chair – the sort not intended to be sat on, that large houses keep in their halls to punish the impudent – and left him alone in the dusty gloom. The house was quite silent, and Benedict began to have fantasies about Sibella being locked up in a tower, prisoner of this sinister servant, and forced to sign away her fortune in exchange for bread and water.

But at last the man returned and with a dark look led the way upstairs. It was like breaking through the surface of water, for up here there was light and air. He was conducted to a small, pleasant sitting-room, and left alone again; but in a moment the door opened, and Sibella was there.

Benedict started towards her, but she held up her hands as if to fend him off, and said quickly, 'No, no, please don't. You shouldn't be here. I shouldn't have seen you, but I couldn't bear—'

'Oh my darling, I'm sorry if you think I am being indiscreet; but I heard you had been bereaved, and when you didn't write, I had to come. Don't worry, there will be no scandal. I quite understand if you want to observe the proprieties, but—'

'It isn't that,' she said, and, biting her lip in agitation she walked a few steps up and down, twisting her hands together nervously. She was in heavy mourning, and now that he observed more closely, she looked pale and unwell. 'I wanted to write to you, but I didn't dare—'

'Didn't dare?' Benedict said, surprised by her agitation. 'Sibella, what is all this? What's frightening you? Or – is it that you have changed your mind about me?'

'No, not that – never that,' she said quickly.

'Thank God! When you didn't write I thought perhaps – but then, why do you say you mustn't see me?'

'It is in the terms of Sir Samuel's Will. He leaves everything to me – but on condition that I do not remarry, or entertain any kind of romantic attachment. I am to live here – certain kinds of visit are allowed but – oh, there are pages of it, all kinds of conditions.'

'Good God! The old monster!'

'Oh, don't say so! It's not safe.'

'Not safe?'

'Munton – the butler – spies on me.' Her face twisted into a grimace, almost comical in its childishness. 'I always hated him! He spied on me when Sir Samuel was alive, and told tales, twisting innocent things to look guilty. But I can't get rid of him – *that* is in the will too. And he is paid a pension as long as he keeps watch over me, so he has every incentive to be a good gaoler.'

'But it's monstrous! How can he think to keep control of you from beyond the grave? Six years of your life were more than enough. Damn his infernal impudence!'

'Oh, don't curse him!' she begged quickly. She glanced towards the door and lowered her voice to a whisper. 'Munton is probably listening. You must go now – it isn't safe. But I had to see you to tell you why, and to tell you I still love you.'

Benedict shook his head to clear it. 'No, wait, wait, this is insanity! Let me think a moment!' She looked at him in a kind of numb hopelessness, and he in his turn walked across the room and back, trying to control his rage at the old man so that he could see past it. 'It's the craziest Will I ever heard of. I am sure it could be contested. We could challenge it in Chancery – I could hire a lawyer—'

'Chancery?' She looked for a moment even more pale. 'It would use up your fortune, and probably uselessly. I can't let you do that.'

'If you break these conditions he has laid down, what happens then?'

'I lose everything. His entire estate goes to a distant cousin – a greengrocer, I believe, in Coventry.'

Benedict stared, the blood returning to his head. 'A greengrocer in Coventry?' Suddenly he began to laugh, a low chuckle which gained strength, changing the atmosphere in the room as if it were breaking a spell. 'My dear, dearest Sibella, if you marry me, you make a greengrocer very rich, and a spying butler very poor, is that it?'

'Yes,' she said, uncertainly, but there was a beginning of understanding in her eyes.

'And should you mind that very much? I rather thought you enjoyed surprising people. Certainly before your marriage you did.'

'You mean—?'

'I mean, if you love me, then marry me, and to hell with Sir Samuel, his Will, his fortune, and Cold Ashby alike!'

She looked at him with dawning joy. 'Would you give up Sir Samuel's fortune for love of me?'

'The question is rather, would you give up me for the love of Sir Samuel's fortune?'

She laughed. 'No! Not if it were ten times as much!'

'I have enough to keep a wife in comfort. You will not lack for fine clothes and handsome horses.'

'Oh Benedict, I wouldn't care if you were a poor man.'

'Well *I* would! And you, live without horses? Pooh!'

'Why didn't I think of it before?' she went on wonderingly. 'It was as if I was bewitched. How could I have thought of obeying his ridiculous rules? But we are brought up to it, to the idea of obedience, and of caring about the money. My mother would be furious if I let it all go.'

'It is rather hard,' Benedict acknowledged with a suppressed grin, 'that you should have had six years of such hard labour for nothing – but if you can bear to disappoint your mother, I think I can.'

'Papa won't be disappointed. He always liked you.'

'Good – then we'll invite him to the wedding.' He reached out and took her hands. 'What would you say to coming away with me now?'

'Now? This minute?'

'I have a horse and gig at the inn in the village. In two hours and a half we can be in Rugby, and if there isn't a train back to York we can catch the first one tomorrow morning.'

'Munton would be furious,' she said, her eyes alight with mischief. 'It would be like an elopement! There would be such a scandal in the village, they wouldn't have done talking about it in a twelvemonth!'

Benedict stepped close, lifted both her hands and kissed them. 'I liked the innkeeper very much – why shouldn't he have something to enliven his life? Will you run away with me, Lady Mayhew?'

Her eyes were shining now like sunlit water. 'Yes, Mr Morland, with all my heart!'

'Then run and pack a bag with anything you can't bear to leave behind, and we'll be off.'

She started away, and then turned back. 'I'm not dreaming, am I? Tell me this is really happening.'

'What went before was a dream. This is real life,' he said; and he took her face between his hands and kissed her. 'Does that convince you?'

'No,' she said, putting her arms round his neck. 'Try again.'

CHAPTER TWENTY-FOUR

Charlotte was puzzled. After the conversation on top of Harrow Hill, she had expected Doctor Anthony to declare himself at the first opportunity, but days passed and nothing happened. She was at home and available to be visited – she even cancelled some engagements to make sure she was available – but he did not call. When she saw him at Mrs Welland's, or in other places in company, he seemed his usual self, with perhaps a degree or two of contentment added, but did not offer her any particular looks or smiles, or find an opportunity to touch her hand or be alone with her. She concluded that he had his own timetable which he meant to adhere to. Her supposition seemed to be borne out when he sent a polite note round to her to say that he would be out of Town for a few days as he was going to Norfolk to visit his father. Evidently he felt he had to consult his parent before proposing marriage to her. It might lack something in spontaneous passion, but after her previous experience, she was impressed with such caution in a lover, glad to think everything would be put on a proper and orderly footing, so that there could be no unhappy surprises to disrupt their future life together.

She began to think she ought to have gone out of Town too, for the continuing dry weather filled London with the haunting smell of sewage from the river, and in the rookeries the usual evils of pests and diseases multiplied more rapidly. With Anthony away and committees suspended for the summer, she again had time to visit the back-slums. It was distressing to rediscover how little she could do to change things. It was plain that Ashley, Batchworth and the others were right, and that a problem on such a scale could only be overcome by Government intervention, a national plan centrally co-ordinated and if necessary backed by legislation. Still, what she did had immediate effect on individual lives, and she could not turn her back on those who came to her for help.

While Anthony was still away, there was an outbreak of cholera in Devil's Acre, and Charlotte, like all the other helpers on the ground, was immediately caught up in the treatment of it. It brought Charlotte in contact with the hospital again, and despite her promise to Doctor Anthony she could not ignore what she found there. The nurses were as unwilling as incapable of caring for the sick she helped bring to the door, and the organisation, such as it was, broke down under the sudden influx of bodies. Newly admitted patients lay on the floor wherever they had been deposited; heaps of soiled bedding lay everywhere, and the floors were awash with ordure. The nurses, drinking more heavily than ever (it was supposed to be a prophylactic against fever) refused to have anything to do with the cholera patients, saying they were not their responsibility; so the victims were left in their own filth without food or water for hours or even days. Not a few died, and the sick lay side by side with corpses.

Charlotte was arguing hopelessly with a nurse when she received reinforcements: a man appeared at her side, a youngish, balding man in the frock-coat and grey trousers and carrying the leather bag of a physician. He had a brisk manner and a flat Yorkshire accent, and put the recalcitrant nurse to the right-about in a moment. Then he turned to Charlotte.

'You are Lady Chelmsford, I take it. I've heard much

about you – you do good work. I'm Doctor Snow – John Snow. I have my practice in Frith Street, very close by.' He offered his hand and she shook it. 'I am acquainted with your friend Doctor Anthony – I know him from Guy's. We've both assisted Doctor Liston.'

'I'm happy to make your acquaintance,' Charlotte said, liking his blunt manners. 'And I'm grateful for your intervention.'

He nodded. 'Well, then, let's get to work,' he said abruptly.

With the authority of the doctor behind them, Charlotte and the handful of her fellow workers who were hard-headed and strong-stomached enough rolled up their sleeves, donned aprons, and got to work. They forced the nurses and orderlies to swab the floors, collect up the soiled linen, drag the dead out and sew them into makeshift shrouds. Relatives of the sick were set to stuffing spare mattress covers with straw, and these paliasses were disposed down the centres of the wards and along the corridors. Those of the original patients who could be moved were dispersed around the hospital so as to make one ward empty for the reception of fever patients alone, who could then be isolated, with the hope that it would stop the fever spreading further.

Through long hours of labour and the bullying and harrying of the nurses, the worst of the muddle was sorted out; but still things were far from satisfactory. The laundry facilities were hopelessly inadequate and the sanitary arrangements more so. There was insufficient water, the privies were overflowing, and there was no provision for feeding the patients. Relatives were expected to bring in food, as was the case for those in prison; and since they used the opportunity to bring in liquor too, the patients were as often drunk as not. This might make it easier for them to bear the conditions, but it did not help their recovery, and often led to drunken brawls, scenes of disgusting licence, and dangerous accidents. In one day one man set fire to his bedclothes when he fell into a drunken stupor while still smoking a pipe, and another fell out of bed and fractured his pelvis. Such incidents were common.

Charlotte worked, organised, and spent her money freely on soap, towels, bedding, mattresses, on special food for the sick, on extra bowls, cups, and spoons. But the building itself worked against her and anything she could hope to achieve. It was old, the fabric of it was filthy, dilapidated and crumbling, and it had no facilities, having been designed simply for the purpose of putting a roof over the heads of the sick poor until they either got better or died. By the time Anthony got back to Town, she had formed a plan which for the moment quite put thoughts of matrimony out of her head.

She tried to explain it to him, but since he first came upon her on his return in the newly created 'fever-ward' of the hospital, it was hard to get him to listen.

'What are you doing here?' he said in horrified astonishment. 'This is no place for you!'

'Oh, don't scold me,' she begged. 'I did not mean to be here, I assure you, but when I brought sick people here I could see they were not going to be looked after unless I did something. I had to help. I couldn't leave them to die.'

'*I* have no right to scold you,' he said, his nostrils white with suppressed anger. 'But it isn't fitting that you should do these things. Nursing is not an activity for a lady, as your own sense must tell you, when you see such sights around you.'

'Oh, I know, I do agree with you – but that is precisely the point on which I have been debating internally, and I have a plan which I think will interest you.'

536

'My only interest is in seeing you removed from this place,' he said, making an effort to smile pleasantly. 'Pray allow me to escort you downstairs and find you a cab to take you home. Apart from the sheer unsuitability of this place, you run the risk of catching the infection yourself. Think how it would affect those who love you – and they are many, let me assure you – if you were to take the sickness yourself. You might take it home and spread it amongst members of your own household. Surely you must see how unfair it is to others – think only of Miss Hobsbawn and you will be convinced – to expose yourself to the miasmas of these back-slum fevers.'

'Ah,' she said eagerly, 'now that is another idea I have had.' His hand was on her elbow and she allowed him to steer her towards the door, largely because she didn't notice the direction, so anxious was she to share her thoughts with him. 'I am not sure that these fevers and infections are carried through the miasma.'

'Are you not?' he asked absently as he picked a way for them through the mattresses on the floor.

'No, not at all. And I must tell you, I have been talking to Doctor Snow, and he agrees with me.'

'John Snow?' Anthony said, frowning.

'Yes, he has been here every day, and we couldn't have got on without him, for the nurses didn't mind us a bit. But he says—'

'I should warn you,' Anthony interrupted, 'that he is not regarded as sound amongst serious-minded medical men. He has odd theories which, if they were applied, could prove dangerous.'

'Oh, but he seems to me a very sensible man altogether,' Charlotte said enthusiastically as they started down the stairs together. 'He has a blunt way of talking which I like very much – though I suppose some people might not like it. But his ideas about cholera fit exactly with what I have been thinking.'

'Indeed?' Anthony said grimly.

She didn't notice the warning. 'He says he's been studying it for years, ever since the epidemic of 'thirty-two, and he doesn't believe the infection passes through inhalation at all, which accords with my observations in the rookeries these two years and more. For one thing, if the fever were caught by breathing in the miasma, people like me – and you, and the missionaries – would fall sick too. We are there day after day breathing the same foul air, but it is very rare for one of us to catch the fevers.'

'It is not to be expected that you would understand the intricacies of medical theory,' he said. 'The sickness passes from one person to another—'

'Yes, of course,' Charlotte interrupted eagerly, 'but suppose it is taken into the healthy body not through the lungs, but through the stomach? Suppose it resides not in the air but in the food or the water, deposited there through contact with the infected person?'

'My dear, ma'am,' he said in vexation, 'you really do not understand what you are talking about. The miasmic theory is accepted by everyone, every physician from the highest to the lowest – by every sensible *person*, indeed. It does not need special medical knowledge to be aware of the particular nature of the foul air that surrounds the places where these infections are bred.'

'But with cholera there are no symptoms of involvement of the lungs or the blood. Doctor Snow is convinced that the infection acts on the alimentary canal, by being brought into direct contact with the mucous surface of the intestines—'

Anthony looked shocked. 'Please, no more! I have warned you that Snow is unsound, and his theories as wild as his manners are unpolished. And I cannot tell you how shocking it is to hear such language on your lips. It is entirely improper for you to know such terms, far less speak them aloud.'

Charlotte's eyes gleamed. 'Is it for you to tell me what is proper, Doctor Anthony?'

'I beg your pardon,' he said stiffly. They walked out of the main door into the comparatively fresh air of the street. There Anthony stopped, and turned to her apologetically. 'I spoke too hastily – I am very sorry. Dear ma'am, I know that you want to do something to help the poor, but believe me you would be very much better advised not to be working here amongst the infected and the depraved, or to go walking about the courts and alleys, but to put your energies into committees and charitable associations, as Miss Hobsbawn does. She is an example to all womankind – and with your fortune at your command, you could do so much good.'

'Yes, I do see your point,' Charlotte said, 'and I have a plan to do just that – to put my money to work for the better treatment of the sick poor. What do you say to my building a hospital?'

Anthony's expression lightened, and he gathered both her hands into his, the most intimate gesture he had ever employed with her, which made her heart jump. He looked into her eyes with deep concern.

'Whatever you wish to spend your money on, it will win my approval if it keeps you away from places like these. Your health is of great concern to me. I would not for the world have you carry an infection home with you. I know I have no right whatever to harangue you—'

'I give you the right,' Charlotte said, smiling. 'You are a very dear friend to me and to Fanny.'

'Well, on that basis, then, let me beg you to go home now, and not to come back here. Miss Hobsbawn is due to return soon, I hope – that is, I suppose?'

'Tomorrow,' Charlotte admitted.

'Very well, then. Let others carry on what you have begun here, and pray, pray do not think of returning to this dreadful place.'

'I should be happy never to set foot in it again,' Charlotte said, her mind on her own plan. She had not yet had a chance to explain it to him. 'Will you come to dinner tomorrow, and help me welcome Fanny home?'

'Tomorrow – oh, I can't,' he said, with satisfactorily profound regret. 'But the following evening—' he added hopefully.

'The following evening, then. Fanny will be glad to see you.'

Charlotte had looked forward to being able to confide in Fanny over her new hopes, but Fanny seemed so despondent when she arrived that Charlotte forbore. However, as soon as they were alone together, Fanny put the question herself.

'Did you see anything of Doctor Anthony while I was away?'

'Oh yes, a little. We had some pleasant rides together – one in particular to Harrow Hill.' She paused, not knowing whether to go on.

'Has he declared himself to you yet?' Fanny asked.

'What makes you think that he means to?'

Fanny looked at her keenly. 'You are in love with him, then,' she said. 'I thought so.'

'I didn't think anyone had noticed.'

'When he spends every spare hour here, or in your company? Mrs Welland says he never used to go out before, that he never accepted dinner invitations. And as for dancing! Well, he seems quite to enjoy the activity when *you* have been there, and he never refuses to eat at Aunt Rosamund's.'

'Oh Fanny! Well, he hasn't declared himself, but – I think he must do so soon.' And she told Fanny about the conversation on Harrow Hill.

'It does sound very pointed,' Fanny said, folding despair in her heart and tucking it away. There was no hope for her now. But above all, Charlotte must never guess how she felt about Anthony. 'I am very happy for you, dearest. He is the best of men. And you are so lovely and good, you will suit each other perfectly.'

'Do you think so?'

'The world will be a better place for the union of two such good people. And his choice endears him to me. I shall be glad to call him cousin.'

Charlotte embraced her hard. 'Thank you, Fanny dear. But he has said nothing yet. He comes to dinner tomorrow, however, and I hope he will take the opportunity, arrive early perhaps—' They were both silent a moment, visualising the scene.

Then Fanny said, 'When you are married, I will go back to Manchester and carry on my good works there.'

'Oh, but I hoped you would stay with me,' Charlotte said in dismay. 'We three have been such good friends, and I shan't stop needing you. I dare say he will be very much occupied with his work, as he is now, and then what shall I do for a companion?'

Fanny smiled faintly, but said, 'I shall visit, of course, if you will have me, but I must make a life for myself elsewhere.'

Charlotte saw no point in arguing about it then, hoping that Fanny would change her mind when the time came. Apart from her selfish desire to secure Fanny as a companion, she still felt that London would offer Fanny more variety of life and more choice of friends than Manchester. Somewhere the man must exist who was handsome and intelligent and virtuous, and good enough for Fanny, and he was more likely to exist in London than elsewhere.

Fanny retired to her room for the afternoon, fatigued from her journey, and Mrs Manvers had gone to a lecture at the Egyptian Rooms, so Charlotte was alone when Tom Weston called.

'Tom! I am so glad to see you! I have an idea to try out on you. It is something rather revolutionary, and I want to know if it has your approval.'

'You know, I might have spoken the self-same words to you,' Tom said.

'What? Have you a plan too?'

'Yes, but yours first.' He glanced towards the table where she had been sitting. 'Is that heap of scribbled paper part of it?'

'Yes, I've just been noting down ideas. I am thinking of building a new hospital for the poor.'

'All on your own?' Tom asked, sitting down ready to give his attention.

'Oh, I think not. There will have to be other sponsors – public support, trustees and patrons and all the other paraphernalia, otherwise the doctors won't have to do with it. But if the worst came to the worst I would be prepared to go on with it alone, because I am sure I have hold of what Doctor Anthony calls a thread – if you pull it, it unties a knot.'

'And what is the knot?' Tom asked.

'This – that the hospitals are filthy and hopeless because only women of the lowest character will under-take nursing, and they are too immoral and drunken and dirty to keep the hospitals clean or run them in good order, so better women will never come near them.'

'It sounds to be what they call a vicious circle,' Tom remarked.

'Yes, and I mean to break it: to build a new hospital on rational lines, with decent facilities – a proper laundry, for instance, and good privies, a clean water supply and efficient drains. Only respectable women of good character will be accepted as nurses, and to ensure they remain decent, they will have separate quarters from the patients, not be expected to live and sleep on the wards, and I'll pay them well, too.'

'Will you!'

'Yes, to make sure they have every incentive to work hard and obey the rules. Everything will be kept clean, and in good order, and there will be no swearing or drinking or indecency. Bedding will be washed between patients – and they won't be put to bed in their own clothes, either, but in a hospital shirt which will be surrendered and washed when they leave. Oh, and there will be a kitchen too, with a cook, to prepare food for the nurses and the patients, so there will be no need for anything to be brought in from outside, and no excuse for liquor to find its way in. In fact,' she added thoughtfully, 'I'm not sure it wouldn't be a good idea to forbid visits from relatives altogether – they bring in dirt and pests as well as drink, and probably take away infections and spread them.'

'My dear Charley,' Tom said with amusement, 'this is not a hospital you describe, it is a combination of hotel and monastery!'

'Don't you think my ideas are sound?' she asked anxiously.

'They may be – I can't judge of that – but you will never get anyone to donate money to an establishment that prescribes such luxury for the sick poor. A dispensary, perhaps; but clean sheets and free meals and clothes and all the rest of it? You would certainly have to pay for it all out of your own purse, and it would cost a fortune – twice a fortune, because you would have every ne-'er-do-well

543

from every back-slum in the country knocking at your door, faking sickness or injury just to get in.'

'No, don't say so.'

'It's true. My dear, don't you see if you make it a better place inside hospital than outside, you will prove an irresistible draw to the lowest classes? Part of the reason hospitals are so loathsome is to persuade people not to be fancying themselves sick all the time. With your system there'll be every incentive for ill health: they'll cut off their own fingers for the sake of a comfortable bed and free meals.'

'There may be some truth in what you say, but there must be a way round that particular problem. My way *is* the right way. It will be necessary perhaps to devise some safeguards—' Charlotte was silent for a moment, and then said, 'Well, I shall think about it. But you said you had a plan, too – a revolutionary plan?'

'Almost as startling as yours,' he said, 'though I hope not so hare-brained. No, no, don't bite my head off, I'm only teasing you! My plan at least has the merit of having been tried before: I mean to get married. What do you think of that?'

'Married? Good heavens!' Charlotte was lost for words. 'I am astonished.'

'That is very unflattering,' Tom said grimly.

'No, no, I beg your pardon, I should say how very pleased I am for you. But I had no idea you – you were—'

'Quite right. I have kept it secret.'

'But who is she? Do I know her?'

'Yes, I think you may do. It is Miss Thorn.'

Charlotte's brow furrowed. 'Miss Thorn? Do I know a Miss Thorn? You don't mean – surely not Miss Thorn from the mission?' She laughed as she said it. 'No, of course you don't, how foolish of me—'

'Dear Charley, please don't say any more, or I may be forced to take offence. Yes, it is Miss Thorn from the mission. I asked her today, and she did me the honour of accepting, and I am very, very happy, which was why I came to share my happiness with you. And also to test your reaction, which I must say has not been all I had hoped.'

'Oh Tom, I'm sorry. I wish you every happiness, of course, and I'm sure she is everything good and delightful.'

'But?' Charlotte wisely kept silent, and Tom went on with a sigh. 'But you think she is unsuitable.'

'No, of course not!'

'She is not of my station in life, and that is what everyone will think. They will laugh.'

'No-one will laugh,' Charlotte said without conviction. 'It is impossible to ridicule what is truly good.' She drew a breath and did her best for him. 'I like Miss Thorn exceedingly. I don't know her very well, to be sure, but she is sensible and pleasant and always good-tempered.'

'But still, people will laugh – not out loud, perhaps, but I shall see it in their eyes, and hear the whispers behind my back.'

'You can't mind about stupid people,' Charlotte told him firmly.

'Oh, not on my own account, of course, but I would not have anything upset my lovely Emily.'

'From what I know of her, I don't think foolishness of that sort will upset her. She will rather upset them, by showing them what she thinks of them.'

Tom grinned suddenly. 'She *is* wonderful, isn't she?'

Charlotte smiled too. 'Everyone who loves you will be delighted: no-one thought you would ever marry now. But tell me all about it. How did you meet? How did you come to fall in love?'

'It was your fault entirely, which was why I wanted you to be the first to know. I met her at your New Year feast, do you remember, at that lodging-house?' He described the course of his romance, and she was as ready to hear every detail as he was to give it, which soothed his prickles somewhat. Her reaction to the news had not been encouraging, especially as she was likely to be the most sympathetic to it; and though Emily was a level-headed, practical person, it did not mean she was insensible. On the contrary, he was sure she had very powerful feelings, which her brisk manner disguised to those who did not know her well.

He had not known that morning that he was going to propose to her. He had gone to take her for a walk in the Park, a proceeding encouraged by Mr and Mrs Thorn for her health's sake. He had found her alone in the parlour, already dressed in mantle and bonnet and waiting patiently for him with her hands in her lap. She had looked like a good little girl told to sit still and not get herself untidy, and his heart had turned such a somersault he had found himself in the middle of his declaration almost before he knew it. She had drawn back a little at first, gravely, but once he had convinced her that he really did wish to make her his wife, her reserve had been replaced by a joyful surprise which had brought him close to tears. He did not want *her* to be grateful to *him*, to think that he was bestowing an honour on her when it was quite the other way round, and he told her so.

'Well, but you are above my station in life,' she said with her most practical look. 'I can't help knowing it – and so will everyone else.'

'Dearest, beloved Emily – oh, now I can call you that, after so long stumbling over *Miss Thorn*! – you had better learn that I am not a great gentleman, nor a rich one. I have my income from my father's fortune, which is enough to keep me, but it will not provide a very lavish establishment for a married man. If you marry me, you will have to live in a very small way.'

'Smaller than this?' she asked succinctly, waving a hand round her father's parlour.

'Well, no.'

'Then you have nothing to apologise for, have you?'

That, Tom told Charlotte, was typical of the practical way she approached all the problems he foresaw. 'The wonderful thing is that she has been in love with me almost as long as I have with her; but she made sure to hide her feelings, seeing no future for them. How can she be so modest?'

Charlotte thought of the little, round, brisk woman she had met about her philanthropic works, and knew exactly how, which made it the more wonderful that these two people had found love together. It would be viewed as an unequal match, and there was no use in Tom shying away from the fact.

'But I am only a sea-captain's son by birth,' he protested. 'There is no inequality there.'

'But your father was a gentleman. And you are Lord Theakston's son by adoption,' Charlotte said. 'The Earl of Aylesbury's brother and the Countess of Batchworth's brother. Don't close your eyes to facts in the hope that they will go away. I'm sure Miss Thorn doesn't.'

'No,' he admitted reluctantly, 'she sees them all with damnable clarity. It makes it all the more wonderful that she has accepted me.' He smiled suddenly. 'If anyone evinces surprise at the match, I shall tell myself they are surprised that such an angel as Miss Thorn should accept a sinner like me. That way I shan't be tempted to floor them.'

'It will make things easier for her around the back-slums, being a married woman,' Charlotte commented.

'Oh, she means to give that up,' Tom said. 'I was at pains to tell her I would not wish to interfere with her good works, and she said in her most down-to-earth manner that no woman on earth would prefer missioneering to keeping house for the man she loved. She didn't do it for pleasure, she told me firmly.'

Charlotte laughed. 'Oh, I long to meet her! I mean, now that I may call her—' She stopped. 'Good heavens, she will be my aunt!'

'I suppose she will. She longs to see you, too. When may I bring her?'

'Bring her to dinner tomorrow,' Charlotte said. 'It will be just us and Doctor Anthony, whom I think she has met, so there will be no strange faces to agitate her.'

'I don't think anything ever agitated my Emily,' Tom said; but he smiled reflectively, remembering how he had kissed her when she had said she would marry him, and how she had trembled in his arms like a bird. *That* discomposure he would make sure to keep to himself.

Doctor Anthony did not come early to dinner, and Charlotte was disappointed again; but when he did arrive he explained that he had been kept late at the hospital dealing with new admissions, so it was no wonder. She would have liked to ask him how things were going there, but the other guests had already arrived.

Miss Thorn had arrived on Tom's arm, looking flushed and younger than her age, and showing her discomposure in talking less than usual. Charlotte had greeted her with a hearty shake of the hand. 'I am so very pleased for you both,' she said. 'It is the nicest news I have heard since I came to London.'

'You don't mind, then?' Miss Thorn asked.

'How could I mind? Make Tom happy, and you'll have the thanks of everyone who loves him.'

548

There then followed a happy half hour while the story of the courtship was told all over again, to an audience which could hardly tire of hearing it. Fanny listened in wistful silence, wondering how everyone in the world should find their happiness but her; Mrs Manvers asked very practical questions about where and when they meant to marry, and where they would live.

'In Emily's parish church, and as soon as possible,' Tom answered. 'And we shall live in London, of course. We are both of us Town birds. I shall have to find a little house for us—'

'There are some pretty places in Brook Street,' Fanny suggested.

'I think Brook Street will be above my touch,' Tom said. 'But there are some nice new houses going up on the other side of the Park, towards Brompton and Knightsbridge – not too far away to visit us, I hope?'

'I'd visit you however far it was,' Charlotte said. 'I don't forget how kind you were to me when I first arrived in London in a state of terror.'

'He *is* kind, isn't he?' Miss Thorn said, looking at him quite as adoringly as Charlotte could have wanted. 'I feel very bad about being the cause of his giving up his rooms in Ryder Street, where he is so comfortable.'

A thought struck Charlotte. 'What about Billington? Will he stay with you, Tom? He's been with you for years, hasn't he?'

'Poor Billingsgate!' Tom laughed. 'He was so stricken when I told him I meant to get married. He had thought he had me for ever. But he swallowed the pill bravely and when I asked him if he would stay on afterwards he said with the most profound expression of gloom that he would be happy to serve me in any capacity I thought fit, sir, but he hoped I would be looking for a house on the *north* side of the river!'

Miss Thorn joined in the laughter good-naturedly, and Charlotte asked her, 'Have you met Billington yet? Did he freeze you with terror? I've heard so much about him.'

'I've had a brush or two with him in the past, when I've knocked at the door soliciting subscriptions, and he's sent me away with a flea in my ear. I don't know what he'll think when he has to call me mistress. Poor man, I feel so sorry for him, I don't think I shall have time to be afraid.'

Tom squeezed her arm in delight. 'Is she original?' he enquired of the air. 'She will have Billington round her thumb in two minutes, I give you odds!'

The family talk ceased when Doctor Anthony arrived, and general topics were pursued in the few minutes remaining until dinner was announced. The evening went pleasantly, though Charlotte thought Anthony rather more subdued than usual. She hoped she might put it down to the right cause, but he was far too correct to give her any hint of his feelings, and indeed paid very proper attention to Fanny all through the meal. He talked to her with persistent kindness, drawing her out so successfully that in the end, with Tom and Miss Thorn being in such good humour, the party became quite merry. After dinner Charlotte proposed a round game, and everyone joined in readily. Miss Thorn introduced them to a new game, a quite ridiculous one, which she played with such an air of solemnity that the company became breathless with laughter. Charlotte had not suspected her of being such a natural comedian, and liked her all the more for it, especially when she saw Doctor Anthony so far seduced from his normal reserve and dignity that he positively *romped*. She had not seen him so happy and relaxed before, and she hoped more sanguinely than before that tonight might be the night he spoke, if only the others would take themselves off before he made the inevitable excuse.

He seemed in no hurry to depart, to be sure. Eventually Mrs Manvers went off to bed, and Tom then took the hint and said that he must escort Miss Thorn home. Charlotte offered her carriage, but he refused to trouble her servants so late at night, and said he would find a cab. He and Miss Thorn said their adieux, and Charlotte accompanied them downstairs for a few minutes' more private conversation, leaving Fanny alone with Doctor Anthony, and hoping she would keep him entertained until she got back, so that he would not feel obliged to leave.

Left alone with Anthony in the drawing-room, Fanny felt the warmth and pleasure of the evening drain away from her like the heat from a bath one has sat in too long. He had been so delightful all evening, talking to her, listening to her, making her feel how vibrant the world could be for the woman at the centre of his attention. She had never known him so chatty, so little on his dignity, and she loved him more than ever; yet the fact that he was evidently in no hurry to leave suggested that it would be tonight that he made his intentions clear to Charlotte, and be lost to her for ever. The thought filled her with misery; but she told herself firmly that if he did not care for her, nothing else could make him more lost. She only wished she had not been left alone with him, for she wanted to look at him, feast her eyes on him for one last time, but as they were alone in the room together, it was not possible.

He broke the silence at last. 'Your cousin Mr Weston seems very happy.'

'Yes,' she answered; and then made an effort. 'A man on the verge of marriage should be happy, don't you think?'

'If he has chosen the right woman,' Anthony said.

His words gave rise to unwelcome thoughts for Fanny. 'Miss Thorn is very amiable.'

Anthony detected something in her tone. 'You don't approve of his choice? You have some reservation?'

'Not at all,' Fanny said, rousing herself again. 'I think he has chosen unexceptionably.'

'But there is some inequality between them; that will be noticed by the world,' he suggested.

'Inequality?'

'Of station – and of fortune.'

'Oh, station! Miss Thorn is perfectly well-behaved, and a great deal more good than most of Society. If they suit each other, what has anyone else to say to it? The world should notice he has chosen a virtuous woman, that's all. As for fortune, no man of character would think for an instant about fortune where his affections were engaged.'

'I'm glad to hear you say so. But in Mr Weston's case, he has the advantage. What would you think if the inequality were the other way, if she had a larger fortune than him?'

Fanny was afraid they were coming too near a certain subject, and felt herself blushing. 'I should say just the same thing. If *he* knows his love is disinterested, why should he care what anyone else thinks?'

Anthony did not answer for a moment, and glancing up, Fanny saw that he was looking at her very intently. Her blush deepened.

'I see from your agitation that you have guessed I am not speaking in complete detachment,' he said.

'No – I suppose – I imagine—' She was too confused and distressed to go on. She supposed he was about to talk about his love for Charlotte, and she didn't want to hear it.

'It encourages me more than you can imagine to hear you say that if a man chooses a virtuous woman, the world must approve. And that inequality of fortune should not deter him from speaking.'

'Doctor Anthony,' Fanny said with an effort, 'I think I should mention that Charlotte has told me about your conversation with her – your particular conversation – at Harrow.'

'Ah!' he said, not displeased. 'Then you know my feelings. And you do not disapprove?'

'Disapprove? No, far from it.'

'Then – have I your permission to proceed?'

'Mine? What have I to say to it?' she exclaimed. She saw that he seemed very disconcerted, and thought she had spoken too hastily. 'I assure you, if my thoughts mean anything to you, that I believe you will suit extremely. But pray, do not say any more to me. You will wish to speak to Charlotte first.'

He seemed quite bewildered. 'But why? Lady Chelmsford is surely not in any position of guardianship over you? I honour your delicacy, but may I not make sure of my happiness before speaking to her?'

Now Fanny was bewildered. Nothing he said made any sense. 'I don't understand you,' she said at last.

He shook his head. 'Perhaps we have been speaking at cross purposes. What was it, may I ask, that you understand me to have said at Harrow?'

Fanny blushed again. 'You asked if a man had any right to love a woman with a greater fortune than his own.'

'Just so! And Lady Chelmsford was good enough to say much what you have just said. She gave me courage to think of you, Miss Hobsbawn, and I have waited impatiently for the opportunity of speaking to you. But have I presumed too much? I thought you were not indifferent to me, but perhaps my own wishes have led me into error. I know you are too good and too generous to toy with me. If I have no chance with you, pray tell me so at once, and I will say no more.'

'With me?' she said, astonished. 'You mean – you love me?'

'With all my heart,' he said. 'These many months. Have I not made it plain?'

'Not quite,' Fanny said, still too stunned to understand it. 'I thought you loved Charlotte. I thought—'

'Lady Chelmsford?' Anthony seemed quite puzzled by the idea. 'Good heavens, no. I like her and admire her tremendously – indeed, I have much affection for her – but it is a brotherly sort of affection. I could never love her in *that* way. She is good, and kind, and full of every sort of merit, but she is not – forgive me – a feminine woman, as you are. As a sister I could love her, but she is too forthright and determined and – forgive me again – too *mannish* for a wife.'

Fanny listened in silence. Poor Charlotte, she thought, poor Charlotte. 'Then – when you spoke to her – when you said—'

'My conversation about my hopes and wishes?' Anthony thought for a moment, and then laughed. 'Why yes, I see now why you mistook my meaning. The inequality of fortune – yes, and it was like your modesty to think I meant her. But she understood me very well, I am sure of it. That is why she has left us alone so long. But it cannot be for much longer. Dear, dearest Miss Hobsbawn – dear Fanny – pray put me out of my misery. Tell me that you love me too! Tell me that you will marry me – poor physician that I am. But not indigent, know! If you can forgive me for not being a rich man, I can assure you that I have a competence, and will inherit my father's estate when he dies, which will not be for many years I hope, but is not a negligible prospect.'

'Oh stop, stop! Don't keep talking about money and estates,' Fanny cried. 'Yes, I love you, and I will marry you gladly, tomorrow if you like; and I would still want to marry you if you had nothing – and if I had nothing too!'

'Fanny!'

'Don't *talk!*' she insisted; and at last his arms were round her, and his lips were on hers, and she felt close to fainting with the bliss of it. But *poor Charlotte* went on in the depths of her mind, a low bourdon to its song of joy. *He must never know that Charlotte had also mistaken him. She must never be exposed to that embarrassment. But how to tell her? Poor Charlotte.*

How to tell her was resolved very soon. The kiss she had waited for so long ended, but Anthony did not permit her to remove herself from his arms. He gazed at her in a kind of bewildered delight, as though love had surprised him, too, as though what he had declared had proved to be only a pale candle to what he had felt. 'Fanny,' he whispered; and then kissed her again. The sound of the door opening was what broke them apart. Fanny was instantly scarlet, but Anthony kept hold of her hand, and turned to Charlotte with calm joy.

'I see you are looking shocked,' he said, 'and I must apologise for using your drawing-room so freely, but I know your generous heart, and how you have been my kind advocate. You will forgive me when I tell you that Miss Hobsbawn has just now consented to be my wife.'

Poor Charlotte. Fanny's usually ready tongue let her down. She could only stare at her cousin, frantically trying to convey with her eyes the things she could not speak of.

'Doctor Anthony, you quite astonish me,' Charlotte managed to say at last. She was as pale as Fanny was flushed.

'Oh, not so very much, I hope,' Anthony said, smiling with his fulfilled joy. 'I find you repeated to my beloved Fanny all I said to you that day in Harrow. You saw through my little subterfuge, as I should have known you

555

would! Foolish of me to say it was a friend I was speaking of, but I felt so unsure then, that I could ever succeed. But it was thanks to you I found Fanny so well prepared for my question! I won't say I spoke to you that day in the hope that you would help my cause, but I am very grateful that you did. You have been a good friend to both of us.'

'I am – I am pleased to have been of use,' Charlotte said, and then managed to pull herself together, to express the pleasure she ought to feel – that she *would* feel, she was determined, when the shock had passed. She had staggered; now, seeing the delight and relief in Fanny's eyes, she understood her unhappiness these past months, and made an effort for her friend. 'I am delighted for you both. I see plainly that your affections are very equally engaged, and I am sure you will be happy together.'

'Thank you.' Anthony drew Fanny's hand through his arm and folded his over it. 'I assure you I know how lucky I am. The benefit will all be to me. Fanny will soften my character and give my temper the openness and generosity I fear it has lacked. I have allowed the misery I encounter in my work to harden me. I had begun to think that there could be no sweetness and virtue in the human character, but she has shown me otherwise. She will bring laughter and lightness to my life. I can only pray,' he bent to kiss the hand reverently, 'that I shall be able to prove myself worthy of her.'

Fanny had nothing to say to all this, but was looking at him with silent, shining joy. Charlotte, still struggling with the shock of having her assumptions turned upside down, and the smart of humiliation and disappointment, was yet able to detect through the storm the faint thought that it would never have suited her to be idolised like that, and that if he had attempted to put her on a pedestal in that way, she would have found it difficult not to say something rather scathing, or laugh out loud.

CHAPTER TWENTY-FIVE

Lucy and Rosamund walked their horses side by side along the tan. It was a chilly morning, and last night's frost had melted only on the centre of the path; the grass was white and sharp with it. The sun hung swollen and orange in the bare branches of the trees, wreathed with fog, and the horses' breath was visible, a little cloud round each neat head, so that it was possible to believe they and the rest of their kind exercising early in the Park had created the morning mist.

Behind them Parslow rode as usual, and Lucy was acutely aware of him. He had had a cold for days, but had refused to stay in bed and let one of the other grooms attend his mistress on her ride. If Lucy was fit to ride, so was Parslow, even if his nose was red and his lips blue. He had even risen early to plait the horses, and when he had brought them to the door and she had protested at his giving himself an extra hour's work, he had said expressionlessly that it was not fitting she should ride an unplaited horse in a public park. And then he sneezed.

She comforted herself that she would not be staying out long. She had worked herself gradually back into the saddle since her fall in the summer, but long rides still made her stiff. She had had her seventieth birthday last week, something she didn't like to think about; and Danby, who had been seventy last February, had expressed doubts about his hunting this season. When she came to think about it, he hadn't ridden since he came back to Town; but she didn't *want* to think about it. She was damned if she would give up riding either for Danby's sake, or Parslow's.

'Well,' she said, and Rosamund returned from her own reverie to look at her enquiringly. 'That was quite a dinner party last night. And what do you think to Benedict's new wife?'

Benedict and Sibella had left Mary with Rosamund while they had their honeymoon in Italy, and had stopped on their way back to collect her. Rosamund had taken the opportunity to have a family dinner; it was the first time Lucy had met Sibella.

'A great improvement on the old one,' Rosamund said. 'One shouldn't speak ill of the dead, but I never liked Rosalind very much.'

'Sibella seems a very nice girl indeed,' Lucy said.

Rosamund smiled. 'You were bound to like her once you discovered she hunts. I don't think you talked of anything but horses all evening.'

'Benedict says she is a very fine horsewoman, and certainly she has the figure and the head for it. And the new horse he gave her for their wedding present sounds quite splendid.'

'It was such a hurried business,' Rosamund said with a faint air of doubt. 'I hope there was nothing – well, odd about it.'

'How could there be? She was widowed, no doubt about that.'

'It smacked of impropriety, though,' Rosamund said. 'Barely three months of widowhood.'

'The old fellow died on the thirtieth of June, and they were married on the first of October. That's a full three months by my reckoning.'

'By special licence. No banns read, and she was living

at Morland Place for ten days before the wedding,' Rosamund pointed out.

'This isn't like you,' Lucy said. 'They have no-one to please but themselves, so why shouldn't they marry at the earliest moment?'

'I have had to learn that what we do affects other people. I never cared about scandal, but see what a cloud it cast on poor Charlotte. Benedict has a daughter, and he may go on to have more children—'

'Certainly will,' Lucy interrupted. 'Sibella is pregnant. Bendy confided in me as they were leaving.'

Rosamund nodded. 'Very well, then. There are scandals enough already surrounding him, and he must think of his children.'

'Mary is a bright little thing, isn't she?' Lucy said. 'Talking to her one quite forgets one is talking to a child. If she were taller, one would take her and Cavendish for the same age.'

Rosamund laughed. 'I take that as a compliment to Mary rather than an insult to Cavendish!'

'One doesn't need very much in the way of brains to be a Hussar,' Lucy said placidly. 'Especially in Prince Albert's Own. Cardigan only cares that his officers' trousers should be tight, their whiskers large and their horses over-corned.'

'Long may it stay that way,' Rosamund said. 'I'd much prefer my boy to remain a Hyde Park soldier. Thank God things seem to be settling down again abroad – although—' She hesitated, frowning. 'Jes says that Louis Bonaparte is almost bound to be elected President of France next month. I must say it makes me nervous to think of the French being led by someone of that name again.'

Lucy nodded agreement. 'We must hope that his sojourn in England has tamed him. He certainly speaks admiringly of our institutions, from what I've read.'

'Cav thought him a very good egg,' Rosamund said. 'And Jes says he is no socialist, and wants a quiet life, so we shall see.'

Lucy's thoughts had gone back to the family party last night. 'Three pairs of lovers in the house at once,' she said, 'and Benedict and Sibella, for all their oddities, were the most conventional.'

Rosamund looked at her sidelong. 'Do you mind about Tom, Mother? I know it seems rather odd—'

She thought of the brisk, cheerful little woman she had met for the first time last night, and had to admire the courage which carried her through the evening, the way she did not try to disguise her origins, nor apologise for them. She had struck a nice balance between being retiring and forthcoming, not shrinking in a corner, nor pushing herself forward.

'I should have minded whoever he married,' Lucy said. She had been closer to Tom than to any of her children, but she had known for years now that he was moving further away from her. Ever since his brother married, really, he had been disentangling the threads of his life from hers, and going his own way. An outsider would have said it was good time, at his age; she'd have said the same about anyone else's son. A man of forty attached to his mother's apron strings was not an edifying sight – but it had never seemed like that with Tom. Still, she wanted him to be happy, and she was trying hard to believe that that odd little woman was the one to do it. It was incomprehensible that he had fallen in love with her; but that, in a way, was Lucy's comfort. She never would have been able to believe in his loving a conventionally suitable girl: she would always have thought her not good enough. But Emily Thorn simply wasn't measurable on any scale, so Lucy had to believe she had some special quality which Tom alone was aware of. 'I hope she doesn't mother him,' she said at last.

'You liked her, though, didn't you?'

'Yes,' Lucy admitted, with a note of puzzlement. 'Yes, I did. Considering who she was meeting yesterday and how she was dressed, I think she coped very well. What I wonder is how she will fit in when they are married.'

'That's Tom's worry,' Rosamund said briskly. 'I shall always be glad to see her.' She laughed suddenly. 'It's her parents one must feel sorry for. Tom says he can't stop them calling him "sir". How will they cope with you and Papa Danby? They must dread the wedding. Has Tom told you when it's to be?'

'In January. I tried to persuade him to have it down at Wolvercote – so much more private – but she wants to marry in her own parish. One can't argue with that, as the Thorns are such pillars of the Church.' Her horse shied at a piece of paper at the side of the track, and she checked it automatically, sitting a few bumps without too much discomfort. Seventy years was nothing, after all, she told herself more cheerfully. 'January for Tom and Miss Thorn, and March for Fanny and Doctor Anthony. And what do you think to *that* arrangement?'

'I'm happy for Fanny, of course. And I'm glad after all that we were wrong about him and Charlotte. He and Fanny will suit much better.'

'I'm surprised Tom got it wrong,' Lucy said. 'He's usually so acute about these things.'

'You don't think—?' Rosamund looked at her mother, and they exchanged a silent question.

'No,' Lucy said at last. 'I suppose she may have fancied herself a little in love at some time – he is very handsome – but he's not good enough for her, and she must have known it.'

'Not good enough? Fanny says he's a saint,' Rosamund said, amused.

'But Charlotte wouldn't be satisfied with rectitude and piety,' Lucy said firmly. 'He was too – too *little* for her.'

'That's not quite the right word,' Rosamund said. 'But I know what you mean. And I'm glad we have her for a little longer. He would have taken her away from us. All the same, I do want her to marry.'

'She'll marry, when she finds the man with enough courage.'

'Enough courage?' Rosamund queried, wrinkling her nose.

'She's turned out rather a lion,' Lucy said. 'It will need a brave man to take her on. Shall we canter as far as the gate and then go home? I just heard Parslow sneeze again.'

Tom's wedding was a cheerful affair, though to avoid frightening Miss Thorn's parents to death, it was kept very small and quiet. On his side there were only Lucy and Danby, Charlotte and Cavendish, and Roland's son Lord Calder representing the Aylesburys. Rosamund and Jes had gone up to Manchester, partly on business and partly to help Fanny prepare for her wedding; they had offered to delay departure until after Tom's wedding, but he had said too many titles in the small church might overpower the minister. For the same reason he begged Roland not to put himself to the trouble of coming up from Wolvercote. 'But I must see you turned off, old chap,' Roland said anxiously. 'Nothing to see, old chap,' Tom assured him. 'I'll bring the bride to visit when we come back from our honeymoon. And you oughtn't to leave Thalia.' Roland accepted that. Thalia was pregnant again, after a gap of nine years and at the age of forty-five, and was taking it very hard, both physically and mentally.

'Calder shall come, then,' Roland said at last, 'so that they shan't think I'm snubbing you.' Calder was Tom's godson, so it was appropriate; and he was far less awful than Aylesbury in all his dignity.

The local church was small but pleasant, an ancient foundation recently refurbished. The local populace packed themselves in to augment the small number of official attendees, and gaped openly at the groom's side which contained more celebrities than they had seen in a lifetime – a countess and three viscounts (George Howard was Tom's groomsman) and four members of Parliament. Miss Thorn arrived on the arm of her father, looking unexpectedly young and pretty in a white velvet mantle trimmed with swansdown and a white bonnet wreathed with silk flowers. Despite Tom's precautions the minister was in such a state of fright at performing in front of so many notables that his usually vibrant voice trembled and finally failed him in the middle of the vow. Tom took over, knowing it by heart, having been groomsman more often than he cared to remember. Miss Thorn made her own vow in a strong, glad voice, the minister rallied and galloped home, and they all retired to a nearby hotel where the wedding feast had been laid on. It was very lavish, Tom having convinced Mr Thorn that it was a family tradition for the wedding breakfast to be paid for by the groom's brother, and under the influence of unaccustomed quantities of champagne and rich food, the bride's father waxed eloquent, and made a speech both moving and funny which had everyone in tears of one sort or another. At last the bride and groom were seen off into a carriage which was to take them to the railway station on the first stage of their wedding journey to Paris. It was a grey and blustery day, and already spitting rain, and many were the jokes about the crossing they would have on the morrow. Tom merely smiled. Today they were going no further than Dover, where in the best bedroom of the Anchor Inn he would at last fulfil his dream and lie with Miss Thorn in his arms, her hair spread across the pillow and her eyes gazing meltingly up into his. Beyond that he saw no reason to think.

When the couple had gone, Cavendish escorted his sister home. He broke the silence in the carriage at last, saying, 'It makes you think, don't it?'

'What does?' Charlotte said, rousing herself from a not entirely satisfactory reverie.

'Seein' Uncle Tom turned off. Never thought it would happen to him.'

'It certainly surprised Grandmama.'

'But they like Miss Thorn – Mrs Weston, I suppose I should say now?'

'Oh yes, I'm sure they do.'

'Glad they ain't havin' to go and live in Kensington,' Cavendish said. Tom and his bride were to have a neat little house in Brook Street after all – much to Billington's relief. Papa Danby had made Tom a wedding gift of some property in Knaresborough which would bring him in sufficient income, added to his own, to maintain a small establishment in Town.

'It would've been yours anyway one day,' Papa Danby had said. 'No point makin' you wait till I'm dead.'

'But are you sure you can manage without the income, sir?' Tom had asked, quite overwhelmed with the generosity.

'Oh, my needs are fewer these days,' Papa Danby said lightly. 'Want to see you and Little Em comfortable. Might make me a Grandpapa Danby, if I'm lucky.'

He and Miss Thorn had taken to each other very strongly, and before the first meeting was over she was calling him Papa Danby so naturally that even Lucy didn't notice; while Danby had found a pet-name for her lying ready on his tongue.

Another silence fell in the carriage, and Charlotte took the opportunity to study her brother, who was staring out at the grey rain, evidently deep in thought. Since joining the Hussars he seemed to have grown taller, and had filled out considerably, so that he no longer looked like a gawky boy. He was on the way to having a splendid figure, and was certainly extremely handsome with his thick fair hair and blue eyes and his finely chiselled features. He had been growing his cavalry whiskers for nine months now, and after a few changes of direction, had settled on a shape which took his fancy. They were blond, too, with a hint of red in them, much the colour of Charlotte's hair. He was very proud of them, and Charlotte had remarked more than once, with some amusement, that he talked about them as though they were a pet dog, and certainly groomed them as much.

The Hussar life plainly suited him – he seemed as happy as a lark – but today there was something on his mind. At last he said, 'This marriage business – what do *you* think?'

'That it is very well if one finds the right person,' Charlotte said, suppressing a smile. 'Have you someone in mind, love? I hope she is handsome and accomplished.'

He turned to look at her with a little anxious frown. 'No, that's just the trouble. I begin to wonder if there's something wrong with me. Here I am, surrounded by pretty women, the whole of London Society to choose from, and when I'm called on in the mess, I have to toast my sister.'

'Do you indeed? I'm very flattered.'

'Not that I don't love you – indeed I do – but I'll be eighteen soon, and I haven't met anyone I could think of marrying.'

'Don't the girls fancy you?' she asked, trying to take his problem seriously.

'Oh, Lord, yes! They're always starin' and gigglin', and the other fellows say I could have my pick – but I don't fancy *them*. They seem so silly compared with you, and Fanny, and Mama, and even cousin Lucilla – all the females of my family. You can't *talk* to them.'

'You've been spoiled, that's what it is,' Charlotte said. 'We Morlands do breed a particularly fine sort of female. But don't worry, there are others in the world. You must be patient, that's all. You'll find them out eventually.'

'Do you think so?'

'Oh, certainly. It takes time to find the right partner. Look at Fanny – she'll be twenty-eight when she marries. Look at Uncle Tom.'

'Lord, I don't want to wait that long!' Cavendish cried in horror, and Charlotte burst out laughing. 'You don't take me seriously,' he complained.

'I do, darling, I do; but you are very young, and you have plenty of time ahead of you.'

'Ah, that's just the thing. I mean, you may be right about that, but I have to find a female for next month, and I don't know how to go about it.'

'For next month? What can you mean?'

He looked at her eagerly, evidently having arrived at the place he was making for in such a roundabout way. 'I wish you will do something for me, Charley – you can absolutely save my bacon, and it will be fun, too, I promise you! You see, our Commander is havin' a house party next month for the huntin', and he's invited a dozen of us from the regiment, but we have to bring a female. It's absolutely respectable, I promise you – Colonel D'Ivery's wife is actin' as hostess, and all the big people from the county will be there, and all sorts of swells besides. Cardigan's parties are famous fun, the best of everythin', loads to eat and drink and entertainment of all sorts – a ball and a concert and I don't know what else. And the huntin' of course: Deene Park is in very fine country, and the old boy leads the field over the best gallops and timber.'

'Well,' Charlotte began, but got no further.

Cavendish bubbled on. 'It's a great honour to be asked when you're only a "bloody sub" like me, and I want so much to go. I daren't *not* go, really, because the Old Man would never forgive me, and that'd be the end of my career – he never forgets a grudge – and if I do go, and make a good impression, he will help me on, I'm sure of it. I've been a miserable cornet for nearly ten months now, and Potter is selling out this spring, which will be my chance to get on, only there's bound to be a dozen men all wanting the lieutenancy, and if I don't get it I shall die! This is my chance to be noticed, and if you will only come with me, it will do me so much credit. You are handsome and clever and nearly as good a rider as Mama – better than most females, anyway, and the Old Man loves the ladies, he really does, but best of all he loves ladies who can ride, and who answer him boldly. So do, do say you will come with me, dearest Charley! You will enjoy it beyond anything, I promise you!'

'You're sure it's respectable?'

'Lord, yes! The Old Man may be violent and quarrelsome, but he's chivalry itself when it comes to females. He would never do anything to dishonour a lady.'

'But he's separated from his wife, is he not?'

'She ran off with another man, but that's hardly his fault, is it? He won't have a mistress there, if that's what you mean. As I said, Lady D'Ivery will be hostess, and she's the greatest stickler in London.'

'Then I'll come and gladly,' Charlotte said. 'Heaven

knows, I need to do something, and I shall enjoy hunting over new country.'

Cavendish's face wreathed itself in blissful smiles. 'Bless you, Charley! A man couldn't have a better sister. It will change my life – and who knows, it might change yours! You might meet the right man that Mama's always talking about.'

'Oh, is she?'

'She wants you to be married more than you can think,' he informed her innocently.

'I'm beginning to think that's all mamas ever think about,' Charlotte said. 'I wonder if it relates to the fable of the tail-less fox?'

Cavendish didn't pick up the clue; he was already off on a further exposition of the splendours to be expected of a house party at Deene Park.

Charlotte needed a change of scene. All had been disappointment recently. Her plan for a new hospital had run into just the sort of barrier Tom had predicted: no-one wanted to contribute to what they saw as needless luxury for the poor, no-one wanted their name associated with something they were convinced would never work. She had hoped the Queen might give the scheme her blessing, and thereby add the allure of royal patronage; but the Queen was firmly of the mind that a good woman's place was in the home, caring for her husband and children, and made some pointed remarks about Charlotte's unmarried state. The nature of the tasks which had to be done for the sick was degrading, and therefore better carried out by men, and men who were fit for nothing else at that.

Even Lord Ashley shook his head. He was all for a hospital with decent drains and privies, but he was convinced no respectable women would take on nursing, and even if they did, they would be corrupted by the circumstances of their work. It would be impossible to keep discipline amongst them, unless they were nuns under religious orders, and the work itself would debase them and drive them to drink and debauchery.

Her grandmother was interested in the idea, but agreed with the general sentiment, that no decent women would be found willing to do the work. 'Though if you could find them, and keep them from the bottle, it might serve very well.' But she pointed out another difficulty, that a hospital was useless without doctors, and doctors were by nature dye-fast traditionalists who resisted anything new, suspected every innovation, and in particular loathed womankind. 'If you found the elixir of life, some doctor would knock the flask out of your hand and grind it under his heel,' she said. 'I remember the trouble I had in Brussels after the battle of Waterloo, and that was with all the urgency of war on my side.'

Charlotte saw the point very well, but said, 'I can't give up my scheme. It is the right way, I am sure. If I can get over the difficulty of the women, is there any way to get over the difficulty of the doctors?'

Lucy thought. 'It is possible that if you could find a young doctor with an idea of his own that he wanted to pursue, you might bribe him to do your work by providing facilities and finances for his. A laboratory or an operating theatre or whatever he needed, a guaranteed income and time for his research, in return for tending your patients.' She glanced at Charlotte's brightening face. 'But before you go coursing after that hare, reflect that if you found such a man, everyone else would consider him a crack-pot with a hobby horse and still refuse to donate funds.'

'Oh dear, it all sounds hopeless,' Charlotte said despondently.

'So it is,' Lucy said with a grim sort of smile. 'But I don't suppose that will stop you.'

569

So far, she had not found a single sponsor for her hospital; though Mrs Saville, whose leg had healed at last and who was again plying her trade, thought it a splendid idea, and offered her services as a nurse should it ever come to fruition. 'You think about it, my lady – you could do worse than take on a few o' my sort. I'm strong, I don't faint easy, and there ain't much I ain't seen. 'T'wouldn't upset my stummick to undress a man and put 'im to bed. And I'd put up with a lot for the sake of a clean bed and three good meals a day.'

Charlotte thought how much more difficult it would make fund-raising if she proposed recruiting a corps of ex-prostitutes for nurses, and thanked her politely, saying she would bear it in mind. Afterwards she imagined what Doctor Anthony's expression would be at the suggestion, and relieved her feelings with a hearty laugh.

She had pretty much got over him now, and was willing to tell herself that he would never have suited. That did very well for her mind, but her feelings were still tender, and seeing him and Fanny so happily involved in their wedding plans increased her sense of isolation. She was lonely; she had been lonely all her life, she realised, except for the brief weeks of her engagement to Oliver Fleetwood. She had had good friends in Ellen and Norton, Doctor Silk and Mrs Welland; she had a family to love and to love her; but those things did not compensate for the want of the intimate love of man and woman.

And now she was losing Fanny, too. They departed for Manchester after Christmas, would be married there, and were to settle there, living in Hobsbawn House to begin with, until they decided where to build a new house for themselves. There were plenty of back-slums in Manchester, and plenty of good work to be done, and Anthony was happy enough to make his life there, while Fanny felt she ought to be taking some of the burden of running the business from Henry's shoulders.

With Fanny gone, Charlotte found the house in Berkeley Street very empty. Even Mrs Manvers commented on it, though she was much engrossed in a new biography of Lady Hester Stanhope, who had gone off to live in the Lebanon, dressing as an Arab, living in a tent and riding a camel. It had inspired her with the desire to do the same thing in Egypt. Of course, she was not independently wealthy, but it furnished her with pleasant daydreams all the same, about discovering an untouched pyramid to excavate.

Mrs Manvers didn't mind in the least being left while Charlotte went with Cavendish to Deene Park. 'I'm sure you will have excellent amusement there,' she said. 'Lord Cardigan is a strange, unaccountable man, but he is very tender towards females. And Deene is in very pretty country. You will have excellent hunting.'

'Do you know Lord Cardigan?' Charlotte asked with interest.

'You forget, my dear, that my late husband was a Northamptonshire man. Everyone in the county knows Lord Cardigan. I lived all my married life in Rockingham, which is not five miles from Deene across country, and many a time I've seen the lord out on one of his fine horses. He took a short cut through our garden once and trampled down all Mr Manvers' hyacinths. He apologised very handsomely afterwards, and sent a brace of pheasants; but he was famous for taking a straight line, and what he couldn't go over he went through.'

'He sounds most alarming!'

'Not a bit. You will have a splendid time. Give yourself over completely to enjoyment for a few days, that's my advice. All the county will be there – he is a famous host.'

Norton, packing for her, was quite excited. 'I wish you would do more of this sort of thing, my lady. I'm sure you've had invitations enough. And I'd sooner see you somewhere like Deene Park than Dead Cat Lane.'

'When I remember how I was when I first came to London,' Charlotte said, watching Norton fold her riding habit. 'How frightened I was of everything! I didn't know the first thing about how to behave, what to do, how to speak, what to expect, how to dress. I was like Gulliver, set off to sea and stumbling on some hidden shore, not knowing whether I would find giants or pygmies.'

'And which did you, miss?' Norton said, looking up. The two women exchanged a long look.

'I don't know,' Charlotte said at last. 'Some of each, perhaps. But mostly – other Gullivers like myself, I suppose.'

'If you've learned that, you've learned all you need,' Norton said, going back to her packing.

'Oh, not all, I hope – otherwise the rest of my life will prove very dull,' Charlotte said lightly.

It seemed quite an expedition. The horses were sent off in advance, with the grooms, who would have to sleep in the village, though the horses were to be stabled at Deene; and then the luggage was taken to the station accompanied by Norton and Cavendish's man; and finally Cavendish came in a cab to collect Charlotte. He was very nervous, and would not settle on the train to reading the Gentleman's Magazine he had bought for the journey, but alternately chattered and stared out of the window, whistling under his breath.

'Ain't you a bit scared?' he asked Charlotte at last, goaded by her air of calm.

'Of course I am,' she said, trying to look it. 'After all, if I commit some dreadful solecism, I might ruin your career.'

'Oh, I dare say it wouldn't be that bad,' he said kindly, and then a faint look of concern crossed his handsome young face. 'Only – it might be better if you didn't talk about back-slums and diseases and lice and such-like – at least, not *all* the time.'

'Not a single louse, I promise!' she said, laughing. 'Not a sore, and not a sewer.'

Deene was a pretty house, long, low and battlemented, of pale honeyed stone, set in fine, gentle parkland with some good timber and an ornamental lake. Inside everything was modern and comfortable. Lady D'Ivery, a placid, comfortable woman very elegantly dressed, greeted Charlotte and Cavendish on their arrival, engaged in a little inconsequential chat, told them everyone would meet in the Great Hall before dinner, and had them shown to their rooms. Charlotte was glad to find Norton there, already busy unpacking. She seemed excited.

'I've been talking to the steward of the bedchambers, my lady, and you're a very important guest. Lord Cardigan himself picked this room for you! It's called the White Bedroom. It's very pretty, don't you think?'

'Very,' Charlotte agreed.

'And I am very important for your sake,' Norton went on. 'Everyone was so polite to me in the servants' hall, and Mrs Hopkins, which is Lady D'Ivery's woman, said she would reserve me first use of the ironing-room if I wished to press your gown for tonight.'

'Ah yes, tonight,' Charlotte said. 'I hope you have been told what I am to do, for no-one has told me.'

'Yes, my lady. Dinner tonight is half-formal, house guests, and gentlemen only from the county. Tomorrow the meet is here on the lawn at ten o'clock, and—'

'But what am I to do now?' Charlotte interrupted the excited flow. 'It's far too early to dress for dinner.

Am I supposed to lie on my bed like an invalid all afternoon?'

'Well, my lady, the gentlemen will all go and look at the horses, I dare say, and see them settled. Lord Blithfield will see yours all right, for certain. And then they will gather somewhere and smoke. And I expect the ladies will all end up in some sitting-room or other, and chat until the dressing-bell.'

'Then I am free to explore,' Charlotte said. She tidied herself, and then sallied forth, wondering again at the difference in her confidence. When she first left Chetton, she would not have dared to venture out of her chamber, for fear of doing the wrong thing and bringing censure down on her head. Now she trod boldly, examining the paintings, peeking into sitting-rooms, hoping rather that she wouldn't find where everyone was gathered, for that would end her solitary exploration. She found a chapel, which smelled as if it was used, and an oak-panelled sitting-room with signs of female occupation, and then, discovering another staircase, trotted down it, arriving in a small hall just as someone entered it from a side door.

He stopped dead, looking as though he had seen a ghost. She froze too, probably just as pale herself, and there was a long moment of palpitating silence. And then Oliver said, 'What are you doing here?'

'I might well ask you the same thing,' Charlotte managed to retort at last. It sounded a trifle cool, but she saw the corners of his lips twitch with amusement.

'A reply of polished courtesy,' he said. 'But I suppose I deserved no better. I beg your pardon if I sounded impertinent, but I was a little discomposed. I was not expecting to see you here – though the pleasure,' he added with a bow, 'is even greater than the surprise.'

Now her lips twitched too. 'I detect the scent of gammon,' she said. 'But to satisfy your curiosity, I have come with my brother, Lord Blithfield, who is a cornet in the Eleventh, and hopes very hard for advancement.'

Southport bowed again. 'You are all generosity; and to prove I can match it, I will remind you that I am a neighbour of Lord Cardigan's, and as a keen huntsman, have been invited to stay, as I have often been before. And now I have satisfied you, I hope, on my credentials – are you going anywhere in particular? May I escort you, or be of service in any way?'

Charlotte could hardly have expected him to be so civil, given that she had jilted him so shockingly. Coolness was the best she would have expected; but though he began with a teasing note, his last words were spoken with a warmth that seemed to be trying to convince her he held no grudge. She would have liked to prove herself equally civilised, but the sight of him had overset her more than a little. If she had thought about it, she might have expected him to be here: if all the swells in the county had been invited, Lord Cardigan would hardly have missed out a duke who was a near neighbour. But the fact was that she had got into the habit of shutting him out from her thoughts, a habit so ingrained she no longer knew she was doing it. Coming upon him like that was a shock; but a worse shock was to discover how her heart fluttered at the sight of him, and how the sound of his voice generated an excitement so intense that she felt rather sick.

All she could do was to stand and stare at him, and try to regain her breath. She was on the bottom stair, he very close to her, so that her face was almost on a level with his. His blue eyes beckoned like cool water on a hot, dusty day. I still love him, she thought with dismay. In spite of everything, in spite of the years between, and all the effort of forgetting him, I still love him just as I did on that last day before his mother came to visit me. It had all been wasted: the sickness was unabated.

'My darling,' he said softly, 'what is it?' His gentleness undid her. She began to tremble. 'You're shaking. Have I frightened you? Upset you? Or are you ill? Tell me. What is it? Let me help you.'

'Don't touch me,' she pleaded in a squeak of a voice. 'I shan't be able to bear it if you touch me.'

Some tension went out of him – she didn't know what or why. He said, 'Bear what?'

'To be – being—' She couldn't find the words. Tears of frustration sprang to her eyes. 'You called me darling,' she said helplessly.

'You are my darling,' he said. 'I'm sorry if it offends you, but in my heart you are my darling. I love you just as I always did. I will never love anyone but you.'

'Liar!' she cried, but it was a weak, unconvinced cry. Near to him she could only feel the heat of his body, the fire they had always generated between them, and it wiped out the truth of the mind. She wanted to touch him, to be touched. She yearned like a salamander for his flame; but she feared it would burn her up and destroy her.

'Why did you run away?' he asked seriously. 'Charlotte, dearest Charlotte, please talk to me, even if it's only for this one last time. Let me at least understand. I have been in hell these five years wondering what went wrong. Don't you owe me that, at least?' She only looked at him with wide eyes, struggling with herself. He smiled sadly. 'No, you don't owe me anything, of course. I take that back. But because you are generous, tell me why you cast me off. I have never loved anyone else, and I never will now. I need to understand how I lost you.'

'You never loved me,' she asserted.

He raised his eyebrows. 'Well,' he said, 'when it comes to it, that must be a matter for your belief. I can't prove it, except to say that I never asked anyone before you to be my wife, and I never asked anyone else after you. That is a matter of recorded fact. And haven't I stayed in the country since that terrible day, for your sake, to save you the embarrassment of meeting me round every corner? Could love do more?'

'You did that for me?' she said incredulously.

'I had news of you, though,' he said. 'I have my agents in London, whose business it is to tell me whenever Lady Chelmsford appears in public, what she says and how she looks. It has been my main comfort – forgive me for this, though it is unredeemed wickedness – that you have not seemed happy either, not had your name linked with another man.'

She thought briefly of Doctor Anthony, and he was utterly unsubstantial, the product of a weak imagination beside this man who seemed to pulse and vibrate with life, as though all the power of the universe passed through him.

'I tried to love someone else,' she said, 'but I see now it was useless. I really tried, but he was never real to me as you were – damn you.'

'You do love me!' he said triumphantly, and took the last step towards her, and took her in his arms. 'I knew it! You couldn't curse me so feelingly otherwise.'

She struggled vainly. 'Let me go!'

'Oh, I think not. Stop wriggling! I shall kiss you in a moment and then it will be all up with you, but tell me first why you left me.'

He was laughing now, and she wanted to hit him for being so confident, but he was much too strong for her. 'Because your mother told me you were marrying me for my fortune. She said you wouldn't dream of marrying someone *like me*,' she put all the dowager's scorn into her voice, 'for any other reason.'

'And you believed her?' he said in amazement. 'You idiot!'

'Abuse me all you like,' she said, ceasing her useless struggles, but turning her head away from him. 'I thought then she was mistaken. So I went to find you, to ask you for the truth. And I found you—'

'Yes?' he asked, gently now.

'With a woman. Going into a restaurant with your *mistress*! Fanny told me afterwards that everyone knew about her. She was even a friend of Tom's mistress. *That* was how much you loved me – from my arms straight to hers.'

'Good God,' he said. He released her, and she felt – fool that she was – a huge stab of disappointment. 'Was that it?'

She looked at him bitterly. 'I couldn't have done that to you if the cases were reversed. I know other men do it, I know it is something people are supposed to accept, but I could not. If loving me wasn't enough for you, then you didn't love me – not as I wanted to be loved. And now, you may call me a romantic fool and go away. I don't regret what I did. I only regret I was so mistaken in you.'

He didn't go. He didn't look defiant or amused or angry, only sad, and it cut her to the heart. 'You should have trusted me,' he said. 'Yes, I did have a mistress – before I met you. I was unmarried and unattached, and it was an arrangement that suited both of us. But once I met you and fell in love with you, you were all I wanted. I *never* went from your arms to hers. That sort of love wouldn't have done for me either.'

'But—'

'The night you saw me with her was the first and only time I met her after dancing with you at your coming-out ball. And I met her only to tell her that our relationship was over, and that I wouldn't be seeing her again. I felt I owed it to her to tell her gently and face to face. Maria was fond of me, and we had been friends for a very long time. So I took her to dinner, and gave her a farewell present, and made sure that she would be adequately cared for. If you think that was wrong, I cannot apologise for it. But once I had fallen in love with you, I never so much as kissed her cheek again.'

Charlotte looked at him long and searchingly. 'Oh,' she said at last.

It tickled his unruly sense of humour, even at this tense moment. His lips twitched again. 'Is that all you have to say – oh!'

'You really did love me, then?'

'I should have thought,' he said slowly, 'that you must have known that, remembering how it was between us.'

'But you did want my money.'

'It would have been useful. But you see, I have managed without it. And if it was money I was after, I hope I might mention without seeming an absolute cad that I have been offered at least a dozen wealthy heiresses since I reached my majority, and I didn't marry any of those.'

'Your mother said—'

'Did *I* ever say, that's the question.'

'I'm sorry,' she said meekly.

'Sorry, I hope, that you have wasted so much time,' he said with mock severity. 'If I had known the frivolity of your objections, I would have come after you and forced you to marry me. But I thought you had changed your mind, and were too afraid to tell me so. And then Grandpa died, and I was so taken up with things. I thought you had mistaken your heart.'

She smiled now, slowly. 'My heart,' she said, 'always knew what it was about. It was my mind that caused the trouble.'

'You should have trusted me,' he said again, and she

579

looked up into his eyes contritely. And then he kissed her, and the world went up in flames.

'It wasn't so bad the first year or so,' he said, later, as they strolled, arms linked, through the garden. It was trying to drizzle, but out of doors was the only place they could secure the privacy they needed to talk. 'Grandpa's death was another reason I didn't come after you. I had expected it for a long time, but I hadn't realised how grieved I would be. I loved him, you see. I'm glad he had the chance to meet you.'

'I liked him very much.'

'Well, after his death I was very much involved with all the estate business, the funeral and the will and seeing the tenants and pensioners and so on. And then the estate proved so much more encumbered even than I had expected. I was determined to get it back into shape. Mama wasn't happy about it, of course – I confined her to the country with me, and she didn't like that at all. But I had to retrench. The two of us, living at Ravendene, with no parties or journeys or London, could economise pretty successfully.'

'It sounds like cruelty to her.'

'Oh, I let her out sometimes, and occasionally we had people to stay. But I suppose it was a little unkind. I had my farming to interest me, and hunting in the winter, but Mama—' He shrugged. 'I suppose I suspected she had had something to do with driving you away. She didn't like you, you know.'

'I guessed as much,' Charlotte said, smiling.

He squeezed her arm. 'God, how I love you! Look, there's a summer-house at the end of this walk. Hurry, I want to kiss you again.'

Rain began to hit the pavement as they hurried inside. Then her arms were round his neck and they were kissing as though they would never stop. At last they broke apart, and sat down together on the bench, arms round each other.

'Considering how I kissed you, how could you think,' he said in amazement, 'that I didn't love you?'

'I don't know,' she said. 'I suppose I knew very little about it then. You must forgive me.'

'Do you know more now?' he asked, narrowing his eyes in mock suspicion. 'Come, tell me. Who have you been dallying with? What fabulous creature took your fancy after me?'

She told him about Doctor Anthony, and was disconcerted when he roared with laughter. 'He is a very handsome man,' she protested. 'And very good.'

'Ha! Because he didn't kiss you?'

'He spends his life doing good works.'

'Very well,' he admitted, 'but how could you explain away the fact that he didn't kiss you, or declare himself?'

'I thought he was being considerate and proper, doing everything as it should be done. I did wonder, after that day in Harrow, why he delayed so long. But he had shown that he liked me, so—'

'And this pawky lover was what you preferred to me? You should have the impudence beaten out of you! Did I ever leave you in the slightest doubt as to how I felt about you – until that day of mistakes?'

'Never,' she said, and he kissed her again.

'You should never have thought him good enough for you. Evidently he knows his own place, though,' he said with satisfaction, 'since he's marrying your cousin.'

'He thinks her more feminine than me. He says he could never think of me as more than a sister, because I'm too mannish,' she confessed with chagrin. Fanny, tactless with happiness, had let it out one evening.

Oliver laughed again, but gently. 'He is a poor fish,

and your cousin deserves better. If he doesn't know a woman when he meets one—' He kissed her again, and this time all her bones seemed to turn to liquid. She felt the change in him, too, a sort of frantic desire for more – a more she knew about now, academically, from her back-slum visiting, but still could not imagine in the context of herself and Oliver, except to think if it was even more exciting than kissing it might well drive her mind right out of her body.

He pulled back at last, looking flushed and dishevelled. 'Look here, we can't go on like this. How soon can we get married?'

She felt impish. 'I haven't said I will marry you yet.'

'I shan't give you the choice, my girl,' he said grimly. 'You won't get away a second time.'

'You want my money.'

'Of course. There's still so much to be done at Ravendene. And I should like to be able to live in London again. But there is a more pressing reason for marriage still.'

'What's that?'

He grinned. 'It will annoy so many people – all the old cats who were pleased when you jilted me, and the other old cats who thought I must secretly have jilted you. You will make such a splendidly untamed duchess!'

She looked serious now. 'But I won't know how to behave. I'm not even very good at being a countess – as a duchess I shall do everything wrong and be in trouble all the time.'

'No, no, that's the whole point. Don't you see, my darling, that as a duchess you are above criticism. You can do anything you like, and everyone else has to grit their teeth and bear it. They even,' he said with a huge smile, 'have to copy you, if they want to be fashionable. You can lead them a tremendous dance.'

She laughed. 'I wouldn't be so cruel. But, seriously now, Oliver—'

'Oh God, you said my name! Say it again!'

'Oliver – no, stop! Seriously, I said – I don't want to give up my work with the sick poor.'

'Why should you?'

'You won't mind?'

'As long as you give me as much time as them.'

'And what about my model hospital? Will you let me go on with setting that up?'

'Yes, I've been hearing about that from my spies. Of course you shall go on with it. I think it would be a splendid way of annoying my mother.'

'I'm not marrying you just to annoy your mother.'

'So you will marry me, then? How soon?'

'My cousin Benedict did it by special licence,' she said demurely. 'Would next week be too soon for you?'

His answer was silent, but eloquent.

Cold and encroaching winter darkness drove them in at last. On their way upstairs they overtook Cavendish, who looked relieved to see Charlotte, but not particularly surprised that she had her arm through that of the Duke of Southport.

'Oh there you are! I thought you had got lost somewhere. No-one has seen you since we arrived.'

'Has the dressing-bell gone?'

'Yes, just.' He looked at Oliver curiously, but his own concerns were too much uppermost. 'I say, Charley, you will make a special effort tonight, won't you?'

'Charley?' said Oliver.

'They call me that,' she said. 'Fanny started it.'

'Good God!' He turned to Cavendish. 'A special effort at what?'

'Oh, to sweeten the Old Man – Lord Cardigan, I should

say. If you butter him up like anything tonight, and then hunt like the very deuce tomorrow, it will make all the difference. So wear your nicest things, won't you, and talk pretty to him?'

'You're after a commission, I take it?' Oliver said.

'Yes, sir. A lieutenancy's going to be on the market in a month or so.'

Oliver nodded. 'I see. Well, I have a certain amount of influence with Lord Cardigan. We are old friends, and he admires my seat on a horse. I shall be sure to put in a good word for you.'

'Thank you very much, sir,' Cavendish said enthusiastically, though with a faint air of puzzlement. 'You are very kind. But why—?'

'Why should I put myself to the trouble?' Oliver anticipated. 'Because, Blithfield, I am going to marry your sister, and how would it look if my only brother-in-law was nothing but a "bloody subaltern"?'

'Not well, sir, I do see,' Cavendish concurred promptly. And then he looked at Charlotte, catching up with what had been said. 'I say, is that true, Charlotte? You're going to be married?' Charlotte nodded. 'Oh, I say, that's splendid,' he said enthusiastically. 'And I tell you what – if you're a duchess, you'll be able to start up your hospital all right. No-one'll be able to say it isn't proper.'

Lord Southport laughed. 'There's no mistaking the blood tie! That was the first thing she thought of too.'